For the boy who helped develop my imagination, the man who encouraged my dreams, and the best little brother a girl could ask for.

SEAN GILLESPIE

-THIS ONE'S FOR YOU-

Hope this makes up for the rocking chair fiasco

PROLOGUE

Darkness. A black so absolute, it nearly drove Marda to insanity with its monotony and the lack of any kind of sight. Marda thought C'Tan had blinded her somehow on the flight from Karsholm. There was no sense of time, no understanding of the days sliding by. She slept when she was tired and ate when food was brought to her.

Ember's mother moved slowly, so as not to hurt herself on the stone walls. A student of the fire magic, especially a disciple of S'Kotos, should have a warm home, comfortable or even hot. But no. The dungeon felt like the frosty start of winter—the kind that requires thick blankets to keep the shivers away and smells of ice. Marda trembled, wrapping her arms around herself, partly for comfort, partly to chase away the cold, her thoughts drifting to the last moments she'd seen her child. The dungeon was miserable, but she'd saved Ember from this fate. At least her daughter was safe and warm. She needed to stay that way.

The darkness was just one weapon in C'Tan's arsenal, Marda knew. There was also the implied and sometimes blatant threat against her daughter, Ember Shandae. C'Tan had wanted the girl since she had discovered Ember was the Wolfchild—the chosen one meant to heal Rasann. She'd tried to capture Ember as a babe, and Jarin sacrificed his own life to save his family from his evil sister. One more reason C'Tan had to punish her ex-sister-in-law.

Marda leaned against the chilly wall and pressed her lips together. C'Tan could not have Ember. Ember was the only chance the world had to overcome the darkness of S'Kotos, C'Tan, and now the shadow weavers.

Feeling around, Marda found the sharpened stone that had cut her fingers so many times. She ignored the pain and scratched into the floor again. Words, unseen and only felt, she continued her letter to Ember, ignoring the blood that made the stone slick and dripped onto the floor, knowing it would only add power to her spell.

Scratching the last word into the smooth rock, she dropped the stone, her fingers trembling with pain and frost. She would wash her cuts if she had water, but did not know when it would be given to her, so she wiped her hands on her shirt, ripped a strip of cloth from the bottom of her skirt and wrapped her fingers. When the pain eased, she reached into her pocket and pulled out a half stone. It was small enough to fit into her palm, rough on the rounded side and smooth as glass on the flat.

Setting the stone flat side down on the floor near the middle of her letter, she said the one word, the only word that would get her letter to Ember. She whispered so none would hear.

"Send," she said.

In an instant, the darkness was gone. Marda blinked, then winced as the light brightened, white at first, and then became a rainbow of colors that took her ragged, bloody words and sucked them into itself before sending them to her daughter. She leaned against the wall with a smile when the light faded away. It was done. Complete. She only hoped Ember could find the keystones before C'Tan or the Shadow Weavers. It was a race, and her daughter needed to be in the lead.

CHAPTER ONE

Kayla wiped a blackened arm across her brow, ash and sweat mixing to form a dark streak that ran from temple to temple. The room was hotter than Helar, and despite two days' effort since C'Tan had tried to drown the mage academy in lava, it still oozed from the walls and floor. Not for the first time, she wished she could walk through stone and freeze the magma at its source. It would be so much simpler than patching never-ending leaks of burning rock.

The lava pushed at her, its magnetic energy of fire affecting the polar opposite magic of air. Without being asked, Brant's spirit-turned-air elemental dove into the wall and spread cold through the heated stone. It still saddened Kayla to see him. Just days before, he'd been her fiancée and best friend. Now he was dead and a permanent part of the sapphire flute, forced to do its bidding and changing him a little more every day. Some days, it hurt more than she could bear. How can you say goodbye to someone when their spirit never left your side?

A balloon of blazing energy surged out of the wall and physically rocked Kayla on her feet. Something big was coming. That was verified seconds later when Brant flew out of the wall and mindspoke to the guardian of the sapphire flute. Fire. Lots of liquid stone coming. Right there. He showed her the picture in her mind, as clear as if she saw it herself.

Kayla called out to the group of teenagers who worked with her, students of the mage academy with nowhere to go. "Behn, Miek. To the left, about three feet. Raech, Aryana, Eden, to your right about half a foot. The surge will come between you. Are you ready?" The kids nodded, grim-faced, as they awaited the fiery blast.

"I thought sending the elemental into the wall would stop the blasts," one of the girls commented. Kayla wasn't sure which one.

"It should have, and usually does," she said, trying very hard not to black out from the conflicting swirl of magical energies between fire and air. "This time, the pressure has to be released before it can be cooled." Nobody said anything else.

The tension built until Kayla thought she might explode, and then the wall blew outward in the exact spot Brant predicted. His elemental form returned to the stone, still spinning cold air in his wake. The students thrust their hands into the stone and helped to break it up and cool it until only chunks of darkened rock remained. Kayla didn't know how they did it. What kind of magic was it that allowed them to literally handle the scorching heat of melted rock? She hadn't had time to ask. She'd barely had time to find a few hours' sleep in the past few days.

Brant's connection with the flute allowed her to see into the stone, to feel it as if she herself spun through rock. The flute pulsed with the energy flowing between them. She used that connection to reach deep and wide, to scan the rock as she would scan a field from a mountainside. She felt into the stone and was relieved. Nothing more stirred. That didn't mean it wouldn't, but for now, this area was clear.

She straightened and looked at her group. They were strong, despite their age, and Kayla was pleased with them. She gave them a half smile—she didn't have the energy for anything more—and put the flute in the leather bag at her hip. "That's it. We're safe, and so is the academy, thanks to you. Hopefully, things will revert to normal and you can resume classes by the end of the week." She clapped the big guy, Behn, on the shoulder. "Why don't you clean up and get some sleep while you can? I'll wake you when we need you again. Thank you for your efforts."

The boys nodded, solemn and bone weary. The girls smiled, their steps heavy with exhaustion, but still they chattered as they made their way out of the room. They all looked as tired as Kayla felt. "And how about you, my friend?" she asked Brant. "Are you as drained as the rest of us?"

Brant tipped his head and looked at her. "I don't become fatigued like I once did. I'm growing stronger, even in this elemental form." He spun in the air, picking up bits of gravel that pelted Kayla and stung her skin. He seemed oblivious to it. Once he would have been so aware of her pain that he would have tripped over himself to apologize and make it stop—just one more way he had changed since his death and new life within the sapphire flute.

Kayla sighed. "Well, I'm beyond tired. How about you recharge yourself for a while so I can sleep?" She held open the top of the bag in invitation, though she knew he didn't need her help. Having no body, he could slide right through the pouch. Still, it made her feel better to pretend things like that were normal.

He began to dive into the flute, but looked over Kayla's shoulder and stopped, then reversed himself and swirled like a living tornado at her side, saying not a word. She turned slowly, afraid of what she might find behind her. C'Tan? A monster? One of the Shadow Weavers? But it was none of those. A group of the magi high council had come through the ruins of the school to talk to her. She'd been told they might. She sighed in relief.

"Counselors," she said, addressing the magi before her. "To what do I owe this honor?" Her voice was pleasant, but something made her wary. She couldn't place it, but somehow she knew something was wrong.

The magi stared at her briefly, then glanced at each other. A man stepped forward. "Miss Kayla, would you please come with us?" His voice was a deep bass that resonated through Kayla's bones.

"And where would you have me go?" she asked, the feeling of wrongness getting stronger, very similar to what she felt whenever she'd been around her grandfather.

"There is a meeting of the mage council and we need you there," he said, but she could feel the lie.

"Why would I need to meet with the mage council? I'm not a member." She was stalling for time, hoping someone would come and assist her. If these truly were members of the mage council, they were traitors, just as Magnet and Seer had been, and those two alone had nearly destroyed the mage academy from the inside out. And if these eight men and women were not members of the mage council...well, she hated to think about what that might mean, and who they could be.

A woman stepped from the rear of the group and gathered magic around her. The man turned to her, surprise apparent on his face. "She already knows," the woman snarled. "We can't afford to waste time. Get the flute." The entire group immediately gathered magic around them. Men and women of every color of magic, but all of it streaked with black.

Shadow Weavers.

Without a word, the Ne'Goi surrounded her, spaced out evenly, so they stood as if points on a compass. Brant's whirlwind picked up speed and the man behind her sang a deep, throbbing note, repeated over and over. Across from her, another man began a rhythm in a tone slightly discordant with the first, and so it continued. The men provided rhythms that struck Kayla clear through, feeling as if she stood on a massive heart. When the women pitched in with wails that sounded half screech and half chant, it brought Kayla to her knees. She felt the life draining from her body, the magic ripping from her soul, and without thinking about it, she put her hand to the pouch at her side.

A shock surged up her arm, energizing her and shooting her to her feet once again. She pulled the flute out, had it to her lips in seconds, and played a counterpoint to their chant. If their sounds were that of the earth tearing apart, hers was the sound of sunshine and healing. If their sound was hot like the lava she'd been fighting for days, hers was the icy cold of the deepest parts of the ocean or the northern lands that held snow year round. The conflicting sounds blended in a strange way, and strength flowed into Kayla despite the heaviness filling the air. Whatever magic these Ne'Goi worked, it was big and would come soon if she didn't do something to stop it. But putting a stop to their chant meant putting an end to the shadow weavers.

It meant taking their lives, the one thing she'd dreaded doing again since the battle of Karsholm. And yet, if she did not, the evil that was the Ne'Goi would gain control over one of the most powerful weapons on Rasann and she knew with no doubt, they would turn the power of the flute to evil.

She had no choice. There was no one else—Kayla and Brant were the only ones there to stop it. Two against eight, but those two had something the others did not: the power of a keystone.

Steeling herself, Kayla drew in a deep breath and visualized a frozen dome over her, much like the one she'd used in battling Sarali's brother, Jihong, then released her breath on a sound so pure, the walls shook with it. The dome formed around her immediately, even sliding beneath her feet so she was completely encased in crystalline ice. The bell-like effect of the tone gave Kayla an idea, and she played the high note again, envisioning the walls trembling and the floor quivering as if an earthquake struck just this one room. Most of the shadow weavers were cowering on the floor before the sound tapered off, and with only a second of hesitation, she played the flute again. This was the instant she dreaded—the moment they would die. Pushing her doubts aside, she sent out the same kind of cold that had frozen the path beneath the ocean in her battle with C'Tan. She sent it to the eight fake magi and farther—into the walls and the ground. Kayla sent the cold as far as it could reach and continued to play, despite her own shivering.

Brant dove into the walls and encircled the group, adding to the disastrous tremors that shook them all. It got colder and colder until the shadow weavers got to their feet and tried to leap into the air and return to wherever they came from—but they would fail this time. Kayla froze their feet to the ground. They weren't going anywhere without taking half the cave with them. Instead of escaping, they cried out and reached toward Kayla, their magic striking her ice bubble with no effect. She had a keystone, and she was its guardian. No one would take it from her.

The anger built in her and surged outward in a concentric ring that froze the shadow weavers in place and penetrated the walls to a depth she couldn't feel, and for the first time in two days, the heat was gone. Everywhere. Her battle with the shadow weavers had sealed all the cracks and frozen the lava.

Slowly, the ice bubble shed itself from around her, and Brant came back to her side. She looked at the frozen men and women, her heart part satisfied and part grieving. She had no idea she could send the cold out that far, nor that it could freeze and seal people in an icy prison that left them immobile, but still alive. Their hearts still beat—slow, but regular.

She and Brant stared at the ice statues. She felt his agitation rushing through the flute and into her. His emotion got her worked up and angry as well. Kayla couldn't believe their audacity. To stride right into the mage academy and attempt to take the flute from her. Brant's anger rose higher, and he spun so fast she could barely see him. In an instant, he leaped into motion, and his intentions became clear.

"Brant! No!" she cried, but it was too late. Spinning in circles around her, he attacked the frozen Ne'Goi. Cracks and snaps assaulted her ears, pieces of ice flying around her. Kayla fell to her knees, eyes welling with tears. She'd disabled the Ne'Goi without killing them, she hadn't been forced to do the thing she dreaded most. She would have found a way for them to be permanently restrained—but Brant had other ideas. He took out his anger on the eight fake magi and Kayla could do nothing—nothing—to stop him. He would not listen to her pleas, and the flute would not interfere.

Finally, he stopped, and all that was left of the eight imposters were bits of fine ice floating in the air and gathering in the corners. Brant had annihilated them. There was nothing left and nothing for her to do.

Her tear-streaked face finally rose, and their eyes met. His were cold—emotionless—but then, what did she expect from a creature changed by the flute? Still, she couldn't help but ask, her voice choked with emotion, "Why?"

Brant tipped his head to one side and answered as if it was the most obvious thing in the world. "Because it needed to be done. Servants of the dark may not live. It is Guardian law."

He spoke of The Guardians—the creators of Haven, Rasann, and the Keystones that rooted magic to the soil and kept the world from flying apart. Their law.

To kill.

And she was a keeper of one of their most powerful stones. The Sapphire Flute.

Wiping her face, Kayla rose to her feet and shook her head. She did not understand it, but though her heart ached, part of her knew it was better this way. Safer.

Brant slowed his whirl and surged into the flute.

Alone, Kayla looked around the room, the ice particles still glistening in the artificial magelight. Those were tiny little pieces of human beings. There should be blood splattered on the wall for the massacre that had just taken place here.

She shook her head again and took a deep, shaky breath. What was done was done. She could do nothing about Brant's attack or the infiltration of the Ne'Goi into the Mage Academy. Feeling powerless, she realized there was one thing she could do—report it. There were people who needed to know.

Starting with her cousin Ember, the white mage. This attack was a sure sign that it was time for them to leave the mage academy and begin their search for the remaining keystones.

With a purpose to distract her, Kayla strode toward the doorway in search of Ember Shandae.

CHAPTER TWO

Ember clamped her hands over her ears as Tiva screamed. She couldn't help the heartache seeing her brother's pain. They may not share blood, but he was her brother nonetheless. His twin, Ren, seemed to be having much the same problem. He squeezed Tiva's hand so hard, Ren's fingers turned white with the pressure. Or maybe it was Tiva squeezing Ren's hand from the pain. She wasn't really sure.

The nurse peeled off more of the bandages covering Tiva's face, chanting all the while, and didn't flinch as another shriek tore from the boy's throat. It had been two days since the attack on Karsholm and the Mage Academy—two days since Tiva had been shoved into the lava and was burned and blinded.

But his healing had been near miraculous. Painful, but miraculous all the same. The burns on his face and hands still looked waxy and scarred, but he had gone from blackened to the bone on both hands and face, his lips gone and teeth forever bared, to almost normal in forty-eight hours. Another practical use for magic Ember had never seen.

Unfortunately, Tiva's eyes could not be healed. They had boiled in his skull and burst like okra seeds. There was nothing left to fix—just an exposed nerve and empty pockets of bone. The healers did their best to bring flesh around to cover the eye sockets and soothe the nerves, but every time they touched the bone around the hollows, he screamed.

After several minutes of rough-voiced wailing, Tiva passed out. The healers could finally work on the most painful parts of his skull.

They took advantage of Tiva's state and changed his bandages, then used their magic to further desensitize the nerve before Tiva awakened. Their long, thin fingers moved quickly across his face. Ember cringed as they dipped into the hollows where his beautiful blue eyes once laughed at her. Using their magic, they burned away the optical nerve.

The smell brought back memories—pulling Tiva from the lava. Carrying him toward the school. Ren taking his twin from her arms and racing to the healers, leaving her with only Tiva's charred scent. Ember fought the nausea that hit her and tried not to remember. Tiva pulled her into the present when he awoke from the pain. His back arched in a soundless screech. She reached for him, but before she could make contact, he returned to oblivion.

Once the nerve was gone, the healers rounded balls of clay and placed them in his eye sockets, adding some here, taking some there, until the spheres fit perfectly. Once sized, they enfolded the clay in their palms, which glowed with orange light, smoke coming from between their fingers. When the smoke stopped, they rolled the clay balls in pale sand and once again heated them in their palms.

When they finished and opened their hands, Ember gasped. What was brown clay had become a white globe, looking very much like an eye—minus the color and pupil. Another healer entered the room. Using a stone stamp, the man took up tinted sand, much the color of Tiva's eyes before his injury, and pushing downward, he embedded the sand into the white, creating colored glass, and then did the same with black sand for the pupils.

With the eyes finished and cooled, the healer set them gently in Tiva's sockets, then gestured for the other two healers to continue. Somehow, they took Tiva's skin and stretched and molded it to create eyelids that almost looked natural. As a final touch, lashes and eyebrows grew from his skin—something Ember never thought she would see again.

It was odd to see Tiva asleep or unconscious with his eyes open, but at least now he looked whole. The female healer spoke. "The waxy texture of his skin will fade with time. If he wishes to have facial hair, that will require a separate healing. It would not be healthy for his skin to deal with it right now. Besides, he is still young. He has time for that." She closed the box containing the colored sands and the instruments of their healing, then looked up. "Our work is done. Now all that is left is for Mistress Vanine to teach him how to see, despite his blindness, and to use the other colors of magic."

The healers backed away, but Ember caught the woman by the hand. "Thank you," she whispered. "You saved his sanity, if not his life. We can never repay you."

The woman smiled, tearing up as she glanced down at Tiva, then back to Ember. "Payment is neither needed nor desired. It is our calling to help those in need. Knowing we have made a difference is payment enough." She squeezed Ember's hand and let go, then walked across the room and out the curtained doorway just as Mistress Vanine stepped to the side and entered the room.

It was always strange seeing the blind woman in the caverns with her darkened glasses, moving as if she saw everything with the brightest of light, and Ember guessed that in her own way, she did. She just didn't use her eyes to see. According to the healer, it was now Mistress Vanine's turn to take Tiva under her wing and teach him how to do the same. The teacher of orange magic approached them and smiled.

"And how is my newest trainee doing?" she asked, putting her hands behind her and rocking on her toes.

Ember glanced at Ren, who gazed at his twin with a mixture of heartache and pride. It was he who answered. "He seems to be doing well, Mistress. His optical nerve was severed and artificial eyes created. He just needs to wake up for us to see how he feels. Last time he awoke, he spent most of the time screaming," Ren said, his emotions apparent in the way he leaned over Tiva as if to protect him.

Mistress Vanine chuckled. "That is to be expected. If what I've seen of Tiva is any indicator of his gifts and determination, I'm sure he will make a fine pupil indeed." She put her hand on Ren's and seemed to look into his eyes, though Ember knew that was impossible. "He's going to be fine, Ren. I promise you. He shall be fine."

Ember left Ren and Mistress Vanine to their discussion and quietly walked away. She had other things that needed to be done, including talking to her cousin Kayla and Headmaster Ezeker.

Heading down the hall to her left, Ember made her way to her quarters, which had, miraculously, remained untouched by the lava that had ravished the caverns. Her clothes smelled of smoke and stone, but it was a small price to pay for her things remaining intact. So many had lost everything and some even their lives. She was very aware of how lucky she was.

She stopped just inside the doorway to let her eyes adjust, unable to cast a magelight like so many others. She still had to depend on candles. Why such a simple spell eluded her, she didn't understand.

Once she could make out the shape of the beds belonging to her and Lily, she went to her dresser and, fumbling a bit, found the candle in its brass stand. She might not be able to create a magelight, but she could make fire. With the touch of her finger, Ember brought the candle to life, then set the three-legged candleholder on her dresser. She took a few minutes to walk around the room and light the other candles. If Lily were here, she would cast a magelight and brighten the room as if they were outdoors in the sunlight, but the girl had been scarce lately. Ember knew little, but from what she'd heard, Ezeker and the council had been questioning Lily about her mother, C'Tan, and were using her to repair some of the damage done to the mage academy.

Ember moved to her bed and sat with a sigh, rubbing her hand over her face and tired eyes. All she wanted to do was take a nap, but she knew if she did, she'd never sleep that night, and she really had things to do. Her eyes closed of their own volition for just a moment, and Ember felt herself sag.

Shaking her head, she lay back and put her head on her pillow. What would an hour of sleep hurt? If she didn't rest, she would be useless to everyone around her. It didn't seem she had a choice. Her body demanded it.

She was about to drift off to sleep when she heard voices outside her room. Two girls. One voice she knew well—her roommate and cousin on her father's side, Lily. The second voice was almost as familiar, though they'd known each other for only two days. The only other cousin she'd met, this one from her mother's side—Kayla, holder of the Sapphire Flute and one of the warriors from her dreams.

Unable to make out their words, Ember opened her eyes with a sigh and glanced at the ceiling, then froze.

Words. Many, many words scribbled across her ceiling and streamed down the wall and beneath the side of her bed, looking almost scratched into the surface. She couldn't help but wonder—how in the world had they gotten onto the ceiling?

And then she remembered—the sending stone had fallen down the side of her bed. It must have slid down the wall, and stopped with the flat side pressed against it. What were the chances of that happening?

But—there was only one person who would have the other half of this stone. Ember knew, because she had given it to her just before the battle in Karsholm. She must have carried it with her during the battle and so had it now.

She knew she was right when she looked again at the scratches in the ceiling, all in handwriting she recognized. Ember leaped to the floor and, grabbing a corner of the footboard, pulled the bed away from the wall so she could read the entire message.

Her mother's.

Ember, I do not know how many days it has been since I was taken. I can only be thankful C'Tan took me instead of you. I need to know you are safe and not on a foolish errand to save me. I know you will come, but come with the keystones, as asked. Don't waste time.

I know how difficult this must be for you, but please heed my wishes. So long as I know you are safe, I can endure.I love you with all my heart, and I am proud of you, Ember. Keep yourself safe—for my sake, if not your own.Always remember you can do anything if you believe enough.

Mum

CHAPTER THREE

Kayla went down the hallway and turned the corner toward Sarali's room. A man with orange tattoos slammed Sarali's door, putting his shirt on as he stormed up the hall toward her, his face and what she could see of his chest beet red as he muttered under his breath. She wasn't positive, but she was pretty sure the man was Ember's stepbrother, though she couldn't remember his name. Why was he leaving Sarali's chambers? And why so angry? Or was he just embarrassed about something? There was only one way to find out.

Passing the man who still cursed under his breath, she went to Sarali's door and knocked. There was no answer. She knocked again, and finally pounded, until the petite MerCat flung the door open. She didn't say a word, but glared when she saw it was Kayla. Thankfully, she didn't slam the door in Kayla's face, though it looked as if she was tempted. Instead, she turned and retreated into the room, leaving the door open for her unwelcome guest.

Kayla stepped into the darkened room and gasped, finally understanding why the man was partially undressed and cursing as he left Sarali's quarters. Kayla covered her mouth as tears burned her eyes. In the middle of the room, on the cold stone floor, lay T'Kato's body, bare of all clothing but a pair of short pants. Sarali had placed burning candles around him—the only light in the dark space. She leaned over him with a paintbrush in hand, retracing the blue tattoos that had been his until death, so he looked the same as he had in life. Sarali must have used Ember's stepbrother to create a template.

Saying nothing, Kayla walked quietly into the room and knelt at the side of her friend and mentor, T'Kato, who had died trying to save the Wolfchild and Karsholm. It was all she could do to support Sarali in her grief. This was not the way of the MerCat, Kayla knew. T'Kato was supposed to be buried where he had fallen. He was supposed to be in the ground, yet here he was, three days later, looking as if he slept. She was grateful for the stasis spell his wife had insisted on—otherwise, the room would be putrid with his stench. Kayla watched as Sarali painted his skin. It was beautiful, in a strange sort of way. Not morbid, but reverently, the brush caressing his skin like Sarali's kisses might have done.

Kayla lost track of time as she watched the MerCat princess in the candlelight. The brushstrokes were mesmerizing—so much so that Kayla barely noticed when Sarali finished and set aside her brush. They knelt together and saw the man, who once again looked as she'd known him.

Sarali did not shed a single tear. Instead, she looked at Kayla and finally spoke, though her voice was rough. "Freeze him."

Kayla glanced up "Excuse me?"

"Freeze him," Sarali repeated. "Like ye did underwater and with Jihong. Freeze him, that I may take him home to me family. Freeze him like ye did yer own love." Her gaze never left Kayla's.

Beyond answering, Kayla nodded.

Sarali dressed her husband and put him in his armor, his sword upon his chest.

Once that was done, Kayla took the flute from her pouch and played. She pulled the cold air and the moisture around her and spun them into a web of glassy ice that surrounded the giant man's body. Just as it had done with Brant, at first the glass was opaque until it grew to the right proportions. Then with a final flourish, Kayla gave the ice a twist that would keep it forever cold and strong and made it transparent. Sarali threw herself atop the ice-covered man and sobbed, her tears becoming part of his casket.

Kayla cried with her, and when the princess was done, she met Kayla's eyes for an instant. "Thank ye," she whispered.

"It's the least I could do," Kayla replied. It was then she remembered her reason for coming here, and though she hesitated to say anything, she needed to tell Sarali sooner rather than later. "We're leaving. Tonight," she said. Maybe not the most delicate way to put it, but she had few words at the moment.

Sarali shook her head. "I won't be going with ye, lass. I be taking me love to MerCato. I have duties there. I have nothing left here."

Though she wanted so much to argue, Kayla saw Sarali's exhaustion and raw grief. She'd already lost Brant and T'Kato, and now to lose Sarali seemed more than she could bear—but it was the princess's decision.

"If that is your wish." Kayla paused. "I understand your reasons, Sarali, but . . . I shall miss you." She got to her feet, embarrassed.

Sarali glanced up at her, then rose to her feet as well. "And I shall miss ye, me friend. If ever ye need the help of the MerCats, ye know where to find me." She stepped around T'Kato to give Kayla a hug. Sarali pulled back and met Kayla's eye in a solid look packed with emotion, then returned to T'Kato.

It was time to withdraw. Slowly, Kayla backed out of the entry, pulling the door shut behind her.

She went to her own quarters and packed the few things she had. Taking her bag in hand, she wound her way back to Ember's room and pulled aside the curtain that acted as a door. Ember and Lily sat on one of the beds, talking. At Kayla's entrance, they quieted and stood, looking to her for answers, but she was a bit at a loss. She hadn't really thought this through. She knew they needed to leave, but not how. "Is there any chance Headmaster Ezeker will allow us to leave? Now? Tonight?"

Lily shook her head. "They've nearly interrogated me these three days. They know Ember needs to leave, but they don't seem to feel the same urgency we do." Lily threw her bag over her shoulder. "And even if he said yes, he would send an escort the size of an army. No. We have to leave on our own, without his knowledge."

"Not even DeMunth?" Ember sounded concerned.

Lily shook her head. "He is your guardian, assigned to protect you by Ezeker. Don't you think the first thing he would do is report our departure?"

"No! He wouldn't do that." But Ember didn't sound completely sure. "He loves me." She looked at the ground, her face red.

Lily put her hand on Ember's shoulder. "That may be, but can we take the chance? If he truly loves you and wants to protect you, he will follow. You'll be together again soon. But we don't have time to waste. We need to leave now."

"Are there means of transportation within the school?" Kayla asked.

Ember looked at Lily, and the girl nodded. "Yes. We have a stable of horses on the far side of the academy. We would have to steal them." She seemed worried.

Kayla was concerned as well. Stealing a horse was no small thing and carried heavy consequence in Peldane. She assumed it was the same here, but what choice did they have? They could not make this journey on foot—not with the limited time they had, and they didn't have the luxury of dragons the way C'Tan did. No, it was the horses or nothing, so she nodded as if she were confident. "Will you lead us then, Lily?"

The girl nodded, picked up her bag, waved a hand to extinguish the candles, and slid through the curtain. The three crept through the empty halls single file, Lily in the front and Kayla bringing up the rear. Several times, she heard rocks fall and thought she heard a footstep behind her, but when she turned, no one was there.

After passing through several portals and running through still-hot rooms—the last remnants of C'Tan's tampering with the fissures leading from Devil's Mount—they emerged into the coolness of a cavern heavy with the smell of horse. None of the animals were as beautiful as the white mare she had left in Peldane after Brant's death, but she would take what she could get. The three quickly saddled and bridled horses for each of them, then Ember led them to the gate of the paddock and let them out, shutting the gate behind them. Once clear, Kayla mounted and took the lead, riding through the wide cavern and out into the cool night just above the village of Karsholm.

Following the road that led west, the girls rode side-by-side, their tempo matching step for step. Kayla was just beginning to relax when, out of nowhere, an orange electric field formed around each of the girls and held them in place as their horses ran out from beneath them. They flipped forward and hit the ground hard, faces to the dust. Kayla felt as if a stone was pressed at her back. She could hardly breathe, especially with her face in the dust, poofing into her eyes and mouth with every gasp. She lay there, furious with whoever had them in his grasp.

"Horse thieves," she heard a male voice growl. He spat in the dirt. "What the Helar do you think you're doing, stealing the academy's horses? Haven't we lost enough already? Now you've got to—" The voice stopped. A man stepped over Kayla to grab Ember by the robe and lift her to her feet. "Ember?" he asked, sounding incredulous. "What are you doing? Don't you know we could have killed you?"

"Well, what do you expect?" She gasped for air. "We're sent on a quest and then we're not allowed to go. If you won't help us, we'll have to depend on our own devices."

The man shoved her, and the orange shields surrounding them melted away.

"You are an idiot!" he shouted at her, completely ignoring the other two.

"No more than you!" Ember's voice matched his in volume and anger. "Hiding out, scouting the road, and attacking us in the dark? What are you? A bunch of bandits?"

"Bandits?" The man moved closer to Ember. "You call us bandits when you are the ones stealing horses? You are the thieves, Ember. Not us."

Kayla's fury grew with each of their words until she ran toward their attacker and leaped into the air, her booted feet catching him mid-back and shoving him to the ground. He flipped over and she sat on him, pinning his arms down while he tried to catch his breath. "You're wasting our time! If we'd been given the help we needed and asked for days ago, we would be long gone. Your headmaster blocks us. The mage council blocks us. And all the while, Ember's mother sits in C'Tan's cells, waiting for her daughter to bring the keystones. And now you block our way!" She picked up a rock, not sure if she did so to protect herself or to attack this enemy who fought with her cousin. She raised her arm threateningly, and a strange tingling sensation traveled across her chest, through her shoulder, and clear to her fingers. When she tried to drop the stone, her hand would not move. She bit down on her fury and the unladylike words that came with it. She was frozen by some outside source. Again.

This time her attacker walked around and stood in front of her, then created a glowing ball of light that hovered just above his head and made her eyes water. "I wouldn't do that if I were you," DeMunth said with his musical silver tongue. "You are about to kill Ember's brother."

Sure enough, she looked down and realized she straddled the young man with the orange tattoos she'd seen coming from Sarali's chamber. If he'd seemed angry then, it was nothing compared to the fury she saw now.

Teeth clenched, he uttered terse words. "Get. Off."

He didn't need to say anything more. As soon as the restraint left her arm, she dropped the rock and scampered to Ember and Lily. She hated that Ember's brother scared her so. The only way she knew how to handle fear like that was to turn it to hate. Make him the enemy. She couldn't be afraid of what she hated.

She never had.

CHAPTER FOUR

Ember didn't want to admit it to herself, but she was happy when Kayla attacked Aldarin. She knew he was upset about being forced to leave the guard because of the magical tattoos T'Kato had passed to him, but he had been getting sullen. She missed the fun brother he used to be, her best friend. He'd become mean since inheriting the tattoos. It was about time someone took him down a notch or three, and Kayla was just the person to do it. He'd hate having a girl send him to the dirt and nearly kill him.

Or maybe it was a bad idea. He would most likely hate Kayla after that. Ember's satisfaction left as quickly as it had formed. According to her dreams, Aldarin was to be a part of the group who destroyed C'Tan and repaired the magic of their world. Kayla was also part of that group. That meant he must travel with them. Ember groaned inwardly. This was bad. Really, really bad.

She put aside those thoughts for now. She could do nothing, so instead, she stood and brushed herself off, then put her hands on her hips and glared at her protector, DeMunth. He should have been escaping with her, not yanking her off a galloping horse and bruising her rear.

He looked angry, but explained anyway. "Ezeker asked us to watch for bandits and for students trying to make their way home without permission. They ordered us to stop any and all travelers on the road, especially those with horses. You were galloping at such a clip, I'm guessing you didn't hear us hail you."

Ember reddened, grateful none could see it in the dark. No, she had heard no one calling them. She shook her head.

"Got the horses," Shad's voice came from the darkness. "Though next time, you might want to consider swapping jobs. Horses and wolves don't really go together, you know?"

That was obvious by the stamping of the animals and the terrified rolling of their eyes. It made Ember grateful that the horses had grown up with her family. They knew her scent.

Shad stopped, his eyes widening. "Ember? You stole the horses?"

She sighed and nodded.

Her wolfen uncle chuckled. "Good for you, pup. It's about time you got your backbone again."

"Shad! Enough!" Aldarin chastised the man twice his age. "Don't encourage her."

Instead of taking offense, Uncle Shad chuckled once again and led the horses past the group. "I'll just return these ladies to the paddock, shall I?" He moved up the roadway toward the Mage Academy and the corral. DeMunth took Ember and Kayla by the elbow, and Aldarin took Lily the same way. Giving Kayla a wide berth, Aldarin walked quickly around the other three and got ahead of them, walking toward the school. DeMunth shook his head and followed with the two fuming girls.

DeMunth spoke quietly as they made their way up the hill, his beautiful silver tongue making the words resonate. "Ember, I know how important it is for you to be on your way. I understand what is at stake, and despite what you may think right now, I am on your side."

"You have a funny way of showing it," she snapped.

He let out a frustrated sigh. "I've done everything in my power to convince the council to give you what you need to go in search of the keystones, but you know how bureaucracies work. Everything goes slow."

"Which is why we left. We don't have time for that mill to grind away. We need to go." She kicked a rock and almost wished she could kick DeMunth. If she was honest with herself, she was more hurt than angry. She felt betrayed, though she knew it wasn't logical.

"I know," he answered. He squeezed her arm in what she assumed was meant to be a reassuring manner. "But stealing horses is not the way to do it."

She really didn't have an answer for that.

DeMunth, Aldarin, and a newly returned Shad escorted the girls into Ezeker's office, pulling in an extra chair so they could all be seated. Ember felt like a prisoner. She was the white mage. The white mage. The first one born in three millennia. They couldn't hold her here, not forever. She didn't understand why the council felt the need to debate everything. Ember needed the keystones to heal Rasann. Only she could find the keystones. Only she could use them. Thus, Ember had to leave, and the sooner the better. The world was falling apart, and the magi high council debated. It was ridiculous.

They waited for the headmaster, Ezeker—or Uncle Ezzie, as Ember called him—to enter his office and speak with them. While waiting, she looked around. She hadn't been to this room before. It must be his "official" office where he conducted business, rather than his more informal dining area where she usually spoke with him.

The room was dusty with ash, but intact. His desk was made of stone rather than wood, but was carved as intricately as the softer material would be. Shelves were formed from the walls themselves, holding books and instruments, some streaming magic she could see when she shut her eyes. She was beginning to see other colors now that she'd been here for a bit. Green had come first, then yellow and purple. Now she could see blue and orange, but not red. Still no red or white, except for the cord that tied her to her master in the Havens, Mahal. The Guardian who created her and watched over her had even taken her father in his death and made him one of her protectors.

Ezeker finally entered the room, pulling Ember from her thoughts. He wore his multi-colored robe and his spectacles, his long beard almost quivering with some form of emotion. Ember guessed anger, but it could be something else. As he came around the desk, the men moved to go, but the ancient magi stopped them with a word. "Stay. Shut the door and stay. This pertains to you as much as to them."

They looked at each other and then did as the headmaster commanded, one man standing behind each of the girls. Aldarin got Kayla by default. There was no one left to stand behind. He did not look pleased. Nor did she.

Ezeker sat down, pulled his chair forward, and looked at each of them. They returned his gaze, none showing remorse for their actions. It was essential to leave—why feel bad? Finally, he leaned forward, took off his glasses and laid them on the desk, then rubbed his eyes.

"Do any of you realize the trouble you have caused tonight?"

No one answered.

He picked up his spectacles and perched them upon his nose. He interlaced his fingers and sat straight. "Horse thieving? Have you no honor?"

Ember couldn't let that go without saying something. "Sir, those horses are school property, and we are students at this school. I don't see where borrowing three mares would—"

He stood, his beard quivering. "Borrowing. Borrowing? You were not borrowing those animals. You stole them!"

Ember stood. "Only because we had to! We've told you repeatedly that we needed to be on our way, that we had a quest to complete, but the council would rather speak to Lily about C'Tan than allow us to heal the world!" She put her palms flat on his desk and leaned forward. "Nobody is listening! You have forced us to sneak like thieves when we would much rather go with your blessing."

Ember stayed standing, glaring at Ezeker with all the energy in her body. He seemed surprised. Of course, it was the first time she'd hadn't backed down with him, so it wasn't really any wonder.

He sat down slowly and ran his hand over his beard, apparently thinking. The silence in the room seemed to last forever, but finally, he spoke. "Perhaps you are right. Perhaps our desire to understand our enemy has overshadowed the need for you to be on your way." He pointed his finger at Ember. "But I will not have you stealing to do it."

The silence continued as he thought his way through something, then, seeming to decide, he leaned forward. "I will make an agreement with you. Perhaps we can help one another." Lily started to say something, but Ezeker put up a finger to silence her. He continued. "I will let you go on your quest, taking whatever you need for your journey. In return, I ask one thing." He looked at all of them, the men included. "I need you to escort the students home."

"What? No!" Ember squawked, and she wasn't alone.

"Unacceptable!" Kayla yelled at the same time.

Lily snapped, "No! There is no time for this!"

All of them objected at once, creating a huge cacophony of sound.

Ezeker rose to his feet and boomed, "Silence!" The entire room shook with his voice, the sound bouncing back and forth off the walls in echoes that grew in strength rather than fading away. It wasn't until they silenced themselves that the painful tone stopped.

Ears ringing, Ember glanced around. Everyone was either rubbing the side of their head or staring at Ezeker with a mixture of awe and fear.

Once he had their attention, he continued. "This is not negotiable. The younger students, in particular, are not safe here. We had a breach just this afternoon that left several of our guard dead."

Kayla looked a bit guilty at that. Ember remembered that Kayla had fought the false magi. Ember had known and hadn't told Uncle Ezzie. She'd meant to, but somehow it was forgotten in their plans to leave.

"I am not asking you to return all the students," Ezeker continued. "Many of them have already used the portals. Others had family come to get them. But until this Academy is running fully, guarded properly, and safe once more, I cannot justify keeping the remaining students here, and I cannot send them home alone. Some students will be your transportation."

He kept talking. "I only ask you to return students to two villages. Only two. It will not take much of your time, and may even give you information about the keystones you would lack otherwise. It will also get you to your destinations thirty times faster than a horse."

Ember gasped. She couldn't imagine anything faster than a horse, aside from a dragon, and she was pretty sure there weren't any dragons at the mage academy. And thirty times faster? Impossible.

But Ezeker said nothing more on the subject. Instead, he asked Shad, DeMunth, and Aldarin, one by one, "Do you agree?"

Each of them said "Yes."

Then Kayla and Lily. "Do you agree?"

They both said "Yes."

And finally, he came to Ember. "Do you agree, Ember?" She was the only one he called by name, and it felt as if the entire thing would be determined by her answer—but if what he said was true, if they could get where they needed to go thirty times faster, it was worth the detour.

She nodded. "I agree."

Ezeker grinned. "Good. Now, in order to get you in the air by sunrise, you'll need to awaken the children who will go with you. I've made lists, telling you where the children can be found." He handed each of them a scrap of parchment. "I will not punish you for your actions tonight, but consider this your penance for taking the horses. Help the children pack. If they do not want to leave, make them want it. Whatever it takes, get them ready. You have three hours until sunrise."

Three hours? Ember yawned and took the paper he set in front of her. As if the night hadn't been long enough, now they had to spend the rest of it prodding younglings.

A knock came at the door.

"Enter," Ezeker called. A guard opened the heavy wood and leaned in.

"Sir, we stopped a woman on the road, and she insists on seeing you. She's looking for her daughter."

Ember's heart sank. It was most likely the mother of a child who had gone missing in the attack on the mage academy. She hoped the child was still alive.

Ezeker looked defeated. It had to be hard telling so many parents that the child you had cared for was gone. "Let her in," he said, dismissing the guard.

The guard opened the door all the way and a blond woman entered, about Ember's mother's age. "Master Ezeker, I beg your pardon, but—" She stopped and stared at Kayla, who had also frozen. Ember looked from one to the other, seeing the resemblance. Could it be?

"Mother?" Kayla sounded completely shocked.

"Kayla?" the woman said, tears coming immediately to her eyes.

"Mother, what are you doing here? How did you find me?" Kayla asked, still not moving.

"I followed your trail. I had a mage guide into Karsholm, then came the rest of the way on my own. I couldn't let you go on your quest alone. Not with all you've been through. Not with all I had to endure. I have nothing else. Nothing but you." Finally, the two moved together and embraced.

"I wasn't sure I'd see you again," Kayla whispered.

Her mother took her hand.

Ezeker cleared his throat, obviously awaiting an introduction.

Kayla reddened. "Excuse me. Headmaster Ezeker, this is my mother, Lady Kalandra of Peldane."

Ezeker bowed his head in her direction. "You've come a long way for your daughter," he said.

"What mother wouldn't come for their child?" she answered, sounding very royal. Kayla continued, introducing each of them. "This is Lily, a student of six colors of magic. She's very gifted. DeMunth, guardian of the yellow keystone, the armor of light." DeMunth took Lady Kalandra's hand and kissed it. She smiled. "The guy with the orange tattoos is Aldarin." She used her thumb to point over her shoulder without turning around. Her voice warmed when she turned to Shad. "This gentleman is Shad of the Bendanatu. Don't ask me what his full name is—I can't pronounce it." Kayla chuckled.

Shad gave Kayla's mother a bow, his eyes shining. "It is an honor to meet such a beautiful lady. Your daughter has done you proud in your absence."

Lady Kalandra beamed and gave Shad a flirty smile.

The chemistry between the two was more than obvious. Shad cleared his throat. "And this is Ember Shandae. Surely you have heard of her?" he asked.

Lady Kalandra tilted her head to the side, looking at Ember, then at her daughter, who grinned like Ember had never seen. "Surely not," she said, but Kayla nodded.

Ember had the lady's full attention then. "You are Brina's daughter?" she asked.

"She has changed her name from Brina to Marda, but yes, I am," Ember answered, taking the lady's outstretched hands.

Lady Kalandra looked pained. "Then we are . . . family?"

"Well, if you and my mum are sisters, I would guess so," Ember answered, and was immediately drawn into a hug.

"Where is your mother?" she asked when she finally released Ember.

Kayla touched her mother's shoulder, and at the lady's look, Kayla shook her head. "She is dead?" Kalandra whispered.

Ember jumped in. "No, no! She's not dead, but she's been kidnapped and is being held hostage by C'Tan."

"Who happens, by unfortunate circumstance, to be my mother," Lily said, joining the conversation.

Lady Kalandra looked overwhelmed by all the information. Shad stepped forward and took the lady by the arm. "Why don't I explain everything to you while the others assist the youngsters in their preparations? We leave on a journey to find more keystones in the morning. I assume you will accompany us?"

Kalandra looked over her shoulder at her daughter. "But of course," she said.

The door shut, and Kayla sighed. "Much as I am happy to see my mother, this is going to place a bit of a burden upon us. She has no magic, she doesn't know how to fight, and she has been pampered most of her life. But she's my mother." She threw her hands up in the air as if she didn't know what to do.

Lily, Ember, Aldarin, and DeMunth surrounded Kayla. Surprisingly, it was Aldarin who spoke. "Family first, Kayla. We'll make sure she stays safe." He scuffed his feet on the stone, looking downward. She turned toward him and Ember expected an argument, but her cousin's face softened and she uttered a simple, "Thank you."

Ezeker clapped his hands, startling them all. "Good. I'm glad that is settled. Now off with you to wake the youngsters. They won't get themselves up for this journey, you know."

Knowing that was all too true, they took their lists and headed out the door.

CHAPTER FIVE

C'Tan stood in her room before the glass mirror, which was still warped and bent from when she last shattered it and fused it together. She opened her robe to drop it, but stopped. For the first time since she had been burned in her fight with her brother, she found she could not use her scars to flare up the anger toward him, not with his wife sitting captive in her dungeon.

It was strange, the feelings having Brina nearby brought up in her. She found herself remembering things she had forgotten. Times when Brina and Jarin and C'Tan had been together. An evening around the table, playing cards after dinner. A picnic in the field near their home, with Mother telling stories about Jarin's father. The night before Brina's wedding, when she and C'Tan had sat and talked for hours about everything under the sun, and how excited she had been to gain Brina as a big sister.

Everything had changed when she'd learned the truth about her father and realized that she was nothing to him. C'Tan had been nineteen when she overheard the man bragging over his ale about taking the mage-mining witch-woman by force. He seemed proud of it, that he had taken away Asana's innocence and left her to raise a child alone.

C'Tan had never known the truth before that night. Whenever she had asked about her father, Asana had made up some story. She'd always made Celena Tan feel loved, but when she heard his boast, put the pieces together, and realized that she was a child of rape—she snapped and did some awful things to the man. Things that had scarred her and changed her and made her open to S'Kotos's power. She hadn't been the same since.

For the first time since she had given in to S'Kotos' charm and become his servant, she felt genuine regret. She could have been so much more, so . . . different. And in one act, she had damned herself for eternity.

Uncomfortable with the turn her thoughts had taken, C'tan banished the mirror and spun, heading to her room. She summoned her wardrobe. It hung before her like the mirror, dangling in the air as if held on a string, but it was only her power holding it in place. She moved down the line of red clothing. She didn't need her riding leathers, or the ball gown given her by a long-gone suitor. Finally, she settled on a simple dress, homespun and rough-cut, but still beautiful. It reminded her of her childhood days and made her feel somehow free.

The necklace about her throat vibrated to notify her of a call coming in from one of her subjects. Annoyed, C'Tan crossed into the other room and dropped the stone into the scrying bowl she kept ready. A woman's face swam up to meet her, and she removed the sunglasses that hid her sightless eyes from the world.

"Report," C'Tan snarled, trying to get a hold of her temper.

"The boy will be an excellent candidate, Mistress," the blind woman said, staring at C'Tan with those eerily blank eyes that could fully see.

"Is he awake?" C'Tan asked, calming at the woman's words.

"He is. He is adjusting to the prosthesis and I am teaching him to use his other colors of magic to see—focusing first on the red, of course. If we are to turn him, he must have full use of his red."

"I know that," C'Tan snapped. "How long until he is ready to be indoctrinated and introduced to S'Kotos?"

The blind woman tipped her head in thought. “I am not sure. It could be days. It could be months. These things take time, Mistress.”

C’Tan stuck her fingers in the bowl and squeezed. The blind woman curled in on herself in obvious pain.

“Make it days, Vani. I don’t have months to train a new spy.” C’Tan cut the connection.

CHAPTER SIX

Kayla looked down at her list of children to awaken and was surprised to find that the last three girls all slept in the same room, though it made sense when she thought about it. Space was rather limited since the attack on the mage academy. Of course, the students would double and triple up, no matter how many had gone home—for comfort, if nothing else.

She was also surprised to note that she knew all three of the girls and had worked with them just that morning.

There was no easy way to wake them—no door to knock upon, no bell to ring—so she stepped through the curtain and sent up a blue magelight without saying a word. The girls startled and sat up almost immediately.

"Mistress Kayla, is it time to work again already?" Aryana rubbed at her eyes and swung her feet to the floor. Raech and Eden did the same.

"No," Kayla answered. "No more working on the caves for you ladies."

The girls objected, but Kayla cut them off and continued. "Master Ezeker has made arrangements for you to return home until the academy is repaired and safe once more. He is arranging transport that is thirty times faster than a horse, he says, though that seems a bit ridiculous to me."

The girls looked at each other and burst out laughing. It made Kayla feel like she had in Peldane, where she was socially awkward and unaccepted. She stiffened and turned to walk away. Let them get home on their own. She refused to be laughed at any longer.

"No, wait!" Raech called. "Please don't be offended. Come, tell us what you need." By the sound of things, the girls were up and packing, bare feet scuffing across the stone floor.

Kayla kept her back to them. "Why should I?" she demanded, exhaustion making her sullen.

"Because *we* are your transportation, silly," Eden answered, giggling once again.

Baffled, Kayla turned and looked at the last girl to speak. "What do you mean?"

Eden looked at the other girls, then at Kayla, her face puzzled. "He didn't tell you?" she asked.

"Tell me what, exactly? That we are to saddle you up and ride you out of here like a horse? Or perhaps you can sprout wings like a dragon and will take us by air?" Kayla snapped. "Seriously, girls, I am not an idiot and I refuse to be treated like one. If you wish to go home, be in the courtyard in thirty minutes." She turned again to leave and reached for the curtain, but a light flashed behind her. Kayla ducked and glanced over her shoulder.

A fiery winged creature hovered in the middle of the cavernous room. All the colors of heat and light shimmered about her—brilliant orange, vibrant pink, and warm yellow. She was full of light, but did not burn—the most beautiful thing Kayla had ever seen. Kayla's legs gave out, and she plopped to the ground, staring in wonder.

Following Eden's example, Raech and Aryana leaped into the air, transforming a few feet off the ground into the same kind of being that flared before Kayla. They spiraled upward, then down to the ground, weaving in and out amongst one another in an intricate winged dance that was breathtaking.

Finally settling to the earth, the girls transformed into their human forms. Raech spoke for them this time. "We are Phoenixian. Phoenix. We are your transportation. I am sorry Ezeker did not tell you before. We are shapeshifters, like the MerCat you brought with you and the Bendanatu you met." The girls continued to pack and change as they spoke.

Dumbfounded, Kayla found the words to ask, "How are we to ride you if you burn with flames?"

Aryana smiled and transformed directly in front of Kayla. She scrambled away, but Aryana came forward, her voice inside Kayla's head. *Touch me. You needn't be afraid. Just touch, and you'll see.*

Shaking, Kayla stopped her crab walk and got up on her knees, reaching toward the colorful bird. Her fingers passed through the flaming aura with nothing more than a tingle and rested on the Phoenixian's head. Astonished, Kayla pulled back and let both her hands play in the fiery-looking aura. Magic. Light. These Phoenixians were the companions to the color yellow. They had to be.

"This . . ." She tried again. "This is incredible. I had no idea phoenix existed. Of course, I'm new to all this. Wow." Unsure what to say or do, she scrambled to her feet. "Is there anything you need? Anything I can do?"

Eden looked at the other two and cinched down her satchel. "No, I think we are ready to go. Is there anything we can do for you?" she asked in return.

Kayla shook her head.

"Then let us go to the meeting place," she said.

Kayla nodded, beginning to get over her awe. Of course there were other shapeshifters. It only made sense. Were there shapeshifters for every color of magic? Air elementals for blue, Phoenixians paired with the yellow, dragons with the red. Did the MerCats pair with the purple? The Bendanatu wolves with the green? And what about orange? Or white, for that matter? Her mind buzzed with possible connections.

In the halls near the courtyard, Kayla met up with Aldarin, and they walked together. She wrinkled her nose with distaste, still angry with him for pulling her off the horse earlier. He didn't seem inclined to speak to her either, but if they were to travel together, she'd have to tolerate the orange tattooed man.

As the halls narrowed, Aldarin fell into step behind her as they made their way toward Ezeker's tower. Kayla followed the spiral staircase, exited the building, and stopped when she saw what was perched in the open space.

People and birds. Gigantic birds of light like Eden, Alayna, and Raech, but much bigger. They alternately thrilled and terrified her, and feeling her terror, Brant spun out from the flute. "What's scaring you, my love?" he asked. Kayla said nothing, but just pointed at the glowing fowl. Brant chuckled. "The Phoenixia? They're nothing to fear. Shapeshifters, just like the Bendanatu and the MerCats. Beautiful, aren't they?"

"Yes. I've seen some of the girls, but they were much smaller. They are pretty to look at, but I don't think I can ride one. They're so *big*, and knowing they have a human form makes the thought of using them as mounts just . . . wrong. It's too odd. Can you take me up in your cyclone? Isn't there some kind of air transportation?"

Brant laughed outright at that. "You can't ride me, no, but there are other air elementals who might be accommodating. Let me call one and see." He went quiet, his eyes staring Havenward, and then a slow smile crept across his face. "There's one coming. I think you'll like this."

"What? What is it?" she asked, her stomach all aflutter once again. She craned her neck, trying to see past the glowing Phoenixia and the students gathered around them, but it was several moments before the glowing blue aura of a serpentine elemental floated into view. It was see-through, like Brant's ghostly aura, but had to be solid or it would be of no use to her as a mount.

A muscular man approached Kayla, speaking as he walked. "Are ye ready to mount up, lass?" He stopped in front of her.

Kayla shook her head, unable to find words as the blue air elemental flowed toward her. It looked much like a small dragon without the wings, its body long and slender. It was actually quite beautiful. She finally spoke to the mount master. "No, I've got my own ride, thank you."

The strong man turned and then stepped away as the air elemental moved toward Kayla, almost as if he were afraid of the thing. She stepped forward and reached out a hand to the mount's head. It leaned into her palm, much like a horse, and rubbed against her hand. Unlike a horse, its breath was not warm, but instead felt like a cool autumn day.

The presence of the strong man disappeared from behind her while Kayla wrapped her arms around the elemental and leaned her cheek against his. "Does he have a name?" she asked Brant, and was surprised to hear an answer in her mind from the dragon itself.

"Yes, of course I have a name, though it is long and unpronounceable for most humans. You may call me Thew. He sniffed at her. *I like you. You smell good."*

Kayla laughed, and Brant disappeared into the flute with a wink in her direction. Ezeker's voice sounded from behind her just then. "Are you sure you won't take one of the Phoenixia? Air elementals are notoriously unreliable."

The dragon hissed at the wizard.

"No offense intended, of course," the old man said, backing up.

Thew snorted, turned, and wrapped himself around a tree.

Kayla fought her laughter. "I am sure, Master Ezeker. I'd be more comfortable with my own color of magic, if you don't mind."

Ezeker shrugged. "If that's what you wish, I won't fight you. Just take care, my child." He turned and walked to the Phoenixia and spoke to one of the largest birds. Instantly, the glowing creatures shrank into humans—men, women, and even young children, Kayla's three young Phoenixians among them. She shouldn't have been surprised but there were others among the birds she knew as well—Behn, the strong boy she'd worked with in the morning, as well as Miek, and some of the younger students, Nayte, Hailey, Lynkyn, Ezra, and Tia, the last four being siblings.

The old wizard then raised his voice above the crowd. He was easy to hear, even as far away as she stood. "People! I need your attention!" he yelled, then waited. The voices faded, and he continued. "Thank you for your patience. I apologize for the need to send you students home, but with the school in such disrepair, we have no choice until it is in operation. We shall retrieve you as soon as possible." A buzz of conversation started up once again. "Now, please, listen for a bit longer," he said. He waited for silence before he spoke and finally got it. "This is Master Ted Finch."

"Call me Finchling," she heard in her own head.

Ezeker continued, as if he'd not been interrupted. "He will be lead mount for Ember's group." The tall, dark-haired man bowed his head and grinned. "DeMunth, he will carry you."

Ezra continued, but Kayla stopped listening. Being so close to leaving, just to have everything delayed was exactly what she'd feared the night before. She let out a sigh and slouched, waiting impatiently.

"That's not very ladylike." Her mother's voice came from behind her.

She jumped, having forgotten her mother was at the school. Embarrassed, she ignored the words and forgetfulness and instead asked, "Have you found a mount yet?" Her mother moved to her side.

"Not as of yet," Lady Kalandra answered. "I am a bit wary of trusting these flaming birds."

"They're not so bad, but I understand. Brant called an elemental for me to ride." A thought occurred to her, and she addressed the glowing, dragon-like creature. "Thew, can you carry more than one?"

The dragon seemed affronted. *"But of course. I am strong and reliable, despite what the magemaster thinks."*

Kayla looked at her mum and grinned. "Will you carry my mother as well?"

The elemental sniffed. *"If you wish it."*

Were all air elementals this rude? She couldn't help but wonder, and it irritated her. Her tone was clipped when she answered. "I do."

"Then it shall be done."

Lady Kalandra squeezed her daughter's arm and leaned close. "Thank you."

Kayla nodded, but said nothing as Ezeker continued his speech.

Leaning to his left, Ezeker put his hand on a woman's shoulder. "This is Mistress Shari Bird and her children, most of whom are students at the school. They will also be mounts." He pointed to the children one by one. "Hailey, Ezra, Tia, and Lynkyn," he said. "Mistress Shari will be mount mistress for Duchess Kayla's group."

Kayla's attention was piqued at that. This woman was a mother to four students? She looked so young, but the resemblance was clear.

"Phoenixia, you may shift into your other form. Students and riders, please step forward and claim a mount," he said. "Use mindspeak while they are in bird form to communicate your needs. Please go directly to the Bendanatu and then to the Phoenixia to return the students to their homes before you go in search of the keystones." He looked at Kayla and Ember. "And under no circumstances will you go to C'Tan's castle. Do you understand?" He stared at Ember. She seemed to hesitate, then nodded.

"Good! Now mount up and be on your way!" Ezeker walked from the courtyard and stood not far from Kayla. Thew unwound himself from the tree and settled to the ground so she and her mother could easily settle themselves astride the elemental. Nervous, Kayla straddled Thew's back, which was about as big around as a human torso, and sat, her mother doing the same behind her. They sank slightly into his form. It surprised her to note he wasn't entirely solid, and finally understood Master Ezeker's concern. She was about to tell Brant she'd changed her mind, but Thew rose into the air and hovered, with no warning. Kayla's stomach twitched, but she had a good seat and his long ears made great handholds. She didn't fall through him, as she'd feared, and released the breath she'd held at his movement.

In mere seconds, everyone had mounted and was ready to go. Ezeker stepped forward again and threw his arms in the air, as if shooing pigeons, sending the Phoenixians and passengers on their way.

The Phoenixia flapped their wings and rose slowly off the ground, some of the younglings squealing at the change of balance. They clung to the glowing birds as they climbed higher, with Thew following close behind.

A male voice sounded in Kayla's head, and by the reaction of the others, they heard it too. *Well, off we go,* one of the Phoenixians said. Kayla thought it might have been DeMunth's mount, Ted Finch.

At least someone was excited.

With the morning sun bright in their eyes, away they went.

CHAPTER SEVEN

As soon as the Phoenix leaped into the air, Ember knew she was in for the ride of her life. One of the Bendanatu students sat behind her. Keyera's grip tightened on Ember's stomach as they gained height. The wind threw Ember's hair from her face, sometimes making it whip around to snap her eyes and probably tickling her fellow passenger, but it was worth it. Riding a horse had always been a thrill, racing from one side of the field to the other or the weightless feeling as she soared over a gate with Brownie, but that was nothing compared to this.

She was flying.

Every dream, every fantasy of flight she'd ever had was a pale comparison. The phoenix spiraled upward, then headed southwest, the forest below them an impenetrable sea of green with only the occasional meadow or stream breaking up the endless field of trees.

Ember glanced to her right. DeMunth, handsome as always and fully bedecked in his crystalline armor of light, flew even with her. It made her happy to see him grinning like a little boy who'd just found a stash of candy. For the first time since she'd met him, he actually looked his age, so much younger than people thought. The weight of responsibility and his history forgotten in the moment, he was just a young man thrilled by his first ride on a Phoenix. No doubt she looked the same, matching his toothy smile that split his face from ear to ear.

Thankful for the ability to cast her thoughts to her guardian, she spoke in her mind. With the wind blowing, there was no one else to talk to. "*Enjoying yourself?*"

DeMunth's head twisted toward her, then turned to the front. He completely ignored her. Ember's stomach dropped. Why would he do that? DeMunth had never shunned her before. He was usually very loving and attentive. Why would he be angry? She puzzled it over for several long minutes as they continued their flight, and finally she sent her thoughts his way once again. "*Are you angry with me?*"

Finally, he looked at her, and if the stiff jaw from gritted teeth wasn't enough to answer her, the look in his eyes certainly did. Once again, he turned his head forward and said nothing.

That hurt.

She thought he loved her. He'd certainly shown her his feelings over the last several days, and his kisses had so much emotion and passion in them, they could nearly power all of Javak. He hadn't spurned her, but was definitely angry. After the silence stretched on and she could stand it no longer, she asked, "*What did I do?*"

He turned and faced her, still angry, but his brows rose in surprise. "*You have to ask that?*" Even his mind voice sounded upset.

"*Well, yes.*" She squirmed in the saddle." *It's obvious that you're mad at me, but I can't for the life of me figure out why.*"

His mindvoice snorted. She wouldn't have heard it if he did it out loud with the wind deafening them in flight. "*Wow.*" He shook his head. "*You really don't know.*" It wasn't a question.

Ember shook her head, still completely baffled.

"*Ember, what am I to you?*" He sent his thoughts across the small distance between their Phoenixian mounts, his musical mind voice once again almost as clear and bell-like as his actual speaking or singing voice.

It still amazed her he could speak again after so many years of being tongueless.

"You're my love. My friend. My guardian—"

He cut her off there. "*Your guardian. Yes. And what exactly does that mean to you?*" His eyes bore into hers as if they would drill a hole through her.

She squirmed in her saddle again and looked away, but she still answered him with her thoughts. "*It means you are my protector. You keep me safe.*" She looked back at him.

DeMunth threw his hands in the air and shot an angry and hurt thought at her so hard she reeled from the emotional and mental blow. "*And how in the world am I supposed to protect you when you leave in the middle of the night without me? I wasn't forgotten—you left me behind. Purposely. What if someone else had attacked you to take the horses? What if the Ne'Goi had returned? Or C'Tan? What would you have done? You have no control over your magic, you don't know how to fight, and though you are strong, you are only one person. I should have been with you! Why can't you trust me?*"

Ember moved as if she'd been punched in the stomach. Oh, the words hurt! And he had every right to say them. Telling him she had wanted to take him wouldn't matter. She had felt the emotion behind his words. Betrayal. Useless. A failure.

All she could offer, really, was sincerity. He would feel it whether or not he wanted to. He would heal and return to her, or he would not. The latter thought made her heart ache, but she could not control his feelings any more than he could control hers. Still, she had to give him something. "*I am sorry,*" she sent, putting all the sincerity she had into the thought. He looked at her again, his eyes softer, but his jaw still tight. He nodded once, but said nothing more.

Ember had to distract herself, or the pain of disappointing DeMunth would drive her to madness. Tyese flew nearby on one of the younger Phoenixians—Ember believed it was Nayte, but she wasn't positive.

Hoping Tyese could still hear her, she sent thoughts to the young redhead. "*Are you enjoying your ride?*"

Tyese turned to her, a goofy grin splattered across her face. "*Oh, yes. This is . . .*" Her voice went silent for a moment. "*I don't even have the words to describe it. This is the most wonderful and exhilarating experience of my life! I must say, I'm very grateful the rumors about the Phoenixia are false.*"

"*What rumors?*" Ember asked.

Her smile grew even wider, if that were possible. "*That they are creatures of fire, of course. I would hate to be astride one of these marvelous beings and have it burst into flames between my legs, wouldn't you?*"

Ember laughed out loud before answering. "*Yes. Yes, I wholeheartedly agree. That would definitely put a damper on things.*"

They rode in silence for a long while, the Phoenixia surfing through the sky like boats on smooth water. Ember felt like a dandelion puff being blown in the wind, and watching the sun rise over the mountains while in the air was something that couldn't have been more beautiful. The clouds turned pink with the light shining through them, and it wasn't until the phoenix flew through the poofs she'd always thought of as cotton that she realized they were, actually, a floating fog. She had never known. It was fascinating. She came out the other side with her clothes slightly damp, and despite the cold autumn wind, she was strangely warm.

That was when she noticed the Phoenix beneath her was glowing. Nervous after Tyese's words, she sent a questioning thought her way. "*Uh, Tyese, are you sure these guys won't burst into flames? Mine is getting awfully warm.*'

"*I have a name, you know.*" A strange voice entered her head.

Ember looked behind her at the student, Keyera, who stared into the distance, then down at the glowing bird. "*Did you say something?*" she asked, Tyese's laughter ringing in her head.

"*Yes, I most certainly did. I have a name. You should use it,*" the bird said.

The shock wearing off Ember grew irritated. "*Well, I would if you would tell me what it is.*" She gripped the handle before her as the phoenix swerved toward the now openly laughing Tyese. Her phoenix veered out of the way and screeched in response.

The phoenix was quiet for a moment before it finally answered. *'Shari. My name is Shari Bird, and I'm not an "it". I'm a woman, and was once a student at the academy, much like you."*

Ember was surprised. "*Nobody is just like me,"* she said, still upset over the scare of her phoenix nearly colliding with Tyese's.

"I may not be a white mage, but I am a shapeshifter too. All the Phoenixia are," Shari Bird said.

Ember nodded. "*I understand. My apologies. I hadn't meant to be rude."* Shari Bird's acknowledgement was felt more than spoken, but it was enough.

The ride was amazing. An occasional bird or cloud passed nearby. Beneath her, the forest canopy grew more dense the farther they flew, and that reminded her of where she was going and why. She knew next to nothing about the Bendanatu, aside from what Uncle Shad had told her, and from her brief stay with them in the caves after her kidnapping and the run to Javak for the mage trials. And so, she turned to the only person who was near enough and actually talking to her, and was sure to have the information she wanted.

"Tyese, can you tell me about the Bendanatu? I don't know your customs, your nature—anything at all." Ember asked Shari to fly closer to the girl. They quickly closed the gap and flew wing to wing with the much smaller Phoenixian.

Tyese glanced at her, then toward the front of her phoenix, but she answered. "*Our lives are spent surviving and finding joy in what ways we can. Some of the Bendanatu stay as wolves, hardly changing to human form at all. Others do the opposite, remaining human and rarely visiting the form of their birth. Most are a mix of both, taking one form or the other, depending on their needs."* She lay down on the neck of her bird, relaxing as if in sleep, though she continued to talk to Ember in her head. Ember didn't blame her. Nobody on this journey had much sleep the night before. She, Kayla, and Lily had none. Weariness pressed at her for a moment until she shook it off to listen.

'Some of us dwell in caves, some in homes. It's just a matter of personal preference as to which we have, and just because we are in wolf form doesn't necessarily mean we choose the cave. We are led by White Shadow's father.

His name is Bahndai, and a more generous and kind-hearted man you will never meet."

Ember vaguely remembered Uncle Shad telling her that his father was the chief of the Bendanatu. That meant Bahndai was her grandfather. Her stomach suddenly fluttered over the possibility of meeting this man she hadn't even known existed until a week or so ago. She was going to meet her father's father. She couldn't get any closer to him than that. Finally, excited to go on this journey for personal reasons and not just obligation, she said, *'Tell me more. Tell me everything!"* It was impossible to keep the excitement from her mindvoice.

Tyese chuckled. "*Well, we're creative and happy by nature. Playful. We have games pretty much all the time. We work the green magic and sometimes the orange all throughout the village, if you want to call it that. It's more a bunch of buildings, with most of the homes being spread around the forest. But at night, almost everybody comes to the village for food and drink, dancing and music. Our musicians are some of the best anywhere."*

Ember felt her eyebrows shoot toward her hairline. *'Really? I would never have thought. I mean, being wolves and all, you'd think it would be all about the hunt, not music."*

Tyese turned her head to face Ember as it still lay on the Phoenix's neck. "*People think that, yes, but it's not true. The hunt is part of the games, but it isn't everything. You'll see."*

Ember put her head on the silky feathers like Tyese had and relaxed. She could fall asleep up here if she wasn't careful. She was strapped in, so even if she did fall asleep, she would be safe. "*How long will it take to get there?"*

Tyese was close enough that Ember could see her brows furrow. "*I don't know. I haven't traveled by Phoenix before. By horse, it is several weeks' travel, but I think flying will get us there in a few days."* Her head turned toward her bird and cocked, as if she was listening, and then she turned back to Ember. "*Nayte says we'll get there by tomorrow evening. Tonight we sleep in a way station and travel on in the morning."*

"Nayte? Is that the name of your phoenix?" she asked, pleased that she'd been right.

Tyese nodded. "*The Phoenixia play games too, but they use those games to determine status within the wing. DeMunth's mount, Finchling, is very good.*" Ember looked at her guardian and love, sad that he wouldn't speak to her. Ted Finch turned his head and playfully nipped at DeMunth before turning back to his flight.

Out of questions, Ember closed her eyes and enjoyed the warmth of the bird and the Bendanatu student, Keyera, behind her. She loved the feel of the cool air tossing her hair. Before she could stop herself, she fell asleep.

With sleep came the dreams, like they hadn't for a few days. She stood in a black room, seemingly made of glass. A stone altar sat across the room beneath a window, red velvet hanging its length. The room was motionless for once, no action distracting Ember from seeing the place for what it was. Or rather, the people were there, but they were all stopped mid-motion, as if an icy breath of air had blown in and frozen them all in place. Ember walked around, taking in the details she'd always missed before. What she'd always thought was one room was actually three. The middle room where the battles always took place was large, a dining hall or meeting room, but at each end, there was a door. One led to a dark room with only a bed covered by red silk sheets. A small library filled the space on the other side of the room, a desk dominating the space. An onyx scrying bowl sat in the exact center of the table-like desk.

It was the first time she realized this was C'Tan's domain. Not just the place she chose to battle, but this area, these three rooms, were her home. Ember chilled to realize she was in the demon's lair. At that moment, the frozen figures burst into action, and once again she watched the battle with a few changes.

She knew all the people here. Not just a few of them, as she had in times past, but every single one of them were known to her. Kayla stood against the woman Ember assumed was C'Tan, playing her flute. Aldarin, with glowing orange symbols swirling about him, battled an old man. Lily fought a black dragon with fluid grace, purple spikes of lightning shooting from her hands. DeMunth was there, of course, fighting beside the dream Ember, who stood with a giant hammer glowing silvery white. A green wolf fought beside Lily, and surprisingly, it wasn't Uncle Shad. It was the girl, Tyese. The young girl who had saved Ember in the battle at the mage academy.Warriors and black dragons surrounded the small group with the keystones.

All of the colors of magic were here but one. And then, a dark and handsome man appeared in the midst of the battle, and without being told, Ember knew this was S'Kotos, the Guardian of fire and C'Tan's evil master. As soon as he arrived, something happened, though Ember didn't see exactly what. Suddenly he was clutching his chest, then reaching toward C'Tan. A glowing red mass floated toward the dream Ember, then suddenly zipped into C'Tan, who burst into flames that did not burn her. S'Kotos disappeared, screaming, leaving behind the motley group of seven of all different colors.

C'Tan turned toward them, looking at her hands as if they had somehow become new, then looked up and met Ember's eyes. Instead of the evil and hate Ember had always seen there, her eyes were full of wonder and surprise before she raised her hands to her face and began to cry.

Ember sat up with a start, throwing Shari off balance. The phoenix screeched at her and Ember steadied herself, though her heart still hammered. She'd never had a dream quite like that before. Some elements repeated. She always saw the battle, but the outcome seemed to change frequently, as well as the players. She'd seen both Lily and Sarali as the purple bearers, and Shad and Tyese as the green. Who would be there in the ending battle? She didn't know. And C'Tan becoming the bearer of the red? Impossible. It would never be. Ember knew it in her bones. She was beginning to wonder if this had actually been an actual dream, not a vision of an unknown future. Except it had felt so real. And the details of C'Tan's quarters were just the way Ember imagined they would be. How could that part be real and the rest of it a dream?

She didn't know, and was afraid there would be no true answer until the final battle.

CHAPTER EIGHT

Kayla's group rose into the sky and skimmed over the tops of the trees, getting as close to the forest's canopy as they could without crashing through the pines. Even seated on Thew's back with her mother behind her, it was a terrifying ride for Kayla. She gripped his long ears tightly, praying she wouldn't fall.

She was acting like the prissy girl she had once been, and she knew it, but fear crippled her. This wasn't the way a warrior was supposed to act. T'Kato wouldn't have been afraid, or if he was, he wouldn't have shown it. He was strong. Why couldn't she be strong like him? Why did she have to be so scared all the time?

The flute buzzed at her. She jumped. It had never done that before. But then again, it had never turned into a sword until the battle at Karsholm, and that had been an interesting, if also terrifying, experience. She pulled the bag around to her front and reached in for the flute. She touched the case and suddenly Brant spun out, fully elemental. He balanced delicately on Thew's neck, the wind not seeming to affect him at all, but then, he was made of wind and air—it was part of him, so it wouldn't bother him in the least.

He spoke to her, his voice sounding as if it echoed from the bottom of a well, resounding in her head. *The Ne'Goi are coming.*

The Shadow Weavers? Kayla asked.

Brant nodded.

Kayla's heart surged to her throat. "*Can you warn the others? How close are the Ne'Goi?*"

Close, he said. "*I'll let them know.*" Brant fell through the trees and then rose to hover next to the Phoenixian leaders of the two groups. Kayla could tell when the news spread through the birds and people as they gathered together and drew their weapons. The birds glowed brighter than before.

The Shadow Weavers appeared. Ember threw up her hands to perform some kind of magic, and Kayla saw two flashes of light fly off in different directions. Ember's bracelets flew from her wrists. One landed almost in the lap of the girl seated behind her. She juggled it for a second, then slapped it on her own wrist. The other flew toward the young Bendanatu, Tyese, who, quick as a hummingbird, snatched the flying bracelet and tucked it in her tunic. Before Ember could say a word, her mount, Shari Bird, gathered her children beneath her and dove through the trees, several Ne'Goi trying to follow. Ted Finch and several of the other Phoenixia interfered and kept the Shadow Weavers engaged so they would forget the children.

The Shadow Weavers fell upon the rest of the group. They came from below as if they were on a string that pulled them into the air. With them were several demon-looking creatures—terrifying winged beings in all colors and shades, the fiercest of all. They attacked DeMunth and Aldarin with the viciousness of a badger or a scorpion. No mercy. Bent not on capture, but destruction of everything in their path.

Some of the Phoenixian girls danced among the Ne'Goi and drew them away and down into the trees, weaving in and out in what seemed like impossible maneuvers. More than one of the demon beasts went down, having slammed into a tree.

And then the word spread through the Phoenixians once again. Brant whispered into Kayla's mind. *'The Bendanatu and humans are going to fight on the ground while the rest of us fight from the air. Do you want to stay here with us or go down with the humans?'*

Kayla debated and then decided. *"I'll stay with you. I can do more here surrounded by air than I could do on the ground."*

Brant nodded, seemingly pleased with her decision, and Kayla watched as the Phoenixia dove into a clearing and deposited their passengers, including her cousin Ember. The two warriors, DeMunth and Aldarin, joined her on the ground. The wolves transformed, including Ember, and they fought the Ne'Goi with tooth and claw. It surprised her at how much damage they could really do with just those two weapons.

The Phoenixia climbed into the air and fought directly against the Shadow Weavers, their light growing brighter and brighter. Kayla played her flute, trying to attack them with music, but just like before, they seemed to eat her magic and leave her with nothing. She needed something tangible, something to throw at the beings. The answer hit her as she watched one of the young humans, Alexa Jade, use a sling to throw rocks at the Ne'Goi.

Kayla changed her tune and began to lob ice balls with hard and fast accuracy at the enemy. One by one, the creatures of darkness fell from the sky and either disappeared mid-fall or hit the ground with sickening thuds.

One of the largest, most disturbing creatures she had seen in her life winged into view. Red welts covered his gray body. He wore a loincloth and had horns coming from his shoulders and head. Leathery maroon wings held him aloft. He grinned, his teeth sharpened as if with a file, and Kayla shivered. He surged toward her faster than she believed possible and clasped her shoulders, trying to pull her off Thew.

Lady Kalandra screamed. Kayla hit and clawed at the creature with her hands and even the flute, but when he tried to snatch it from her, she realized she was jeopardizing her greatest weapon, and instead, she began to play. She played a harsh, sharp whistle of sound, and just as the demon creature was about to pull her from Thew's back, despite the thick straps that held her in the saddle, Brant appeared. He wrapped his enormous arms around the ugly creature and pulled, disengaging the beast from her.

Ferocious in his anger, Brant spun out in a cyclone—nearly as frightening as the Ne'Goi he fought. They surged toward one another and wrestled in the air, spinning around and colliding with trees, stray Phoenixians, and the other Ne'Goi. Kayla wanted to help, but there was nothing she could do but watch, powerless. She only hoped Brant would survive the power of the magic-eating Ne'Goi.

CHAPTER NINE

Ember nearly panicked when the bracelets fell from her wrists. That wasn't supposed to happen. Last she had seen, they were tattoos, though if she thought about it, they had been drawn upward, close to the surface of her skin since she had been sliced in the battle at Karsholm. The cut had bisected the bracelet. That was the only thing that had been different. It had to be what pulled them from her skin.

But no time to think about that. A large Ne'Goi with bat-like wings dove toward her, and he was fast. He opened his claws to tackle her and take her to the ground. Ember threw her hands up, willing the monster to stop, slow down, anything. A rush of energy left her, and the demon smashed into an invisible dome that hurled him back into the air like a rubber ball. Despite the growing distance between them, he drew himself up and bellowed at her. She recognized him, and a spike of fear stabbed through her soul.

Laerdish. The evil spy who had been integrated into the mage council for twenty years. The spy she had revealed. She'd thought he was gone for good. She'd also thought he worked for C'Tan.

Evidently, she was wrong. Laerdish was one of the Ne'Goi, and a strong one, it appeared. Probably a leader. He'd definitely shown leadership potential when he tried to shut Ezeker out of the voting to let her into the mage academy.

Shari dove through the trees, and pulled up quickly just before she reached the ground, back-winging and making her children scatter. She looked around and then called out a bird-like whistle. Her children came quickly, and she pulled apart the bushes to expose a shallow cave. The little Phoenixia gathered in together, shivering, and then suddenly there were more children, the humans who had been riding them, huddling with the younglings. Shari and Ember put the bushes in place to hide the children. Then Shari launched herself into the air and Ember looked around, wondering what to do.

Several others dropped to the earth and immediately turned wolf. Ember kicked herself for not thinking to do the same. It was only a matter of a few seconds and she had joined them in form, but with a few changes. Shad had taught her that she could change any part of herself, so she changed herself for battle. She gave more strength to her hindquarters. She lengthened her teeth and made them strong and sharp, and as a final change, she made her claws into long razors—just in time.

The Ne'Goi landed. Not all of them, but enough. Ember immediately launched herself and annihilated one with a swipe of her paw and her teeth at his throat. When the other wolves saw what she had done, they too changed themselves to be better warriors. She didn't know why *they* hadn't thought of it before. One of their own had taught her, after all. But it didn't matter. She was just grateful to have a team of real warriors at her side protecting the little ones.

A big crash came from above and Ember watched three of the Phoenixia tumble from the sky, entrapped by the Ne'Goi. She hoped they would be all right, but that was all the thought she could spare them before the next enemy was upon her. Shadow Weavers fell at her feet, but more came on like the tide, wounding her companions. Some of the students were hurt, but they continued to fight. They were Bendanatu. There was no word for "defeat" in their language. They would fight to the death.

Another crash came from above, one of the younger Phoenixia this time, but she regained her wings before she hit the ground.

A demon-like Ne'Goi rushed Ember. Again, it was Laerdish. Why did he have such a hate for her? He had tried to destroy her even before he met her. Ember snarled and leaped at him, trying to tear his throat with her teeth, but he knocked her aside with an armored fist.

That hurt.

Ember stood and shook herself, her ribs aching from his attack. She was more cautious this time, and they circled one another before she darted in. He swung too late, and she leaped high and bit into his shoulder. The coppery blood sprang to her tongue and he bellowed, reaching over his shoulder for her. Before he could get a grip, she let go and dropped to the ground, then lunged for his hamstrings. Her teeth sank past the leather straps, and though it did little damage, he still grunted in pain.

Laerdish stepped back and stomped down on her right paw. She yelped and retreated, her foot in the air. He lunged toward her. She rolled sideways through the dirt and the grass and came up hard against the bush that hid the littles. Panicked, she rolled in the other direction as the demon's foot came down hard. It shook the ground, and one of the young Phoenixia cried out.

"What have we here?" he said, his voice gravelly. He pushed his hands into the bushes and made an opening, exposing the younglings with nowhere to go. Ember leaped at him, her hind legs still strong, and bit deep into his shoulder again. His bellow shook the cones from the trees. He swatted her away, then stalked toward her. Ember knew it was finished. She was done.

From her left, Uncle Shad attacked the demon as if he were nothing more than a mouse. They fought hard as a Phoenix, Ember's mount, dove in to protect her children. For a while, the group did well against the Shadow Weavers—until the many more Ne'Goi settled to the ground and surrounded the three of them. They alternated their attacks with Laerdish's, and the battle swung in their direction.

Ember tried to get up and help, but pain lanced up her paw. With no way to use it or heal, she sat in front of the cavern between the demons and the children. No one would get past her unless it was with her dying breath. She would protect these littles with everything she had left.

The battle between the Bendanatu and Ne'Goi intensified, the smell of dirt and blood and pine mixing until she sneezed. At that moment, when her head was down and her eyes closed, something flew past her from behind. Startled, she turned, but saw nothing until she spun toward the battle and Shari Bird's cry.

One of her children, little Ezra, hovered before the Ne'Goi, separating his mother from their reach. He grew brighter and brighter until he shone like the moon and then the sun. Ember found her eyes watering, but she couldn't look away as the little one protected his mother. Laerdish screamed into the air, fleeing before the light as the Ne'Goi surrounding Shari and the injured Shad screeched and poofed into dust. The rest of the Ne'Goi disappeared in a flash of darkness.

Ezra's light went out, and he fell to the earth, still and unmoving.

CHAPTER TEN

For the second day in a row, C'Tan pulled the mirror into existence and stared at her reflection. Ever since she had shattered the mirror, the experience of reliving her pain at her brother's hands hadn't been the same. She could go through the motions: disrobe, let down her illusion of beauty, and show her scars, but instead of anger and bitterness, she just felt—empty. It wasn't a feeling she understood or could use. How could she fill the emptiness? Anger didn't work any longer. Hate was gone. And the idea of forgiveness and peace were so foreign to her, they seemed impossible. How could she ever find peace with all the evil things she'd done?

Unable to summon the energy to go through her routine, she dismissed the mirror and dressed, then walked to the kitchens and waited for the cook to prepare Brina's evening meal, early though it was.

C'Tan wasn't sure why she insisted on taking Brina's meals to her personally. It wasn't as if she liked the woman. She wanted to hate her, but there was still that family tie that had been lacking in her life for so many years. She couldn't let it go and found it softening her, which would not please S'Kotos—but she couldn't help the way she felt.

She felt drawn to Brina, like a bee to nectar. She was everything light and whole—everything C'Tan was not and would never be, however she might wish things to be different. C'Tan pulled the key from her bodice, placed it in the lock, and waited. She grinned with anticipation, wondering what Brina would try this this time. Another flying leap? Perhaps a trap set above the door? A thrown chair? She had destroyed two already in her desperate attempts to hurt C'Tan.

Readying herself, she drew up a mage shield, turned the key in the lock, and pushed open the door.

Nothing happened.

Slightly disappointed and even irritated, she threw a red magelight into the air and entered the room—only to find Brina on her cot, fast asleep. C'Tan put her hands on her hips. How could the woman sleep when she knew she was in danger? Not understanding, C'Tan summoned a chair and sat down beside the bed. When Brina still didn't move, C'Tan put her hand on Brina's hip to wake her.

Ember's mother awoke slowly, blinking, rubbing her eyes. When she was finally alert, she froze, staring at C'Tan with a flash of fear and then hatred burning in her eyes.

"Ah, there you are, I see. I had wondered when I'd see that look again. You were so peaceful in your sleep. I had thought you might have forgiven me." C'Tan wasn't sure why she said that, but she felt it. Damn this woman. She made her feel things she had set aside long ago and would prefer to stay that way.

"Never," Brina replied.

The part of C'Tan that was still Celena ached with that truth. Brina never would forgive her, and why should she? The fire that had taken C'Tan's beauty had claimed both Jarin's and Brina's lives. One in death, one in a living death full of fear and hate.

C'Tan nodded and pulled her hand away, interlacing her fingers around her knee. Neither of them moved as they stared into each other's eyes. C'Tan broke the silence, though she wasn't sure why. Things just bubbled out, no matter how she tried to stop them. "Do you remember the night before your wedding when we talked for hours? I was so excited to have a big sister. I loved you, you know. Even before you married Jarin, I loved you, and envied you for the time you would spend with him." She fell quiet, introspective.

Brina's eyes were troubled when C'Tan glanced at them again. "Yes, I remember. It was a wonderful evening. I was desperately nervous, and hearing all your stories of Jarin calmed me." Brina paused, her mouth chewing on whatever she wanted to ask. It came out in a rush. "Celena, what happened?"

For once, C'Tan didn't detest the name she'd been born with. She sighed and turned away, not wanting to answer, but finding herself unable to resist the pleading in those eyes that had hated her but a second ago. "I don't know that I am ready to talk about it yet. I made some mistakes that I can never rectify, but I never stopped loving you or Jarin." She twisted at her pants now, creating little mountains of fabric on her thighs.

"If you loved us so, why do you keep trying to kill my daughter?" Brina asked, the bitterness returning.

"I don't want to kill her," C'Tan answered. "I don't want to do anything to her at all. It is S'Kotos who wants her, and not dead, but sealed, so she will be powerless to destroy him for the eternities. I don't have a choice—can't you see that?" C'Tan pleaded, wanting so much for Brina to understand.

"My name is Marda now because of you," she said, sitting up. "You took everything I had left. Everything but Ember Shandae. You turned me into the being I am now, renamed for my murdered mother and sister because of the pain you caused me. I can't understand your choices, C'Tan, and I don't want to. You have hurt me to my very being—have changed me with your actions. You *always* have a choice, so don't tell me otherwise. I don't care who you serve. You may not be able to choose the consequences, but the choice of what you do is always in your hands."

Brina's words echoed through her mind. *You may not be able to choose the consequences, but the choice of what you do is always in your hands.* She didn't want to hear that, didn't want to think about it—but she felt the truth of it.

C'Tan stood, the walls that kept her emotions at bay comfortably returning. "I see. Perhaps now is not the best time to visit with you. I shall return at a later hour." She turned and walked to the door. "I *will* have Shandae, one way or another, or die trying. You are wrong, Brina, Marda, or whatever you call yourself now. Sometimes choice is taken from us and there is nothing we can do."

It surprised her when a knock sounded at Brina's door, and it swung open. Kardon stood with his head down.

Pulling her emotional mask back into place, she spoke with an icy voice. "I hope you have a good reason for disturbing me."

"Yes, Mistress," he said. "The girl, Ember, is under attack by the Shadow Weavers, and I thought you might want to see your enemy destroyed." He shuffled his feet.

That was not at all what she wanted, but she *did* want to see what was happening. "I shall go to the scrying bowl at once. You may be excused." The man turned and left.

C'Tan turned to Marda and, with surprising softness, said, "I'll find out what I can and let you know. She must survive until she has the keystones." She turned and pulled the door shut, locking it behind her.

CHAPTER ELEVEN

The Ne'Goi surged in numbers and ferocity as Kayla fired ice balls at them. Lady Kalandra clung to Kayla so tightly, the girl could hardly breathe, and her mother's sobs wet her shirt between her shoulder blades. Kayla pried her whimpering mother off and sighed. A week before, she would have responded the same way.

A searing pain jolted Kayla back to the battle, and she cried out in pain. An arrow had sliced through her arm. Seething at the distraction, she fired back, the injury fading into the background of her reality. She built an ice ball the size of a pumpkin and hurled it at the demon creature. It collided with his head in a wet explosion. The sight was sure to haunt her for years.

Just as the shadow weaver fell, the ugly red-and-black Ne'Goi burst straight up through the trees and screeched to the others. The sound was horrific, like the highest, most discordant combination of notes she'd ever heard. Nails on slate, perhaps. It was hard to describe. Kayla slapped her hands over her ears. Lady Kalandra did the same, as did all the other riders. In an instant, the sound stopped, and the weavers disappeared.

Something on the ground had made the Ne'Goi retreat. What could scare the shadow weavers so terribly? Whatever it was, it must have been bad.

Really bad.

As if they all shared a common mind, Kayla and the Phoenixians dove toward the ground, where the wolves stood in a circle around a woman. She knelt over a small bird-like creature, sobbing as if her heart were broken.

The Phoenixians turned human when they were still a few feet up, their riders falling to the ground. The humans cried out when they hit the packed dirt, but the Phoenixians didn't seem to hear. They raced toward the broken-hearted woman and gathered around her, cooing but not touching. Kayla asked Thew to move closer to the wolves, and she leaned toward the one she thought was Ember. "What happened?" she asked. The wolf's masculine voice resonated in her mind. Not Ember, then. Shad.

One of Shari's younglings tried to protect his mother and gave all his power to destroy the Ne'Goi. He's dying, Ember's uncle answered.

"What can we do?" she whispered, but the only response was silence.

Kayla looked around at the odd assortment of people, mostly children—a few humans, Bendanatu, human shaped Phoenixians, and of course Thew, her air elemental. There had to be something that could be done, but what? What?

In a moment, she knew. She softly stepped to Shari's side, then knelt down. "Shari."

She didn't answer.

Kayla put her hand on the woman's arm. "Shari," she said more loudly and finally got a response, though not the one she expected.

Shari turned, snarling, and shoved Kayla with both hands. "Leave me alone!" she screamed. "My son is dying! Dying!"

Kayla slammed into the dirt and skidded away with the force of the thrust. She was astonished by the woman's strength. Giving Shari a few moments, Kayla finally stood, brushed off her pants, then took three steps back. "Shari," she said firmly, though not without kindness. "Listen to me. Is there any chance your son—"

"Ezra," the grieving mother interrupted.

Kayla started again. "Is there any chance Ezra can be saved? Anything we can do? Let us help."

There was a murmur of assent around the group, and Shari looked up as if just realizing she was not alone. Her eyes went to Kayla as she wiped her tears. "I don't know! I don't know, I don't know!" Shari began to rock. It was obvious she was out of her mind with grief. Surely, someone else had to know. Kayla turned to the nearest Phoenixian, who just happened to be one of the girls she'd worked with earlier. Eden, she thought. Taking the teenager by the shoulder, she said, "You tell me. Is there any way to save the boy? Can he be healed?"

Eden seemed to have trouble coming back to herself, her eyes distant and teary for a moment before they cleared. "I . . . I think so," she said. She straightened, her eyes sharply focused and excited. "Yes! If we can get him to Phoenixia in time, there is a healer who can give him some light until he can create his own. But we'd have to leave now, and even then—" She didn't finish.

She didn't have to.

Kayla went into action. "Okay then, let's make this happen. Ember!" she shouted, at which her cousin lifted her wolfen head and looked at Kayla, her ears perked as if she were listening. "Can you lead the Bendanatu to their home?"

Ember glanced at her uncle Shad, who nodded. Kayla took that as a yes.

"Great. We need a few Phoenixians to go with the Bendanatu and provide transportation for the humans. Let's split up and save Ezra. Agreed?"

Heads nodded all around.

Shad spoke up. "The Bendanatu can run. We need only a few of the Phoenixians to carry the young humans and the injured. As many of your people as can go with you should do so. You'll need protection, as your primary intent will be speed. Yes?"

Shari nodded.

Shad looked around as if gauging the strength of his people. "Good. DeMunth can come with us. Kayla, go with them. That will give each group a keystone for protection. Lady Kalandra, will you go with your daughter, or would you like to journey with us? She will meet us there at a later time, I am sure."

Kayla was surprised at the offer. This race to save the boy was not suited for the lady. She needed safety and comfort, and would find that much more quickly with the Bendanatu than she would with Kayla. Their eyes met and it was as if Lady Kalandra read her daughter's mind.

She responded with a sigh. "I shall go with you, Master Shad. I don't think I can manage another battle such as that. Kayla . . . be careful," she almost whispered, a single tear escaping to run down her cheek.

Kayla went to her mother and embraced her. "I will. You be safe as well. Now go."

Lady Kalandra nodded and went to Shad, a few Phoenixians also joining the wolves and humans.

With things settled, Shari Bird changed form, gathered up Ezra, and placed him in a pouch at her breast. The other Phoenixians changed form as well. Only two other humans chose to travel with the Phoenixians.

Lily and Aldarin both clambered aboard their mounts, and with stubborn gazes and lifted chins, they dared her to make them leave. Not that she would. Actually, despite her irritation with Aldarin, he would be very good in a fight, and Lily's magic was already well known. She was glad to have them.

Let's go, Shari said, surging into the air with a burst of wings. The rest of the group followed quickly behind.

CHAPTER TWELVE

After Kayla and the Phoenixians disappeared in the distance, silence settled over the clearing. Not even the insects sounded in the battle's wake and the near death of the Phoenixian boy. One by one, the Bendanatu transformed into human shape, utterly silent. It wasn't until Ember began to change and the pain in her foot caused her to first howl and then cry out in human form that any sound broke the stillness.

She fell to the ground, cradling her foot. Tears poured down her face as she rocked without making another sound. Uncle Shad cradled her foot in his hands, closed his eyes, and concentrated. Ember felt the touch of his energy probing gently and cried out when he reached the middle of her foot, gasping when he moved to her toes.

Shaking his head, he called out to the others without opening his eyes. "I need moss, and lots of it. Vines. Some kind of fruit, preferably juicy."

Ember hissed as he found a particularly excruciating spot.

"And I need them *now.*" He continued to cradle Ember's foot. She felt the pressure as it swelled, the bones grinding against one another as he pressed them back into alignment.

"Did you know that there are twenty-six bones in the human foot?" he asked.

She shook her head, trying to let the pain drift through her and back out.

"It's true. Between your two feet, you've got fifty-two bones. That's about a quarter of all the bones in your body. Interesting, huh?" One of the students came up behind him with hands full of green moss, dirt still clinging to the bottom. Shad took it and placed the moist layers over the top of Ember's foot. "I think you broke nearly every bone in that one small appendage," he said casually, as if it didn't matter.

But it did. It mattered a lot.

One of the human girls hurried to Shad, her shirt held like a basket overflowing with berries. He gestured with his chin for her to put them on the ground to his right. Lady Kalandra stepped lightly to Shad's left and unwound loop after loop of vine from her arms and shoulders. He smiled up at her, and then, continuing his pointless prattle, he encased Ember's entire foot in moss, smashed a massive amount of berries into it, then covered it with another layer of moss and looped the vines around her foot until they covered it from toe to heel and partway up her ankle.

Ember had no idea what Shad was doing. He gestured for the Bendanatu to come forward. They gathered around Shad and Ember, touching her foot, her leg, his shoulder, back, and arm until every Bendanatu was somehow connected to her. They took a collective breath, and energy poured into her foot like a beaver's dam that had been suddenly swept away. She couldn't help herself. She screamed.

Just before the darkness took her, the pain eased. The bones in her foot shifted, moving back into place, the rightness of healing sweeping over her. Amazed, she stared at the Bendanatu around her. Tyese, straining, the energy flowing from her. Several of the students whose names she did not know. Uncle Shad. Sweat streaked his dusty face as he collected the energy from each of the wolflings and poured it into her crushed foot.

As she felt the healing and understood the damage, she realized they had just saved her from being crippled for life.

It was very humbling.

Finally, the group pulled their hands away as if they were one. Their legs gave out, and they collapsed onto the ground, breathing hard like they'd run for hours. Ember choked up. They had done that for her. All Shad had to do was ask, and each of them had come to her aid. If this was what the rest of the Bendanatu were like, she knew that being a part of them would be almost like coming home.

"You didn't have to do that," Ember said, seeing what a drain it was on everyone.

She heard shuffling and felt Shad's hand on her shoulder, then his presence as he crouched beside her. "Yes, we did. Ember, you have no idea how priceless you are. Any one of us would give up anything, even our lives, to ensure your safety." He squeezed gently. "So, yes, we had to." He stood and walked back to her wrapped foot and squatted down, letting his hand hover over the vines. He smiled. Evidently, good things were happening. "Just leave that on until we're ready to go. It's healed, but the bones came together so quickly, it's going to pain you for a while to come. I wish it could be otherwise." He tapped her foot, and she cringed, then realized it hadn't hurt at all. Standing, he walked over to Lady Kalandra and spoke to her, leaving Ember to herself for a few minutes before he gathered the entire group around her.

"Now that the healing's done, we need to be on our way. Bendanatu is quite a distance from here. Ember, you are our leader. What would you have us do?" Shad asked, his arms crossed and eyes twinkling.

Ember looked around at the children, both young and mature. They met her eye with varying emotions—fear, expectation, pride. She cleared her throat and glanced at Shad. She was unfamiliar with many of these younglings. How was she supposed to lead them? She didn't know, but she could at least learn their names.

"Hi," she croaked, then tried again, pulling her shoulders back as best she could while seated on a mound of pine needles. She had to seem strong for these children, even if inside she was a quivering, slippery vat of mud. "I'm sure you all know that I'm new around here and haven't had the chance to meet you young magelings. Would you mind giving me your names?"

The oldest girl looked around her, then met Ember's eye with only a slight hesitation. "Alexa Jade. Human. I lost my parents in the caverns. These are my younger sisters, Elaisha and Aislyn," she said, pointing to a girl who looked about ten and another about seven. They came closer, and Ember reached up to shake their hands.

"I'm pleased to meet you," she said.

The leader of her Phoenixians stepped forward in human form. "I'm Ted Finch, also known as Finchling, and this little egg is Lex," he said, patting his chest where an obvious lump was hidden beneath his skin. "It looks like we are left with three birds—Aryana, Eden, and Naythan." He introduced them in turn, the girls nodding and the young boy bowing before her.

Shad took over from there. "Not to be rude, but time is short, Ember Shandae. Let me introduce you to the Bendanatu. You know Tyese." The girl nodded briefly. "And Keyera." The girl who had ridden behind Ember smiled and waved, a bit shy now that they were on the ground. "And this is Abbey, Kymber, and Mandalin. All fine warriors. You can trust that you'll be safe in their hands."

One of the older Phoenixian girls, Aryana, turned to Ember's aunt. "Lady Kalandra, it would honor me to be your mount." It sounded strange coming from human lips, but Kayla's mother looked relieved when she nodded and placed a hand on the girl's shoulder. "Thank you. Yes, if you would not mind."

"Not at all," Aryana answered, and shifted form.

That was when Ember noticed someone was missing. Alarmed, she turned to Shad and asked, "Where is DeMunth?"

Shad startled and spun, looking around him. "I don't know. He's missing?" Her uncle smacked his forehead. "Of course he's missing! Why didn't I notice?" he muttered. "Let's spread out!" He yelled to the group. "Find DeMunth!"

Finchling gasped and started muttering under his breath. Ember couldn't hear all he said, but it sounded as if he was giving himself a good talking-to for losing his rider.

It was the youngest Phoenixian, Naythan, who found him. "Over here!" he squealed, and everyone ran. DeMunth lay in the bushes unconscious, the greenery flattened by his weight. It looked as if he had tumbled from Ted Finch's back as they dove toward the earth. And most likely, it was the Armor of Light which had saved him. Not enough to keep him conscious, but he still breathed, despite deep gashes across his chest and a particularly deep cut in his leg. Evidently, not even the Armor of Light could protect him from everything. Most likely, battling the Ne'Goi had drained the keystone of some of its power. They did eat magic, after all.

Shad unstrapped Ember's foot and took the berry-smeared pieces of moss to DeMunth. Finally able to stand, she limped over to help bind the energy-packed moss onto DeMunth's injuries.

She knelt at the side of this man who had given her so much. She'd hurt him by trying to leave and hadn't spoken to her since the incident with the horses. Panic surged and her stomach felt as if it were about to claw its way out of her throat. She touched his hair, brushing it back like he did so often to her. She couldn't lose him, especially without resolving their issues. Just the thought nearly undid her. She leaned over and kissed him on the forehead and muttered, "Don't leave me. Heal. I need you." Tears filled her eyes, and she had to turn away to put the mask of composure back in place once again.

She and several others levered DeMunth into Ted Finch's saddle, then strapped the guardian down so it would be near impossible for him to tumble from the Phoenixian's back again.

Ember looked at the sky. Almost Midday, and the group needed to be on its way.

The human, Alexa Jade, sat astride Eden, while the two youngest girls doubled up on Naythan. He was so small, Ember wasn't sure he could handle their combined weight, but he seemed to manage. The Phoenixians hovered in the air while the Bendanatu shifted to their wolf form and prepared to run. It felt very much the same as her run to Javak with Shad and his pack. Had it only been a week? It seemed impossible. So much had changed—surely it was a year, at least. But no. One week for her life to change completely.

Shifting slowly so as to avoid the pain, Ember crouched as her clothing transformed into long, white fur that extended up her neck and across her hands and face. In only a few moments, she went from girl to wolf, and thrilled at the changes it brought into her body. Every sense was exaggerated. She could hear the ants in the nearby tree. Her nose smelled the faint trail of another pack of wolves—a familiar one. Her mind again went to her run to Javak, and she knew this was the path the other wolves had taken home. She worried about her foot, but there were no more Phoenixia available to carry her. She had no choice but to run, so she put her faith in Uncle Shad's healing and readied herself for the long journey.

Shad looked behind him, and at her nod, he began to run, taking a position as the point runner. Ember brought up the rear so she would have time to adapt to running on her painful limb with no one watching. It didn't take long to gain the effortless lope that took them through the forest, up and down the hills and rocks, the Phoenixians circling overhead, trying to hold their pace back without falling from the sky.

Well past noon, the Phoenixians landed in front of the Bendanatu, bringing the entire group to a halt. Ted Finch mindspoke to Shad and Ember. *"We can eat on the fly, as can you on the run, but the humans need to eat and empty themselves."*

Shad chuckled. *"All right. Let's take a quick break and bring out the rations."* The Bendanatu shifted to their human form and went to work, unlatching the satchels on the Phoenixians' backs and retrieving rations for the humans and for Ember. Shad knew she wouldn't eat the rabbits and mice she passed on her way. Thankfully, he'd quit fighting her on that.

The humans unbuckled themselves from the backs of the Phoenixians and dispersed to find private places to relieve themselves. Ember checked on a still-unconscious DeMunth. His last words to her as they flew the skies haunted her. *Why don't you trust me?* She wished so much she had time to talk to him and reassure him that she trusted him with her life. But then she wondered—if that were true, why had she let Kayla and Lily talk her into leaving him behind when they stole the horses? It had taken little for her to go without him. If she could do that, did she really trust him?

There was no answer, but it ate at her like a leprous disease.

She left DeMunth and went into the woods, but it was more an excuse to get away from the bustle of people than anything else.

Finding a quiet copse of trees, Ember sat, her back to the group far behind her, and listened to the music of the forest. The leaves stirred. The cicadas sang their constant chirruping song. A squirrel chattered as it scampered up a tree, obviously disturbed by her presence.

In much too short a time, Shad called for her. Ember stood with a sigh. She turned to rejoin the group, but a man stood in front of her, his hulking frame and malicious grin stopping her as if she'd hit a wall. Nothing had alerted her to his presence. Not the surrounding animals, not her magic, nor instinct. It was as if he'd stepped through a portal, and perhaps he had—but she hadn't felt it. Looking closer, she realized she knew this man. Her jaw clenched and palms began to sweat. He was tall and bald, with freakishly large muscles and eyes so blue they were almost white.

"Ian Covainis," she whispered, her heart pounding nearly out of her chest as she backed away. He came toward her, a slow smile spreading across his face.

"I'm not here to harm you, girlie. Your aunt sent me to help. She saw the battle with the Ne'Goi and wanted to send another powerful arm to help in the fight."

Ember stopped moving. That. Was. Impossible.

"C'Tan. Sent you. To *help* me?"

He picked a piece of dry grass and stuck it between his teeth. "You're smarter than you look, girlie," he said, grinning the evil smile that haunted her dreams.

"I don't believe you," she said, pulling energy into herself.

Ian threw something at her, and she caught it automatically. "Ask her yourself."

Ember opened her hand to find a black, glassy stone threaded with a leather cord. The thing vibrated in her hand and she almost dropped it until a voice sounded in her head. *"Shandae?"* C'Tan's voice echoed inside her.

Ember did drop the amulet then. Ian laughed and picked it up. "Just talk to her. She can't bite you here." He put the stone back in her hand, his rough fingertips brushing hers. She shivered, but not the same way she did when DeMunth touched her. She took two steps back and sent her thoughts toward the stone.

C'Tan? she asked, unsure and feeling a bit silly.

The woman harrumphed. "*Finally!*"

That got Ember's back up fast. "*You kidnapped my mother, sent a killer to help me, and still expect me to be happy to talk to you?*"

Silence reigned at the other end, and then C'Tan chuckled. "*Well, aren't you your father's daughter? You are correct in all the above, and Ian probably would pursue you still if not for one thing—you are an investment, and I keep my investments safe and happy. Ian will help you—*"

"No, I don't think so," Ember interrupted, speaking out loud. "I don't trust him."

Ian laughed and crossed his arms as if he couldn't wait to crush her with them.

C'Tan's voice turned to ice. "*Yes. He will. Trust him or not, that is your prerogative, but he will stay, because I am his master, not you. I don't care if you are the Wolfchild. You will remain safe until the keystones arrive here. We can battle out ownership then, but until that time, I will do what I wish, how I wish, to keep you safe.*"

Ember didn't know what to say. Evidently her silence stretched on too long because C'Tan spoke again, softer this time.

"*Your mother is safe. I have not harmed her, though there is no love lost between us. She is well fed and housed. I made sure of that.*" Ember stole a picture from C'Tan's mind of her mother shivering in a blackened dungeon.

Ember's anger flared again, but she held it within. "*If you want Ian to protect me so badly, I want something from you.*"

"*I will not release your mother,*" C'Tan said, her voice sharp.

"*If you won't release her, at least give her a room and sunlight. Get her out of the cold. I'm not asking you to treat her like a queen, but if you are willing to sacrifice Ian for me when I don't want him here, make this concession and give her a place of her own."* Ember waited, tense, as the silence stretched long enough to make her uncomfortable.

"Ember!" Shad's voice came from not far away. "Where are you? We're leaving!"

"Well?" Ember asked, wanting to be done with this before Shad arrived.

"It will be as you ask," C'Tan's voice sour. *"But if you do anything to harm Ian or his soldiers, I will find the darkest, coldest spot in my dungeon for your mother. Do you understand?"*

Ember nodded, then realized C'Tan couldn't see her and answered. *"I understand."* And then she said the last thing she ever expected to say to the woman who had killed her father. *"Thank you."*

C'Tan severed the connection and Ember tossed the necklace back to Ian, who put it around his neck. "This here communication stone," he said while tying the ends at the back of his neck, "is the same one your father used with C'Tan the day he saved your life and ran from the mistress before she killed him. He wore it for a year before that. Now it's mine." He smirked, as if he knew how much that revelation would hurt Ember—and oh, it did.

Knowing that, even knowing who was on the other end of the stone, Ember decided then and there that she would have the amulet. She didn't know how it could happen without hurting Ian and making her mother face the consequences, but she would get it somehow.

Shad stepped into the clearing. "Ember, where have you been? Everyone is waiting for you." He spotted Ian and went half wolf, standing on his hind legs, his teeth huge. He growled and prepared to leap. The big man just stood there with his arms across his chest.

Ember's uncle snarled and charged. Ember shouted out. "No!" and threw the energy she'd collected at her uncle. He flew backwards as if he had hit a rubber wall and skidded in the dirt. He sat up, shook, and readied himself for another attack, but Ember stepped in front of Ian, much as it felt like snakes had crawled up her spine to have him behind her. "Uncle, stop! He's here to help! If you harm him, C'Tan will hurt my mum."

Shad froze. He looked from Ember to Ian and back again, and then, without saying another word, he stormed back to the group.

Sighing, Ember followed him, hearing others stepping out of the bushes, mounts following behind as they trailed behind her. Not at all surprised, she realized Ian had brought his own private army. She gritted her teeth and marched on.

When she got back to the group, evidently Shad had filled them in, for they were looking at her and Ian expectantly. Their eyes widened at the people following the immense man. Ember made her shift to wolf quick, hating the pain but feeling the need to be armed as quickly as possible, and her teeth and claws were her best weapon. Her right foot throbbed as if she'd just kicked a tree, but she ignored it and finally turned to see how many of Ian's guards there were. Eighteen men with mounts. Eighteen men who were their enemy and had been asked to fight *with* them.

She wanted to shake her head. It was too much, but if it would make her mother's life easier until Ember could unite the keystones and bring them to C'Tan, it was worth living with the enemy for a while.

But that didn't mean she had to like it.

CHAPTER THIRTEEN

Kayla sat astride Thew and tried not to lose the Phoenixians. Shari Bird flew hard and fast, her son's body clutched in her claws. She led the pack of Phoenixians as if she were alone, seemingly unaware that anyone flew with her. They followed in silence, only the wind howling past and the beat of their wings breaking the silence.

Kayla battled the wind and opened the case of the Sapphire Flute just enough to slip a finger inside. The connection was instantaneous, the energy filling the empty places inside of her. After a moment, she sent her thoughts to Brant's spirit. "*Is there any way to make the wind flow with us? Any way to speed up the journey?*"

He was quiet for a moment and then answered, uncertainty coloring his thoughts. "*I can try, but I cannot make promises. The winds are fickle and more prone to choosing their own path than helping those in need.*"

A gust nearly pulled her out of her straps and caught Kayla off guard. She focused her thoughts on the elemental who was the servant of the flute. "*Can you at least ask?*"

A mental nod, and in a flash of blue light, he streaked away from her, higher than she thought possible, until she could see him no longer. With him out of sight, she focused on matching her pace with the Phoenixians in front of her. Their speed seemed to increase every hour. Aldarin and Lily clung to their mounts as if the wind would rip them from their seats if they dared release their grips on the pommels. They hunched low over the shoulders of their mounts.

The gale blowing in their faces began to taper, and then Kayla felt a breeze start up and grow stronger until it blew them from behind nearly as hard as it had from the front.

Brant streaked down from the Havens and hovered at Kayla's side. His smile could have challenged the sun for warmth. "*The lords of the wind have agreed to help our cause, but only because it was you who asked through the flute, and not because of the injured child.*" He seemed very pleased with his report.

Kayla was appalled. "*What? That can't be right. A child's life has more worth than a guardian or the flute. Don't they?*"

"*Not in the eyes of the wind. No,*" he said, his smile fading. "*I told you they were fickle.*"

The elemental-charged gale blew them swiftly onward for another hour or two. The sun was just sinking into the distant mountains when Shari cried out. Her wings dipped, then dipped again, and with no warning, she dove toward an opening in the trees. The entire group followed, and upon landing, they found the mother bird cradling Ezra in her claws. She wept crystalline tears that collected on her feathers like beads.

Little Ezra's light pulsed faintly, his breath coming in gasps that sounded painful. One thing was evident—he was dying.

Shari looked around at the group, her eyes growing large. She darted to the nearest Phoenixians, using her beak to pull them toward her, joining their claws together, then brought another over. The rest of the group looked at each other, evidently understanding what she wanted.

Everyone, including humans, entered or was pulled into a circle around Ezra's failing body. Shari Bird joined the claws of the Phoenixians on each side of her, which started a ripple of hand-and-claw holding all the way around the circle. Once complete, the grieving mother went back to her son. She closed her eyes, pointed her face toward the setting sun, and somehow drew energy from its light. Kayla wasn't sure what it was, but she felt as if a piece of her streamed into the hand clutched in hers, only to be filled and immediately emptied by those to her left. She watched as Ezra's light brightened and his breathing grew smoother. He opened his beautiful eyes, still in his small Phoenixian form, and looked at his mother.

The connection between mother and son flowed through the circle. Love overwhelmed them and none could help the tears trailing down their faces. Shari's chick held on to life for several moments, staring into his mother's eyes, and then his voice sounded in all their heads.

"Mum, it hurts. It hurts so bad. But I couldn't. I couldn't . . . let them . . . hurt you." He said, gasping once again with the mental effort.

"Shhh," his mother mindspoke, still crying. *"Don't speak. We're trying to get you home to the healers. Just hold on, son. Hold on until you are home. Then we'll make you well."* She cradled him in her claws.

T"rying, he said. *But Mum. Hard. Don't know . . . can't . . . ."* He was quiet for a long moment, his light dimming once more. *"Love you. Always love you."* And then his light went out.

Shari's muffled sob turned into a tortured screech as Ezra's essence dissolved into particles of light that floated upward in a steady stream. Kayla's heart broke at the mother's pain. She knew the pain of loss all too well. The tears that wouldn't stop, the weakness in her knees, the clenching gut—they all resonated with Shari Bird's pain.

Kayla was the first to break the circle. She couldn't help herself. Shari's unending scream was more than she could bear, and stumbling forward, she fell to her knees in front of the giant bird and threw her arms around her, not caring that the sound nearly deafened her. This mother needed comfort, and though Kayla did not really know her, she knew her pain and had to do something.

Slowly, the screeching turned into a whimpering sob until Shari transformed right in Kayla's arms and embraced her in return. It seemed she didn't realize who was before her, but Kayla knew she felt the comfort and understanding of a fellow sufferer. She felt the resonance between them. The others faded into the background, almost as if they ceased to exist. Nobody moved. She felt the weight of their eyes, but they did not matter. Shari's heart had been ripped from her chest, filled with agony, the longing for death just to make the pain stop.

Kayla knew.

She also knew that Shari would be useless for the rest of the journey, and they still needed to go to Phoenixia. She wouldn't have this distraught woman turning back to join the Bendanatu. She needed to be among her people and loved ones.

Her arms still around a crying Shari, Kayla looked up to meet Lily's eyes. "We need to camp here for the night. She's in no condition to go on."

Lily shook her head. "You don't know the Phoenixians. If we don't get her home, she will end her life just to be with her son, and she has other children." Lily gestured with her chin to three younglings not far away, all crying almost as hard as their mother. "Hayley, Lynkyn, and Tia will follow their mother if she chooses to die. It will wipe an entire family from existence if we do not get them home and into the caring hands of the healers. Don't let Ezra's sacrifice be in vain."

Kayla looked at the children, horrified. Then, coming to a decision, she nodded. "Who can carry Shari Bird? We travel on to Phoenixia tonight."

There was no shortage of volunteers, and in minutes, they were back in the air. Aldarin supported the weeping mother, now in human form, on the back of his big mount, Behn. Kayla once again rode a silent Thew.

The air flowed with them, pushing them on faster than ever. One of the students, Miek, took the lead. He was one of the boys she had worked with the day before. Thankfully, they knew their way home. She wondered if it was a bird thing or familiarity with their path that made their flight so sure.

And that question was a sign of how tired she truly was. Her thoughts were no longer focused on any one thing, but rambled like a cow path. Knowing she would be awakened if there was more trouble, and although the sun still peeked over the mountains, Kayla leaned forward on her elemental mount.

As she faded into an achy, sorrow-filled slumber, a whisper of thought came from Thew. "*So sad.*"

She didn't have time to acknowledge it before she was fully asleep.

CHAPTER FOURTEEN

Ian and his horsemen dramatically slowed the run to Bendanatu, and everyone's tempers were high long before they stopped for the evening. The wolves and Phoenixia could have continued through the night, but the horses were near exhaustion, and Ember was not without compassion. After all, it was the rider she hated, not the horse.

Ember sent a thought to her uncle. "*The horses need to rest before they fall over dead.*" Shad nodded and slowed, then stopped completely. He shifted into human form and called out to the group. "We're stopping here for the night. Everyone set up camp and eat something , then get some rest. We'll leave before dawn."

In a matter of minutes, they had staked out places for themselves to sleep, several of the younger children too tired to even take the time to eat. They were asleep almost as soon as they pulled a blanket about themselves and tucked their satchels under their heads for pillows.

Ember took a moment to check on DeMunth, but he was still unconscious. "*Leave him*," Finchling told her. "*He will not affect my sleep and it will not hurt him to remain strapped for the night.*" Ember wanted to argue, but then realized if anything went wrong, she wouldn't have time to buckle him back into place, so she grimaced, thanked Ted, and left. Starving, she gathered sticks and small logs for a fire and brought them to the center of the clearing, surprised to discover she was the only one to do so.

Shad approached her and spoke in low tones. "No fire tonight. I don't trust Ian and his group, and it's easier for all but the humans to see in the dark. I'll set a watch amongst the Bendanatu and we'll rotate throughout the night. You have the first shift. Wake me in two hours." He turned and went back to his own makeshift bed. Before long, most of the group was asleep, Ian included.

Making do with jerky, travel rations, and water, Ember found a copse of trees within a trio of boulders and settled herself to watch for danger, though she was more concerned about Ian than she'd be about a bear or the Ne'Goi. She watched the men who had intruded on their comfortable group, not sure if they slept or only pretended. It didn't help that her recently healed foot was aching so badly that she wanted to cry. Shad wasn't kidding when he said it would be painful for a while.

She was so focused on her foot and on watching Ian's men that she jumped and nearly blasted Tyese and Keyera with her magic when they hopped over the boulders and approached her.

"What are you girls doing up?" She pulled her knees to her chest and leaned against a tree, making room for the younglings to join her amidst the stone.

They quietly sat in the hollow facing Ember, looking embarrassed and a little scared. Ember couldn't imagine why in the world they would fear her. She was not scary at all—unless she was facing an enemy, and Tyese and Keyera were anything but. The girls looked at each other, staring silently, waiting for the other one to speak. The silence stretched on. Finally Ember spoke.

"What is it? You look upset." She picked up a twig and began breaking it into little pieces, hoping that avoiding eye contact would get the girls to open up sooner.

It worked.

Keyera looked at Ember and blurted out, "We have your bracelets."

Ember sighed with relief. She'd completely forgotten that they'd fallen off her wrists during the battle with the Ne'Goi. "Wonderful! Can I have them?"

"Ummmm, actually . . . no," Keyera continued and Ember could see her face turn red, even in the dark. "It's not that we don't want to give them to you. It's just that—"

Tyese interrupted and continued the story. "When we caught the bracelets, it was in the middle of the battle and we didn't have any place to put them. I didn't even think about it. I put one on my wrist and kept fighting. It wasn't until we were on the ground that I realized . . ." She faded off and stuck her arm out toward Ember. "Well, see for yourself."

Ember's breath stopped. The bracelet that had graced her arm since her birthday had embedded itself in Tyese's hand and wrist and somehow shrunk down to fit her. The tattooed lines gleamed silver in the moonlight.

Keyera took up the tale once again. "When I caught the bracelet, it was broken—slashed as if by a knife." Ember remembered the battle at Karsholm when she had been struck in the leg by a Ne'Goi sword, bisecting the lines of the slave bracelet. "I played with it, trying to fix it for you, but it was so hard to do in the air and I was afraid I would drop it, so I put it on my wrist to join the ends together again. It took a while, but then I fixed it, and it sank into my skin just like Tyese's did. I'm sorry, Ember. I didn't mean for it to happen." Keyera was near tears, and though upset, Ember knew she had to say something. She wanted to chastise the girls. She wanted her bracelets back. They were hers! But she knew the bracelets well enough to know that they could not be coerced. They chose whom they would, and for some reason they had chosen Tyese and Keyera to be their bearers—for the moment, she hoped.

"I can't say I'm happy, but I can't decide whom the bracelets choose. If they chose you, then you are their current bearers. The three of us, together, create a whole—the two of you with the bracelets, and me with the necklace. At least you caught them when I thought they were lost." She looked at Keyera. "And thank you for fixing the damage done to the bracelet in the battle at Karshsholm. For that alone, you have earned the right to wear it." Ember stretched her legs out between the girls and tossed away the last of the twig she'd been snapping.

"Now, is there anything else?" she asked.

"What do they do?" Tyese asked, her head cocked as she glanced at Ember with bashful eyes.

Ember shrugged. "I have no idea. I'm sure they have a purpose, but I have yet to find it."

She was about to tell the girls to go back to bed when she heard someone's muffled cry. She stood and looked around the clearing, the girls following suit.

Ian's men were gone.

Ember sent a loud thought to Shad. She knew what was happening—she'd known all along that Ian was not to be trusted. *"Shad! We're under attack! Wake everyone!"*

Immediately his mind met hers, saw with her eyes. He had slept in wolf form, so waking everyone was easy—he howled.

Ember heard curses as Ian's men dropped the bound children they'd thrown over their shoulders and drew their weapons. Seeing their blindness, Ember had an idea and whispered to the girls. "Go and wake the Phoenixians, but tell them to leave their lights dimmed. It's our one advantage over so large a foe. Once done, join us in the fight. Ian's men must be killed."

Keyera and Tyese nodded, leaping over the boulders with grace and racing toward where the Phoenixians perched in the trees. Ember shifted to wolf and ran toward the largest man in the bunch, the one she hoped would be Ian. He had to die. This was one time too many he had tried to capture or kill her.

Sure enough, the bald man loomed in her sight. He swung almost blindly as Uncle Shad leaped upon him. Another wolf crept from behind the leader and tore into his legs, hamstringing him in the worst of ways. Ian yelled out and tried to spin, but the wolf darted away fast and his injured leg gave out, sending him to one knee. Ember leaped forward and put her teeth around his neck. As soon as he felt her teeth, he stilled, and she didn't press down. She wanted him to know the terror he had forced upon her when she was held prisoner in the cave and when he held her before the mage trials.

He laughed. "Too scared to bite down, girlie? Even laying flat I'm too big an opponent for you. Why don't you back off and let the real men fight?"

Ember tried very hard not to let his words sink in.

"Ember," Shad mindspoke. *"Leave him to us. There is no need for you to take his life."*

"I owe him," she said. *"I want him for myself."*

"You don't need to do this," he said, pacing back and forth as the fight began its end.

"Yes. I do," she said, and with no further thought, she tore out his throat. Ian's eyes widened in shock and pain. He gurgled, his hands to his throat as she stepped away.

It was strange watching him die. She felt a great mixture of satisfaction and relief, but also sorrow and disgust. Ember hated herself for taking a life, but she knew Ian would have killed her somehow, someday—it was just the man he was. She'd had to kill him.

Hadn't she?

It was hard to justify it now that it was done.

Finally, all of Ian's guard was either dead or on the run and had taken the horses with them. Once the battle was over, the Phoenixians glowed from within to light the area. Everyone agreed these men were not worth burying, so they dragged them into a copse of trees and left for the elements and animals to find. The Bendanatu were not ones to let needed items go unclaimed, so they scavenged the bodies before leaving them. Some claimed leather vests. Others, weapons and food. They handed all coins and gems over to Shad to give to his father to help rebuild Bendanatu.

Shad stood on the same rocks where Ember hid earlier and spoke to everyone. "We must make a decision. Do we stay here for the remainder of the evening to rest, or do you wish to move on and away from this soon-to-be haunted place?"

A murmur of voices went through the group, and finally a consensus was reached. Surprisingly, it was Lady Kalandra who spoke for them all.

"We all agree. Let us move on. I, for one, would not sleep at all with the bodies of our enemy nearby." She held herself tall and regal. It made Ember proud to be her niece, and she looked forward to getting to know her better.

Shad smiled, bowing to the woman. "Then move on, we shall, Lady Kalandra."

Ember grinned. Despite the battle, it was obvious by the way he said her name that Uncle Shad was rather taken by Kayla's mother. It was cute, watching these older people flirting with one another. She wasn't old enough to remember her mother's courtship with Paeder. Somehow, it seemed strange to see such mature people flustered and trying to impress one another. She'd only ever thought of it for people her own age.

Still smiling, joined Shad as the humans mounted the Phoenixians, who took to the air.

With Ian gone, they could at last race toward Bendanatu, and race they did, flying through the night as if their legs had wings. It was exhilarating, but one thought continued to haunt Ember. Ian was evil, self-serving, malicious, and a danger to all. He had needed to be killed.

Hadn't he?

CHAPATER FIFTEEN

C'Tan watched in her scrying bowl as Ian met Ember and offered his assistance. She'd spoken to the girl and given her word that Ian was there on her orders—that she was safe.

And then the man had made a liar out of her.

When all was done and Ember was on the move once more, C'Tan gripped her desk so hard that she left scorched handprints on its edges. She summoned one of her servants using her communication stone. She had an entire batch all made from the same rock so her voice could carry to anyone she chose. *"Fetch Kardon for me."*

She stood at her desk, hunched over the scrying bowl, until the man who had once been her master shuffled into the room. The old-man act was exactly that—an act. He wasn't much older than she, and the magi lived long lives if they so chose. He stepped inside and hesitated by the door, unwilling to come closer than he had to with the tension in the room.

"You called, Mistress?" he asked, his voice completely devoid of emotion. Wise on his part.

She didn't say anything, willing him to come closer. Showing the only emotion she had seen in years, he sighed, then shuffled to stand before her with his head bowed.

With everything in her, she wanted to grab his hair and bash his head into the scrying bowl until it was a bloody pulp, heal it, and then smash it again—but that would accomplish nothing. She needed answers.

"Do you have any idea what your son just did?" she asked in almost a whisper.

Kardon said nothing and C'Tan looked up, her eyes flaming red with the fury burning inside her.

"You know. I can see it in you. You planned this together, did you not?" She gripped the desk's edge once more, smoke rising from her smoldering hands.

Again, Kardon did not answer, would not even meet her eyes.

"The answer is in your very frame, Kardon. Your son betrayed me. He made a liar out of me and may have destroyed my chance to retrieve the keystones. Answer me one question. Just one." She leaned in close until she was barely inches from his face. "Why?" she whispered.

His head came up at that, and his eyes surprised her. No regret. No shame. No fear. Just a mocking anger. "Why?" his gravelly voice repeated. "You really need to ask why?"

She nodded once.

He gave one short bark of laughter. "Several reasons. First, do you really trust the Wolfchild to bring the most powerful artifacts in creation to you?" He let that sink in. "Second, S'Kotos wants her bound to the soulstone. You've known that for sixteen years and have done nothing to make it happen. You know where she is, and yet you let her run free. Ian was to bring her in. Third, if I can reveal your incompetence to our master, so much the better." His malicious smirk fueled her rage.

She nodded. "I see. So you challenge me now when the most is at stake. I should not be surprised. You are a snake, Kardon. That has never changed. Why I kept you alive is a wonder to me." She took his head in her hands and pulled his eyes to hers. "Now, let me give you a few pieces of information."

With that, her hand flashed out and her nails, like talons, embedded in his scalp, wrenching his head down until his nose touched the water of the scrying bowl. Heat seeped from her fingers, scorching his hair as she forced him to face the images. Using her power of fire, she created an obsidian vice that fit his head and held it in place so he couldn't look away from the pictures the water would show him.

She commanded the bowl to replay all the interactions between Ian and Ember from the moment he approached her until the moment of his death. When the battle started, Kardon chuckled as the students were gathered up. As soon as Shad and Ember entered the fray, he quieted, and when Ian was hamstrung, he gasped.

As Ember placed her teeth around Ian's neck and he insulted her, Kardon sobbed. "No, son, don't taunt her. Don't do it."

But he couldn't change the past.

At Ian's last gurgling breath, C'Tan stopped the playback and said, "This is what happens when you betray me, Kardon. This is what happens when you try to capture the Wolfchild. This is why I choose to work with her rather than against her. Do you see it now? Your stupidity has lost you your son, and a very good tool in my arsenal." She began the projection of the past again, forcing Kardon to watch it once more, as his head was in an obsidian grasp that wouldn't release until C'Tan commanded it.

She came out from behind the desk and leaned close to Kardon's ear. "Enjoy the show, slave. It will play until it is burned into your brain."

Kardon cried out and struggled futilely against the vise holding him in place.

"You've a lesson to learn, so watch it well."

Her grin sharp and feral, C'Tan left the room

CHAPTER SIXTEEN

Birds singing with . . . humans? Human birds harmonizing? No, that wasn't possible. Kayla stretched and sat up. But instead of finding herself on Thew's back, a comfortable bed in a round room greeted her. There were no windows—only frames that brought the outside in. Instead of the trilling birdsong she was used to, a hybrid of human and bird voice wafted in. A beautiful melancholic song wove in and out, twining with wordless voices, surging in and out of the group theme. She sat transfixed, mesmerized by the sound, and wondered if the song was for little Ezra, for Shari Bird and her other children, Hayley, Lynkyn, and Tia, or if it was a constant part of the environment in Phoenixia.

The sound faded away, and the silence was almost painful after the beauty of the music. Kayla sighed and swung her legs over the side of the bed, only then realizing that she wore the same clothes she had been in for two days now, thick with dust and sweat from the battle with the shadow weavers—and something heavy on her shoulder. She brushed at it, and little crystalline pebbles fell to her bed. "What in the . . ." she said, then trailed off, thinking. Shari Bird cried on that shoulder. Were those her tears? Phoenix tears?

She'd have to ask. But if so, they were worth a fortune. Only the extremely wealthy of Peldane had been able to afford them. Like diamonds, they sparkled amidst her rumpled blankets. She reached to pick up the largest, but a knock sounded on the open doorframe, and she looked up. It was Shari Bird's oldest daughter, Hailey. Kayla's heart immediately melted and she gestured for the girl to come in and sit beside her. Hailey appeared to do so with a heavy heart, her gait slow and eyes on the ground. She hesitantly sat on the edge of the bed, silent until Kayla spoke.

"What can I do for you, Hayley?" she asked, fidgeting with the Phoenix tears.

Hailey glanced over, and instead of answering, gave a sad little smile. "Are those my mother's?"

"I don't know. They were on my shirt when I awoke. Is this what happens when a Phoenix cries?" Kayla asked, gathering up a handful.

Hailey nodded. "Yes. It is how we can release our emotions without turning to dust and light ourselves. Each stone is packed with emotion that is magic unto itself."

Kayla's hand froze as she thought. "So, if I broke one open—"

"The emotion that created it would overwhelm you," the girl finished. "But it is near to impossible to break them open without magic. They are as hard as diamonds to hold the emotion inside. It is a protection."

Kayla nodded and pulled her hand away, wiping it on her pillow just to be safe. She looked at the girl and asked, "How are you doing this morning? And how is your mother?"

Hailey sighed. "We are better, though sorrow is still a knife in my heart. The healers have taken Ezra's light force and shared it with us, so a piece of my brother now lives within me. It helps. Mother got the largest part, as she hurts the most. Still, they put her with a healer and she is under constant guard until she shows she is stable enough to walk amongst us without her own light dispersing into Sha'iim."

Kayla was not sure how to describe her feelings about these strange people, that they could die and "disperse their light" because of the deep sorrow of loss. She did not doubt that if she could have done so when Brant died, she would have done the same. She was almost jealous.

"Thank you for asking after us, but I came to summon you. There is one here who wishes to see you. Will you come?"

Curious, Kayla nodded, and despite the dirt and sweat, she didn't bother to change. She just stood and followed the girl through the open doorway and along the wooden trail that hovered high above the ground. She shouldn't have been surprised, but was still filled with awe when she discovered the Phoenixians lived high in the tallest of trees. They must be nearly invisible from the ground.

She was so busy looking down and trying to figure out how far it was to the ground that she didn't realize when Hailey stopped. Kayla plowed into the back of the girl, just as she had Pedran when being introduced to the king. Both of them stumbled into the ropes that ran along each side.

"Sorry!" Kayla said, worried when the girl glared at her. Her emotions must still be so volatile and tender from the loss of her brother. Hailey said nothing, but pointed to a man standing in the distance. "There," she said, then turned and walked away.

Curious, Kayla moved toward the man. With his back to her and a helmet on, she couldn't identify him. It wasn't until she stood at his side and he turned to face her she recognized him. Familiar disappointment and a twinge of anger settling in her stomach. Ember's stepbrother, Aldarin. His orange tattoos seemed to move across his face, though she knew it was only an illusion. It still made her ill to see T'Kato's tattoos on the face of this man. No doubt he had some wonderful traits, but she missed T'Kato, and Aldarin was a constant reminder of his absence.

It made it very hard to like him, and he seemed to feel antagonistic toward her as well. His bearing was formal as he finally spoke. "Since you were so instrumental in getting Shari Bird and her children home safely, I thought you deserved to know how they are doing. Hailey was desperate for distractions and volunteered. Did she explain things?"

Kayla nodded. "She told me a bit. The healers took Ezra's light and gave a part to each of them, the largest part going to his mother. I don't exactly understand what that means, but if it brings them comfort and will keep them alive, that is all that matters." She was stiff in her speech as well. She'd spent her life surrounded by people who hated her for who she was. Aldarin's treatment of her was neither a surprise nor any different from she was used to. "Is that all?"

Aldarin's rough façade cracked just a little. "No. It's not." The soldier removed his helmet and tucked it under his arm, fidgeting with what looked like nervousness. "I wondered . . ." He paused, cleared his throat, and started again. "I wondered if I could ask for your help."

Kayla's walls fell with her surprise. "Whatever for? I was an outcast in an aristocratic society until a week ago. What could you possibly want from me?"

Aldarin looked down, his face reddening. It took a moment for him to raise his eyes to meet hers and say, "Magic."

Kayla squinted her eyes and tipped her head. "What about magic?"

Aldarin's color deepened, if that were possible. He took a deep breath and visibly steeled himself, then blurted, "I want you to teach me magic."

Kayla's mouth fell open, then snapped shut. "You want *me* to teach *you* magic?"

Aldarin seemed frustrated at that point. "Yes! I've been surrounded by magic most of my life, but I was a guard to the Magi. There are no guards who also carry magic. They kept it a secret from us." He paced, then turned back to her. "I've lost a position I loved because of all this ugliness embedded in my skin. The least I can do is learn to use it."

Now Kayla understood why he had been so rigid and formal. He was angry and hurt and trying to hold all that emotion inside. But calling T'Kato's tattoos "ugly" was an insult to a man she revered. She took a step forward until she was right in his face. "Sure. I'll teach you. The first thing you need to learn is . . ." she waited for a few seconds and then leaned in even closer and in a very quiet voice said, ". . . respect."

She spun on her heel and walked away.

Aldarin followed and called out. "Wait! What do you mean, 'respect'? Respect for the magic? That I have already."

Furious, Kayla turned again, and he stopped quickly. "Respect for the magic, yes, but where do you think that magic comes from?" She glared at him until he reddened, though he didn't drop his head.

"I understand what you are saying and I know T'Kato was a friend to you, but to me, these tattoos are sheer ugliness. Ugly like childish scribbles on a newly whitewashed wall. I hate them. I will use them for the good of the group, but I cannot make myself love something that has taken away nearly everything I love." It was Aldarin's turn to spin on his heel and walk back to the overlook where they had met.

Kayla stood in place, thinking and trying to tame her emotions. It was difficult to separate her love for T'Kato from his tattoos. She knew they were what gave him power, and without them, he would have been just a man. But setting that aside, how did she feel about the markings themselves? If it was her body that had claimed T'Kato's magic, how would she react?

Much like Aldarin had, she imagined.

Tucking her pride away, she walked forward until she was once again at Aldarin's side.

They stood there, silent, for the longest time, staring out into the canopy of trees and the morning sky beyond. The Phoenixians soared over the treetops, occasionally dipping into the foliage and coming back up with a squirming animal in their claws. They returned to a dais that rose above the trees and dropped their catch, much like a seagull does a fish onto the rocks below. It finally dawned on her they were collecting dinner.

Thinking of food made her stomach growl, and Aldarin turned to her with a smirk. "Hungry, are we?"

"Starving," she answered, her stomach rumbling again. "I've got an enormous appetite, and I don't remember the last time I ate."

He gave her a full smile this time. "Me neither. Here," he said, pulling a paper wrapped fruity nut bar from his pocket. "That should quiet your stomach—for a moment."

Chagrined, Kayla took the bar and ate it as quickly as she could chew. It wasn't enough, but he was right—it would tide her over until she could get some proper food.

"Sooo," Aldarin drawled when she was done. "Will you help me? I'm serious. And I'll do what I can to respect the tattoos. It's just going to take some time."

Kayla nodded before he even finished. "I don't know what I can teach you. I'm so new to this myself, but I can at least give you some basics that will hopefully help."

With a sincere smile, Aldarin extended his hand. "Shake on it?"

Kayla reached for his hand. As their palms met, a surge of energy sparked between them, and for a moment, Aldarin's orange tattoos turned blue. She pulled back quickly. "Wow. That was odd."

Aldarin rubbed at his hand. "Definitely," he said. "It felt like my skin was crawling."

"It turned your tattoos blue—like T'Kato's," Kayla said, taking a step back.

Aldarin looked stunned. "Really? Odd indeed."

At that moment, a cloaked figured overshadowed the two of them and Aldarin quickly stepped to his side.

"Oh, this gentleman was asking for you. I apologize for the delay, sir. We had business to discuss. Will you join us for breakfast?" he offered. "Kayla is starving."

"Certainly." The cloaked man followed the two of them across another bridge. Kayla was too distracted by her stomach to pay much attention to the man who'd been looking for her, and even more so by the delicious smells wafting from an open doorway. She stopped, closed her eyes for a moment and breathed deep. Aldarin noticed and chuckled, but she said nothing. She was too focused on the aromas to care that he was laughing at her.

Aldarin and the cowled man entered the room first and found an empty table. Kayla followed them and sat, wondering what to do next. The room reminded her of a pub, but much cleaner and without the alcohol.

A servant approached their table and addressed the stranger first. "What do you desire?" he asked.

The man steepled his fingers and said, "What do you have?" Kayla was glad he asked because she had no idea how this worked. In a pub, you took what was in the pot or on the spit. There were no other choices.

The other man recited a list of several items so fast that she couldn't catch it all. She heard something about a fish and root vegetables, soup, assorted meats and vegetables on a stick, and several drinks—some hot and some cold.

The stranger ordered for all of them. "I'll have the hot cacao and the soup. The gentleman will have the assorted meats and vegetables on a stick and your cool, sweet mint tea. For the lady, one of everything, including drinks." The man leaned back in his chair, his long fingers intertwined over his stomach.

Kayla's jaw dropped once again. How did he know? The man taking their order seemed just as surprised. "Are you sure, sir?"

The cowled man nodded and made a shooing gesture for him to be gone.

As soon as he left, Kayla leaned forward. "Who are you? No one knows my appetite. None but my mother, my uncle, and my love. How do you know?" she asked again.

He sat up and chuckled. "You forgot one person on that list." He put his hand to the hood of his cloak and pushed it back. Kayla gasped at the Evahn ears peeking through his long, dark hair and looked into eyes as blue as her own.

"Your father." He smiled. "Hello, Kayla. It's been a long time."

CHAPTER SEVENTEEN

Ember watched the young wolf, Keyera, stumble and pull herself up before she could fall completely. That was the third time in an hour. Looking around, Ember could see the others were almost as exhausted. They couldn't continue—not at this pace, and especially not the younglings. She blinked against the first rays of dawn peeking over the mountains as deep weariness seeped into her paws. They'd run all night from memories of Ian and his men. Putting on a burst of speed, she raced past the Bendanatu and slowed beside Shad. *They can't go on any longer. We need to rest.*

He huffed as he leaped over a fallen log. *If we continue on, we'll be there by afternoon.*

She growled. *Uncle! Look at them! They are exhausted, and frankly, so am I. Let us rest. Just a few hours, I promise. But if we don't sleep, someone will break a neck or a leg.*

He slowed a little and looked behind him. Whatever he saw was more convincing than her words, for he stopped and turned toward the group. He waited for the Phoenixians to land with the others before he changed back to human form to speak to everyone. "If we continue, we will make Bendanatu in a few hours. Do you want to go on, or stop and rest for a bit?"

Nobody answered. They stood there, looking at one another, silent. Exasperated, Ember turned to the Bendanatu girl who had stumbled so much this past hour. "Keyera, are you tired? Because you sure looked tired back there when you almost broke your neck for the third time." Keyera hung her head. "Tyese, aren't you tired? You're staggering around as if you were drunk!" Tyese's tongue lolled out of her mouth as if she didn't even have the strength to change. "Any of you humans up there want to sleep? Because I sure do. Am I the only one?"

"No, you are not," Lady Kalandra called out. "I am about to fall out of my straps with exhaustion. Give me a rock for a pillow and some leaves to cover myself, and I will sleep for hours." Kayla's mother stayed on her mount as she spoke.

Emboldened by Lady Kalandra, the others nodded or gave muffled affirmations. Shad sighed, though whether with disgust or resignation, Ember didn't know. "All right. Let's take until the second hour past noon and sleep. We are in Bendanatu woods, so we needn't fear attack. We can all rest peacefully."

Ember melted back into her wolf shape, walked into the woods, and found a shady spot not far from their landing place to curl up. Her shoulders, haunches, and especially her foot ached as she tried to relax.

Footsteps sounded near Ember, but she was too tired to open her eyes. Soon she could smell the human standing over her. She opened one eye and peeked upward to verify. Yes. It was her aunt, the Lady Kalandra.

The tall woman squatted down beside Ember and asked quietly, "May I join you?"

Ember tried sending a thought to her aunt's mind, but Kalandra was deaf to it. Instead, Ember nodded and scooted over. The woman knelt down and rested her hand on Ember's neck. The wolf tensed. "May I?" the tall woman asked.

May I what? Ember wondered, then remembered DeMunth scratching Uncle Shad behind the ears. Was she asking if she could pet Ember? Like a dog? If it were anyone else, Ember would have bitten their hand off, but with her aunt, for some reason, she felt safe. Once again, she nodded and her aunt's long fingers gently caressed Ember's white fur, tentatively at first, then with more confidence.

It was one of the most comforting things Ember had ever felt.

She wished she could mindspeak with her aunt. She didn't even know what to call her. But even with the lack of familiarity with each other, the call of blood bound them. Lady Kalandra lay down behind Ember and wrapped her arms around the wolf-shaped girl. Despite the difference in size and shape, and even temperament, having her aunt's arms around her felt very much like being in her mother's embrace. A single tear slipped from Ember's eye.

Oh, how she missed her mum and prayed that C'Tan was taking care of her. Ian's betrayal made it doubtful. If he worked for C'Tan, or was even her son, as so many rumors said, chances were good that C'Tan had sent him to capture or kill Ember. At the very least, C'Tan was going to be furious when she discovered Ember had killed him.

She tried not to think about it, but she was terrified that her actions the night before had cost her mother her life. With Lady Kalandra's arms around her, Ember could not hold her feelings inside any longer, and for the first time, as a wolf, she sobbed—or at least the wolfen equivalent of a sob. Tears, whines, and even a soft howl escaped. She had no control. It felt strange.

Somehow, Lady Kalandra sensed what was going on and tried to comfort Ember. She caressed her fur, then gave her what could only be a hug, whispering, "It will be all right, Ember. It will be okay. Have faith, child. Sometimes bad things happen, but The Guardians watch over us more than we know. They will take care of her. It will be okay."

She hadn't thought the words would help, but somehow they did, and before long, both Ember and Lady Kalandra were fast asleep. The lady's arms wrapped protectively around her niece.

Ember woke enough to realize her fur made her sweltering hot, then felt Shad nuzzle her with his nose. *It's time to wake,* he said, then went around behind Ember and licked Lady Kalandra's neck. She cringed, not really awake, then giggled in her sleep. The giggling just made Shad lick more. Ember pulled away and watched, trying not to laugh as well. Boy, Uncle Shad must really be crazy about Ember's aunt. She'd never seen him lick anyone before. Finally, Lady Kalandra wiped the slobber off her neck and sat up, still laughing. Ember was sure she would be angry, but when she saw who had been licking her, she reddened and smiled, rubbing Shad behind the ears with affection.

Shad sat down on his haunches and watched her walk away, his tongue lolling. His eyes never left her.

You must really like her, Uncle.

He turned and cocked his head. *I do believe that is true.* He grinned. *She is one amazing woman. You don't object, do you?*

Ember laughed. *Of course not! I totally approve, though Kayla might feel otherwise.*

Shad winked at her. *Perhaps, but she's not here at the moment, is she?*

Leaving his niece, Shad continued to wake the Bendanatu while Ember's aunt woke the humans and Phoenixians.

After a quick meal of travel rations for those who would eat them, the group continued on once more, feeling refreshed, if not completely rested.

The run was long and arduous, with steep climbs and sliding descents, but they made progress.

We should arrive within the hour, Shad announced later that day, the sun still high in the sky.

Wonderful! she answered, definitely tired of this endless run.

They topped another hill and burst into the trees, and that was when she smelled it.

Death.

Ember slowed and Shad shortly after, the rest of the group following suit. *Do you smell that?* she asked him.

He didn't answer, but put his nose to the ground and turned to the right, zig-zagging back and forth until he came to a large pile of branches and stones. He shifted to human form and pulled the cover away with a desperate frenzy Ember had never seen in him. Everyone quickly joined him. The smell was sweet and sickening, and more than one of them turned away to vomit what little they had eaten that day.

When they finished, they'd uncovered seventeen Bendanatu wolves buried in a mass grave.

Ember looked more closely at the bodies, not even buried properly, and realized why he was so hurt by this loss.

She knew these wolves.

In the caves above Karsholm, they had slept in a massive room, all sharing warmth and comfort. They had run from the caves to Paeder's farm and on to the giant willow. They had turned human and heated stones to cook her food, so she didn't have to eat it raw. The first Bendanatu she had known, good and kind beings. They deserved better than this.

Even in human form, Shad howled his grief, tears streaming down his face. He fell to his knees at the edge of the grave and sobbed. Lady Kalandra moved behind him and gently pulled his head against her stomach, caressing his hair. He finally turned and wrapped his arms around her, still crying as if his heart had burst.

"I thought you said we were safe in the Bendanatu woods," Ember said without thinking.

One of the younglings, the quiet one, Abbey, answered. "The woods are patrolled and usually safe, but it is a lot of ground to cover, and the Bendanatu have been decimated by attacks from the Ne'Goi as of late. It is possible that some of the shadow weavers broke through and followed them home." The girl had tears on her face as she stared at the grave.

Ember thought she understood. "Do you know any of them?" she asked.

"All of them," Abbey answered. "I know all of them. My uncle. My cousin. My father—" she choked.

At the last, Ember stopped breathing, went to the girl and took her in her arms, giving the girl a safe place to cry. Over Abbey's shoulder, she asked the other Bendanatu, "Is it this way for all of you? Do you know them?"

They nodded. Kymber stared at the grave somberly, but never shed a tear. Tyese and Keyera clung to one another, crying and nearly going to the decaying wolves. Mandalin would not look at them, but it was her voice that lifted in song. It started low, a long note that pulsed like a heartbeat, then soared up into a near howl. The melody was eerie, unlike anything Ember had ever heard, but it was mournful, beautiful.

And then another familiar voice joined in, intertwining with Mandalin's and creating a harmony that brought the song from despair to longing and then to hope.

Ember spun to see DeMunth sitting up in his harness, his eyes closed as he used his music to perform magic. Everyone backed away as the heat around the area intensified, though the song continued. Mandalin's magic and music joined with DeMunth's, and together they created a pyre of light and land within which they encased all the dead wolves.

Once built, DeMunth hit a particularly high note that matched Mandalin's pitch for pitch, as if it were a massive howl created through the power flowing in them. As the howl died off and the song ended, the magical structure caught fire, but it was like no fire Ember had ever seen. It was a fire of light and land magic. The flames touched nothing green, nothing growing, but acted much as Ezra's body had when he died. They turned into particles of light that floated upwards and toward the north until only stone and dirt remained, the smell and wolves gone with the light.

Shad sat down, Lady Kalandra behind him as he leaned against her for support. His eyes, hollow with grief, closed as he began his own song. Ember had never heard him sing before, and though his voice was rough from the tears, it was still beautiful. His song seemed a traditional dirge, something sung at a funeral, but also a kind of purging. With his song, the feelings of despair dissipated, and the memories Ember had of this group came to the front of her mind—things she had forgotten.

And when the song was over, the tears were gone. All of them. There was still sadness in her heart and on the faces of the other Bendanatu in particular, but the ache that was so debilitating was gone.

Shad stood and turned to hug Lady Kalandra—his way of giving thanks—before he addressed the group.

"We ride on. The chief and priestess must know of this. Come." He became wolf again and ran, not looking behind him to see if any of them followed.

One by one, they left the scene behind and followed the path toward home.

CHAPTER EIGHTEEN

Kayla's breakfast was delightful and very filling—lunch much the same. Aldarin left father and daughter alone after the morning hours, and Felandian and Kayla had spent much of that time speaking of the Sapphire Flute and the blue magic.

Having come across a quiet fountain away from the bustle of the Phoenixian city, they sat upon the wooden bench surrounding the fountain and talked, despite the lateness of the day.

"But how did the flute pull Brant into it? Why was he changed into an air elemental when his spirit left his body? I still don't understand," Kayla asked.

Felandian stood and paced in front of her. "Consider the flute as a hollow reed. You know the kind you played with as a child and insisted on using to drink your milk?"

Kayla reddened, but nodded.

"The flute is like that reed, pulling things through it that may be powerful and of use. You may not feel it, but it is constantly recharging itself." He stopped and looked at her, a twinkle in his eye.

"Do you remember the time you got a fly in your milk and sucked it up your straw?"

Kayla wanted to gag at the memory. "Yes. Thank you so very much for bringing that up. I would put that memory on my list of the worst things to happen to me. Ever."

Her father chuckled.

"So if the flute is a reed, consider Brant's spirit as the fly," he began, but Kayla interrupted.

"You're saying Brant is a fly? Really, Father?"

He laughed again. "Not at all, but it is the best I can do without showing you, and if I touch the flute, my people will know. I am taking a chance with our safety just coming to visit you. Now pay attention."

Kayla grew serious and nodded.

"If Brant was a fly sucked into the reed of a flute, what was the flute to do with it? The fly was stuck. And so the flute made the fly into something it could use. It turned Brant into an instrument that would work for its purposes. Does that make sense?" he asked.

Kayla thought it over. It made sense in an odd sort of way. "Okay, I think I understand. He has certainly acted the way a soldier would in following the biddings of his master."

"Yes, you see it now!" Felandian's eyes lit up, and he paced, his cloak snapping with every turn. "He is, in reality, an extension of the flute, his memories and personality being pulled into the instrument itself. The unfortunate side effect is that Brant is drained of the person he was and becomes more a creature of the Sapphire Flute as time passes." He sat down, took her hand, and spoke with his head down. "I am sorry for that, Kayla. I know how much you loved him."

She pulled her hand from his and stood, her back to her father. "I don't wish to speak of that." The pain was still too fresh and raw, and though Brant dwelt in the flute at her hip, her father was right—he lost more of himself every day until a single week had made him a changed person, a stranger—yet her oldest friend.

She took several deep breaths to pull herself together. It was easier to see Brant as the elemental he was now than to remember him as the man he had been. Kayla took three steps forward and put her hands on the railing, looking out over the woodland as she had with Aldarin earlier that day. She felt guilty for not giving the guard the magical instruction he had requested, but seeing her father had erased the thought from her mind until now. She would have time with Aldarin. She wasn't sure if she would ever see her father again.

The thought brought the tears that memories of Brant had not. She had never expected to see her father in the flesh. He had said it was impossible, and yet, here he was.

"Lord Felandian." A voice came from behind her. Kayla didn't turn, but listened as her father answered.

"Yes?"

"The grand council requests your distinguished presence in their honoring the child gone to light."

Kayla's heart gave a pang of regret. Ezra.

"I shall be there momentarily," her father responded, and the footsteps retreated in the distance.

Finally she turned. "You must go. Take my heart with you. I was there and saw the boy give his light to save us all. He may have been young, but he is a hero." She paused and then took a single, longing step toward her father. "Will I see you again?"

He raised his hands. "I do not know. I hope that once the white mage brings the keystones together and heals Rasann, there will no longer be a need for the individual stones and the Evahn will give up their tired attempt to retrieve what was anciently theirs. If that happens, there will no longer be a need for me to stay away. I pray, with all my heart, that we can be together again." He stepped forward and wrapped his arms around her, cradling her head in the palm of his hand.

She fought a losing battle against tears and finally gave in, throwing her arms around him and taking in his scent. It might be all she would have for the remainder of her life.

He patted her on the back and then pulled away. His eyes were not any drier than her own. He leaned forward and kissed her forehead, then pressed his cheek to hers. "Farewell, daughter. I'll see you in our dreams." He spun on his heel and walked away without looking behind him. Kayla didn't take offense. It was the Evahn way.

Instead, she sighed. Walking toward the center of the community, she turned left, hoping to find someone to direct her to a bath. Instead, she found Aldarin. He cleared his throat as she was about to walk past him, and she looked up to meet his boyish grin.

She was starting to see the handsome man behind the orange markings and didn't know why she hadn't liked him before. Well, other than his keeping Ember's group from leaving the school and turning them in to Ezeker. He was different out here in the wild. Kinder, actually.

"Sorry about the interruption earlier. I never did get to talk to you about magic."

Aldarin shrugged. "It's all right. I figured talking to your father was more important. It seemed like you hadn't seen each other for a while." He turned and walked with her.

"Since I was seven, actually. It's a long story," she said, a little embarrassed that it *had* been so long. It was strange—it rarely bothered her to talk about her father.

"My mum died when I was about that age, so I know how it feels not to see someone you love for a long time. You're lucky you still have him, even with the long distance." Aldarin kicked a pebble from the walk. Kayla watched it tumble into the canopy of trees below them and then disappear, but she could still hear it ricochet from branch to branch.

"I hadn't thought of it like that, but you're right," she said. Silence fell between them as they walked across three adjoining bridges. Kayla broke the silence. "Do you know where I can bathe? I'm not used to going so long in dirty clothes."

Aldarin looked sideways at her. "Actually, I do, but it's different from anything you've experienced, I'm sure. No baths. I mean, really, how would they haul water up here?"

"Really?" Kayla looked up, surprised. "Then what about the fountains?"

Aldarin chuckled. "Rain water, believe it or not. If it doesn't rain, they don't run. So, no bath, but they have these things called showers that Lily swears are 'divine'. Her word, not mine. Want to try them?"

Kayla shrugged. "Sure. I was about to use the fountain if I didn't find something more ideal."

Aldarin reddened and looked away. "Well . . . uh . . . the . . . uh . . . showers are close to our quarters, so how about we get a change of clothes and clean up?"

Kayla felt a moment of panic. "Is it an open bath, like the mage academy? Please don't tell me it's mixed gender."

Aldarin laughed. "No, they are individual stalls about as big as a small closet. You'll see. Just get your clothes and meet me back here." He stopped near the room she had awakened in. Despite its similarity to most of the other buildings, she recognized it. In her room, she opened her satchel and pulled out her only change of clothes. She'd have to find a way to wash her dirty things before she left.

Heading out the open doorway, she found Aldarin waited, having returned ahead of her. Without a word, they turned to the left, crossed two bridges, and came to the only building she had seen that was rectangular instead of round.

Inside, a woman standing at a counter did not speak, but took their clothes from them and handed each of them a thick robe and towel, then a wooden chip with a shower number stamped on both sides. Six and seven. She pointed to the left and Kayla and Aldarin shuffled off in that direction, finding their showers easily.

"Well, here goes nothing," Aldarin mumbled, winking at Kayla. She smiled at him and stepped through the curtain into her changing area. She hung up the robe on one hook and the towel on another, then undressed quickly and left her clothes on the floor. No point in folding them when they needed to be washed anyway.

The water turned on in Aldarin's shower and steam rose into the air above their adjoining wall. He whistled a nameless tune that made her smile.

She stepped through the second curtain and looked at the knobs in her room. She finally experimented, getting a blast of cold water that elicited a yelp from her and a chuckle from Aldarin next door, but after a few twists, she got the temperature just right.

Soap for hair and body were provided, so she wet her long blond locks and had lathered up when she heard a terrified yell from Aldarin.

"What is it?" she hollered. For an answer, he yelled again, sounding distraught. Something was very wrong.

Shampoo in her hair and dripping wet, Kayla leaped out of the water, pulled on the robe, and tied the belt as she dashed past the exterior curtain. She took three running steps to Aldarin's shower and pushed aside the first curtain, surprised when she saw that his inner curtain was open and Aldarin stood in the water with his pants on. He had a stiff-bristled brush and was scrubbing at his arm. Then he yelled again and scrubbed at his left shoulder, and then backed into the wall, scrubbing at his chest. He didn't seem to know she was there, though he faced her straight on.

He was going to scrub himself to shreds if he didn't stop. Still unsure what was happening, she stepped into the water and took him by the shoulder, only vaguely noticing how strong it was. "Aldarin! Stop your yelling! What is wrong with you?" She grabbed the brush away from him. He cried out and grabbed it back, continuing to scrub at his chest and then his washboard stomach.

"Get out! Get out!" he yelled, still sounding panicked.

"Not until you tell me what's going on!" she yelled right back. When he didn't answer, she reached toward the brush again, but he lifted it above his head, looking distraught.

"No! No, you can't have it! I have to get them off! They're alive—can't you see? They're moving!"

The voice of the robe lady out front echoed from the distance. "No funny business back there, chicks. I'll toss you out on your naked backsides if you don't tone it down!"

He silenced and added more soap to the bristles, scrubbing his body again, a low chant coming from his lips. "Get it off, get it off, get it off, get it off!" Over and over again.

Kayla felt sorry for him despite herself. He was out of his mind with terror over the orange tattoos covering his body. She stepped forward, then startled. He was right. They *were* moving! Some gently waved as if the wind caught them, others completely rearranging themselves like a silk scarf in rough waters. Did it have something to do with the flash of blue from when they touched earlier? The tattoos hadn't moved before—she was sure of it. Did she have something to do with this?

Curious, she reached slowly toward his chest and barely rested her fingers on his sternum.

Just like before, the tattoos flashed blue, then returned to orange—and stilled.

He stopped scrubbing, looking at his shoulders, his arms, chest, stomach, and as much of his back as he could see, then finally turned around and asked her, "Are they moving? Did it stop?"

She nodded, then realizing he couldn't see her with his back turned, she answered, "Yes. They stopped. Now, please tell me what happened."

He looked around him, as if suddenly realizing where the two of them were, and reddened. "Aldarin," she said again, but quietly this time. "Tell me what's wrong. Let me help you fix it."

He shook his head back and forth. "There is no fixing this. I'm stuck with it until we get to your friend T'Kato's village and they take back his magical tattoos."

She didn't understand at all. "What have the tattoos got to do with anything? You've had them for days! You should be used to them by now."

"I was—until they started moving. I could feel it, Kayla! It was like being covered with bugs of all sizes, constantly moving and walking on my skin." He shivered, then looked at her. "What did you do to me? Why did it stop?"

Kayla tipped her head and wanted to touch him again, but didn't want to reawaken the terror in him. "I just touched you. That's all."

He leaned against the wall just outside of the water's reach. "Why would your touch stop it? And why did it start to begin with?" He wiped the beads of water or sweat off his forehead.

"I think the answers to both questions come back to me," she said, looking at the ground. "Do you remember when we shook hands before and your tattoos turned blue for a moment?"

He nodded when she looked at him from the corner of her eye.

"They flashed again when I touched your sternum. I think somehow the colors of our magic are interacting and the blue in mine brings the orange in yours to life. Literally."

Aldarin was quiet for a long moment, then softly said, "Kayla, why would the colors interact like that? It makes little sense to me."

She scratched her head, her hand coming away soapy. She'd forgotten about the shampoo in her hair until that moment. "Opposites in all things?" she guessed.

Aldarin pursed his lips, thinking. "That makes a strange kind of sense. If you think about the nature of magic, the different types affect each other in a circular fashion—three positive, the other three negative. For example, fire eats land, but is extinguished by water, air feeds it, it creates light, and when it is gone, all that remains is change. Does that make sense?"

Kayla's brain was swimming. She'd learned none of this. He must have seen her boggled look because he sighed and tried again. "Okay. How about color? Everything has an opposite, right? Like red is the opposite of green. One is a primary color, the other is a combination of the other two primary colors. Well, blue and orange are opposites. Maybe there is something in that magic that makes them affect each other."

That made more sense. Kayla nodded. "I can understand that. But if our magic affects each other, why hasn't yours affected me?"

He pushed away from the wall. "My guess? You have a keystone. I don't. Your power is a lot stronger than mine, so I get the effect." His well-formed shoulders drooped.

She was quiet for a moment. "I'm sorry, Aldarin. I wish I could change that."

He sighed and stepped back into the shower. "Me too. Now, I'm going to finish my shower, if you don't mind. My skin is a bit raw." He pulled the inner curtain closed and within seconds, his pants flew over the bar holding the curtain and smacked her in the head.

"Ow!" she muttered, then turned quickly, embarrassed that he cared so little that she stood right outside his shower curtain. Knowing it was all her fault he'd been in such a panic kept her from leaving without saying something. She spoke up so he could hear her over the water.

"Umm, I'm going to go wash the soap out of my hair now. I'm glad you're not dying," she said and turned to leave. Unable to think of anything more to comfort him, she went back to her shower, rinsed her hair, washed it again, then washed her body and turned the water as warm as it would go and just stood there. She didn't want to think. Thinking took her places her mind shouldn't go. She couldn't think about a relationship. She couldn't think of Aldarin that way. It was too soon. It felt like a betrayal to Brant.

A knock sounded on the doorframe. "Are you ever coming out?" Aldarin asked, trying to mask the embarrassment that still leaked through his gruff exterior.

"No," she answered, letting the water wash away the thoughts of Aldarin.

"They're going to yank you out of there when the next group of Phoenixians comes in. They just landed. Evidently there's an Evahn hunting party racing this way. They don't know why."

Kayla went cold. She knew why. Flipping the water off, she scrambled past the curtain, dried herself with the towel, and put on her robe. She reached, meaning to gather her clothes, but they were gone. Frustrated, she ran through the other curtain, Aldarin trailing behind her. She stopped at the front desk and retrieved her clean set. "What happened to my dirty clothes?"

"We have taken them to the cleaners," the woman said. "With as long as you were in the shower, they should be near done. Other side of the building. You can dress in there." She pointed to the right.

Kayla darted into one of the rooms and pulled her things on as quickly as possible, then rushed to the cleaners. Her clothes were still damp, but they were the only spare she had.

Aldarin caught up with her. "What's going on?"

"The Evahn are coming for me. The Sapphire Flute belonged to them eons ago, and my father told me that if they had the chance, they would steal it back, even if it meant my life. We have to leave for Bendanatu now. Do you know where the others are?" she asked, jogging toward her room.

Aldarin grasped the situation quickly. "Yes, they're all near. We'll need Phoenixian rides, though, and I'm not sure if we can persuade anyone to take us."

"Can you try?" Kayla stepped through her doorway and spun.

"Yes. I'll try. I'll send them here as quickly as possible."

Kayla nodded, then stuffed her damp clothes in her bag, cinching it tight once she'd retrieved her few things. She tossed the satchel on the bed and turned around in time to see Lily stroll through the door. She nodded to Kayla and then sat on the bed. Next came three of the Phoenixian students—Raech, Behn, and Miek. Thew, the air elemental, hovered outside the door. And last of all, accompanying Aldarin and surprising Kayla beyond anything, was Shari Bird. Kayla quickly went to the doorway to talk to the woman before she came into the room. "Are you sure you can do this? You've suffered a horrific loss."

Shari Bird met her eyes, and though they were full of sadness, there was also a raging determination that Kayla knew she could not fight. It was the kind of determination that got things done. "I ache for my son. My other children shall remain here, safe with their father. I will find my son's killers and they will feel my wrath. But I will not let that impede your mission. I will help. I *need* to help. Being here is . . . hard." She moved past Kayla and into the room.

Kayla turned to Aldarin. "Is this everyone?"

He nodded.

"It's more than I expected. Much more. Thank you." She turned to the group. "The Evahn are sending a hunting party, I'm sure you've heard." Nods came from every direction. "They come for the Sapphire Flute. They come for me, and they cannot have either of us. Will you ride with me to Bendanatu? Now?"

Not a single person said no.

Kayla actually smiled. "Then let's go!"

CHAPTER NINETEEN

It was nearing dark before Ember's group encountered any local Bendanatu. They ran and flew for what seemed like forever. Then Ember heard several twangs and the distinctive swishing whir of arrows in flight. The Phoenixia above them cried out as one, then circled down to the ground and landed roughly, almost throwing the humans from their backs.

Five wolves darted silently from the trees, aimed straight for the Phoenixian students and Ted Finch. The flyers were about to be murdered by the very people they'd come to for help. As one, the Bendanatu banded together and moved in front of the magical birds. The wolves never slowed. Shad leaped and tackled the lead wolf, and following his lead, Ember, Tyese, Keyera, Mandalin, and Kymber did the same. The other wolves, outnumbered and small, were taken down easily. The girls had their teeth to the attacker's throats but did not bite, waiting for Shad's instructions.

When the lead wolf rolled over and bared his neck to Shad, Ember watched her uncle's posture relax, and he backed away. He shifted to human and so did the other wolf. Ember gasped to see the attacker was only a boy. They were all young.

Shad put his hands on his hips and yelled at the young Bendanatu. "What were you thinking? You could have killed our friends. I know you are the Moningers, and having lost all have nothing to lose. I know you love and protect Bendanatu with all you are, but you can't shoot everyone. Part of being a good guard is diplomacy. You can't just take everyone by surprise." They hung their heads as they listened.

Leaving Shad to speak with the guards, Ember went to the Phoenixians to see what kind of damage had been done. The humans had dismounted, but could not hear the birds speaking to them. Just like the Lady Kalandra, they were deaf to mindspeech—all but DeMunth.

Ember longed to go to him. They hadn't spoken since he regained consciousness. There hadn't been time. She moved past him with a gentle touch on his shoulder. He nodded to her and continued directing things as best he could, but Ember could help too.

DeMunth was working on several arrows embedded in the left wing of Ted Finch. Kymber, Alexa Jade, and her sisters, Elaisha and Aislyn, held his wing open and still so that DeMunth could work. He obviously didn't need her. Ember grabbed her aunt and Mandalin to help with the other two Phoenixians. She approached Eden first, mindspeaking to be sure she would allow their contact. Considering the pain she must be in, Ember wanted to be sure the girl was in her right mind. *Where does it hurt, Eden? Let us help.*

My wing. Oh, my wing. They punctured it. Is the arrow still there?

I don't know. May I touch you and see?

The great bird nodded, and Ember approached slowly, looking for the puncture wound. She easily found it once she got near. The arrow protruded halfway through the wing. She instantly felt a knot in her stomach, knowing she was going to have to pull the arrow out. But why were they attacked in the first place? And why only the Phoenixians?

It is still there, Eden. It is in your wing. Do you want me to remove it? Ember asked. The bird girl whimpered, but nodded, and Ember put her hands on each side of the arrow to break it in half. If she didn't, whichever end went through the hole would cause more damage.

Ember pulled her hands back, as they were shaking. Composing herself and putting all her focus on the arrow, she reached with her right hand and got a grip on the shaft with her fingertips just below the arrowhead, surprised when she pinched right through the wood. The stone head fell off. Wondering if it would continue to work, she pinched down next to the wound. The remaining portion of the top of the staff fell, then the bottom half, leaving only a small plug in the hole.

She prayed that the injury was not near a vein and that she was not doing more damage by helping. Using her index finger, she pushed the wooden plug through the bottom of the wound.

Eden hissed at her and snapped her beak inches from Ember's ear.

She jerked away, then went back to the wound, focusing her emotion on speeding up the healing and using heat to sear the wound closed. In an instant, it was done, with only a single bellow of pain from the girl.

Moving on to Aryana, Ember repeated the process, then went to Ted Finch and finished what DeMunth had already started and healed his wound. She didn't know if she could ever do this again, but for now, her magic was working and she would use it.

Once healed, the Phoenixians shifted to their human form and moved their arms around. They grimaced at the residual pain. Ember knew all too well how that felt, her foot twinging at the thought, but they were healed and seemed pleased with that.

Ember went back to Shad to find out what had happened. He stood with hands on hips, his voice still angry as he finished lecturing the teenaged wolves who'd attacked them.

The boy, who seemed to be the leader, raised his eyes. "We are most sorry, Chieftain-elect White Shadow. But you don't know how bad it's been. Almost all the grown-ups are dead or missing. There are only a few adults and younglings left, most not old enough to help. That's why we took it into our hands. We were some of the oldest, and the only ones passionate enough to take a chance. We're all orphaned, sir." He hung his head again and kicked at the dirt. "We're doing our best."

Shad put his hand on the boy's shoulder. "I know. And you're doing a good job. Just make sure you are shooting at the enemy before you release the arrow, understood? Phoenixians are good. Watch for the light within them. Shadow weavers are bad. They fly too, yes, but they are dark and ugly. Can you not see the difference?"

The boy shook his head. "We have yet to see the Ne'Goi, sir. Always before, the adults made us hide."

Ember's heart ached. She was still upset they had shot her friends, but these younglings had been through Helar. She couldn't blame them for shooting in fear.

Shad shook the boy's shoulder, then released. "Enough for now. We'll talk more later. Now that I'm here, I'll make sure you get some training so you can do more. We're depending on you. Now, take us to my father and Priestess Adrienne. We have much to speak with them about."

The boy nodded, and the group of five shifted to wolf and ran. Shad looked at the others behind him. The Bendanatu scrambled to his side and followed suit. The Phoenixians shifted and took to the air, though more slowly than before, the humans astride their backs, and last of all, Ember changed form and tried to catch up with her uncle.

Bendanatu. They had arrived at last.

Ember took a cup of herbal tea from the Priestess Adrienne, fascinated by her coppery red hair and pale blue eyes. Tall and thin, like a willow, she barely made a sound as she moved. Ember blew her tea and sat in this woman's home, waiting for Shad to finish with his father—her grandfather. Her stomach was a mass of butterflies in anticipation of meeting this man she'd not known about until Uncle Shad told her a week or so ago. Her father's father. This was quite the week for meeting family. First Uncle Shad, then her cousins, Lily and Kayla, then Kayla's mother, Lady Kalandra. Now her grandfather. It was so much to take in.

Nervous, Ember spoke to Adrienne, though they were words of little consequence. "So, are you married to the chief?"

Adrienne laughed, her voice like chimes in the wind. "Oh, Havens no! I serve the Bendanatu just as he does—but in a different capacity. I take care of their spiritual needs, being the mediator between the Bendanatu and their Guardian, Bendanatu."

Baffled, Ember asked, "Why is everything called Bendanatu? The people, the village, the Guardian. Isn't it confusing?"

The priestess chuckled, stirring something in a black kettle over the fire. "To outsiders, yes, it can be very confusing, but to us, it is as it is. We know the difference. When we say the Bendanatu, we mean the people. When we say we are going to Bendanatu, it is the village. When we speak of the Guardian, he is just Bendanatu, or Lord Bendanatu, or Master Bendanatu. It is all in how the name is used."

A young girl entered the room with a bowl full of something she dumped into the pot.

Adrienne picked up a pair of tongs and used them to grasp a clean stone from the fire oven and drop it in the water. The kettle's contents immediately began to boil. "Have you met my daughter?" She glanced up at Ember, who shook her head. "This is Agrobel. Agrobel, this is Miss Ember. She is Chieftain Bahndai's granddaughter."

The girl gave a small curtsey, her eyes bashful, her mouth silent. She left the room as quickly as she'd entered it.

"She's beautiful," Ember said, watching the girl's retreating back, dark hair swaying with her walk.

Adrienne smiled and stirred the contents of the pot. "Thank you. It's just the two of us now, but we do well."

Not knowing what to say, Ember stood, walked over to the pot, and looked in. The water was light brown and full of carrots and potatoes and bits of floating meat, among other vegetables. "You're making soup?"

"Yes. What did you think I was making?" Adrienne answered, distracted.

"I don't know. Some kind of potion, I guess." Ember felt stupid saying it out loud, but at least Adrienne had the decency not to laugh.

"I'm a priestess, Ember Shandae, not a witch. I don't deal in potions. Only in the power and magic of my Guardian." She was quiet a moment, then asked, "How is that you are one of us, have never been to Bendanatu, know nothing of our cultures and customs, and have not become acquainted with our deity?" Adrienne stirred the soup, then tapped the wooden spoon on the side of the bowl and set it across the lip of the pot while dinner simmered. She sat on one of the benches across from Ember and crossed her legs, very prim for a backwoods priestess.

Ember sighed. "It is such a long story, and I don't want to slander Bahndai's name."

Adrienne chuckled. "The Bendanatu are very earthy people. We follow our nature, though it may not always sit well with human society. It is an extension of the magic within us. You cannot slander his name. Besides, I believe I know most of the chieftain's secrets."

That was a relief, at least. Ember continued. "Well then, knowing that, I'll just say that Bahndai is my grandfather, though I didn't know it until recently. He partnered with a human woman, Asana, and they had a son—my father, Jarin."

Adrienne nodded as if none of this was news to her. Ember shifted in her seat, a little uncomfortable spilling her family secrets to a stranger, but still she went on. "My father grew up and married my mother, Brina, who has since changed her name to Marda. He got a job as a stone sculptor from his half-sister and worked for her for a year, then found out she worked for S'Kotos and my parents tried to run away. He saved me and my mother, but died in the battle with his sister. My mum never knew he was a Bendanatu, so she never taught me your ways. I only met Uncle Shad a week ago, and he's taught me what little I know. Without him, I would still be oblivious, never knowing the blood I carried."

Adrienne shook her head. "That is quite a story, I'll admit. I knew about Asana and your father, but not what happened after. That must have been hard for your mother to lose him like that. And you, growing up without a father. I'm glad you've come to us now. We'll celebrate, welcoming you home as a sister of the Bendanatu while we celebrate the lives of those lost in the forest. It is a good balance, I believe." Adrienne went back to her soup, stirring the chunks up from the bottom.

Shad chose that moment to return. "Did you have a pleasant visit with Adrienne?"

The priestess answered for both of them. "It was very enlightening. Thank you for returning this lost sister to us." She outlined her plan to him.

Shad didn't smile, though his eyes danced a bit. "Beautiful idea. If you weren't family, I'd kiss you."

Adrienne smacked him on the arm. "Oh, hush, cousin. You always were such a flirt. And speaking of, when are you going to marry? You're getting awfully old."

Ember watched the insults fly back and forth and grinned. Adrienne was a different person with Shad around.

He glanced at Ember and winked. "Well, what's the point when you're not available? Who on earth could ever top you?" He plucked the spoon from her hand, had a bite of her soup, and gave a growling sign of approval.

Adrienne grabbed her spoon back and thwacked him with it. "I've noticed a certain lady who may have finally pinned down our renowned bachelor."

Shad actually turned red. "I don't know what you're talking about," he said a little stiffly.

Adrienne laughed. "Ooooo, struck a nerve, have we? I think you really have found your match in the lady, human or not. She doesn't seem to care much about race. I hear her first husband was Evahn."

He ignored his cousin and turned to Ember. "Are you ready to go?"

She nodded and stood. "Did you have time to talk to Grandfather about me?" she asked as they stepped out the door of Adrienne's hut.

Shad shook his head and said nothing more.

Ember's stomach felt like someone had dropped a stone in it. "Why not?"

"It just . . . wasn't the right time," he said. "We were talking about war and the funeral, and it just . . . well, you never came up."

Ember said nothing. That hurt. She'd been forgotten. It seemed she'd spent her life being forgotten, and here she'd finally found a grandparent and might never have the chance to get to know him.

Shad must have sensed her disappointment because he put his arm around her and said, “I think the best way to introduce you would be at the celebration tonight. He knows you, but he doesn’t know who you belong to. He doesn’t know you are family. So, tonight at the celebration, let’s get him up there with you and introduce you publicly. Claim you not just as a Bendanatu sister, but as the granddaughter of the chieftain. He loves surprises. It will be amazing!” He squeezed her shoulder before letting go.

Part of Ember loved the idea, but the other part wanted a quiet introduction where they could just talk and be away from everyone. She would not get it, she could tell, so she’d resign herself to the other—but it wasn’t ideal. “So, what time is this celebration?”

“We start just after sunset. Let’s get some food in you and find someone to fix you up. Everyone will wear their best tonight!” Shad whistled as they made their way to his cavern. Ember only hoped she didn’t have to go dressed in sticks and bushes.

CHAPTER TWENTY

C'Tan made Kardon suffer, watching his son die hour after hour. When his fingers bled from clawing at the vise and his sobs had turned to nonsensical gibberish, she released him and personally escorted him to the dungeon. She unlatched the door and threw the man in with her ex-sister-in-law, then waited, staring into the darkness. Her old master blubbered, nearly mad from his grief and torment, but C'Tan ignored him.

She had a promise to keep. "Brina," she called.

"Call me Marda," the woman's voice answered from the other side of the room.

"Marda, then," C'Tan answered, slightly irritated. She didn't care what the woman called herself. "I've spoken with your daughter and struck a deal. My servant undermined that deal and got his son killed for it, but I keep my promises."

Quiet came from the woman. "Oh?" she finally asked, guarded and wary.

"You are to have a comfortable room, with a bed and sunlight. Those were her demands." C'Tan stepped aside and gestured for Brina or Marda or whatever she was called to exit the room.

"How do I know you speak the truth?" Ember's mother asked.

C'Tan was getting annoyed. "You don't. You can choose to stay here with the babbling madman, stuck in the dark forever, or you can have a nice room upstairs. You'll still be locked away, but it will be much more comfortable. Trust me or don't, but can it really be worse than where you are now?"

There was silence for a long moment, and C'Tan started to shut the door.

"Wait!" Brina called out. C'Tan heard shuffling sounds, and finally Brina stepped into the dim light, her hand on the wall to guide her. Smart woman to accept the offer.

C'Tan opened the door again, and Marda shuffled out and immediately pressed against the wall. C'Tan snorted, shut the door and locked it, then turned her back and walked away. Marda scuttled to get behind C'Tan and followed her.

Once they reached the next floor, C'Tan unlocked another door and the two women spiraled up a tower until they reached the top. Another door was unlocked and C'Tan held the door open, waiting for Marda to enter. As her prisoner stepped across the threshold, C'Tan heard a sigh of relief escape Marda's lips. Her fingers ran along the obsidian walls and touched the scarlet blankets on the bed. Last of all, she went to the open window and looked out and down. C'Tan knew the drop from the windows was deadly, which was why they were left open year round, except at the coldest of times. Of all the rooms, this one had the most sunshine, which was why C'Tan picked it. Ember could not accuse C'Tan of not following through on her promises. She only hoped the girl would follow through on hers, despite Ian's treachery.

"What do you need?" C'Tan asked.

Brina spun, as if she'd forgotten C'Tan was there. She looked her captor up and down and grimaced. "A shower," she said, almost reluctantly, "then food and water? Medicine for my injuries?" She said it as if she expected C'Tan to say no, but she needn't fear. C'Tan kept her promises, and she did have good memories with this woman. She'd tried to forget them, but they were still there.

"Done, done, and done. Follow me," the mistress of fire ordered, and walked across the room. Behind the obsidian wall was a large pool of water piped up from the hot springs below the castle. Clean towels, soap for body, and soap for hair in multiple fragrances adorned the shelves—and there was even a change of clothing in Marda's size. C'Tan had the tailor send it up an hour before. Marda ogled the water as if it sang to her like a siren. Another moment, and she'd get in even with C'Tan standing there.

"I'll leave you to your bath and bring you the food, water, and medical supplies you requested. Anything else?" It almost felt like she was a servant again. Strange that she didn't resent it.

Brina wanted to ask something, but seemed almost afraid. Finally, she blurted it out. "Something to write on, and . . . and a book to read? Is that too much?"

C'Tan laughed for the first time in ages. Not the kind of laughter she used on her subjects—the evil laugh of a servant of S'Kotos—but genuine laughter. She didn't know why, but Brina asking for those things was so familiar and struck her as funny. She calmed enough to answer when she saw Brina cringe. "No. It's not too much. I'll pull something from the library myself and bring parchment and a blackstick with your dinner. Now bathe. You're stinking up the place," she said, trying to gain back some of the fearful demeanor she usually carried.

She did not know why being around Brina made her happy. It was strange and unfamiliar, which always set her teeth on edge.

Pulling the door closed behind her, she went in search of the few items Brina needed, humming all the way.

CHAPTER TWENTY-ONE

"Are they still back there?" Shari Bird asked as they wove among the trees toward Bendanatu. They had been flying for hours, the Evahn guard racing after them on flying creatures of their own like a cross between a lion and a giant bat, charging across the sky.

Kayla had seen nothing like them before.

She looked behind her, searching the dark, and saw flitting, dark figures, then turned to the front and hollered, "Yes." She sounded calm, but was actually rather panicked that they hadn't been able to outrun the chasing guard. The Phoenixians couldn't go on forever. Exhaustion wore on them, but if they stopped, the guard would catch up, and Kayla was pretty sure they wouldn't be satisfied with taking the flute and killing her alone. The entire group shared her danger now that they had helped her.

What could she do? What could the group do? They couldn't battle in the air—there were too many of the Evahn guard. They would kill the Phoenixians, no matter how good they and their riders were at fighting. What about magic?

Kayla glanced down at her hip and smacked herself in the head with her palm. She had the tool to battle them with magic right there and hadn't even thought to use it. Sending a mental note to Thew, Kayla came to a stop and circled around. The Phoenixians went on without her, and she hoped they wouldn't notice her absence as she turned to face the enemy.

Putting the flute to her lips, she called forth Brant. As the guard came ever closer by the second, excitedly yelling and pointing at her hovering form, she pleaded, "I need your help, love." The swirling mass of blue at her side bowed.

"Whatever you desire, Mistress," Brant said, his voice emotionless. Her heart cracked. He'd never called her "Mistress" before. He lost more of himself to the flute every hour, just as her father had said.

"Those men behind us want to cause harm to the flute and to myself. They must be stopped. Air or ice?"

Brant swirled faster, his anger at her pursuers clear as his momentum increased and he grew in mass. "Both, Mistress. Let us do both. I shall handle the wind. You handle the ice."

She grinned. Kayla loved this kind of battle. Brant flew toward the oncoming guard while she drew her breath to play the flute, releasing it on a high note that lowered the surrounding temperature. The sound built, pulling moisture from the air to collect in small, pebble-sized balls of ice. She created more, and more, until they hung in the air around her like hail. She took one last breath and pushed the balls of ice toward Brant, who pulled them into his miniature hurricane and spun them faster and faster until they whipped about him. The ice pieces grew in size as it got colder until they had grown from pebbles to walnuts to the size of lemons.

Brant let go. Kayla watched the trail of blue magic as the ice balls flew toward the Evahn guard, cracking against trees, breaking branches, and finally, when they reached the men, annihilating them in one volley. The ice blasted holes through armor and took out the winged creatures, so men fell to their death. It killed every single man and woman following her in an instant. It wasn't pleasant, watching their life force get snuffed out by the ice balls, but it was necessary.

She'd never have succeeded if one of the Evahn had been watching for a magical attack. She'd only won because the rain of hail was near invisible in the dark, but a win was a win.

She'd take it.

Kayla turned around and flew after her friends. They'd never stopped, never even realized the murder that had taken place behind them, and now that it was done, she felt sick to her stomach. The guard hadn't stood a chance. It was to protect herself and her friends, yes, but it still felt like murder, and it was a feeling she hated with all her being. Kayla wasn't born for this, wasn't meant for the warrior's life. She was too gentle, born to aristocracy. It just wasn't right. She shouldn't have to use music to kill.

It was that which bothered her more than anything. In gaining the flute, she had often been forced to use the thing she loved most in the world—the beauty of music—in destructive and murderous ways. Why couldn't music just stay music? It was powerful in and of itself. Why did it have to become something so ugly?

She still had no answers when she caught up with the group and pulled even with Shari Bird. "They're gone. We can slow down now."

Shari looked at her with disbelief.

"Truly, they are gone. Look for yourself," Kayla said, knowing Shari's magic of light would allow her to see in the darkness.

Shari slowed, then turned and hovered in place, the rest of the group following suit. She stayed there for what seemed like forever, but was probably only a minute or two, before she looked at Kayla asked, "Your doing?"

Reluctantly, she nodded. "Mine and Brant's. I didn't know what else to do."

Shari nodded and gave a Phoenixian grin that was more terrifying than beautiful. "Well done. It is difficult to face one's enemy in battle, and harder still to be one against a multitude. Do not let guilt cripple you. You are right. It was the only thing to do."

Kayla wished words would remove the guilt as easily as they were said, but they did provide some small measure of comfort.

Looking around, Shari inspected the younglings and then murmured. "They are beyond tired. We must find a place to rest or they will fall from the sky."

Kayla nodded, and the group continued on, more slowly this time, dropping lower into the trees so they might better find a cave or barn. Somewhere that would accommodate both human and Phoenixian.

They never expected to find a glorious cabin hidden in the woods, built right next to a magestone mine. The Phoenixians could recover quickly with such fine accommodations.

One by one, they landed on the ground in front of the cabin, releasing their humans from their backs before rising to the rooftop to perch and sleep.

Aldarin leaped from Shari Bird's back before she landed and stormed over to Kayla, Lily trailing in his wake. "You took care of them all on your own, didn't you?"

Kayla didn't answer right at first. One, his anger startled her, and two, she wasn't sure what to say.

"Hey, I'm talking to you!" he said, grabbing her arm. Brant swirled up from the flute and pushed Aldarin back, then centered his swirling vortex over the tattooed man. Aldarin coughed and hacked, falling to his knees as the oxygen was sucked from the center of Brant's cyclone.

"Stop!" she yelled at the elemental. He ignored her. "I said, stop!" She pushed out with her hands. Her voice echoed as her power shoved Brant away from Aldarin.

The elemental looked at her in surprise. "Why did you do that? He was hurting you. I was helping. That is my duty. Protect Kayla. That is what the flute called me to do. Why?" He seemed almost hurt in his child-like speech.

Aldarin gasped for air, and finally slowed his breathing when the oxygen returned. He stood, glaring at the swirling elemental.

"Brant, I know you want to protect me, and I appreciate it. You're a great warrior and help, and you have always been a wonderful friend—but you can't attack people just because you don't like the way they touch me. Aldarin was within his rights to grasp my arm. Did I like it?" She purposely glared at the tattooed warrior as she answered her own question. "No. Not at all. But he asked a question, and I didn't answer. He was frustrated. That's what people do. Don't you remember?"

Brant's face scrunched up as if he was trying to regain the memories that the flute had stolen. His voice changed. "I think . . . perhaps . . . yes, I remember a little. I'm sorry, Kay. It is so hard to remember what it was to be human. I told you. I told you the flute would change me," he said in his old voice, almost looking like himself for a second—and then he disappeared and let the flute pull him inside.

Kayla's heart broke all over again, and she couldn't help the tears that started. In a moment, her single, trailing tear became full-on sobbing as she dropped to her knees in the dirt.

Aldarin caught her as she tipped sideways, his thigh cradling her head. She curled in on herself and cried. She wasn't even sure why she cried. The stress of the past week? Losing Brant? The deaths caused at her hand—Jihong, the Ne'Goi, and now the Evahn guard? Her own people. She had slaughtered her own people as if they were nothing but rabbits to be skinned after the hunt. It didn't matter that they would have killed her to gain the flute. She had not seen an Evahn aside from her father in her entire life, and she had slaughtered a dozen or more without thought.

The tears wouldn't stop. Aldarin laid his hand on her head and hesitantly, then gently caressed her hair, pulling it back from her tear-streaked face and exposing her ear. She didn't even notice until he traced it with his callused finger, lingering on the point near the top. She stopped crying then, expecting any moment to feel the shame and embarrassment that usually came when someone realized she was different.

But it never came.

Surprised, she lay there quietly and let him touch her hair, her face, her ear as he tried to console her. It was very comforting. Despite how brusque he was at times, Aldarin was a gentle soul, a kind man, and he revealed it in this moment. Maybe she had misjudged him. The longer she lay there, the more she realized he was a truly good person.

It was too soon to fall in love. Brant's loss still broke her heart, but feelings stirred within her. She could love this man. It surprised her. He was a working man, a guard of the magi. He was not one of her kind. And yet, she also was not one of her kind—not really. She was a half-breed and one who had been an outcast. And now she was a warrior herself. If she, an aristocrat who had never touched a weapon, could become a warrior, why couldn't a warrior become an aristocrat?

It was something to think about.

Kayla sat up and Aldarin scrambled back, embarrassed. She reached out and grasped his shoulder, meeting his eye. "Thank you."

He nodded, though his face reddened in the blue glow of the elemental Thew.

A door in the cabin opened, and a magelight soared Havenward. It sprang to life with a bright orange light that pierced Kayla's eyes like daggers. She turned away, squinting and blinking until her sight adjusted to the brightness. She looked at the doorway and froze.

An old woman, her hair long and silver, stood in the entry. Dressed in only a nightgown, she radiated fury, each hand glowing with a burning light.

"Who are you? And what are you doing on my property?" she snapped.

Kayla glanced at her friends—everyone was frozen in place, not by magic but by fear—took her courage in hand, and stepped forward. "We're but humble travelers from Phoenixia looking for a place to rest. We've been chased by the Evahn guard half the night and are exhausted. Please, may we rest in your barn and on your rooftop?" She ignored the implied threat in the woman's burning hands and addressed her as if she were weaponless.

The old woman cocked her head and looked Kayla over from top to bottom. "The Evahn guard gave chase, you say?" At Kayla's nod, she asked, "Why?"

Dreading what would happen when she gave the truth, she said, "Because I hold a keystone they believe belongs to them and will kill all of us to get it."

The woman's eyes widened, and the fire in her hands went out. She stepped off the porch and took several steps toward Kayla. "the Sapphire Flute? You have it?" Her voice was filled with longing and excitement.

Nodding, Kayla pulled the instrument from the satchel at her waist and stepped forward, holding it out with both hands toward the old woman. It seemed foolish, but she somehow knew she could trust her.

The woman reached out, then snatched her hand back before touching the instrument. She tucked her hands beneath her chin and met Kayla's eyes. "May I? Please?" she almost begged.

Kayla extended the instrument, so it was within the woman's reach. She took it reverently, inspecting the flute from the mouthpiece to fingering holes to the opening at the end. She turned it over in her hand, running her fingers down its length, and last of all, gave the flute a single blow. The sound resonated as if within a cave—the purest, most powerful sound created by Haven. Her voice full of awe, she said, "I find myself without words. They truly made it of one piece of magestone. I hadn't believed it possible." She handed the instrument back to Kayla, who secured it in her pouch.

The old woman extended her hand. "I am Asana, miner of magestone, and this is my humble cabin. I would be honored if you slept here this night. Are you hungry? Your friends? Please, let me feed you. Bring them down from the rooftop and let me serve you properly. It is the least I can do for one of the keystone guardians. Come! Come!"

She stepped back through the door, magelights illuminating the place enough for it to be seen for miles. Kayla turned to Aldarin and Lily. "Anyone know how to get the birds down from the roof?" Aldarin called up to Shari Bird, waking her from her slumber. She went roused the rest of the Phoenixians. The exhausted birds landed on the porch and shifted to their human forms, then filed inside one by one.

Kayla looked at Lily, who hadn't moved since the old woman introduced herself. "Come on. Aren't you hungry?"

Lily didn't answer. Her face was slack, as if she was in a stupor of absolute shock.

Worried, Kayla move until she stood directly in front of the girl and put a hand on her shoulder. "Lily? Lily, are you all right?"

The girl nodded slowly, and then a slow grin spread across her face. "Do you know who that is?"

Stumped, Kayla shook her head. Lily's grin continued to grow.

"Asana. Once wed to Bahndai of the Bendanatu. They had a son, Jarin, who had a daughter, Ember Shandae."

Shocked beyond measure, Kayla said, "No! You can't be serious!"

Lily nodded, smiling from ear to ear now. "Oh, I'm completely serious. And it gets better. Asana had another child. A child of rape, I've been told. She named her Celena Tan. She went by that name until she was taken and turned to evil by S'Kotos. You might know her better by C'Tan."

Kayla gasped.

"My mother," Lily continued.

At that, Kayla felt like someone had kicked her in the stomach. "C'Tan is your mother?"

Lily nodded and walked forward, Kayla at her side. "Yes. She is, unfortunately. But you know what that makes Asana?" She stopped on the porch and faced Kayla.

Realization spread across Kayla's face. She felt it as the blood drained from her skin and her eyes widened.

"Your grandmother," she whispered.

"Yep!" Lily grinned and skipped through the doorway.

CHAPTER TWENTY-TWO

Ember had three women working on her hair and another two on her costume—all at once. She felt like a doll being dressed and crimped and rouged, but in Bendanatu, that translated to having feathers and beads woven into her hair, a crown of leaves, berries, and flowers, and a leather dress and shoes. It was . . . interesting. She couldn't help but wonder what she would look like when they were done with her. She only put up with it because of the celebration for the Bendanatu who had run with her from Karsholm to Javak. They had been kind when she was so new to shapeshifting and the ways of Bendanatu. Was it only a week since she had last seen them alive?

Adrienne, the priestess, was one of the women working on her hair. Her daughter, Agrobel, played with a sock doll on the ground near the door. The woman was behind her, so Ember didn't know what she was doing, only that her hair was off her neck.

And then they were finished. The women stood her up and turned her around to see the full effect, oohing and aaahing. Ember wanted to see, blast it! She didn't want to go out there looking like a fool, especially knowing she was about to meet her grandfather. The women put a white cloth around her shoulders and let it fall almost to her feet. They spread it open wide, then tied another white cloth around her waist to hold the first in place. Thankfully, they didn't put an enormous bow in it like her mother would have done, but instead tied a simple knot and let the ends dangle on her left hip.

Intriguing.

Finally, after dabbing a few things on Ember's face, they put her in front of a full-length glass mirror, something she had never seen before. She gasped when she saw what they had done.

She almost didn't recognize the beauty in the mirror as herself—didn't know she could even look like that.

Her hair was piled on top of her head in ringlets with white ribbons, vines, and flowers running through it. Beaded knotwork adorned her creamy leather dress, similar to her father's designs in the stone room she'd nearly destroyed. A hint of red brushed her cheekbones, and her lips were the color of rubies. Her eyes somehow stood out, showing the deep emerald green they had become—more the color when she was wolf than human.

"I don't know what to say," she finally whispered.

Adrienne turned her around and smiled. "How about 'thank you'?"

Ember laughed. "Thank you! I have no idea what you did, but it's beautiful!"

Agrobel tugged at her sash, and Ember looked down at the darling girl. Looking up at Ember with bright eyes, she said, "You look amazing, Miss Ember! I hope I can grow up to be as pretty as you."

Ember blushed, then hugged the girl to her leg. "Thank you, Agrobel. That means a lot."

The girl nodded, grinned, then ran to her mother. Adrienne winked at Ember. The women giggled and all but Adrienne and her daughter left the room, probably to get themselves ready. The priestess grew serious then. “I have a surprise for you. Shad is ignorant of what a woman needs and so I went behind his back and did something that needs doing. I hope you do not mind.”

Curious, Ember shook her head. “I’m sure it will be fine.”

Adrienne smiled, a curious glint in her eye. “Good. I’d hoped you would say that. Wait here.” She then left the room, Agrobel trailing behind and looking over her shoulder every few steps. Once they were out of the chamber, Ember turned and walked back to the mirror, admiring the intricacy of the beadwork and what they had done to her hair. It was almost . . . magic.

“You look stunning,” a male voice said from behind her.

Ember spun, then froze when she realized who was in the room.

Grandfather.

Did he know? Had he been told who she was? Is that what Adrienne had meant?

He opened his arms and walked to her. “I’d never thought to see grandchildren of my own, and here you are. Welcome home, Ember Shandae. Welcome home.” He took her in his arms.

Ember threw her arms around him and fought the tears, not wanting to mess up her eyes. She held him gingerly, like he might break or disappear. She’d never had a grandfather and had wanted family so badly, especially from her father’s side. She’d known nothing of him until she had met Uncle Shad, and now, here she was in her grandfather’s arms.

He pushed her to arm's length, then hugged her again. “Oh, Ember. You are so beautiful, child! And you, the Chosen one. I have been richly blessed. Richly blessed. If only your father were here to see you now,” he said, leading her to one of the benches along the wall. They sat together, and she grinned.

“He may not be here now, but I’ve seen him,” she said.

Bahndai looked shocked. “How is that possible? Did he not die in a fire fifteen years gone?”

She nodded. “He did. It’s crazy and beautiful and so mixed up, but I saw him. When he died, instead of going to Haven or wherever it is The Guardians keep the spirits from this world, they gave him a choice. He could go to the beautiful Haven, or he could come back here as a servant of Mahal and be my protector throughout the years, never telling me who he was. I only found out because he healed my stepfather, Paeder, from lung sickness as payment for delivering a message to the mage council. He showed me his true form. He spoke with me, Grandfather. It meant so much. I don't remember him from before, but I will never forget him now. Never!" she said, taking Bahndai by the hand and squeezing tight.

Her grandfather had tears running down his face. "You saw him. In what form, besides his human one?"

Ember beamed. "A white hawk with glowing green eyes."

Bahndai laughed. "It was indeed my son. That was his favorite form. Do you still see him?"

"From time to time," she answered. "I haven't seen him at all since the battle at Karsholm. He always seems to be near, but I don't know where he is. I'm sure he'll show up sometime—probably when I need him most."

"Soooo," Bahndai drawled, looking down. "There is a chance I might see him too?"

It suddenly dawned on Ember how much her grandfather must miss his son. Knowing how she felt about missing her mother, she squeezed his hand again. "I'm sure of it."

She stared at his face, memorizing every wrinkle and age freckle on his face. He had Shad's firm jaw and nose, but his eyes were different. Still green, but a different shade. Full white hair fell down over his flat forehead. If it wasn't for the wrinkles, she would swear he was maybe forty. The wrinkles put him closer to sixty, but she wasn't about to ask him.

He looked at her, his eyes squinted. "What?"

"I'm just memorizing your face. I've never had a grandfather before and I want to remember you forever," she said.

He took both her hands and gently squeezed. "You can stay here, you know. There is no need to leave." His eyes implored her to say yes.

She shook her head. "C'Tan has my mum, and in order to get her back, I have to gather the keystones and combine them to heal the world.

C'Tan expects me to give them to her, but I won't. She wouldn't be able to use them, anyway." Ember was quiet for a moment, then opened up and talk to her grandfather about her fears. "I don't understand C'Tan. She's supposed to be my aunt. You knew that, right?"

Bahndai had gone white at her words. "I did not know,"

"Oh. Sorry for telling you like that, then. I thought you knew. I guess my grandma had another babe after you left. My cousin tells me they raped her."

He gasped, his hand going to his mouth.

For a moment, it felt like a dragon stepped on Ember's chest. She wasn't handling this right. "And I'm guessing you didn't know that either. Wow. I'm not doing very well."

He patted her hand. "You're fine. You have no way of knowing what I do and don't know. Go on."

"Are you sure?" she asked, concerned.

"Yes," he said, collecting himself, though he was still pale.

Ember told her grandfather about her dealings with C'Tan, then told him about Ian's betrayal.

"But, see, I bartered with C'Tan." Ember was near tears, remembering. "I said I'd accept Ian's help if she'd make sure my mum was taken good care of, and she agreed, but said if I crossed her, Mum would be in the dungeon with no light or anything. Then I killed Ian. I ripped his throat out."

"Good," Bahndai said viciously.

"But what if she hurts Mum? He broke the deal, not me. But she's C'Tan. She's evil. What if she goes back on her word? What if—"

He stopped her with an upraised hand. "I hear what you are saying, child, but there is nothing you can do. Is there a way to speak with C'Tan?" He almost spat her name.

"Well, there was, but I don't know what happened to it. Ian had a speaking stone." She stopped and thought for a moment. "I wonder if any of the group picked it up when they were scavenging the bodies."

Bahndai cocked his head. "That is a good question. If you have a way to speak to her, take it. Clear your mind. Clear your conscience. You know this is not your fault, but who knows what C'Tan thinks? The woman is half mad."

Ember bit her lip. The Bendanatu had stripped those bodies of everything of worth or use. Surely someone had the speaking stone. She'd have to talk to them and see if they would give it to her, or at least trade for it. Whatever worked.

A bell sounded from outside.

Bahndai smiled. "It is time, Granddaughter. May I present you to the Bendanatu? Will you take my arm and let me show you off just a bit?"

Ember laughed. "I don't know about the showing off, but I would love to go with you. Thank you." She placed her hand in the crook of his elbow, and, following his stately pace, left the main caverns where the highest of the Bendanatu lived.

Upon exiting the final cave, the sound of many voices singing—some human, some wolf, some Phoenixian, but all beautiful—met Ember. What was it about shapeshifters that made their voices so magical? Perfect pitch, every one. Even the youngest of the young.

And there sat DeMunth, in the very front row, his silvery voice blending with the rest, though he didn't know the words. He didn't have to. Ember's heart melted again, just as it had the first time she'd heard him sing in the caverns near Karsholm as he knelt in musical worship.

His eyes widened, scanning her from head to toe and back to her eyes. They showed only appreciation for what he saw.

Bahndai's voice rang out over the crowd. "Behold! The newest of our family. Ember Shandae Jarin Bahndai Bendanatu!" The crowd roared, Shad probably loudest of all, and surprisingly her aunt, the Lady Kalandra nearly as loud. She and Shad sat together. Ember smiled and waved, unsure what the etiquette was, but it seemed to be mostly casual.

Once she was introduced, her grandfather took her to a seat in the front row, putting her between DeMunth and her grandfather. She couldn't talk to her silver tongued hero. Adrienne walked to the middle of the half circle, a bonfire behind her. "A moment of silence to remember our fallen brothers," she said, and the crowd became so quiet, it seemed there was no one there. After a minute or two, Adrienne spoke again. "Let us remember our brethren and sisters now as they once were—mighty hunters, wondrous jokesters, kind caregivers, and friends to all. We shall miss them, but honor them in the sharing of their magic." She dumped a vase into the fire and green sparks arose and covered the people. They skipped the humans and Phoenixians and instead went to the Bendanatu, covering them and then immersing themselves within their skin. Even Ember had the honor of being covered with the green essence of the wolves who had passed. She closed her eyes and remembered memories that were not her own. A race of cubs. Midnight howling. Human-formed wolves walking amongst the non-shifters. Lives lived away from hers, and yet, close to the end, they each had the memory of her as she learned to shift, as she refused to eat raw meat, as she slept in the cavern and ran with them. They remembered her.

And so she remembered them.

When the memories stopped, she had tears streaming down her face, and no longer cared what she looked like. Glancing around, she saw she was not the only one. A howl started in the back, and then another, and another. They moved forward in a wave until her grandfather howled and Adrienne howled and she, who had never done so as a human, threw back her head and let the emotion soar into the sky.

They stopped as one.

DeMunth took her hand as she sat down. Ember froze, then glanced over at him. Despite his not sharing the memories of the dead wolves, he had tear stains. He squeezed her hand, then turned to the front. Adrienne had disappeared—sitting somewhere amongst the crowd, Ember guessed. Shad stood and began to sing. A song of joy and longing. When he was done, Mandalin strode to the front with a stringed instrument in hand. The girl began to play, and Ember had heard nothing like it before. The girl's fingers nearly danced across the instrument, and after a few minutes of that, the pace slowed, and her voice swept out.

It was the first Ember realized that a celebration didn't have to be all fun and laughter. It could be joyous and melancholy at the same time. That was Mandalin's music. It made Ember want to join her in song and cry at the same time.

Behind her, a flutter of wings sounded. Ember and DeMunth turned as one and watched as Eden took to the sky in her Phoenixian form. She dove and swirled, twisting in feats that seemed impossible, but fit Mandalin's music so beautifully. Soon, Aryana joined her and they danced together, adding to the celebration. Ember was pretty sure Mandalin stretched out her performance just so the Phoenixia could continue their dance that much longer. It was beautiful.

The evening continued in much the same vein. Eventually, tables were brought out and loaded with food, and the center areas opened for dancing. Mandalin and several others were the primary instrumentalists, while Shad and Lady Kalandra had the eye of everyone there. They really did make a striking couple. Ember watched her aunt and uncle as they leaped, dipped, and swirled around the bonfire, laughing as if they had no cares. It was nice to see them forget their trials for a bit. She wished she could do so as easily, and very much wished DeMunth would take her onto the floor. But he sat and watched, the only connection between them that of their hands.

Her grandfather leaned down shortly after, his hand extended. "May I have this dance, Lady Ember?"

She fought a smile and took his hand, letting go of DeMunth's. "Of course." They walked to the center and began a slow dance. They didn't say a word to each other. Impulsively, Ember put her head on Bahndai's chest and danced with him like that. It was incredibly comforting, and when the song was done and she pulled away, she looked up to see his eyes brimming. He hugged her, then turned to escort her from the dance floor, but paused.

DeMunth didn't use words. His hand extended toward Ember and he mindspoke to her. *Would you give me the pleasure of this dance?*

Ember shivered at the emotional echo his mindvoice held. She nodded and sent her own thoughts. *Of course.*

Taking his hand, he took Bahndai's place in her arms, but the feeling was completely different. Both of the men felt awkward to her, but her grandfather was more because he was unfamiliar. With DeMunth, she'd never had the chance to work out his anger and her resentment. She didn't know what to say, and so they swayed together, distance between their bodies she longed to close.

Her heart pounded, her palms sweaty as she looked up into DeMunth's eyes and saw the same conflicted emotion. She opened her mouth to say something when a commotion came from the back. Several young boys, probably only seven or eight, except for one young teenage boy, stumbled into the camp. "Help!" one of them croaked. "We need help. Can you help us? Please?" he begged, tears in his eyes. "Our parents are gone. We have no one but each other. Help us, please. Flying men attacked our wagon and killed them all. Mum. Da. My little sister," he sobbed.

Everyone had surrounded the group by then and murmurs came from all around. A tall man, sturdy and strong, stepped forward. He looked to the chieftain in a questioning manner. Ember's grandfather nodded slightly and the man looked at the boys. "I am Justesen. Please, come with me and I will take care of your needs until we can make more permanent arrangements. Come," he said again, beckoning for them to follow. The boys looked relieved and followed the tall man. Justesen, he'd called himself.

The young teenage boy looked back, met Ember's eyes and gave her a slight nod and grin, then turned back to the others and followed the man, who had agreed to take them in.

A sinking feeling swept over her, despite the joys of the evening. Something was not right with those boys. She didn't know what, had no proof, but no good would come from taking them in. She said nothing because she knew none would believe her.

She glanced across the amphitheater to DeMunth, who was watching the boys with the same wariness she felt. Their eyes met, and she suspected he knew the same.

The boys were not what they seemed. They were dangerous, like baby snakes so poisonous, they would kill with one bite.

CHAPTER TWENTY-THREE

Dinner was buffet-style, late-night sandwiches, but it was perfect. With three different species in the room, everyone created what was best for them. And thankfully, Asana was intuitive enough not to include eggs in the mix. Kayla wasn't sure how that would affect the Phoenixians.

Lily couldn't stop staring at Asana. It was almost embarrassing. The old woman didn't seem to notice, though Kayla was betting she was aware of the mild version of hero worship going on and chose to ignore it for the moment.

It was still beyond believing that of all the places where they could have stopped for the night, they had chosen Ember and Lily's grandmother's home. None of the group had known where she lived. They'd had no guide and yet, here they were. Kayla had never really been a believer in

The Guardians. She had sort of known they were there, that something was out there creating things and directing lives, but she hadn't thought of them in terms of being a part of her life. Of being even aware of her as an individual—and yet, again, she had ended up here with Asana. There had to be a reason, a purpose, behind it. But why?

She felt a bit overwhelmed knowing Klii'kunn, the Guardian of blue magic, of wind and air, was aware of her. How did this work, anyway? Was she automatically assigned to her Guardian because of the keystone? Or could she worship any Guardian she chose? And did she want to?

This was going to take more thought than she really wanted or could afford right now.

Asana finished the last few dishes in the sink and turned around, quirking an eyebrow at Lily. "Okay, young lady. Out with it. You've been watching me for over an hour. Do I have mud in my hair? Too many wrinkles? Surely I'm not that ugly that you can't stop your staring." Asana's eyes had twinkles in them.

Lily turned red and looked away. "I'm sorry. I, uh, I just . . ." She trailed off and looked at Asana helplessly. It wasn't like Lily to be so shy. With a sigh, Kayla took over, hoping Lily wouldn't kill her later.

"She's your granddaughter," Kayla said. Lily's head turned sharply, her face red. "What? You wanted her to know or you wouldn't have been looking at her like a lost puppy for so long." Lily's brows dropped and her red face changed from embarrassment to anger.

"Granddaughter?" Asana whispered, as pale as Lily had been red. "I have a granddaughter?" She found her way to the table and sat down shakily on the end of the bench.

Lily turned away from Kayla with a sigh and took Asana's hand. "You have two granddaughters, actually, and your other granddaughter is cousin to Kayla there, so she's but one step away from being family."

Asana breathed rapidly and bent over. "Are you okay?" Kayla squatted in front of her. "I know it's a lot to take in. I don't know how we ended up here—"

Asana interrupted her, spinning toward Lily. "Who?" she whispered. "Which of my children is your parent?" Her eyes were intense.

Lily looked down, and it seemed that she didn't want to answer. Finally, reluctantly, she said the name that had kept her from telling Asana earlier. "Celena Tan."

Asana sucked in a sharp breath and pulled away.

Lily raised her head, almost looking panicked. "I'm not like her. I was raised by one of her servants at the mage academy, and when I realized he was not my father, I abandoned her and her plans. I didn't want to follow through anyway. I want good, and I want to *be* good. Though I love my mother, I choose to fight for the side of The Guardians against her. She is my mother after all—but she is wrong. Her choices are evil and hurt people, and I cannot side with that. I *will* not!" Lily's tears ran down her face almost from the moment she began to speak.

Asana stared at her granddaughter. At first, Kayla couldn't tell what she was feeling, and then the old woman's tears fell. She opened her arms, and Lily scooted into them. Grandmother and granddaughter hugged for the first time and Lily sobbed, much as Kayla had in the dirt out front. It was the releasing of a thousand emotions, and knowing Lily's story, how she had been emotionally abandoned her entire life, Kayla knew that being accepted by her grandmother had to be doing all kinds of things to heal that ache and hole that had been in her heart.

One by one, the others wandered off to find a place to sleep, but Kayla stayed, watching grandmother and granddaughter begin to bond as they spoke. She wanted that kind of relationship with a grandparent for herself, but it could never happen. At least she had a good relationship with her mother now.

Finally, unable to keep her eyes open any longer, Kayla lay down in the corner, tucked her bag beneath her head, and fell asleep.

CHAPTER TWENTY-FOUR

"Uncle," Ember said, dropping the gaming stones into their cup and setting it on the game board, "this is boring. Can't we do something interesting? Like maybe you could show me around the village or something. Anything to get out of the caves and into the sunlight."

Shad chuckled, setting down his own gaming stones and standing. "That is a marvelous idea. I'm rather tired of getting beat by you in a game I've played all my life. Let's walk, and I'll introduce you to the rest of your family."

Ember startled, then stood, scooting out from behind the stone bench. "You mean I have more family here? Who?"

Uncle Shad laughed out loud. "No, my dear. Not family by blood, but the Bendanatu all consider themselves a family, whether or not there is an actual relationship."

A twinge of disappointment tugged on Ember's heart, even so, it was exciting to get out and away from the boredom of the morning. After all the excitement and drama of getting here, just sitting to play a game felt like a waste of time. Besides that, she had to find out about the emerald keystone and how to retrieve it. She couldn't do that sitting behind a game board.

Shad led Ember through the maze of caves to the exit. The minute Ember reached the main floor and saw sunlight, she broke into a run. She couldn't help herself—she needed her sunshine. Ten steps outside of the cave, she stopped and spread her arms like the branches of a tree and swayed back and forth, her head back, her eyes closed, and the sun filling her with its light and warmth. It was almost a spiritual moment for her, and she felt a peace that had been missing for quite some time.

It didn't take long for her to get her fill and be ready to move on. She lowered her arms and chin and opened her eyes to see Shad watching her, serious for once.

"What?" she asked, a little embarrassed that he had seen her so open to the world.

He said nothing. He just shook his head and took her arm, leading her down the hill and to the left, to the only actual building Ember had seen in Bendanatu. They walked past the remains of the fire pit near the amphitheater where they'd had their celebration the night before, and Ember remembered the amazing events of the evening. For the first time, she wanted to live somewhere besides her family farm. She wanted to stay here. She felt so at one with these people, more than she had anywhere else in her life. If it wasn't for the people she loved back in Karsholm, she might have indeed stayed here.

Well, that and the fact that her mother was still in C'Tan's power.

That reminded her. "Uncle, do you remember if any of the Bendanatu took a necklace with a black stone from Ian when they scavenged?"

Shad's brow wrinkled. She could see his brain working, trying to remember. He nodded slowly. "I think so. Yes," he said, gaining confidence. "I do believe that Kymber has it. Why?"

"It's a communication stone linked with C'Tan," she said, and he sucked in a breath. "I don't think it's anything your people will want to keep, and it could be valuable to me." She didn't need to explain why. "Do you think Kymber would be willing to part with it?"

Shad shrugged. "One never knows. I imagine that if you offered something in exchange, something that would be equally valuable to her, she might."

Frustration grew in Ember as they neared the building. "But I don't have anything. What could I give her?"

"It doesn't have to be a material item. It could be a service. Let's ask her and see what she says," he said. They arrived, and Shad knocked. Light footsteps ran across the floor. Grunting sounded from the other side, and finally a click as the door slowly swung open. But nobody was there. Ember wrinkled her brow, perplexed by the whole thing, and then she looked down.

A young boy, about three or four years old, stood there with his hands on his hips. "Who are you?" he asked, looking straight at Ember. Shad stifled a chuckle.

"I'm Ember Shandae. Shad is my uncle."

"How come I never seed you here before?" he asked, mistrust written all over his face.

She crouched down in front of him. "Because I've never been here before. I didn't even know I was Bendanatu until a week ago. Would you believe that?" she said, making her voice light and disbelieving herself.

His mouth opened. "No! Really? But weren't you born a pup?"

Ember shook her head. "No. My da was Bendanatu, but my mum is human. I'm a half-breed."

Instead of being upset by that, all of his defenses lowered and he stepped out through the doorway. "Really? I never meeted a half-breed before. That's neat."

"Yeah, it has some advantages," she said, then asked, "What's your name?"

"I'm Ronan," he said, his chest puffed out, "And that boy behind the door is my twin brudder William." He cupped his hand around his mouth and whispered loudly. "He's kinda shy."

"No, I'm not." William's voice echoed from behind Ronan. "He just says that so he can meet people first. He always beats me to the door." Another face, similar to Ronan's but not exact, peeked around the entrance. "Hi," he said, definitely more shy than his brother.

"Hello, William. Ronan and William. It's nice to meet you both. Do you live here?" Ember asked.

Both boys nodded. William continued, "Us and a bunch of other kids who don't have mums and das. This is the orphan place."

Ember's heart panged. It was hard enough living without a parent, but to lose them both? Oh, these poor children.

It surprised ember when Shad asked, "Is Kymber here?"

The boys nodded in tandem again.

"Can we talk to her?" he asked. Ronan pulled the door open further, though it was obviously an effort for the small boy.

"Sure. She's in the back helping Gamma Dawnna and Gawpa Roahnald. They're fixin' dinner. I hope its venison again. But no carrots. I hate carrots," Ronan said.

William nodded. "Carrots and beets. Yuck!"

Shad chuckled and pulled something out of his pocket. "Thanks, boys. We'll just head back there. Don't ruin your appetite with those!" They had already stuffed the treats in their mouths, their cheeks bulging. They nodded solemnly, then scampered off.

Ember looked at him, curious. "Dried berries," he answered her unspoken question and crossed the room. "Dawnna and Roahnald run the orphanage. I wanted you to meet them—they are some of the best Bendanatu has to offer and they love these children as if they were their own, and right now they have quite a few." He headed toward an opening blocked by a curtain. "The Ne'Goi have not been kind to our village. Some of the younglings have taken over the job of guarding the forest like their parents did, and they are surprisingly good at it. They call themselves the Moningers, after one of their teachers who died in the first attack."

Ember remembered the Moningers all too well, but knowing their history, she didn't know what to say. Children shouldn't have to do what these did, but if they didn't protect the village, who would? There weren't enough adults to go around. It felt like the world had reversed itself here and the younglings held the most important positions.

Sad. And scary. What an awful way to live.

CHAPTER TWENTY-FIVE

C'Tan gestured for Yidun to continue his work and Kardon screamed, only stopping to breathe when the man in black leather lifted the flaming brand from his blistering skin. She almost felt sorry for him. The mighty Kardon brought to screams after a few simple torture techniques. His emotional armor had been stripped away and he sobbed, gripping his hand as the man in black took two steps back and waited for C'Tan's command.

She stepped forward, leaned over until she was about an inch from his ear, and asked her question again. "Why did you betray me, Kardon? Was it your idea? Ian's?"

She waited for his answer and was about to gesture for Yidun to return to his work when her former master whispered. She straightened, waiting for his answer. "Neither. Not us. Following orders."

That was all he said, but she could piece together the rest. She turned and walked to the other side of the room, nervously chewing her nails as she worked it out. She muttered, "Following orders. Can't follow orders if I didn't give the order. It had to be one of them. Maybe he's lying. That's it—he's got to be lying. No. No, that can't be it. What if he's telling the truth? What then? Who would give him orders if I didn't?" She went utterly still as the answer came to her.

"S'Kotos," she said aloud, and Kardon nodded. She stormed back to him and lifted his head up by his hair. "Really? S'Kotos?"

He whimpered, and she pulled harder.

"Yes, Mistress!" he almost yelled. "I don't know why, but he ordered us to kill the Wolfchild."

She slammed his head down on the wooden chopping block, then pulled it back up by his hair again. "Without telling me? Me? Why would he do that?"

"He knew you would try to save her. He said you were too soft and so he turned to me and Ian to handle matters. And now he is dead. My son is dead." Kardon sobbed once again, and she knew she would get nothing more from him, but she couldn't bring herself to have him killed. He might still be of some use.

Instead, she gestured with her chin toward the cage, and ever the faithful servant, her torture master, Yidun, picked up Kardon and threw him back inside. The old man didn't even seem to notice. He was so lost in his pain, both emotional and physical.

She didn't have the luxury of caring at the moment. Too soft, was she? She'd show S'Kotos how hard she could be.

She would let Kardon live.

CHAPTER TWENTY-SIX

The Phoenixians woke with the sun, then transformed and moved to the roof to nap in the sunlight. During the night, Asana and Lily had disappeared, presumably to sleep. Kayla awoke only long enough to realize what was happening and notice the absence of her friend and her grandmother, then went back to sleep on the kitchen floor.

She didn't wake again until afternoon, with the smell of herbed meat roasting on the spit over the fire. It was her stomach grumbling that actually woke her. She sat up with a yawn and stretched, her back popping, then rubbed her eyes before she got up. At some point during the night, someone had draped a blanket across her, and it fell to a puddle around her feet. She picked it up and folded it. She was nearly done when Asana came from the back with her arms full of vegetables.

"Thanks for the blanket," Kayla said, setting it on the bench at the end of the table.

"Oh, that wasn't me," she said, chuckling. "It was going to be me—I came in here not long after Lily faded off to sleep, knowing you'd get cold in the night, as skinny as you are, but that young man with the orange tattoos had already taken care of it. He seemed a little embarrassed that I'd caught him." Asana moved to the sink basin and dropped the vegetables in, turning on the magic-pumped water and scrubbing the dirt away. She must have a garden in the back.

Kayla fought a blush. Aldarin had covered her? Ever since she'd witnessed his panic in the shower over the tattoos, they'd gained an awkward closeness. She wasn't sure if it was their symbiotic magic or the quiet moment shared, but he'd been acting a little strangely toward her since then. Why would that bond them? She liked him, sure, but he had shown nothing that would let her know he felt the same way. She decided not to think about it any longer. It made her uncomfortable in ways she wasn't ready for.

"Asana, can I help you with those?" she asked the old woman.

"Sure. I'm just scrubbing off the dirt, but you're more than welcome to help." Asana never stopped—her hands were constantly moving. It fascinated Kayla. She hadn't really had the chance to do much cooking. They had a chef for that, and he would never in a million years have allowed her to help.

It was kind of exciting.

"What do I do? Just scrub?" Kayla asked, picking up a carrot, pushing it under the water, and brushing at the dirt.

Asana looked at her like there was something wrong with her. "You have no idea what you are doing, do you?"

Kayla reddened. "No, not really."

"Have you ever cooked?" Asana seemed astonished.

"Well . . . no . . ." Kayla answered.

Now curiosity laced Asana's voice. "Why ever not?" And then guessed at the answer to her own question. "You grew up in a wealthy home."

Kayla nodded, letting the carrot drop into the sink. She turned, stepped away, and was about to leave when Asana grabbed her wrist with her wet hand. "That wasn't meant as an insult. You can't help what you weren't taught. Let me show you," she said, and gently, she pulled Kayla back to the sink, picked up her carrot, and handed her a stiff-bristled brush. "Now watch." She took the carrot, placed it under the running water, and using a second brush, she scrubbed away the dirt and mud. The stiff bristles took part of the carrot skin with it so that when finished, the carrot shone with a bright orange color that was completely free of the earth that had housed it. "Now you try," she said, stepping aside and giving Kayla access to the water.

Kayla tried to imitate Asana's motions and did pretty well, except for one crease in the carrot that wouldn't relent. It was frustrating. She wanted to cut that part out, but when she had cleaned all the vegetable but that one spot, Asana took it from her, broke it in half at that juncture, and scrubbed the ends.

"And that is that," the grandmother said, smiling at Kayla. "Still want to help?"

She nodded. "Absolutely. Potatoes?"

Asana nodded. "Ready to move on to something new already, eh?" Without waiting for an answer, she handed a potato to Kayla, and they both scrubbed away.

It was harder than she'd thought it would be, but satisfying in its own way. Kayla scrubbed carrots, potatoes, and turnips. She washed peppers, mushrooms, and tomatoes, and then peeled onions. When the washing was complete, they took all the vegetables to the table and chopped them into bite-sized pieces.

Kayla was slow compared to Asana, who handled a knife like Aldarin did a sword. It was amazing. But regardless of the speed, eventually all the vegetables were cut, thrown into a pot with the meat, a bit of water, and some herbs and salt.

"There now. That wasn't so bad, was it?" Asana asked.

"Actually, that was fun in its own sort of way. Thank you for teaching me. It's definitely something important to learn. What was that you put in at the end? Salt, I know, but what were the spices?" Kayla sat at the table and picked at a sliver of wood sticking up.

Asana went back to the sink to clean up the remnants and the mud. "Oh, a bit of this and a bit of that. Fresh basil, primarily. Some diced garlic. Rosemary and sage. Nothing fancy."

Kayla didn't even know what most of that was, but she nodded her head and tried to ignore her protesting stomach. "About how long will it take to cook?" she asked.

"Probably about thirty minutes more. It doesn't take long once the meat is done. Why? Are you hungry?" she asked, turning around to face Kayla.

"Yes, but I can wait." Her stomach grumbled loudly.

Asana pursed her lips. "You're part Evahn, aren't you?"

Kayla ducked her head, trying to hide her red cheeks, but finally nodded.

The grandmother chuckled. "Well, of course you're hungry then. You missed breakfast, and the Evahn have a very high metabolism. I'll bet you're hungry all the time." She went to the cupboard and pulled out a few things.

"Pretty much, yes. But I didn't know that was an Evahn trait. How do you know that?"

Asana began slathering something brown on a slice of bread, then took a banana and sliced it up, covering the brown mix with the banana pieces. She put it on a plate and carried it over to Kayla. "A little snack. Give it a try. You'll be surprised." She sat down across from Kayla and finally answered her question. "I know about the Evahn because their largest village is but a day's ride from here. I do a lot of trading with them and have come to know their ways. One of them even courted me for a while, but gave up when he saw I wasn't interested. I've only ever loved one man in my life, and that's the way it will stay."

Kayla knew who she meant, but said nothing. Curious she asked, "Have you met Felandian in your dealings?" She took a bite of the sandwich, chewed twice and stopped, letting the flavor caress her tongue. It was magnificent. She knew bananas and bread, but what was this brown stuff? It was glorious!

The old woman saw her face and laughed. "Good, huh? I thought you'd like it. Peanut mash and banana. It was my long-gone husband's favorite."

Peanut mash? That was poor man's food. Kayla had never actually seen it, let alone tried it. She shook her head. She had learned much this past week, one of the greatest being not to judge anyone or anything by its label alone. Peanut mash was now one thing to add to that list.

"It's the best sandwich I've had in my entire life," she said around a sticky mouthful.

"Thank you," Asana answered, beaming. "Now, Felandian. Let me see. Tall man? Long dark hair? Son of the chieftain?"

Kayla nodded.

"Oh, yes, we've had many dealings over the years. The Evahn are crazy about their magestone, and since I mine it, they come directly to me to save on the price. He seems like a nice man—better than most of the Evahn. Why? Do you know him?"

"He's my father," Kayla answered. She finished up the last bite of sandwich and wished for more, but knew dinner would be ready soon. "I haven't seen him but once since I was seven years old, but he's my da. And yes, he's a good man. He wouldn't have left Mum except for his father's illness and the demands of the Evahn council."

"Yes, I can see how that would force a man onto a different path," Asana said, nodding, "especially with the alternatives that were there at the time."

Kayla perked up. "Alternatives? What do you mean?"

"Oh? You haven't heard?" Asana grinned. "Well, let me share the story with you, then. It's rarely I get to be the first to tell of things." She ran her fingers across her lips, then spoke. "About ten years ago, the Evahn were divided. Felandian's father—I guess your grandfather—wished to live peacefully and let the Sapphire Flute find its way home to them when it would. Another man, your uncle, Kalaphis, wanted to overthrow your grandfather and go out searching for the flute and take it by whatever force necessary."

"Why did they want it so badly?" Kayla asked.

"Because just like the Phoenixians, the Evahn live within the trees, and their mother tree was dying. It needed the magic of the Sapphire Flute to give it life once more."

She'd just killed a dozen or more of their guard who were looking to retrieve it. "So, let me get this right. You say that they need the flute in order to save their home?"

Asana shook her head. "Not anymore, no. Your father went home to save his own father's life and to stop his brother. It's amazing he didn't kill him—I would have. But regardless, they extended the life of the tree by using the blue magestone I have here and embedding it within her trunk. It may not make her live as long as she would with the flute, but she will live several hundred years more doing this. Your father is a genius."

Kayla calmed a bit, but in that moment, she decided that when this was all over, she was going to the Evahn home, no matter what, and she would play the flute and heal their home. It was the least she could do for killing their soldiers.

The old woman stood, swung her leg over the bench, and went to check on the vegetables. She smiled, satisfied. "Kayla, would you mind letting everyone know that lunch is ready?"

She didn't mind at all. The smell was about to drive her insane. Stepping out the front door, Kayla called up to the rooftop and the snoozing Phoenixians. "Hey! Shari! Lunch is ready." Shari Bird shook herself and looked down at Kayla, then nodded and leaped from the roof to circle over the clearing for a moment.

Next, Kayla searched for the boys. Baen, Miek, and Aldarin were down by the mine examining remnants of magestone that littered the ground. She did not know what they were talking about and didn't care. She wanted to eat. "Boys! Lunch is on the table!" They nodded to her, continuing their conversation as they ambled toward the house. Not sure where Lily was, Kayla walked back into the house to ask Asana, but found Lily already there and setting the table for lunch. She went to the sink to wash her hands once more, the boys filing in behind her to do the same, and then Shari. By the time she was done, everything was on the table and Lily and Asana sat at each end, leaving the benches for the rest of them. The boys sat on one bench, regardless of species, and the girls on the other.

Asana demanded their plates and everyone handed them down the line to be stacked just below the meat spit. Asana held one end of the rod with a hand towel and cut meat onto each of their plates with the other. When she got to Kayla's plate, she glanced up and sliced off three times the amount she'd given anyone else. Reddening at the special attention, Kayla hoped the boys wouldn't complain, but nobody but Aldarin even seemed to notice. There was laughter in his eyes, but not condemnation.

Everyone received a healthy portion of vegetables, and the plates were passed back down the line. Again, Kayla got a much larger portion than anyone else, but she didn't care anymore. She was too hungry. Once they got their food, they began to eat, and there was no sound but that of chewing, knives and forks scraping across plates, and sounds of delight as everyone partook of Asana's food. She beamed at the wordless praise and enjoyed her own portion. The boys finished quickly and asked for more, and though embarrassed, so did Kayla.

She was nearly done with her second plate of food when crashing came from outside, then shouting and maniacal laughter. Asana froze as a wave of dark magic flowed through the room. The candles dimmed and a soft howl of wind rattled the windows. Face hardening, she went to the doorway, everyone quickly following, but instead of going out on the porch, she twitched aside the curtain and looked outside. She pulled back quickly and faced the others.

"Shadow weavers," she said.

CHAPTER TWENTY-SEVEN

"And here we are!" Shad pushed aside a beaded curtain and led Ember into the roomy kitchen. Kymber, Keyera, Abbey, Tyese, and a girl who looked like her sister were all there helping wash, chop, and cook food. There were more younglings there as well, but Ember had no idea who they were. She had a pretty good idea who the two older people at the stove were, though.

Shad led her directly to them and proved her right. "Dawnna, Roahnald, I'd like you to meet my niece, Ember Shandae." In the noisy kitchen, Ember thought they would jump at Shad's silent approach, but they turned as if it was perfectly normal for him to be there. Smiling, each of them gave him a hug, then gave Ember a hug in turn. It was a little awkward, but they were so grandparent-like that Ember couldn't help but immediately like them. They oozed kindness and love like jelly from the inside of a pastry.

"We saw you at the celebration last night," Dawnna said, "but we didn't get the chance to introduce ourselves. Had to get the pups to bed and all, but such a pleasure to meet you! I know Bahndai has been worried about handing his power to this one without a grandchild to carry on the family name." She looked at Shad like some teachers at the mage academy looked at particularly unruly students.

Shad reddened under her glare and muttered, "I'm working on it."

Dawnna smiled then and said, "So I've seen."

Shad reddened and Ember decided to save him. He'd done it for her often enough—it was time to return the favor. "Would you mind if we borrowed Kymber for a moment? I need to ask her about something."

Dawnna and Roahnald looked at each other. He shrugged. Evidently, he was a man of few words. Dawnna answered for the both of them. "Certainly. She'll probably be happy to get out of the kitchen for a bit. She hates scrubbing vegetables." She said the last quietly, but Kymber's voice rose from the other side of the kitchen.

"I heard that!"

Dawnna and Roahnald chuckled, and she asked Shad about Lady Kalandra. His eyes went soft and Ember stepped away. She didn't need to be a part of that conversation. It was kind of weird, anyway. Instead, she crossed the room to Kymber and was about to touch her on the arm when Tyese grabbed Ember's vest in excitement.

"Ember! Have you met my sister? I want you to meet her. I hardly ever get to see her, and I don't even care that I'm around lots of people because I'm with her." She hugged the younger girl around the neck, both of them grinning. "This is Tabitha. Tabitha, this is Miss Ember I was telling you about. You can totally trust her."

When Tyese said that, Ember's heart warmed. Such blind faith. She hoped she would never let this girl down.

Ember extended her hand to Tabitha, and the girl took it, if a bit shyly. "It's nice to meet you, Tabitha. Did you know your sister saved my life? Twice?" Tyese puffed up a little at that.

Tabitha's eyes went big. "Really? Tyese, you saved the Wolfchild's life?"

Tyese flushed, but nodded. “I did. She needed help, and I knew how to give it.”

“And I would have been dead without it.” Ember leaned down, so she was on Tabitha’s eye level. “I’m serious. Your sister is a hero and I would do anything for her.”

Tabitha beamed, bounced into the air, and spun around with a little foot flick. Ember had seen nothing like it before. “Do that again. That was beautiful!” she said. Tabitha’s smile got even brighter, if that were possible. She repeated the action. “Wow! That is amazing! Are you a dancer?”

“Sort of,” Tabitha said, losing her shyness. “I dance on ice. Have you ever seen ice skates?”

Ember shook her head.

“Well, in the winter, it gets so cold that the lake freezes, and sometimes Bahndai will flood an empty field and freeze it just so I can skate. It’s not something most of the Bendanatu do—I learned it from my mother. She spent a lot of time in the northern countries. I have a pair of shoes with metal on the bottom, but not flat. The metal stands up, like a sword on the bottom of my feet, and it lets me glide on the ice. I leap and spin and do all kinds of neat things.” She sighed. “It is very happy-making.”

“I’m glad it’s happy-making for you, Tabitha. Horses are happy-making for me. And DeMunth. He’s very happy-making. Have you seen him yet?”

She nodded and giggled.

“Isn’t he beautiful?” Ember asked.

Tabitha and Tyese giggled, then nodded.

“I’m glad you agree.” She straightened and put a hand on each girl’s shoulder. “Now, if you’ll excuse me, I need a minute with Kymber.”

“All right,” Tyese said, then impulsively threw her arms around Ember’s waist. “Thank you for being nice to my sister,” she whispered.

Ember hugged her back. “She’s easy to be nice to.”

Letting her go, Tyese and Tabitha went back to work, and Ember turned to find Kymber directly in front of her. “Is there a quiet place we can talk?” Ember asked her.

Kymber nodded and led Ember out of the back of the kitchen and outside. There were a few boys kicking a ball in the distance, but for the most part, they were completely alone. Turning, the tall girl asked, "What did you need?"

Ember wasn't sure how to phrase this, especially with the necklace being so important to her. It made the thought of negotiations difficult. Finally, she just spat it out. "When you scavenged Ian's corpse, did you find a leather necklace with a triangular black stone?"

Kymber's eyes narrowed, and her lips pursed. "Maybe. Why?"

Ember sighed. This was going to be harder than she'd hoped. "I'm going to be honest with you here. That necklace will do nothing for you. It's not even pretty. It's a speaking stone, but it's tuned to three people, one of which is dead. The only person you would find on the other end if you could even use it is C'Tan." The girl's eyes widened, and she took a step back. "Like I said, it's of no use to you—but C'Tan has my mother, and it could be of great use to me. Is there anything I can give you, trade you, do for you to get that necklace?"

Kymber looked at Ember in silence for a moment, then dug into her pocket. "If the only person on the other end is C'Tan, I don't want it. Take it," she said, dangling it before Ember.

But she wouldn't touch it. "I can't take it without giving you something in return. It wouldn't be right. I have little, but I'll give what I can. If there is a service I can perform for you, I'll do it."

"Can you bring my parents back to life?" she asked, her voice bitter.

Ember's heart nearly broke. "No," she whispered, "Though I wish with everything in me I could." Then she had an idea. "I can't bring them back, but I might be able to create something for you that would hold their picture, but not a flat picture—this would be almost real, as if they stood before you. Would that be of value?"

Kymber's eyes welled up with tears. "Yes," she choked. "It would mean the world to me."

"As that necklace does to me. Will you entrust me with it until I can make the projecting stone of your parents?"

Kymber put it in her hand and closed her fingers around it. "Yes. I trust you."

Ember pulled her fist up to her chest. "Thank you," she said. "You do whatever you can to remember every detail of your parents because I'm going to have to pluck that picture from your mind, okay?"

Kymber nodded, sober. "That shouldn't be difficult. I think of them every moment of the day. How can I not?"

Shad stepped out the back door right then. Kymber left without another word.

"How do you do that?" Ember asked him.

"Do what?" Shad took her by the elbow and steered her toward another cave opening across the field.

"How do you know when to step out and interrupt a conversation like you just did? How do you know when to interrupt? You always have perfect timing."

He glanced at her with a mischievous grin. "I listen at the door."

Ember's jaw dropped. "You do not!"

The corner of his mouth twitched upward. "I do. My father always said it was a terrible habit, but I've found it rather handy."

Ember laughed out loud. "I can't believe you! I mean, thank you, but eavesdropping? I'd thought better of you, Uncle."

"Ah, even the best of us have our weaknesses," he said. His eyes twinkled.

Ember laughed all the way across the field.

CHAPTER TWENTY-EIGHT

"Shadow weavers? Here?" Kayla asked as Aldarin reached for the door.

Asana slapped her arm across the wood. "Don't go out there. They'll eat the magestone they need and go away. They've been here before. It's a good thing magestone grows back or they would put me out of business," she muttered. "Just wish it didn't take so long."

Aldarin looked at the others, the question obvious in his eyes, and they nodded back at him. He met Asana's eye and said, "I'm sorry, Grandmother, but we can't let them do this to you." With that, he jerked open the door and ran toward the mine, all the travelers following behind and Asana in the back.

The Ne'Goi hadn't been expecting resistance, so they were taken by surprise. Aldarin touched the fence lining the mining cart rails, turning it into some moving, slithering being that whipped into the Ne'Goi and bit them as if it were a serpent. Kayla heard a scream, and then another as Lily sent lightning into the tunnel.

And then the shadow weavers surged out of the tunnel en masse to meet their attackers. Kayla had thought there were maybe five or six of the demons taking Asana's magestone, but she had been wrong.

Dozens swarmed out of the tunnel and straight toward the group.

"Oh, Helar," Aldarin said, then yelled at the Phoenixians. "Change. Change! There is nothing we can do here. Let's go!"

The Phoenixians changed mid step, and the humans leaped to the mounts without saddle or straps to hold them in, leaving Asana standing alone. She squared her shoulders and turned to meet the torrent of angry shadow weavers heading her way. But then Shari Bird swooped down, snatched Asana from the ground, and flipped her up onto Raech's back.

The Ne'Goi took to the air and started after them. Behn, Raech, Miek, and Shari stopped just above Asana's home and let their inner light explode outward. The front Ne'Goi cowered back, but the light of Sha'iim hit them anyway, and in an instant, six of the shadow weavers had turned to ash that floated slowly to the ground.

The next wave of Ne'Goi were more cautious and tried to circle around the Phoenixians, but the light that burst from them this time expanded outward in a sphere that almost touched the ground and the far side of Asana's house. Another dozen of the shadow weavers turned to ash, and Kayla had hope that they might eliminate the enemy after all.

A tremendous roar shook the ground, rocks falling around the magestone tunnel. Kayla's hope turned to surprise and then fear as a huge shadow weaver burst right out of the top of the tunnel, magestone tumbling around him. He turned toward the group, inhaled, and then blew out a blast of fire that raced toward the group. With no time to pull the flute from its bag, she reached her hand inside and hummed a note, imagining a tremendous wall of ice. Fire hit ice, and at once, the wall began to melt.

Kayla willed the ice to grow stronger, but the more she tried, the faster it melted. A burst of flame got through a hole in the ice, and the Phoenixia scattered. Instead of hitting the group, it hit the front of

Asana's beautiful home, breaking the windows and catching the curtains and wood on fire.

"No! Oh, no, no, no!" Asana cried, watching her home disappear in flames.

The giant Ne'Goi saw her pain and grinned. "You cannot fight the Ne'Goi! We are stronger than magestone. Stronger than The Guardians. Stronger than Rasann! Rasann will die and be reborn with Ne'Goi as lord of all. And you, tiny mortals, will die with it. Just like this house, you will burn in the fire!" He breathed out more flame, aimed not at Kayla or the others, but at the house, his flame burning so hot, something exploded in the kitchen.

The Phoenixians spoke to one another, though too quickly for Kayla to understand, and then they took off in a burst of speed, separating into individual flyers. Kayla sincerely hoped they would meet up again somewhere. She had no idea how to get to Bendanatu.

Shari Bird—at least Kayla thought it was Shari—sent a picture to Kayla's mind. A map, she thought, though it took her a moment to decipher it. When she did, she sighed with relief. It was a map to Bendanatu. It may not be home, but it was as close as she was going to get to it for the next little while.

Satisfied, she separated herself farther from the others and flew through the trees, the mental map guiding her like a magnet toward Bendanatu.

CHAPTER TWENTY-NINE

After leaving Kymber and with the issue of the speaking stone resolved, Ember and Shad came to a new cave, a round, wooden door sealing the stone from the outside elements. Only the chieftain had one as ornate. The owner must be important to warrant the same kinds of luxuries.

Shad knocked.

This time, instead of childish running, she heard a tired shuffle approach the door. It opened fully to reveal the man who had taken in the strange youngling boys from the night before. He'd said his name—what was it? Jamison? No. Justesen. That's right.

Justesen said nothing, but invited them in with a sweep of his arm. Shad nodded and Ember watched warily as they came inside. Justesen shut the door behind them.

"Please. Sit," he said, gesturing toward a small table much like the game table Ember had been at all morning. She quietly sighed, then sat in the back corner, Justesen across from her. "To what do I owe this honor?" he asked Shad.

"To be honest, Ember wanted to see the village, and with the calling you have and the mission she must carry out, I thought it important that you meet." Shad was very respectful to this man. He was never respectful—Ember couldn't puzzle it out. Shad continued speaking to her then. "Justesen is guardian of the emerald maze. He watches the door that would eventually lead to the emerald keystone."

And then it all became clear.

Justesen glared at Shad. "That is supposed to be a sacred secret! What are you doing, White Shadow? Have you no honor?" The man almost quivered with anger.

Shad kept his head down until Justesen was done, then raised it and spoke. "Do you know who Ember Shandae is?"

"Of course I do. She is Bahndai's granddaughter, and she's sitting right there. What is your point?"

"No, Justesen. Do you know who she is? Or maybe I should ask, do you know *what* she is?"

The guardian calmed as he looked quizzically at Ember. "She is a half-breed Bendanatu. That is all I know."

Shad leaned forward, his hands on the table. "Justesen. Think. Then close your eyes and look at her. What do you see?" His voice was intense.

The man hesitated, either cantankerous or stubborn, she didn't know, but eventually he humored Shad with a sigh. He closed his eyes and pointed his face toward Ember. His brow crinkled up as he looked with his magical sight, and then his jaw dropped in what looked like shock. He sat back from the table and opened his eyes, staring at Ember and completely speechless.

"Did you see it?" Shad asked, though it was obvious Justesen had seen something. "You have been trained for this your entire life. You know what it means. You know what she is. The door must open for her." If Shad leaned any further into the table, he was going to push it over.

Ember was tired of the men talking over her head. “What did you see?” she asked Justesen directly. Evidently, the idea that she was speaking to him loosened his tongue.

He whispered. “White. I saw white. You are the Wolfchild.”

Now she understood.

“Yes. That is what I am told. The first white mage in three thousand years, and it is my job, my duty, mission, or calling to unite the keystones and heal Rasann. Do you know where the emerald keystone is?” she asked.

He nodded and used his chin to gesture to a stone door in the wall, symbols carved into the surface and looking like sigils of power. “It’s in the maze. It’s called the Emerald Wolf and can be worn only by one of the Bendanatu. Three keys are required to enter, one necklace and two bracelets."

Ember’s heart sank. “Oh, no,” she said.

Justesen looked worried. “What? What is it? I see the necklace, but—” He broke off and pulled her hands forward. “Where are the bracelets? I was told the Wolfchild would have them.”

“I did,” Ember answered. “And before you get angry, they are here. They just aren’t attached to me.”

Shad groaned and smacked his forehead. “Tyese and Keyera. I thought they had given them back.”

“They won’t come off,” Ember said. Turning to Justesen, she explained, “In the battle at Karsholm, I was cut directly across one of the bracelets. As we flew here and engaged the Ne’Goi in another battle, the bracelets that had been embedded in my skin rose to the surface and flew off my wrists. Two of the Bendanatu girls caught them. One placed the bracelet on her wrist for safekeeping, and before she thought about the consequences, it had sunk below her skin. The other retrieved the broken bracelet and worked at fixing it. She was successful, but at one intricate point, she had to put it on her wrist to keep the shape intact, and when the metal rejoined, that bracelet sank below her skin as well. It was not intentional, but they will not rise to the surface like they did before. I am sorry.”

Justesen looked thoughtful, his fingers pinching his pursed lips. He got up from the table and went to a shelf of books on the wall, muttering to himself, then pulled an age-darkened leather-bound book from the depths of the shelf and brought it back to the table. He sat down and set the book in front of him, flipping pages quickly, stopping when he seemed to find what he was looking for. "There!" he almost shouted. "There is the answer. Why didn't I see it before?" he asked himself. "The words of Kezyan the third. Prophet of Bendanatu over three millennia ago."

He cleared his throat and read from the book. "And the Wolfchild shall come unto the cave of the emerald maze, and upon her chest shall be the emerald key. And the white of the Wolfchild shall be blinding to her enemies, for her enemies are many and hidden, but into the maze she shall not go alone. The signs shall be upon their wrists, and together, three shall become one, enter the maze, and retrieve the Emerald Wolf."

He continued. "But beware, for there are demons among you, and when the time comes for the cave to be opened, they shall battle the Wolfchild and would take the Emerald Wolf if they could. Caution, my son. Beware the demons and keep them at bay."

Justesen shut the book. Ember was a bit scared after hearing the last part. Demons? She would battle demons to get into the maze?

"Did you hear it?" Justesen asked. "Three shall become one, and her other parts shall be upon their wrist. They prophesied this, Ember! All three of you must enter the maze."

Shad spoke up. "Are you insane? The others are only children! The three of them together to conquer the maze that is supposed to be possible only for the Wolfchild? It's a suicide mission!"

Justesen nodded. "I feel the same, White Shadow, but it has been prophesied, and what choice does she have? All the keys must enter. If she cannot wear all three, then all three must go within."

Shad's head fell to the table. He banged it once. "This is wrong. We can't lose any more of us, especially the children."

"Again, I agree. But there is no other choice. The door will not open without the keys." Justesen took the book off the table and walked back to the shelf, placing it carefully inside.

Shad sighed. "I think we'd better call a council on this. It is not a decision we should make alone, especially with the lives of two of our children at risk. There are so few of us left. We have to protect every life. What do you think?"

Justesen steepled his fingers in front of him and nodded. "Absolutely."

CHAPTER THIRTY

The reports came in to C'Tan despite Kardon's betrayal. The dragons had always been her best spies, and they continued to be now.

"Mistress, the Ne'Goi follow the guardian of the Sapphire Flute to Bendanatu. Wyciskalla is with them. It is a battle that will destroy all you have worked for, and they will claim three keystones. I worry about Ember's safety. You shall never have the keystones if they kill her."

"I know that, Drake," C'Tan snapped, pacing the roof of her keep while she spoke to the dragon. "What do I do? What do I do?"

And then she knew.

"Call all the dragons. We shall ride and battle with the Bendanatu against the Ne'Goi." She could feel Drake's displeasure, but he was smart enough not to say anything. Instead, he pulled himself aloft and dove from the top of the tower to carry her message.

C'Tan hurried down the stairs, calling her captain of the guard along the way. He was at the bottom of the tower when she arrived. "Gather all the soldiers. We ride within the hour," she said. She could feel his displeasure as well, but he said nothing.

And now the most difficult of all. C'Tan climbed another set of steps, unlocked the door to Brina's room, and stepped inside, then froze.

A white hawk with glowing green eyes sat on the window ledge. He seemed to be waiting for her. She knew who it was the instant she saw him, and the battle within her was monumental. It thrilled her to see her brother. Furious with him for the scarring she underwent. Happy, sad, mad, jealous, and so much more.

His voice sounded in her head. *Hello, Celena Tan.*

For once, she didn't correct him. "What are you doing here?" she nearly whispered.

I've come to get you. There is someone we both want to protect. I have power you don't, and you have power I don't. Let's set aside this animosity and work together this once. He hopped from the ledge to Brina's shoulder.

C'Tan didn't even look at the woman—she was so focused on the bird who was her brother.

"I plan to go to Bendanatu to defend my investment. If you wish to accompany me, that is your choice," she said.

He bobbed his head. *Brina needs to go with us.*

C'Tan finally looked at her. "What? No! She is my prisoner, and the only thing keeping Ember in my power."

Ember isn't, you know. Not really. She'll get the keystones, and yes, she will bring them here, but unless you change, that day will be your last. It has already been spoken. The choice is yours. Show some compassion, and she may show you the same, Jarin said, preening under his wing.

C'Tan growled, picked up a bowl, and threw it against the wall. It smashed into tiny pieces, the wall not denting at all. She began pacing again and finally faced the bird.

"Fine, then. She may come."

I knew you'd see it my way, he said, just a bit smugly.

C'Tan hated it.

I believe I heard we depart within the hour? he asked.

She stormed down the stairs.

CHAPTER THIRTY-ONE

Kayla thought the Ne'Goi would stay with the magestone and feed. She'd thought she and the others would be safe once they were away from Asana's farm.

She was wrong.

Weaving through the trees for hours, she tried to lose the Ne'Goi that ran and flew hard on her trail. One by one they dropped away, seemingly either from her well-aimed ice balls or because they lost interest in the chase. Only one continued, dauntlessly following her when no other Ne'Goi were left. She wasn't sure if it was for vengeance or because of the Sapphire Flute, but he wanted her and made it very apparent that he wasn't giving up.

The giant Ne'Goi followed her, sometimes close enough to singe Thew's tail and other times falling back, nearly out of sight. Kayla was tired, but she didn't dare stop. She continued to weave through the trees, hoping to lose the Ne'Goi if she made enough turns. She dove into a lake and swam beneath the water to the other side. She dove over a waterfall, raced down a cavern trail, and climbed into the mountains, all to no avail. Kayla had to get to the Bendanatu and meet up with the others. There was strength in numbers, and if Bendanatu was the center city for the wolves, they should have enough people to fight.

She hoped.

Regardless, all she could do was fly on, hoping she could make it before the shadow weavers caught up with her. "You stop for Wyciskalla, tiny half-breed!" the giant demon yelled from the top of the mountain behind her. "Wyciskalla hungry for Evahn blood. Magic blood. And you have keystone! Hungry! Wyciskalla hungry!"

The giant demon thing scared her beyond anything she'd experienced, probably because he was so immediate and so huge. He scared her more than C'Tan. More than continuing to lose Brant. More than her mother's near death. She had to get away from the beast, but Thew was already going his fastest, and Kayla didn't dare use the flute or Brant to protect herself, not when the Ne'Goi ate magic. They would swallow Brant up as if he were a gnat.

She remembered facing the Ne'Goi who disguised themselves as the mage council. Brant had handled himself well then, and so had she and the flute. So why was she so worried? The answer was right behind her. Wyciskalla was no ordinary Ne'Goi, and she did not know what to expect from such a giant shadow weaver. Was his magic as strong as his body? Could he destroy Brant and the Sapphire Flute without a thought?

She had no idea.

All she could do was fly hard and fast.

She swept over another mountain crest and dove for the ground, skimming the golden grass that waved with their passing. A line of woods quickly approached and she flew low, threading in and out amongst the trees again, hoping to lose the shadow weaver, but it didn't work. He'd be to her left one second, then her right another, zig-zagging in that sickening way the shadow weavers do, hopping from one place to the next using teleportation. Why he didn't just land in front of her, she didn't know.

Once again, her tactics weren't working, so this time she urged Thew higher, up above the canopy of trees but, still they flew in a straight race for Bendanatu. The giant Ne'Goi fell farther and farther behind, but Kayla knew she hadn't lost him. He was back there, still following. She could feel it. They flew at that same breakneck pace, even when she couldn't see him. They went so high it became difficult to breathe, and gasping, Kayla lay across Thew's back. The elemental air dragon accommodated her by feeding her oxygen, and her chest loosened enough to suck in some real air.

A familiar Phoenixian with the lump of an egg in his pouch appeared from beneath them and drew near, Aldarin upon his back. What was he doing? Didn't he know the Ne'Goi were more likely to find them if they were together? And how was he breathing where the air was so thin?

As if reading her mind, he led Ted Finch within touching distance of Kayla and her mount and yelled through blue lips. "We may not be able to fight right now, but they know where we're going regardless, and I'd rather stand together with you than be alone. Wouldn't you?" So close to Thew, Aldarin's color returned to normal, and he seemed to breathe easier.

She nodded and couldn't help the smile that spread across her face. She desperately wanted to hold his hand, but not only would it be dangerous, it would be inappropriate. Brant had been gone less than a week. She couldn't allow herself to feel this way about Aldarin. She just couldn't.

She turned to Thew. "Can you share breath with Finchling and Aldarin too?"

Thew answered in her mind. "I cannot, but the elemental in your flute can."

Kayla called Brant from the flute and asked him to help Ted and Aldarin breathe. He flew across the way and did something that placed a blue glow around their heads, then returned to the flute without a word.

Finally, the giant Ne'Goi quit screaming after Kayla. She wasn't sure whether to be relieved or nervous at his absence. If he had rejoined his fellow Ne'Goi, there was bound to be a battle, and they were heading straight for Bendanatu. That wasn't what she'd wanted when they set out to go there, but it looked as if they had no choice. At least they could arrive ahead of the Ne'Goi and warn the Bendanatu of what was coming. She was incredibly grateful the Ne'Goi didn't seem able to transport long distances. According to Tyese, the shadow weavers had nearly annihilated her village and there were hardly any adults left. The phoenixian and human help would probably be appreciated if there were a battle to come.

Brant spun out of the flute and hovered in front of Kayla, the wind not affecting him at all. For that matter, it didn't seem to affect Thew, either. She hadn't noticed until now. It must be part of being air elementals. Brant rarely surfaced from the flute unless she called him or he was warning or protecting her, so why appear now? He stood in the air, his ankles crossed, almost looking like his old self, except for the blue glow. Aldarin watched the two of them with a hard look in his eyes and a jutting jaw. He didn't like Brant—that was obvious—but she didn't know why.

Brant spoke, the echoing bottom-of-the-well sound very apparent in his voice today. "He likes you."

She didn't have to ask who he meant. Her face grew warm, and she looked away. "No, he doesn't. He's just a friend." She glanced at the tattooed warrior and her heart beat a little faster.

"No," Brant said, coming closer and sitting backward on Thew's neck, directly in front of her. "He likes you. I can tell. For some reason, he was totally himself today. The old Brant—not the servant of the flute. She couldn't admit anything to him, not regarding another man. It just felt wrong.

Her ex-fiancè grinned. "Oh, there is no doubt. He likes you. You like him too. It's in every line of your body, every look in your eye. Your face speaks what words cannot. You love him." Brant said it as if it were fact.

Kayla was indignant. "No! That's not true. I love you! Forever! I can't love anyone else. I am already given to you!" She was shouting without realizing it, almost unaware that Aldarin was even there. Her anger only grew hotter when Brant laughed.

When he quieted, he said, "Love, it is all right. I cannot have you, nor you me, and I do not doubt your love for me just because you've come to love him too." He reached out and gently caressed her cheek with a cool, nearly insubstantial hand. "He's a good man and will make a fine husband."

Kayla spluttered, unable to find words for what she felt. Love? She might find Aldarin attractive, but how could Brant think she would fall in love so soon?

Brant laughed again and spun back into the flute. Kayla spent a long time staring straight ahead, trying very hard not to think. Finally, the realization crept in, despite her attempts to strangle it. Had Brant just given his blessing for her to love Aldarin?

She refused to think about it, but there was a part of her, a tiny part, that was giddy. Brant took away a huge burden by letting her go.

CHAPTER THIRTY-TWO

Ember sat in a large cave, domed and smooth. It looked very much like the council chambers in Javak, where she had been falsely accused and imprisoned by Laerdish before Uncle Ezzie came to her rescue and proved the truth.

But this time she was not on trial, and she definitely was not alone. Around her were many Bendanatu—her grandfather, Chief Bahndai. Uncle Shad. Justesen, guardian of the emerald maze. Adrienne, priestess of the Bendanatu, and her young friends—redheaded Tyese, so shy and gifted, and lastly Keyera, her usual sunshine dimmed by the solemnity of the meeting. Oh, and then there was DeMunth. Now that he was well, he left her side only when necessary. She didn't mind. She loved being near him. He held her hand as they listened to Justesen present the same information he had given Ember near the cave entrance.

"Chieftain, we must allow the three girls to enter the cave together. It is prophesied, and the door will not open without all three keys present," the tall man said. Ember was beginning to realize he was younger than she'd first thought. The weight of his responsibility made him seem older.

Bahndai pursed his lips and scraped a hand through his short hair, much like his son Shad did so often. "I hear your words, Justesen," he said. "Adrienne, your thoughts?"

Bahndai turned to the priestess, who had her hands clasped, her index fingers pointed upward and pressed against her mouth. "Do you ask for my opinion, or the knowledge of the Guardian?" She met his eye, and he hesitated, glancing at Ember.

"Both," he answered. "It would be a lie if I didn't admit to being reluctant to send my granddaughter and two of our youngest and finest into the darkness of the maze, but if this is what Bendanatu requires of us, I shall be in full support." He squirmed in his chair, then stilled as he waited for Adrienne.

The priestess let her hands slip apart. She raised them above her, and burst into blue flames, part mist and part fire. It was the strangest and most beautiful thing Ember had seen. Once the nimbus surrounded her, Adrienne raised her head and opened her eyes. Ember gasped. The woman's eyes had been lovely before, but a pale, washed-out blue that said little about her. Now her eyes were the color of Kayla's Sapphire Flute. Ember was surprised. She thought that someone who was supposed to be so close to the Guardian of green magic would have green eyes and flames, not blue.

Evidently, there was still a lot for Ember to learn.

Adrienne stood in that position for an uncomfortable amount of time, looking as if she listened to an unknown voice. After about ten minutes, the glowing swirls stopped and Adrienne's head fell forward. Everything pulled back into her, and when she raised her head, her eyes had gone back to their normal pale blue and immediately met Bahndai's. "They must go, sir, and they must go now. There is evil coming to us and it can only be stopped with the Emerald Wolf. These three together are destined to find it, despite the obstacles in their path."

Bahndai lowered his chin for a moment, then looked up and nodded. Everyone stood and followed Justesen. DeMunth leaned over and whispered in Ember's ear. "The three of you? Is she saying those children are to go in there and I cannot?"

Ember nodded.

DeMunth pulled away. "Alone?" he fumed. "You should have a protector—a guard, if not a companion. It is the mage academy all over again. Why can't you trust I will care for you?" He turned away, his jaw clenching, but she touched his arm and he stilled.

"It has nothing to do with trusting you. I've given you my heart. There *is* no greater trust! I cannot help was Bendanatu says, not can I change a prophecy written three thousand years ago. Following a prophecy is never easy, and leaping into the unknown is even harder, but for the sake of the Bendanatu, for the sake of our world, Rasann, I have to go."

"But why the younglings and not me? I can better protect you!" His jaw jutted, but there were tears in his eyes.

She stepped in front of him, letting her fingers trail down his arm until she took one hand and then the other and looked up into his stormy eyes. "They have the keys and you do not. DeMunth, hardest of all is to stay behind and let those you love fly into the darkness without you. But you must let me go." He was her guardian, her best friend, and the person she loved and trusted most in this world. She knew how it would feel if it were him going into the cave and she who was left behind. She imagined it was torture for him.

He searched her eyes, unasked questions pressed against her, but remained unspoken. Finally, he nodded his head slowly, as if it took every bit of will to do that much. She squeezed his hands, and together they turned and hurried after the others.

They entered Justesen's quarters and looked around. Bahndai, Adrienne, Tyese, Keyera, and the tall maze guardian stood near the symbols engraved on the wall. The five boys who had come in the night before sat around the table, eating. She still felt uncomfortable around them, but she couldn't understand why. They looked like normal younglings, and they had certainly done nothing to harm anyone. The boys looked up when Ember and DeMunth entered. Ember shivered.

Justesen ignored the children as if they were harmless. He ignored the boys, gesturing to Ember to come forward. He stood her directly in front of the middle carving, then brought Tyese to the right and Keyera to the left.

The carved sigils began to glow. Ember didn't know what the others felt, but, for her, it filled her with green light and the taste of grass—and then the door completely disappeared, leaving a dark cave-like opening. Startled, the girls stood there and did nothing, and then there was a commotion behind them. Ember turned, but was shoved aside as one of the five strange boys darted past her and into the cavern leading to the Emerald Wolf. In an instant, they were all gone, having shifted shape into what looked like a cross between a giant frog and a hyena.

Justesen groaned and fell to his knees. "The book warned me. It warned me and I didn't listen. I knew there was something wrong with those boys, but they were disguised so well, I thought they were Bendanatu. They were the demons, the demons the books warned of!" He turned his attention to Ember, Keyera, and Tyese. "Girls, you must hurry. If the Ne'Goi reach the Emerald Wolf before you, they will destroy it with their black magic. You must pursue them and get ahead of them."

"Ne'Goi?" DeMunth asked. "Those were shadow weavers?"

Justesen nodded. "Yes. Lesser demons, but yes, they are Ne'Goi."

DeMunth started toward the opening. "That does it. I'm going in there whether or not you like it!" As he moved forward, the door began to rematerialize. Shad tackled DeMunth and took him to the floor. The door held its place for a moment. Why had the Ne'Goi gotten through when DeMunth could not? Was it truly the prophecy?

Ember didn't know and right now, it didn't matter. She looked at DeMunth and said, "I'm sorry, but this time *you* have to trust *me* and stay behind. We'll take care of each other." She took Keyera and Tyese by the hand and stepped forward, still looking over her shoulder at him. "I love you. Take care of Grandfather for me," she said, then taking three steps forward, the girls moved beyond the doorway and turned around.

DeMunth yelled. "Noooo!" He pulled himself away from Shad and ran toward Ember, but it was too late. The girls moved beyond the doorway. The cave door slammed shut just before he reached it. Ember could hear him pounding against the wall, and saw a flash of light even from this side as he most likely pulled his Guardian-made sword and struck the wall as he'd done at the mage academy. Evidently, the magic of this place would have none of it.

Not letting go of the girls' hands, Ember turned once again, the door to her back, though she could no longer see it. They were in blind darkness and didn't know where to go. Only the scrabbling sounds of the Ne'Goi ahead gave them any sense of direction.

"Well, it looks like we're on our own. Tyese. Keyera. Are you ready for this? You are as much a part of this as I am." Ember tried to calm her racing heart and was sure the girls could feel the sweat on her palms.

Keyera squeezed her hand and then pulled away long enough to throw a magelight into the air. She turned to Ember with a grin as her yellow light shone down. Tyese looked at them both, then threw three more magelights up. One yellow, one orange, and one green. They created a dazzling and colorful mosaic on the ground to lead the way. It was Tyese who finally answered with words.

"Ready? I think I was born for this moment. Let's go," she said, taking the first step.

Ember nodded in satisfaction. Together, the three of them moved down the path amid the rubble into the unknown.

CHAPTER THIRTY-THREE

It was dusk before Kayla and Aldarin neared Bendanatu. Finally, the map in her head overlapped the structures and cartography below. Caves, an amphitheater, and a strange stone building dotted the land, but very few people. Most of the phoenixians had already arrived and waited for her in the amphitheater with a small group of armed younglings. Kayla paid them no mind as she and Thew glided in for a quick landing.

"They're coming," Kayla said, winded, as if she had just run the entire way instead of riding, but the terror wouldn't let her breathe. "The big one, Wyciskalla, he followed me the all the way. He fell back, but I know he's still coming. We have to organize an army or something."

Shari spoke. "We can't. We can do our best, but the Ne'Goi have massacred this village. They have little to offer but younglings and old men."

The armed Bendanatu growled at that, drawing the strings of their bows back farther in response. It finally hit Kayla that she was in danger here, too. She addressed the young warriors. "Please. We mean you no harm. We are here to help—"

One of the tall girls cut her off. Kayla recognized her from the academy. Kymber? "Not if you led the Ne'Goi to our doorstep. Only the enemy does that."

Kayla's heart sank. "No! It was an accident! We were told to come here, and they followed. There has to be something we can do together. Please. Isn't there someone we can speak to? We are here to offer our help."

The younglings looked at one another, then nodded. The tall girl put down her bow and beckoned with her chin, not saying a word.

Shari drew even with Kayla and murmured. "This is not good. We come to offer aid and return their people, and instead, we bring the enemy to their door. If we had known how diminished their forces were, would could have done something else. They have next to nothing, and we are but a small army—though we will fight. It is our battle, too." She leaned over to Aldarin and continued in her soft voice. "Aldarin, go and speak to the chieftain and see what he can spare in the way of warriors and supplies. Give him a warning and our heartfelt apologies. The battle is on its way to us, whether or not we are ready."

Aldarin nodded and headed toward one of the younglings on the field in front of him. He knelt and talked to the kid for a few brief seconds, and when the boy pointed toward a cavern across the meadow and at the top of some stairs, he ran in that direction. Kymber watched him, but said nothing.

Shari spoke again. "Kayla. Lily. Go to the square building and tell them what is happening. I saw younglings going in and out of the building, and they need protecting. The older ones may be able to help."

Kayla was surprised Shari had taken over and was giving orders, but it was nice not to have to think for a moment. She and Lily separated from the group and ran to the building, knocking on the door. Two very young boys answered. "Whatcha want?" said one.

"Yeah, whatcha want," the other repeated.

"Are there grown-ups here? Adults? We need to talk to an adult." Kayla was flustered and knew it, but couldn't stop the panic racing through her veins.

The first boy's brow furrowed. "Yeah. Gamma Dawnna and Gawpa Roahnald. You need them?" He asked.

Lily answered this time. "Please yes. It's very important."

The girls moved to step inside, and the two boys stood in front of them. "We don't know you."

Kayla was getting frustrated. "No, you don't know me, but my name is Kayla, and this is Lily. Can I play a song for you?" she asked.

The boys perked up and nodded.

Kayla pulled out the flute and thought sleepy thoughts toward the boys. It only took half a minute, and they had fallen to the floor, fast asleep.

"Good thinking," Lily said. Kayla didn't even smile, just stepped across the boys and raced to the back. She darted through a beaded curtain and into a kitchen full of people—younglings. Children. There were only two adults in the room, but everyone stared when the girls entered, a few of them growling, though they never morphed into wolf.

"We're not a threat, we promise." Kayla said, feeling panicked again. "We're here to help and to warn you. The Ne'Goi are on their way. Are there any who can fight? And what can we do to help protect the littles?"

Dawnna and Roahnald turned, concern on their faces. The older man, Roahnald, spoke to the surrounding younglings. "Madison, Tayten, Tabitha, gather the youngest and bring them here. The rest of you, get ready for war. We knew this day would come again, but you've practiced and prepared. You'll do well." He then crossed the room in three long strides and took Kayla and Lily by the arms, escorting them into the next room. He stopped and faced them. "Tell me," was all he said.

And so they did. They left out all the personal happenings at Asana's home and began with hearing and then seeing the Ne'Goi in the magestone tunnel, and then their flight and separation and the pursuit of the Ne'Goi, and eventually their arrival in Bendanatu.

"So you brought them to us," he said accusingly.

Before Kayla could say a word, Lily spoke. "Not intentionally. If we had known how sparse your forces were, how much you'd suffered already, we would have taken them elsewhere or died trying to fight them on our own. But we'd heard about the mighty Bendanatu, and believed this was the place to come. I'm sorry to see we were proven wrong."

Kayla was appalled at Lily's lack of tact, but Roahnald rose to the bait.

He straightened his shoulders and puffed out his chest. "The Bendanatu are mighty and strong. We may be low in numbers, but we are not unsurprised this time, thanks to you, and we have learned how to fight them. We may be mostly children, but we'll help in whatever way we can."

Lily smiled then. "Thank you. I knew you would rise to the occasion. The Bendanatu are noble, graceful, and strong. The best fighters I've seen. It will be an honor to stand beside you." She extended her arm and their palms met in a grip that looked like it would crush Lily's small hand.

Roahnald turned away and strode back to the kitchen. The girls leaped over the still- sleeping boys, darted out the front door, and ran back to the group of Phoenixians and humans who had been traveling together for these three days.

A graying man had joined the group since last they'd been there, and Kayla knew him as soon as he turned and she saw his eyes. She walked toward him soberly, but with her hand extended. "You must be Bahndai. It's an honor to meet you, Chieftain."

He looked surprised, examining her face. "Do I know you?"

"No, but you know my cousin Ember. I'm Kayla. Her mother and mine are sisters," she explained, and something like delight came across his face. He took her in his arms for just a moment.

"Welcome, Kayla," he said. "I'm sorry to meet under such dire circumstances, but it is truly a pleasure to meet the guardian of The Sapphire Flute, and for you to be family makes this even more of an honor."

They weren't family. Not really. But it didn't matter. She'd sort it out with him later. Right now, they had a battle to fight.

The sound of wings came from overhead and dust blew as the last three Phoenixians landed, lowering humans onto Bendanatu soil. Asana's legs were wobbly as she first slid off the Phoenix, but she quickly regained her balance and walked to Kayla.

Kayla glanced at Bahndai and froze. Asana. Bahndai. Jarin's parents. Ember's grandparents. Asana's husband.

She thought he was dead.

Oh boy.

Bahndai watched Asana with a puzzled expression, as if he knew her, but couldn't remember where. The old woman made her way toward the chieftain and Kayla watched with a mixture of excitement and dread. Asana looked at the grizzled leader of the Bendanatu with no recognition whatsoever. Her husband, the first and only man she'd ever loved, and she didn't recognize him—but then why should she? She believed Bahndai was dead. Glancing back at the old man, Kayla saw when the realization hit. Surprise flashed across his face, then the thrill of seeing a long-lost love, then shame and embarrassment. He looked around as if he'd rather be anywhere but there at that moment.

Asana stepped between Shari and Kayla and addressed the Bendanatu chieftain. "Are we too late to help?" she asked, her brave voice masking her shaking knees.

Bahndai looked at her, seemingly in shock, tipping his head like a hound, but did not answer.

Asana looked at Kayla and whispered out of the side of her mouth, "Is he deaf?"

Kayla nearly burst out laughing. She hid her snort of laughter behind a hand and clearing her throat while shaking her head.

Asana imitated his cocked head without seeming to realize it. "Then what's wrong with him? Why won't he speak?"

Shari, oblivious to what was happening between the two old lovers, said, "He spoke clearly but a moment ago. Perhaps he is taken with you."

Now it was Asana's turn to snort. "These old bones? That would be the day." She turned to face him again. Bahndai alternated between shades of red and white and he almost panted, he breathed so fast.

"Sir," Asana said loudly, despite being told he was not deaf. "Are you all right?" She emphasized each word.

It was all Kayla could do not to laugh.

Bahndai finally spoke. A whisper, nothing else. "Asana?"

The old woman jerked back and looked at his face with suspicion. "How do you know me, wolf man? I don't know your face."

Bahndai chuckled. "It has aged much since last we met. It is you, Asana. I thought I would never see you again." He stepped forward, took her in his arms, and twirled her about.

She yelled at him, and as soon as her feet touched the ground, she shoved him. Hard.

He released her, and she stumbled and fell, skidding in the soft dirt. He reached for her, but she scrambled away. "I don't know you," she snarled. "Don't touch my person again."

His smile was charming as he reached a hand to her. "Asana, it's me. It's Bahndai," he said, expecting a warm welcome, or so it seemed, with his smile and outstretched hand.

Asana froze, searching his face, as if she could not believe it. For a moment, Kayla thought it would be a beautiful reunion, but with recognition came anger. Asana surged to her feet with a scream and lunged toward Bahndai. She slapped him across the face, then doubled her fists and swung at him. He wrapped his arms around her and all she could do was pummel uselessly at his chest. His cheek was a brilliant red, but it didn't seem to bother him at all, as distracted as he was by his estranged wife trying to escape his grasp.

Kayla did not know what to do. She looked at Shari, and the Phoenixian shrugged. They watched the chieftain and the little grandmother battle it out until the woman slumped against Bahndai and stilled. He looked down at Asana and chuckled, which was the last thing Kayla expected to hear from him. "You haven't changed much, have you?" he whispered. "I always did love the ferocity in you. It's so Bendanatu. Welcome, love, to my home at last. I've missed you." She hit his shoulder once more. He winced, then leaned over and gently kissed her on the top of the head.

Bahndai pushed her to arm's length and smiled. Asana spat at him, but it landed in the dirt. He let go and turned his back, ignoring her. He gestured to the others. "Come, come! Enjoy our hospitality while you can. Who knows how long it will be available? Please—enter my home and consider yourselves my guests. Kymber, you may go now. Thank you for your service."

The girl bowed to the chieftain, pivoted on her heel, and loped back to the square building that housed the orphans.

Asana followed Aldarin and DeMunth, entering the caves and climbing the stairs to Bahndai's quarters. There was much to talk about, and who knew how long they had to prepare for the Ne'Goi. Kayla was just grateful they had any time at all. Evidently the Ne'Goi had pulled back to make their own preparations, but no doubt, they were coming—and soon.

CHAPTER THIRTY-FOUR

The multi-colored magelights cast a strange glow on the stone walls, shadows popping up in odd places as the girls moved forward down the tunnel. Tyese sniffed the air, then bent over and sniffed again at the rubble at the base of the walls, then crouched and picked up a handful of pebbles and brought it to her face. Inhaling deeply, she closed her eyes. "They were here," she said, then dropped it and brushed her hands together.

"Well, of course they were," Keyera snapped at her. "We've walked in nothing but a straight line for an hour. Where else could they go?" She kicked at the rocks, scattering them with pings as they bounced off the walls.

Tyese reddened and opened her mouth to respond. Just then, Ember saw the opening ahead and to their left. "It looks like that's about to change." She stepped forward, almost running, to the break in the monotonous wall, then sucked in a breath. "Crap." That's all she needed to say upon sight of the endless bends and turns ahead of them. The girls came up behind her with hardly a sound. It must be a Bendanatu trait.

Keyera groaned. "Is that what I think it is?"

"A maze," Tyese answered for her, almost breathless. "It is the Bendanatu maze. Somewhere down there is the emerald keystone."

Hyena-type laughter sounded from the deep caverns, and Ember caught sight of the shadow weaver boys not far in the distance. They couldn't reach the Emerald Wolf first. There was no way she could let that happen. The three girls were going to have to move faster and rid themselves of the shadow weavers permanently. It would be devastating if a single keystone fell into the hands of the darkness. They would eat it like candy and destroy Rasann with the act.

Ember pulled her shoulders back and started ahead at a jog. "Come on! We may not like it, but it is a race to the keystone. We have got to reach it before those boys do."

Tyese and Keyera immediately broke into a run, following close on Ember's heels, and she picked up the pace. They entered the maze, took a left, a right, and another right, and ran smack into a stone wall.

"Ooof!" Keyera stepped back and rubbed her nose. "Where did that come from?"

Ember shook her head. "Well, it is a maze. What would a maze be without some dead ends?"

Tyese snickered, and Keyera glared at her.

Ember ignored them, turned around, and went back to the last turn, this time going straight until she hit a 'T' intersection and had to go left or right. She picked left, then right, then straight, left and right, before she hit a dead end once more. When she turned around to go back, she was surprised to find her way blocked by a new stone wall covered with growing vines.

"How did that get there?" she asked, feeling beneath the vines to determine their thickness. The vines seemed to get more dense by the second, pinning the girls to the wall behind them.

Keyera pushed back, her eyes wide and scared. "What do we do? How do we get past that?"

Tyese shook her head and kept looking at Ember, just as helpless as Keyera.

That was when it struck Ember. This was her problem to fix. This was one of the tests she had to pass to get them to the emerald keystone. But how? She had no control of her magic, and though the green had been her first color of magic, she still didn't know how to control the magic of life. But weren't the tests supposed to be for the Wolfchild only? Something only she could solve?

If that was the case, there was more to this test than getting past some thorny vines and a stone wall.

Closing her eyes, Ember looked at the vines, the stone wall, and then through it. She didn't know how she did it, but somehow her sight shifted and she saw the energy that fed everything, all in their various colors. If her eyes had been open, they would have widened with surprise. This spell was complicated. What she saw wasn't just vines and a wall, but magic continually fed the vines and made them grow at a very accelerated pace, and that same magic fed into the wall, making it more than stone cut from a mountain. It was impenetrable.

And to make matters worse, behind the wall was a fire spell that would burn them like chicken left too long on the spit. How could she take down the wall without getting burned? How could she take down the wall at all?

Perhaps if she could create a fist-sized hole through the vines and then the stone, she could control the fire coming through. They would still get warm, but hopefully it would keep them alive. A memory came back then. Lily teaching her the orange magic and Ember practicing. She had a very distinct image of putting her fists into the stone wall and popping pieces out when she twisted her fist.

She chewed it over in her mind for several moments before Keyera cried out, "Ember, do something! We're going to die!"

Ember shook her head. "No, you will not die . . . I hope." She muttered the last under her breath.

Ember reached for the vines to push them out of the way, but several sharp pricks gouged her thumb. She screamed and yanked away, long strands of vine coming with her. She looked at the joint to see blood welling up in what looked like teeth marks. Tyese and Keyera were at her side in an instant, turning her hand over to see the red marks darkening and veins of purple creep up her arm. Ember's heart beat fast, the adrenaline pumping, and she felt faint pain as the lines moved quickly from thumb to wrist to elbow.

Poison. The vines were poisonous, and she had attacked them like an idiot. Her heart was beating fast, but her mind was still clear, despite the dizziness. Poison was something she was very familiar with after dealing with herds of horses constantly getting into the creeping briars, and Uncle Ezzie with his various healing concoctions.

Unfortunately, all healing potions were at the mage academy, far from her reach. Panic overwhelmed her. The girls alternately screamed and asked questions. Ember could tell by their tone, but she didn't hear the words. Instead, her mind raced for an answer. The poison crept upward. Her elbow twinged as the lines collected there and spread in a circle around the joint.

What could she do? She scanned the surrounding area. Nothing but stone, dirt, and poisonous vines. She looked over the girls. Skin, clothing, and hair. Nothing more. She was on her own and had nothing—nothing that could halt the flow of the acid flowing toward her heart.

And then her mind stilled. She had something. She just didn't know how to control it.

She had her magic.

She looked at her hand, now the vibrant color of blueberries, and tried to find an answer, something the mage academy might have taught her in the short time she was there.

Nothing.

Nothing!

But she had broken stone with only a thought. She had pushed her hands through rock, popped it out of its place, then melted it together again. She had healed one of the shadow weavers from near death and magically tied him to the ground. If she could do that, surely there was an answer to her dilemma here.

"Think, Ember, just think," she muttered to herself. The girls quieted at last and Ember's mind raced. Finally, it stopped, still unable to find an answer. She had no training for this, no understanding of her power. In trying to heal herself, she could very well make her arm explode or fall off or turn into a hissing snake.

But she had to try.

Taking a deep breath, Ember put all her attention on the bite in her thumb and whispered, "change!"

Once again—nothing.

Frustrated, she turned to the cold stone wall behind her and put her head against it. She had to break this down further. If the maze held everyone but the Wolfchild at bay, then wouldn't that mean only a white mage could overcome the challenges? It made sense. So what could she do that was impossible for any other mage?

And then the answer came, so simple she felt stupid for not thinking of it before.

Ember could combine colors of magic. Other magi could use their powers one at a time, but she could make them all work together. So, what colors of magic did she need to rid herself of this poison and get the wall of shrubs out of the way so the three of them could pass? Well, she needed to slow the progress of the poison first. If she didn't, she would be unconscious or dead before she had a chance to do anything more. What would slow poison?

Ember racked her brain. Well, an antidote would do it, but she didn't have one. Depending on the poison, fire could kill or feed it, not to mention that it could kill Ember herself. Cold? Ember lifted her head from the stone. Cold could slow any kind of liquid. The trick would be to slow it without turning her blood to ice. For the first time since being bitten, she felt a shred of hope.

Turning, she put her back against the cold stone and pulled the cool through her body. Starting at the top near her shoulder where the dark lines continued to surge upward, she pushed cold into her veins. Instantly, the progress of the toxin stopped, but the pain was exquisite.

It felt as if Ember's arm had turned to ice from the inside out. Ember screamed.

"Too much! Too much!" she yelled to no one in particular. She pulled her magic back, just a bit, until the agony of a frozen limb thawing diminished to a barely tolerable feeling of numbing cold.

The spread of the deadly toxin had stopped, but it was still in her blood. How was she to get it out? Fire was as much out of the question as it had been before. Not only might she kill herself with the flame, but fire would only undo all that she had done with the cold by thawing it out. She'd used cold. Healing hadn't worked the first time. Maybe it would now? It certainly couldn't hurt to try.

Closing her eyes, Ember pushed the color of green into her blood. There was a slight change, but when she looked, all she saw was that her entire arm, from shoulder to finger, was the vivid green of spring grass. Not what she had meant to accomplish at all. Keyera snickered, and when Ember glanced over with a glare, Tyese looked away with a quirk to her mouth.

Ember shook her head and tried not to laugh herself, though her laughter was more out of hysteria than humor. There had to be a way to get this poison out of her. It wouldn't have been the first challenge otherwise. She combed through her mind, the sound of the wind a constant whistle overhead. It pulled at her hair and gave her an idea. What if she used the power of the green for healing and combined it with the power of blue in the wind to suck the poison from the bite marks like a reed used as a straw? Again, what could it hurt to try? If she didn't get the poison out, she would die. She had to do something, anything, to keep that from happening.

Gathering her concentration, she again pulled on the power of green and nudged it into her veins near her shoulder, just above the sluggish poison still advancing toward her heart. She pushed the energy into her blood and held it there, then pulled the power of the wind above her and thinned it into small straws that attached to the vicious tooth marks. Immediately, the toxin flowed out of the entrance wounds in large drops of something looking a bit like blood and something else that seemed to flail as it left her body. Something alive. Ember tried not to squirm as it pushed the toxin from her body, the green healing of earth following behind—still turning her arm green—but cleansing the veins so thoroughly she could feel the purity seeping into the rest of her system. It strengthened her in ways she'd never thought possible.

When the drops coming from her injury turned into the bright red of blood tinted with magical green, Ember turned the healing power on the wounds themselves, and in seconds they had pulled inward and disappeared, only small white dots left in an oval pattern to show that the injury had been there at all.

"Wow," Tyese whispered. "That was amazing. I didn't know you could do that."

Ember gave a single bark of a laugh and pushed herself away from the wall, her legs still a bit shaky. "Yeah, neither did I. You never know what you can do until you try."

Keyera nodded and said, "Your arm is still green."

Ember nodded. "I know, but I getting out of here is more important. I'll fix it later."

The immediate problem had been taken care of, but raising her eyes, Ember realized there was another that had to be dealt with and she was the only one who could do it. With a sigh, she stepped toward the wall of snarling, snapping vines, closed her eyes, and looked beyond the physical to what lay beyond. Green. Yes, lots of green. Tainted green mixed with something dark and indescribable, but green nonetheless. And what was the opposite of green? Its greatest enemy and destructor?

Red—fire. Ember pulled heat in to her and was about to release it on the vines when she hesitated. Could it really be that easy? Weren't all the tests designed for her to overcome? That meant she needed one more color to overcome this challenge, but what could it be? Blue would feed them, as would purple and yellow. Air, water, and sunshine feed all plant life, so it made sense that they would feed this monstrosity as well. What was left? The orange of change? That was useless. All that was remained was more of the green. The plants were born of green—it flowed through their stalks. How would that help?

And suddenly she knew. She needed to invert some of the colors of magic. Use their opposites, just as she had used cold instead of fire.

Opposite sides of the same coin. Water would begin. Ember gathered the color of purple into her soul, then sent a tendril of magic to the plant, where it drank as if it hadn't been watered in decades. Perhaps it hadn't.

As soon as the vicious plant latched on to the water magic, Ember slowly pulled. No actual water flowed from either of them, but the power of one of the greatest elements of the earth was so strong, it was as if it was actually there. As the power of water drew away, the plant stretched for it, its green magic separating a bit from the thick vines to follow the nectar Ember enticed them with. As their life essence stretched farther, the moisture in their cells began to evaporate and shrivel the plant bit by bit. Ember tugged a little faster as the suckers got close to her, and finally tried to wrench away as they noticed something wrong.

Ember lunged away from a particularly aggressive flower head. Evidently, sucking the water out of them wasn't enough. What else could she do? A slow killing like this might take too long, and might get the three of them poisoned to death. She needed something faster—something that would destroy them in a flash. Without even thinking about it, she felt energy leave her and surge through the wall to the fire behind it. Like a grappling hook, the fire moved through the stone, the heat evaporating all liquid, though the fire itself never manifest. The vines instantly dried completely and thrashed around, crackles and snaps following their movement as dried pieces broke away. She almost felt sorry for them in that moment, and to put them out of their misery, she imagined a bright flash of sunlight. The moment she saw it in her mind it appeared so bright Ember and the two girls had to shield their eyes.

There was a sharp squeal of pain that was instantly silenced. Ember blinked rapidly a few times, trying to clear her eyes of the tears the light caused, then glanced at the wall of vines and stopped breathing for just a moment. She'd expected them to be dead. She had not expected the vines to hang lifeless, bleached an ivory white. No ash. No blackened char. Just bone-white sticks and crumpled flower heads with sharp teeth, all dead. The fire behind them was gone, consumed by her magic.

Once again, she'd been forced to kill. The three of them moved forward together and pushed the vines aside, thorns and teeth now harmless against their skin. Nothing stood behind the wall of vines, and within moments, they were once again on their way through the maze and headed toward the center. They found more correct turns than wrong ones for a change, and within a few hours, they arrived at the bank of a small lake.

Tyese and Keyera collapsed on the soft sand, exhausted from the long walk. Ember had to admit, she was tired herself.

Keyera looked up and met Ember's eyes. "Can we stay here for tonight? I don't think I can take another step and I didn't sleep well last night."

"Me neither," Tyese echoed. "This sand looks perfect for a nap. I don't even need to eat. Just let me sleep. Please?" she said, her eyes actually filling with tears.

Ember couldn't have agreed more. She had no idea what time of day it was, but her body demanded sleep after the trying day, so she sat on the shore with a sigh, the quiet lap of water hitting land lulling the three of them into a deep sleep.

Ember wasn't sure if it was the fireball that hit the sand near her feet or the screaming of Tyese and Keyera that woke her. All she knew was that she went from a very sound, dreamless state to wide awake and on her feet in an instant.

Still confused and befuddled by sleep, she looked around, trying to understand what was happening. It was bad, whatever it was. The girls dodged fireballs lofted from somewhere across the water, and laughter rang through the cavern. Ember recognized that laughter.

The Shadow Weaver boys had returned.

Understanding brought action, and in mere seconds she had dashed across the sand to the girls, taken them by the hand, and crossed the shore to safety behind the rocky crags. The fireballs soared toward them a few more times, falling far short of their goal.

When enough time had passed that the girls knew the barrage was over, Keyera growled and darted forward, Ember barely catching her in time. "No!" Ember whispered, her voice quiet iron.

Keyera growled again, then whispered back in something close to a snarl. "They killed my family. Vengeance. Justice. They must be destroyed."

Ember's heart ached for the Bendanatu girl, but she couldn't find any words to comfort her. Didn't know if she should. She was half tempted to let her fight the Ne'Goi boys.

"They killed all of our families," Tyese said, stepping to Keyera and putting a tentative hand on her arm. "But would you become like them? Is vengeance worth the price you will pay? Is it worth your sanity? Your soul?" The two young girls stood frozen for a moment, one waiting for an answer and the other thinking. Keyera's shoulders slumped, and she shook her head after a moment. That was all the answer she could give, it seemed.

Ember found tears brimming in her eyes as she watched these two girls who had been, if not enemies, at least distant rivals, come together with an understanding only they could share. And then realization created an understanding in Ember. Keyera might have been wrong to want to attack the Ne'Goi in vengeance, but there was absolutely nothing wrong with defending yourself and those you love. She opened her mouth to speak to the girls, but then something moved in the shadows.

By instinct, Ember gathered light and threw it into the air above them. It spread out in a flat disk, very unlike the magelights others created, but it worked all the same. Better, actually.

The Ne'Goi, or at least what Ember assumed were the Ne'Goi, crept toward the girls, hidden in the rocky shadows. For the first time since entering the cavern, she longed for DeMunth's presence. He would have known how to battle these vicious creatures.

The demon beings stopped completely when the light appeared above them, but when Ember's eyes met the Ne'Goi leader's, the enemy surged toward her as if they shared a hive mind. Ironic that Ember's last thought had been that of defending yourself versus vengeance, because now, the battle was all about survival. Keyera screamed as she turned wolf and leaped at the oddly shaped creatures before her. Ember modified her thought. A little vengeful anger didn't hurt when fighting for your life.

CHAPTER THIRTY-FIVE

C'Tan's dragons and soldiers had flown with her through the night in their race to get to Bendanatu ahead of the Ne'Goi. She was tired—tired of sitting, tired of having to do things she really didn't want to do because of S'Kotos's demands—just plain tired. And hungry. She sent a request to her mount. "Notify the others that we are stopping for breakfast and to take care of any personal matters. No fires. We won't be long."

The beast nodded, and within seconds, the entire wing of dragons began their descent to an open field in the woods. They landed gracefully, with hardly a bump—as they always did—and C'Tan dismounted stiffly, waving off any help from the captain of her guard. She wanted to be alone to think. Both Marda and Jarin had said things to her these past few days—things that pierced her toughened heart and made her feel again.

She wasn't sure if she liked it, but it was what it was. She could not change what had been said or what had been done.

Digging in the saddlebags, she pulled out some leftover rolls, still soft, though cold. An apple and a wedge of cheese finished her meal, and she set to eating it quickly. She didn't want to be the one to hold up the group when she had called for a quick break.

The necklace at her throat buzzed. Annoyed, she reached up to activate it. "What?" she nearly snarled.

The guard she had left to watch over Kardon stammered. "The man . . . Kardon . . . He . . . he. . . ."

Impatiently, she sent him a jolt of pain to speed things up. "Spit it out, man! What about Kardon?"

"He is dead," the man said, his voice choked with tears.

C'Tan stilled, shock sending her ramrod straight. "Explain," she whispered.

"He took his own life, Mistress. He hung himself with his pants. We did not know." The man was openly trembling now. Unable to cope with his emotion, she cut off the connection and paced. Kardon was dead. What was she going to do? S'Kotos was going to be furious when he found out. How could she twist this to stay alive?

And then he was there, almost as if she had called him, though she knew she had not. She turned slowly to face her master. Flames licked about his normally handsome frame. Today his eyes were black, his clothing black, his skin blood red, and then the orange flames. Oh . . . so ferociously beautiful. She tried to look away, but she could not. He crooked a finger and beckoned her to come closer, not seeming to notice that his fire had set the meadow aflame. She came, unable to say no. When she was in reaching distance, he leaned in slowly and asked her a question.

"Why did you kill my faithful servant?"

"Master, I did not. He killed himself," she said, unable to stop the words.

"What?" he roared, leaning back and spitting fire into the sky. When finished, he turned to her.

"Why would he kill himself? He had everything to live for." His breath was of burnt oil scorched in a pan.

"Because the Wolfchild killed his son when he defied my orders to leave her alone." She wanted to crouch and cower in fear. None of this would make him happy, but she couldn't stop the things that came out of her mouth when the master asked.

S'Kotos leaned in even closer, so their noses almost touched. "He did so on my orders."

"I know, Master. I don't understand why, but I know." Again, she wanted to clamp her hand over her mouth or cut out her tongue so she wouldn't have to answer.

"Because the Wolfchild must die," he answered, backing away a little. "She has become too dangerous. I can't afford for her to come into her true power and use the keystones against me, which is why I don't understand why you are heading to Bendanatu to help her." His voice echoed across the field with the power of his anger.

C'Tan quivered. "Master, I only wish to protect our investment. She is our best hope for finding all the keystones. It is her power that reveals them. How can we find them all otherwise?"

S'Kotos growled. "I do not condone this! You take a monumental risk, C'Tan. If she confronts me with the keystones, I will lose everything. Everything!" He leaned close again, placing fiery hands on her shoulders. "You. Will. Not. Fail. Me! Understand?"

C'Tan nodded, struck dumb in his presence. His brutal hand lashed out, striking her full in the face, another to her gut. The blows rained down, such as she'd never endured before. She bit her lip and tasted blood, fighting the urge to cry out. That only made things worse. He kicked, punched, slapped, and burned her until she lay a quivering, sobbing heap amid the flaming grass.

"I marked you, C'Tan. I marked you in the fire that nearly took your life. Do you remember? You are mine. If you fail, I will lose everything." He glanced across the field to the men who stood at the ready next to their dragon mounts, and an evil smile crept across his face. "Here. Let me give you a taste of what may be," he said.

"No!" she cried out, but he laughed. Curled on the ground and facing the wing of dragons, C'Tan watched as one by one, her soldiers dropped to the ground as ashes and bones. Every single one of her men was destroyed in seconds by the thing she called "Master". It was the first time she truly hated him. Not that she cared for the soldiers as men, but they were hers—hers! No one had the right to take them from her, let alone cripple her in front of them. Worst of all, he had just shown how little he cared for her. She knew he had no heart, but he had never shown his cruelty to her directly. There was nothing to draw her to him any longer. He had just destroyed that, and he would pay.

S'Kotos disappeared with the snap of his fingers.

C'Tan lay there and cried quietly. Oh, yes, he would pay.

CHAPTER THIRTY-SIX

The sun hadn't even begun to rise when Kayla awoke, her mind on the coming battle, her heart full of worries and fear. She had led the Ne'Goi here and could do nothing to stop them—nothing but fight alongside her new friends. They had lost so much, facing death herself was nothing if it meant saving the few Bendanatu who remained.

Below Kayla's cave window, people moved about, some wolfen, some human, some phoenixian, and who knew what else. Curious, she made her way down the stairs and joined the group, heading toward the square building where the orphans lived. A hand clasped her shoulder, and she jumped. "Sorry to startle you," came the familiar voice of Chieftain Bahndai. "You'll be joining us in breaking our night fast?"

She looked at him, seeing his outline in the dark, only the moon casting any kind of light. "You mean you get up this early every day?" She couldn't believe it.

He nodded. "Some of us, yes. Most, actually. There are others who stand guard at night who sleep now, so they will join us for lunch or dinner. The eatery is always open."

Kayla's jaw dropped. "It never closes?"

He shook his head. "Never."

They entered the doorway where she had played the two young boys to sleep the day before. Kayla felt a little guilty for doing so, but made her way to a table in the well-lit room. A wide mix of Bendanatu, human, and Phoenixian gathered here—people she knew and desperately needed at the moment for familiarity. A man scooted in next to her. Aldarin. She could tell it was him by the feel of his energy and the smell of burning wood and stone his skin gave off. There was a different kind of energy about him that others did not have, probably from wearing T'Kato's tattoos. His spirit soothed her. She smiled, and he took her hand beneath the table, smiling back, though a bit shy—as if he expected her to thrust his hand away at any moment. But Brant had said he approved. She still felt guilty, but clung to the hand Ember's brother offered her. The tension in his shoulders eased, and he turned to her with his tentative smile. He seemed relieved that she hadn't rejected him.

Food passed from the opposite end of the table. Bowl after plate after steaming spit made their way toward them. Raw meat, cooked meat, tall piles of fluffy pancakes, assorted fruits and vegetables, eggs, and hot cereal—what Kayla's mother used to call mush. People on both sides of the table grabbed whatever they wanted as it came past, but plenty remained by the time things reached her. Kayla took some meat from the spit, several pancakes, fruit, some vegetables, and three eggs still in the shell.

Kayla took an egg in her hand and cracked it on the side of her plate, intending to peel it. Instead of being boiled, as she expected, raw, runny yolk and slimy egg white splattered across her plate, across the table, and onto Shari Bird's hand. Kayla was horrified. She hadn't even realized the woman was there until that moment. The Phoenixian lifted her hand

and watched the egg run down her arm and drip onto the table. She turned pale white, then somehow spun in place and raced out the door of the eatery. Kayla could hear her body purging as she threw up time and time again, sobbing in between.

Kayla's face burned, and her eyes threatened tears. She stared at the mess the egg had made as, one by one, the Phoenixians left the table and walked out the door without touching their food. The tears fell then, and Aldarin let go of her hand to put an arm around her. He whispered into her ear, "Come on. Let's get you cleaned up." She nodded and let him pull her away from the table and toward the kitchen. He spoke to someone, then led her through a curtain and into a private wash area, took her arm, turned on the magic-pumped water, and rinsed away the slime. The tears continued to fall. Kayla had known how sensitive Shari was about losing Ezra. She should have thought before taking an egg. Stupid, stupid, stupid!

Aldarin got her arm and hand cleaned, then gave her a wet rag to scrub her shirt. When she was done, he took the rag, rinsed it again, and wiped her face, erasing the tracks of tears and traces of yolk. He draped the rag over the side of the sink, turned, and took her face in his hands, trying to force her eyes to his. She didn't want to look, but his patience and the intensity of his gaze finally forced her eyes up. He finally spoke. "Do not feel bad, Mishon. You didn't know. It was not your fault."

She couldn't move. His gaze was so electric.

And then it hit her. He had just called her Mishon.

My love.

The tears began once more as she threw herself into his arms and held him tight. Brant had called her 'my love'. But he was gone, and now here was this amazing man, strong, kind, willing to help and defend her at all costs. He'd taken on a burden not his own to help a dying man and now wore tattoos he despised, but tried to use for good. And realization hit her like lightning—I love this man.

Knowing that, feeling that, and letting it linger in her heart this time, she pulled back just enough to look into his eyes. Aldarin and Kayla were nearly equal in height. He reached up and brushed away a tear, then tucked a stray piece of hair behind her ear, stopping on the pointed tip and caressing it with his thumb.

Her heart beat fast, her stomach a mass of butterflies. She couldn't wait for him to take this last step.

Slowly, he leaned in, letting their breath mingle for a moment, and then their lips met with a surge of energy. If Brant's kisses had made the world stop spinning, Aldarin's took her to another realm, far in the reaches of the darkness beyond the sun and moon. The instant their lips met, she felt the unity. Their hearts beat as one, their souls intertwined. It had to be the sharing of their complementary magic. That was the only thing that made sense. It lasted less than a minute, but in that time, her entire world changed.

Brant was not her soul mate. He had been her best friend, yes, but she had mistaken that kind of love for what she felt now with Aldarin.

He was her chosen one. A new best friend who could never take Brant's place, but filled the space in her heart with his own kind of understanding and love. He was everything a true best friend should be.

A soulmate—but not in the way so many others thought of it. This was a man she could confide every thought to, could trust and depend on, lean on in her times of sorrow and know that he would be there—but a man with whom she also wanted to share her heart and soul and kiss all day long.

The kiss broke and she pressed her cheek to his shoulder, the tears still falling, but they were now happy tears. "Don't cry, Mishon," he whispered in her ear, his breath stirring the fine hairs on her face. "It couldn't have been that bad of a kiss, could it?"

Kayla giggled. "Aldarin." She put her hands on the sides of his face, his whiskers a bristly comfort across her palm. "Mishon," she said, repeating his phrase. His eyes were huge. "It was not bad at all." She kissed him softly once more. "That was the most incredible kiss I have ever experienced. It was beautiful," she whispered, resting her cheek against his.

He melted against her. "I know the timing is terrible, but I can't help the way I feel." Kayla Kalandra Felandian, I love you."

She grinned from ear to ear. "Aldarin . . . " She trailed off, then laughed. "I don't know your middle name, or if you even have one."

"Our people don't follow after yours. We have a first name, and then a last name based on our profession, or our father's profession, when we were young. I was once Aldarin Paeder Horsemaster. Then I became Aldarin Mageguard. But for you—" He looked into her eyes and took both her hands. "Vierra. My mother's name was Vierra. Aldarin Vierra Paeder," he said with pride.

Kayla was touched. "You don't have to do that," she whispered.

"I know," was all he said in return. He squeezed her hand and led her back out to the table where they had been sitting. Most of the people were gone, so Kayla didn't have to relive the embarrassment of her mistake. Someone had cleaned the egg from her place and left her a clean plate with food nearby. Kayla reached for the food and filled her plate once again, something bothering her until she finally asked Aldarin, "Why in the world were there raw eggs on the table? Especially with Phoenixians in the room? That was either mean or in poor taste." She stabbed a strawberry and put the whole thing in her mouth.

Aldarin didn't answer. His mouth was full, but he pointed down the table, and Kayla followed his finger. Near the middle of the long table, a Bendanatu sat sucking on the end of an egg. Several empty shells lay nearby. His mouth finally empty, Aldarin said, "I think they are a delicacy here. The Bendanatu seem to love them raw." Kayla watched the man pick up another egg, and using the tip of a sharp knife, bore a hole in each end, placing a finger over the open end. When ready, he tipped the egg up and sucked the liquid from inside.

Kayla shuddered. Bad enough watching him eat raw eggs, but knowing what it must have felt like for Shari Bird was horrifying. Cooked or raw, the eggs needed to be put away so long as the Phoenixians were in Bendanatu. She needed to speak to someone before the next meal or the Phoenixians were going to have to eat somewhere else. The Bendanatu, for all their welcome and courtesy, seemed oblivious to the dietary needs and sensitivities of others.

Kayla's stomach growled at her, now that she had a plan in place and was calming from the egg issue. She wished her stomach was more in tune to the needs of her heart, but it worked on its own time, and right now, she needed to eat.

It seemed Kayla couldn't get enough, that her appetite had finally reached a bottomless state, and she'd be hungry forever. Aldarin finished long before her and sat and watched with a growing smile as she devoured plate after plate of food. Finally, there was little left around her and she felt full. That was an incredible relief. She sat back and let out an enormous belch—in Evahn culture, the best compliment she could give the chef. Aldarin laughed.

"What?" she asked, genuinely confused.

He stopped his laughter and bit his lips. "Nothing. That took me by surprise, is all."

She shook her head, then stood and made her way to the kitchen to find the cook. Rhoanald and Dawnna were there with a dozen or so younglings. Kayla told them about the incident with the egg and Shari Bird's reaction. The two looked embarrassed. "We hadn't even thought of it, to be honest," Dawnna said. "We'll take eggs off the menu until the Phoenixians are gone. Thank you for telling us."

"Thank you. I know it will mean much to my Phoenixian friends, especially the one who lost her son recently." She shook their hands and left the room, winding her way past the tables and out the door into the beautiful light of sunrise. She stopped for a moment, closed her eyes, and let the sun soak into her. Aldarin said nothing, but took her hand and stood with her for a long moment. It made her smile to feel him so close, both in body and soul. She didn't know how she had missed it before. Probably because she was determined to cling to Brant, despite his lack of a body and losing himself.

They made their way back to Bahndai's caverns and eventually into his meeting room, where it seemed everyone she knew had gathered. The two found an empty corner and settled themselves on a large, flat pillow that kept away the cold from the stone floor and provided a bit of padding for her saddle-sore backside.

Bahndai spoke to the two of them. "I was just informing your family and friends here about the things that have taken place before. The Ne'Goi have attacked our village many times, always destroying my people with ease. Nothing has worked in the battle against them. Not magic. Not arrows. Not traps. Not direct attack. Nothing. Many have left to find help, but none have returned. My son, White Shadow, has informed me of the loss of a large group who traveled with him. They were our greatest hope for success." Bahndai sat forward, looking down as he pursed his lips, then quietly said, "I do not know how we can win a single battle, let alone this war with the shadow weavers. They are indestructible."

Kayla spoke up. "Sir—"

"Grandfather," he insisted.

It felt strange, but she honored his wishes. "Grandfather." He smiled. "There is a way to destroy them. We fought them in Karsholm, and though there were many casualties, we defeated them there. We have engaged them on our journey here and lost not a single soul."

Bahndai looked up, his eyes intense. "Tell me."

And so she did, recounting the battle in Karsholm, describing how the Ne'Goi ate magic as if it were air to breathe. "The secret to defeating them is not to use magic against them."

He growled. "We've tried that! It doesn't work."

She grinned. "I didn't say don't use magic. I said don't use magic against them."

Bahndai cocked his head. "How is that possible?"

"By using the magic on things around them, things that can do damage. It is much more difficult to stop a sharpened tree from flying at you with magical force than to eat a fireball. Rocks. Trees. Boulders. Arrows. Fire. Sticks. Glass. Anything sharp, anything that can attack. We can use anything that can be lifted and thrown with magic against them." Kayla leaned back against the cool stone wall.

Bahndai looked skeptical. "So we can't send magic against them directly. We can't send weapons against them directly with no magic. Only the two combined will kill them?"

Kayla nodded.

The chieftain looked thoughtful. "White Shadow, DeMunth, have you found this to be true?" Both of the warriors nodded.

White Shadow spoke. "It is absolute truth, Father. The force of the magic not only seems to send the objects toward them with incredible speed and force, but somehow using the magic attaches something to the objects—something that makes the hungry Ne'Goi lower their defenses unwittingly. I have seen it kill them many, many times."

Bahndai nodded, then began to smile. It wasn't a pretty one, his sharp canines showing. "That is good to know. Very good to know."

Kayla had a thought. "Sir—I mean, Grandfather—I have been here for hours and have yet to see my cousin Ember. Has something happened?"

Bahndai looked distraught. "Well, yes—but no," he said, looking to the others for help. Nobody spoke up. DeMunth sat stiff and stoic, his jaw locked and eyes angry. He looked ready to chew stone. The chieftain sighed. "She came searching for the Emerald Wolf and she found the entrance to the maze where it is guarded. Unfortunately, five young Ne'Goi came to our camp disguised as humans in need of help, and when Ember, Tyese, and Keyera opened the door to the maze, the young shadow weavers darted through. The girls followed after, and the door sealed behind them."

Kayla sat up straight. "You mean she is in the caves with not one, but five Ne'Goi? And she's in there with only two young Bendanatu as companion warriors?"

Bahndai nodded slowly. "We tried to pursue them, but the maze would not let us pass. I do not know why the Ne'Goi were allowed to enter, but not her protectors." DeMunth growled at Bahndai's words, and now his demeanor made sense. He was Ember's guard, and he could not help her. He must be going mad with worry and fear. She shot him a sympathetic look.

"If Ember can find the Emerald Wolf and use it in time, she can help us win this war. If not—" He left it hanging, but Kayla knew what he meant. "If not" meant she would be dead. Ember had known that going in, but she hadn't planned to take anyone with her. Why Tyese and Keyera? What was Ember thinking? There had to be a reason, but Kayla couldn't see it. Before she could ask, DeMunth reluctantly spoke, explaining what had happened to Ember's bracelets and how Tyese and Keyera became involved.

He continued. "All three of the Emerald keystone keys must be present when opening the maze and searching for the Emerald Wolf. Ember had no choice but to take the girls."

Kayla shook her head. So many things going wrong. So many people dying. She hoped with all her heart Ember wouldn't be one of them.

Bahndai broke the long silence with a clap of his hands, rubbing them together. "So! What do we do to prepare for this battle? Let's use the time we've got and make this a war the Ne'Goi will never forget."

CHAPTER THIRTY-SEVEN

The five creatures that approached the girls looked nothing like the boys who had entered the cavern. Part hyena, part boar, with rows of jagged teeth in a frog-like mouth—more shark than anything—the creatures lurched closer. Their tailless hindquarters and lanky legs put their back end higher in the air than the front. Bodies thick with wiry hair, surrounded slightly canine faces, but with wide mouths that seemed capable of swallowing a man whole. They moved in bounds and leaps, yipping and snarling as they raced toward Ember, Keyera, and Tyese. The younger girls had both gone wolf the instant they spotted the young shadow weavers and though Ember was tempted to change herself, all she could focus on was those teeth and the young wolf cubs racing toward them.

Fear for the girls overwhelmed her instinct, and instead of attacking with her teeth, as she was wont to do, she used the same tactics she'd used in the battle at Karsholm. She used her magic to gather up anything sharp, anything hard, and threw them at the Ne'Goi. Pebbles, sand, head-sized stones all catapulted into the bodies of the attackers, throwing them back and halting their progress. One lay on the ground, blood seeping into the sand, a jagged stone near his head and gashes on his skull.

With grim satisfaction, she pulled her focus back into herself and reached for another round of ammunition.

The girls met three of the Ne'Goi in a collision that should have killed the girls and left Ember alone with the shadow weavers, but Tyese and Keyera were more wily and experienced than she'd realized. They twisted in the air, grabbing hold of the Ne'Goi by the back of their necks and landed on their shoulders, biting furiously where the shadow weaver boys could not reach them because of their short necks. The girls couldn't kill them like that, but they could do some damage, and it distracted two of the enemy long enough for Ember to gather ammunition. Instead of using stones that might hurt the girls, she sought the cave spikes high above her, and found two that were small enough to break but heavy enough to do what had to be done. She waited for the Ne'Goi to be directly beneath them, then pulled on the spikes and guided them in a free fall toward the two shadow weavers. She yelled at the girls. "Off! Now!"

The girls flung themselves from the backs of the Ne'Goi and the spikes hit just as Ember willed. They pinned the two creatures to the sand, large cave spikes completely impaled through their bodies. They each coughed blood, whimpered, their lips drawing back from the rows of teeth as they cried out, sounding eerily like screaming children—and then the sound cut off. Their heads hung silent and still.

The remaining Shadow Weavers looked at each other, then at Ember. She pulled several more cave spikes from the roof to rain toward the last two boys, but they moved before the weapons could reach their target. Sharp stones falling around them, they dove into the water and disappeared, a few brief bubbles marking their trail.

Ember looked at the surrounding carnage—all that was left of three young men who would never grow old. They had followed a dark master and paid for it with their lives. Such a tragic waste should matter, but honestly, she was just too exhausted to care. She was tired. Bone weary. Sucked completely dry.

Ember staggered and fell to her side, staring at nothing. Tyese and Keyera raced toward her in their wolf forms, transforming back to human just before reaching her.

"Are you all right?" Keyera asked as Tyese knelt and stared at Ember, brow wrinkled and eyes full of worry.

Ember shook herself like a dog. "I'm not injured, no." The girls looked at each other with some kind of understanding and went to work. Tyese gathered driftwood that had come from somewhere outside the cavern, placing it in a large pile close to Ember. Keyera went to the dark lake and stood still, watching the water, then swiped a fish from below the small waves in a blur of motion. It landed in the dirt a few feet away and Keyera went back to her attentive stance.

Tyese collected the thrashing thing and put it out of its misery with a smack against a nearby rock. Keyera sent another fish her way shortly after, and they continued the pattern for a good half hour, Ember watching but barely aware. She wasn't sure if it was the smell of the fish, the dead Ne'Goi, or remnants from her poisoning, but she just couldn't seem to focus, much as she tried. She felt nothing. So she let the girls gather the fish and hoped she'd be able to contribute more later. All she wanted to do at the moment was go to sleep and forget the entire day.

Tyese crouched down and stared at the stacked driftwood with fierce intensity. Ripples of glowing embers spread over the logs like molten lava coursed through their veins before they burst into fire. The girls put the fish on spits and set them over the flames. In the back of her mind, Ember knew they did this for her. They were Bendanatu and would probably like the fish raw. All Bendanatu did. Except for Ember—but then, she hadn't been raised as a wolf.

The fish cooked swiftly, and the smell brought Ember back to herself. That happened completely the moment they placed a spit of fish in her hands and she bit into the delicate flesh. It was hot, and with the first bite, she sucked in and nearly inhaled the fish. Choking, she pursed her lips and tried to cool the food in her mouth. She burned her tongue a dozen times over, but kept eating. Her stomach growled, and she devoured the meal without seasoning or variety. Ember didn't keep track of exact numbers, but looking at the piles of sticks beside each of them, Ember ate the largest portion.

Once the fish were gone, she licked her fingers clean and scooted closer to the fire. The three of them sat quietly like that for a bit before Tyese glanced down at the strange underground beach and asked, "What about them? What do we do with the bodies?" She voiced the one thing Ember didn't want to face at the moment, but they couldn't just leave them there.

Ember sighed and got to her feet. "Come on. Let's get this over with. We can at least drag them back into the rocks where we don't have to look at them."

Tyese and Keyera followed her, Tyese casting a magelight as they neared the spot where the first Ne'Goi had fallen. "What in the world?" Ember said. She stepped closer to the rock that had hit the shadow weaver's head and Tyese, ever accommodating, brought the magelight closer.

The Ne'Goi was gone. A black, greasy stain in the shape of his body was all that remained, with ash settled over the outline. Stunned, Ember moved to the place the other two bodies had been, only to find much the same. Black stains and ash in the shape of their bodies, the cave spikes tipped on their sides. Ember looked at the girls. "Have you ever seen anything like this?"

Keyera shook her head, but Tyese nodded. "In the battle that took my parents. I saw things like this, but didn't know what it was. We took their lives too. There were no bodies, so I never knew. I never knew," she repeated, nearly whispering.

Ember chewed at the corner of her lip in thought. "So this is a Ne'Goi trait, something seen only among the shadow weavers. I wonder where their bodies go, and why. Does it strengthen their leader somehow? Or are they so full of corruption that it eats their remains in death?"

Tyese shrugged, though Ember had really only been asking herself the question. "Does it matter?"

Ember hesitated. "I don't know. Perhaps."

Ember blinked as a raindrop caught in her lashes. Another drop traced down her cheek as she lifted her face to the ceiling. Rain? In a cave? The drops trickled into a deluge, and in seconds it soaked the girls through. Driftwood swirled as water from the small lake rose. Panic surged in Ember's throat, but she stuffed it down. This was obviously another test. A piece of ceiling fell, and a waterfall poured through, changing the ground into a roiling cauldron as water covered their ankles, knees, and then waists in less than a minute.

The water surged to her hips, and she gritted her teeth—only minutes more until she'd be dead. If only there was a way for her to breathe underwater, she could have the time she needed to find a way out.

Breathe underwater. The stories Kayla told her came to mind. She'd been given gills. Ember had seen them. Kayla had told her there was air inside the water and the gills found it. They let the lungs absorb the air and let the water pass through. She understood the concept, but this was something she could mess up so easily. Her memory of the accident in the orange classroom came to mind. Her power was strong, but uncontrolled. How could she do this?

What choice did she have?

Well, she would be her own test subject before trying it on the girls. Concentrating, Ember went to that place in her mind that allowed her body to change the way she wanted it. She pictured the gills on a fish and imagined them on her neck behind her ear, much like Kayla's. She felt the change happen as slits tore within her skin. It hurt a bit, but if it would save their lives, it was worth the pain. With a grin, she ducked her head underwater and let the water in through the gills.

She came up spluttering and choking.

Okay, she was missing something, and she was running out of time. The water had risen to their chins, and they were treading water now, the girls frantic in their cries. "Just stay close to me. I'm working on something," Ember said. The girls listened, whimpering.

Something brushed Ember's knee, and she reached down, unthinking, to find a fish nibbling at her boot tops. Instead of darting away as fish usually do, it stayed under her touch. Ember felt a feather of thought coming from the little being and pursued it. The simple mind of a fish fed her memories. Laying eggs in the sand. Nibbling on plants at the bottom. The feel of water flowing through gills and mouth. The heaviness in the lungs. All happy things.

Ember pulled her mind away and thought about what she'd just seen. Eggs and plants didn't matter, but the heaviness in the lungs, the feel of water through mouth and gills—those things were important. The connection between the mouth, lungs, and gills was missing. She used her magic to examine the fish and saw the problem. She had the connection from lungs to gills, but not mouth to lungs, and a change needed to be made there to allow air to filter into the lungs and the water to be expelled through the gills. A small shift, but an important one. She pulled the magic in and slowly made the change, then ducked her head below water once again, opened her mouth, and, against all her better judgment, breathed in.

Her body fought it at first. She felt like she was drowning and she kicked and thrashed, wanting to rise back to the surface, but she made herself stay down. She was still alive. That meant it was working, right? Ember calmed herself and made a few other modifications to her hands, so they became webbed. She removed her boots and socks and tucked them into her belt, then changed her feet to imitate a fish's fin, only sideways. She moved much faster under the water that way.

Once satisfied, she surfaced near the girls. They screamed when she came up. "We thought you were dead!" Tyese sobbed.

"That you'd given up," Keyera finished for the younger girl.

Ember grinned. "Nope. I just found a way for us to survive this trial. Come here, Tyese. This is going to hurt a little." She made the same changes to Tyese that she had to herself, having the girl remove her boots and socks, and then did the same for Keyera. "Okay. This is the hardest part of all. I need you to go underwater and breathe through your mouth." The girls immediately objected, but Ember would have none of it. "Do you want to live? Then do it!" She didn't leave them any choice when she dove beneath the water and waited for them.

It took a few minutes, but Keyera put her head under the water and breathed, jerking back out first, then trying again and finally staying.

Tyese took a little longer and then ducked under the water all at once, holding her breath at first and sinking, then finally gasping for air as if drowning. She did just as Ember had, kicking and thrashing, but Ember and Keyera raced over and held her under the water long enough for the panic to pass. Once it did, a look of wonder came over her face. She examined her hands and feet, and tentatively moved forward. Then she surged far and fast with a single flip of her feet. She turned around and tried to say something, but the sound from her mouth was unintelligible. Ember hadn't thought of that. Communication was going to be a challenge.

Well, there were always hand signals. And mindspeech.

Signaling for the girls to join her, she mimicked swimming around the perimeter and looking for an exit, wanting to test the hand signals. It took a few tries, but the girls finally understood, and they began a swim around the edge of the cavern looking for a way out. It was a much larger cavern than she had originally thought, but when they had gone a full circle and come back to their starting place, they began to panic. They had found nothing. They swam up the walls, thinking there might be something higher up, but again, nothing.

As a last resort, they swam to the floor of the cavern and began scouring it for anything that might look like an exit. They started on the outside edges and worked their way inward, spiraling toward the middle. As they got close to the center of the spiral, they saw a white light flashing. Drawn to the light, the girls swam directly to the center and stopped, puzzled, as they stared at a stone cube about three feet square floating in the water, a magelight hovering over it. There was a small door on each side, including the bottom, each with a symbol on it.

Not wanting to believe it, Ember realized that this was their exit.

Why couldn't anything be easy?

CHAPTER THIRTY-EIGHT

Kayla crouched down behind the netted blind the Moninger Guard had set up with vines, leaves, and branches, so it looked incredibly natural, but still allowed her to see. "You've got dozens of these throughout the woods, you say?" she asked.

The four boys and two girls who protected Bendanatu nodded as one, grinning with their canines showing.

"Can you set up some more down in the village?" she asked.

They huddled together and had a short, muttered conversation before turning toward her. The dark-haired boy who seemed to be their leader spoke. "We think so. It will be a lot harder because of the open land and stone instead of all the trees, but we should be able to work something out—if we have enough time."

And that was the clincher. No one knew exactly how much time they had to prepare for this battle. Kayla startled at every sound, terrified it was the Ne'Goi coming before they were ready. She needed every bit of knowledge these boys had. A sly grin spread across her face. "Would a little magic help with your disguises?"

The lead boy's eyes widened. A sly grin spread, and he nodded thoughtfully. "So long as it's something the Ne'Goi can't see through, yeah, I think it would. Is there anyone who can do orange magic, so it's actual change and not just an illusion?"

Kayla thought of Aldarin with all those orange tattoos and nodded. "I think we just might."

Sweat rolled off Aldarin's back—his shirt soaked and discarded long ago. As his forehead beaded with moisture, Kayla watched his muscles flex and relax in turn as he wrestled the orange magic inside. Power tempered by uncertainty, his body strained to master the magic she asked for. There was no doubting his strength. At all. A nervous kind of happiness skittered through her insides; he did it all for her.

"Kayla," he said, slightly exasperated, by the sound of it. "I've got a hold of the magic. Now what do I do with it?" The sweat rolled down his face like raindrops on a window.

She pulled her gaze from his torso and focused. "Touch the blind. Tell it to look like stone. Not to make it stone, just *look* like stone. Make the colors the same so it blends in. Put the picture in your mind and then tell it to change.

"Like, actually tell it. Say 'change.'"

"Yep."

He shrugged, turned back to the net, and grabbed hold of it with his powerful hands. He closed his eyes a moment, concentration furrowing his brow as orange lights raced over his tattoos like glowing embers through coal. His chest swelled with breath, and he yelled, "Change!"

Oh, and change it did! Stone flowed across the net, covering it completely. It was a total success—except that Aldarin's hands were embedded in that stone. He couldn't stand up. Panic flashed through his eyes as he turned to her.

Kayla fought the laughter that welled up from her belly and threatened to burst out of her mouth. "Okay, it looks like stone, that's for sure."

He growled. "That's because it *is* stone," he said through clenched teeth.

Kayla giggled, then got herself under control. "Okay. Try this. Imagine the stone like water. There, but able to pass through it. Just put some kind of skin on it or it will splash through the net. Go slow. Feel the change."

Aldarin steeled himself and spread his legs for balance. The furrow in his brow returned and the surface of the stone rippled. It moved like jelly that had set too hard. His hands pulled out an inch or so and stopped. He grunted, pulling until his veins bulged, but nothing happened.

Kayla put a hand on his shoulder, and he relaxed. "You're trying too hard. Feel the change. Make it feel like soft custard and ask it to release your hands."

The tattooed man cocked his head at her and his posture eased. He stared at the spot where his hands were embedded in tar-like stone and slowly, like a straw pulled from cold molasses, his hands came free. The instant his fingers hit the air, he staggered back, breathing hard, wiping a hand across his dripping brow. "Who knew magic could be this hard?"

Doing all she could not to laugh, Kayla tested the "boulder" in front of her. It was thin, movable, transparent, and, most importantly, impermeable. It would be a great place to hide when things got dangerous. A gradual smile radiated across her face and Kayla squeezed Aldarin's perspiring shoulder. "You did it! Perfect. Now we just need you to do that seventeen more times. Think you can do it?" His super-heated skin almost burned and she pulled her hand away, self- conscious.

Aldarin groaned, then picked up his shirt, tucked it through his belt, and gestured forward. "Lead the way, my lady."

One of the Moningers approached her, and she beckoned him closer while replying to Aldarin. "I would love to, but I have to instruct some of the others in setting up traps and poisoning weapons. This gentleman will guide you to the rest. Just do what you did here, and it will all be good."

His smile fell, but he followed the boy, glancing over his shoulder by way of farewell.

Kayla headed toward the orphanage, then navigated through the eatery and to the kitchen. "How go things here?"

Dawnna stirred a steaming pot, her face positioned away from the contents. "I wouldn't say exactly well, but we have done as you asked. Does this have to smell so terrible?" She coughed.

Kayla tried to smile, but it was hard in the toxic landscape of the kitchen. "I'm afraid so. Between poison and pitch for the arrows and stakes, it may smell bad, but could very well be the thing that turns this war. I appreciate your trial on our behalf." Kayla was trying very hard to be tactful when in reality, her heart whispered doubts to her mind. *It's pointless. What you are doing is a waste of time and will only slow them down, not do any real damage. We're going to die!* But she swallowed the bitter words. She was here to offer encouragement—support—not bring them down into despair. Everyone had to feel as if what they did was important, and those in the kitchen were no different.

"I'll never be able to use these pots again," Dawnna mumbled. "Wasted. Pots this size don't come cheap. But then, if we don't survive, it won't matter, anyway." She clamped her lips shut when some of the younglings glanced at her.

Afraid the girls may have heard, Kayla turned back to Dawnna and pointed at some of the young Bendanatu. "Are you using these three at the moment? I could really use some hands setting up the other weapons. And is any of the poison or pitch ready?"

Dawnna waved without saying a word, pointing at four pots sitting by the back door. Kayla beckoned for the girls to each take a pot and follow her up the hill outside, to where the young men had been sharpening thick stakes and laying them on the ground in neat rows. The girls set their buckets down with relief and backed away. Kayla took from her belt three sticks with strips of cloth tied to the ends and gave one to each of the girls. She pointed at the stakes. "Take a bucket of poison, dip your brush into it, and slather it on the sharp ends of the stakes to about three feet down from the point."

The girls looked at the pile as if it was impossible.

"You can do it," Kayla said with false confidence. "It won't take as long as you think. Just be sure not to get any of the poison on your face and especially not in your mouth or eyes. It will kill you." The girls looked at each and then the buckets with cautious respect. Then, acting like the Bendanatu warriors they were, they shrugged and got to work.

Kayla picked up half a dozen stakes once the poison was applied, and carried them to the men and boys standing nearby. "Where do you want these placed?"

One of the men, Justesen, she thought, turned to her. "Well, we had a thought, Miss Kayla. It would be more work, but I think it could be really effective. Really effective." He rubbed his hands, his eyes lit up with excitement.

"Okay." Kayla set down the stakes and turned her attention to the tall man. "Tell me what you have in mind."

"Pits," he said, as if very pleased with himself.

"Pardon?" Kayla asked, thoroughly confused.

He spread his hands. "Dig pits. Put the sharp stakes in the bottom. Put some dirt in or stone. If someone can do orange magic, then cover it up with a net and leaves or grass, so it looks natural. They step on it, fall in, and get impaled and poisoned at once. What do you think?"

Kayla bit her tongue. Time was of the essence, and this man wanted to complicate things with an elaborate plan that would take days to implement. She didn't want to deflate him or toss away his idea, but how would it even be possible? What if the Ne'Goi came tomorrow? Tonight? In an hour? Everything had to be simple.

Something occurred to her, and she stiffened. It was a good plan, a great idea, really, but she was so used to thinking of things in physical hours that she often forgot her other tools. She had magic. She had control over the power of air—wind, temperature, elementals and more. Why couldn't they dig the holes and move the stakes? For that matter, why couldn't someone use their magic to sharpen the stakes and speed things up? She shook her head at herself.

Justesen's face fell. He must have thought she disliked the idea.

She smiled at him, putting her hand on his shoulder. "I think it's brilliant." The man beamed. "I just had to work out the logistics. If we are going to do this, and fast, we have to use magic. If we dig holes by hand, we'll be at it for days."

"Well, of course!" the tall man said, sounding offended.

Kayla chuckled and shook her head. "Okay, then! Let's get to work. If I handle the holes and freeze the stakes into place, can you and your team position them?"

Justesen nodded.

With the new plan in place, Kayla turned to the ground near the stakes, the girls continuing to slather the stakes with poison and set them aside. Pulling her attention away from the others, Kayla directed it to the flute and to Brant within. He surged from the flute in an instant, ready to work. The flute most likely knew what she needed already, which meant Brant knew as well. "Are you ready to dig some holes?" she asked.

With a devious grin and nod, Brant spun. Faster and faster he went, until Kayla's hair was a snarled mass and she almost had to grab the trees to keep from being pulled forward. Once he was up to speed, Brant pushed down against the earth, dust and debris flying around them. Everyone backed away, taking cover behind the trees. Brant sank slowly into the ground until he disappeared entirely for a bit. Kayla was beginning to worry, but then he surged back to the top, and, still spinning, his echoing voice asked, "More? Do I need to dig more?" He sounded as if there could be nothing better in the world. Her heart panged. He lost more of himself every day. She hated seeing it—but there was no time to dwell on it.

"Yes, Brant. I need—" she glanced at Justesen. He mouthed a number, and she continued. "Twenty-seven more holes. Can you do that for me?"

"Yes, Mistress. Where do you desire these holes?" he asked in that deep monotone.

She looked across the area to see. There were people sharpening stakes in nearly every direction. "Anywhere you see a pile of sharpened stakes. Make some holes bigger, some smaller. Can you do that?" He didn't answer, but took off for the next location, the men working there running away as he approached. She wanted to laugh. She probably should have warned them before sending an air elemental their way, especially one as powerful as Brant.

She turned back to the hole that had already been formed to find the gloved men lowering the stakes into the ground in random patterns, leaving about six feet from the end of the stake to the top of the hole. A net had somehow been attached to the wall and held the stakes straight up. Kayla shivered. This was a nasty trap. She was certainly grateful she wasn't a Ne'Goi.

Pulling the flute from its case at her side, Kayla played, first drawing wind into the hole, dragging some of the refuse that had flown out in its digging back in, just enough to hold the stakes in position. Changing her tune, she pulled moisture into the upper layers of dirt, then used the song of cold to freeze it into place. With a magical twist, she locked it so the ice was as solid as stone. Someone pulled a rope, releasing the net, and drew it up the side of the pit. The men criss-crossed thin sticks across the top, then loaded them with grass still embedded in the soil, even adding some growing flowers and fallen leaves to the disguise.

When they were done, the pit seemed indistinguishable from the surrounding area. It was almost as good as an illusion. Actually, it was better than illusion—and there was no way the shadow weavers could detect it until they fell through the roof and onto the stakes.

As a final precaution, she set up a barrier that would activate for anyone and anything that was not Ne'Goi. It would be impossible for any of the Bendanatu to fall in by mistake.

Only twenty-seven more to freeze in place. Maybe they had a chance in this battle after all. A small one, but a chance was a chance.

She'd take it.

CHAPTER THIRTY-NINE

After nearly an hour of swimming around the cube and finding no clue as to how to activate the doors, Ember stopped and stilled her mind, floating in the water as if she'd been born there. A stone. Six doors, each divided and too small to enter. Symbols on each side. She stopped. The symbols—those she could decipher. One door for each of the six colors of magic, but why were they divided? What was she supposed to do? And even if she could open one of the doors, how could they fit through it? And where would they go? The cube wasn't connected to anything. It hovered in the water. It would move in a circle if pushed even gently, but would not stray from its position above the ground.

She mentally shook herself. It had to come back to the doors. Maybe the cube itself wasn't the exit, but was the key to the exit? Again, she didn't know—but she had to get those doors open somehow. She took what she thought was a deep breath and almost choked with the water entering her lungs. Sometimes she forgot that her body was extracting air from the water and would convulse with the influx of heavy liquid.

Once she had herself under control, she moved closer to the cube to examine the doors again. This time she stuck with just one. It had the volcanic symbol for change chiseled above it. The door itself was about two feet tall and just as wide, arched, with a large circle in the center as if it were a window.

Something moved in that stone window, and she looked closer. Her heart beat a little faster. She could have sworn the picture in the window had been an owl but a moment before. Now a lizard blinked at her from the circle.

Blinked.

Ember pulled back for a second, then leaned in closer until her nose was almost against the pane. The lizard turned its head to meet her eyes, its tongue flickering in and out, then scampered in a circle within the boundaries of the stone window.

She almost pulled away again, her heart beating a fast rhythm now. The lizard glanced at her once more, then, mid tongue flicker, it transformed into a snake that hissed and curled in upon itself in a defensive posture, almost as if it would strike at her.

So the window within the door was about change. That made sense—the symbol was all about the magic of change and shifting. Okay, so what about the door itself? She looked closer at the gray stone carved to look like wood. It was surrounded by movement held in stasis. Birds and Phoenixians in flight. A squirrel stopped mid leap between trees. A herd of deer running across a meadow. All of that and more. It was as if someone had caught an instant of movement and imprinted it upon the stone.

Now she did pull back, her mind racing. A door stuck in stasis, but depicting movement. A window of stone with changing creatures that moved within the circle. Could it be? This was two elements of the same color of magic held within one door. Did the other doors hold the same concept? She quickly glanced at them, but couldn't be sure. The door of orange magic seemed the most obvious, so that was where she would start. If she was right, she had to find a way to balance the two opposite aspects of that particular color of magic at the same time. That meant freezing the moving and changing creature in the window while freeing the movement of the animals and plants on the rest of the door. Change and stasis at the same time.

Oh, boy.

It seemed an impossible task, and yet she had accomplished it with air in healing herself of the poison earlier. So why not now? If this was the next test, she had to try.

Taking another deep breath, this time not choking, she set her mind to the task at hand. At least she was familiar with orange magic. It was what controlled her ability to shift form and read minds. But this kind of control—she held her breath for a moment to calm the panic that swept over her. She could do this. Mahal had given her the gift of white magic and she was meant to use it. If he had such faith in her, shouldn't she have that kind of faith in herself? She wanted to, but wow, it was hard.

She stopped, the emotion overwhelming her. She had to rid herself of it completely for the moment. Let go of the fear and self-doubt or she would never succeed. For her mother's freedom. For Mahal. For her world, Rasann. She needed the Emerald Wolf, and it could only be found if she passed these tests.

Using a technique Lily had taught her, Ember breathed deeply, water or air, it didn't matter. She calmed herself and focused her thoughts on the stone. Only on the stone. All other thoughts, feelings, and desires floated away as a kite on the wind. There was only the stone, and upon that stone was a door. One door. Only one mattered for now. The orange door of change, no matter that it had no color. It was the orange door.

To begin, she focused on freeing the animals held in stasis. She pulled energy to her and fed it slowly into the stone door, imagining movement. Nothing happened for a long while and the frustration built, but she remembered Lily's teachings and let the frustration go. The door. Focus on the door, she told herself. She continued to feed the orange magic into the stone and push the picture in her mind into some form of life. Still, nothing happened.

And then, the trees began to move in the invisible wind. She focused harder and fed the magic a little faster. A flock of birds erupted from the stone trees and circled in the sky. The deer leaped across the door and out of sight. The squirrel completed its jump, the branch it landed upon dipping and swaying with the weight. Satisfied, Ember twisted the magic and locked it into place. The door glowed a brilliant, magma-rich orange, though it gave off no heat.

Turning her attention to the round window, Ember was surprised to see that the figure had changed once again. This time it was a beautiful wolf, shaped much like Uncle Shad. That didn't help. The idea of putting such a beautiful creature or someone she loved in stasis was appalling. She couldn't do it.

And yet she had to.

Pulling more of the orange magic to her, she focused on the wolf. He sat up and howled, fighting the stasis spell she tried so hard to lock upon him. He glared at her and snarled, then changed into a mountain lion, tail lashing back and forth. It got easier now with the wolf gone, but the mountain lion gathered itself to spring. Startled, Ember pushed at the animal, shoving it into the stone. It stopped moving, frozen in place at last. She once again twisted and locked the magic into place, then backed away.

The window glowed the same beautiful orange, and then the whole door shifted until it no longer looked made of stone, but as if it were wood. A door with moving images, and a transparent window with a mountain lion gathered to strike etched in its glass.

The door swung open.

One down, five to go.

Now that she understood what she was supposed to do, she turned the cube, searching for another door that would be nearly as simple as the orange had been. There wasn't one, but she had an idea about the blue door and so tried that one next. The symbol of wind above the door showed air going in and out of a mouth. If the orange door had been about movement and stasis, it made sense that the blue door was about pushing and pulling at the same time while using wind. This was a new one for her. Kayla was more familiar with the blue magic than Ember was, but Ember had been born to use all magic, so try she would.

This door had no window, but instead, was divided in half the middle split from side to side. The top showed air breathed in, or in other words, suction, and the bottom showed air blowing out, or wind. She focused first on the bottom, pulling the color of blue to her and filling her energy well. She reached out a hand, touched the bottom of the door, and exhaled. The wind immediately began. Just a breeze, but a start. She put her focus on the upper half of the door and, again touching it, inhaled, and though it was water entering her lungs, she felt a current pulling against her. The door lit up blue, just as the orange had, and opened.

Well, that was easier than I expected.

That was really neat, Tyese mindspoke from over Ember's shoulder.

Ember spun. She'd forgotten all about the girls in her focus on the stone. She smiled once her heart calmed. *Thank you. Now if I can just figure out how to open the rest of these, maybe we can get out of here.* She refocused on the cube and turned it again, looking for another simple door.

Tyese touched her on the shoulder. *I have an idea,* she said, a bit shy.

Oh? Let's hear it, Ember said.

Well, you know my main magic is yellow, right?

Ember nodded.

Well, yellow is all about light. And what's the opposite of light? she asked, a twinkle in her eye.

Ember laughed. It was so obvious. *Darkness. Tyese, you're brilliant! Thank you!* She quickly turned back to the stone and found the door with the symbol for light overhead. This one had a window in the door, much like the orange door, but this window was rectangular and ran almost the entire length, from top to bottom, with only a narrow strip of "wood" framing it. The window had lines crossing it into patterns like stained glass. This had to be the place for light, then. She could not imagine a darkened window, especially one so beautiful.

Pulling the color of yellow was not too hard after spending so much time with DeMunth. Her heart panged. She missed him, and could no more help the feelings she had for him than she could stop the moon from shining.

She pulled the yellow magic to her and focused it slowly toward the window, infusing the glass with light so it glowed from within. When it was full, she twisted and locked the magic into place and admired the beauty before her. Light shone, yes, but not just sunshine yellow. It held the color in all its shades, from the palest cream to mustard to nearly brown, and all of them beautiful. It formed a geometric pattern of the symbol for light—a circle with arrows pointed downward, a half diamond at the bottom. It was stunning.

But now it was time to turn her attention to the door. It reflected the light of the window, and that could not be. It must be dark. Pure dark. Black showed off all colors at their very best, and what better time to use it than now?

More yellow magic, but this time she pulled it from the door itself, creating a void of light darker than the deepest cavern. When she could not pull anymore light from the door, she twisted it and locked it into place. The door glowed around the edges and through the glass until it seemed almost real and opened into a room filled with white light.

Excited now, Ember moved on to another door. Green? No, that one was still beyond her. Purple? Maybe. But it was the red that called her next. She had already used fire and ice this day. It seemed simple to do so once again, and she was right. The red was nearly as quick and simple as the blue. With the window covered in ice and the wood aflame, the door opened. Purple was much the same. The window became an island in a sea of door. Once the light of purple arrived, Ember knew she was nearly done.

All that remained was the green, and it puzzled and frustrated her. How could she be so close and yet not understand this one last door? The girls had stayed back and remained silent most of this time, but perhaps now was the time to use their wisdom, young though they might be. Tyese had proven herself with the yellow. Perhaps they could see something Ember could not in her rush to finish the task. She turned and beckoned to the girls. Immediately they surged closer, floating in the water.

I am stuck, Ember admitted. *I don't understand the green door. What is green about, anyway? You are Bendanatu. Your Guardian holds the green. What do you know that I don't? What is green and what is its opposite?*

Tyese and Keyera looked at each other, then back at Ember. Keyera gave a shrug and spoke. *Green magic is mostly known for its healing ability. I'm sure you already know that—but do you know where it gets the ability from?* The girl pulled her feet up under her backside, as if sitting on her heels.

Ember shook her head, then racked her brain. Healing. Where would healing come from? She broke down the different kinds of magic, vocalizing through mindspeech. *Well, blue deals with air and sound. Yellow with light and dark and sight. Red is fire and ice and taste. Orange is the magic of change and touch. Purple is water and emotion. Air, Fire, Water, Light, Change, and . . . Land?*

Keyera nodded. *Yes, but even more. What does land produce?*

And then Ember understood. *Life,* she whispered.

The wolfling did not smile. *That is correct. Life. And its opposite is—*

Death, Ember answered for her.

Yes. Keyera didn't need to say more.

How in the world was Ember supposed to infuse life and death into the door without killing something? Hadn't there been enough killing already? What would she kill? A fish? After her interchange with the fish who had helped her understand breathing underwater, she was loath to do that. Then what?

Nothing came. Life was easy. She could do that. She could do that right now and figure out the death part later, and so she did. Pulling on the green magic, she infused the door with living, breathing life. Vines grew from the door, flowers at the base, ladybugs and bees flitting from flower to flower. Done, she locked it into place, but the diamond window remained blank. Life surrounding death, but how did she implant the magic of death into the window?

She floated in place and stared. If she sucked the life from the plants around the window to infuse it with death, she would no longer have life upon the door. But the thought of killing something to activate the magic of death was abhorrent to her. Hadn't she killed enough? Three

Ne'Goi just this afternoon, and they were young boys at that. Their deaths were such a loss and weighed heavily on her soul, almost killing her a little with the burden.

She stilled.

Could it be that easy? Surely not—but she had to try. Ember pulled on those emotions she had buried deep. The death of her father. Paeder's near death. Killing in the battles against the Ne'Goi. T'Kato's death. And now the death of the three young Ne'Goi. The pain of loss surfaced and she felt the tears well, despite the water surrounding her. No one else would see, but she knew they were there.

Having gathered up all the pain, the dark, the absence of life that death had caused, she shoved it into the window and felt the black trickle out of her. The vines and flowers pulled back from the window, giving it plenty of room as the magic of death surged out of Ember in a torrent of emotion. She sobbed, not even really aware of anything beyond the window as it filled with her pain—the pain of death.

And then it was gone.

The tears stopped and Ember looked up as the door glowed with green, the window a dark shade that was sad even to glance at, and then it creaked open.

The stone holding all six doors began to glow a brilliant white and stretched upward, combining to form one large entry with six windows stacked in two rows. The human- sized door opened, but they could see only white light beyond. Ember glanced at Tyese and Keyera, and with a nod, the three girls stepped through the entry and onto dry land, the door and the beautiful light disappearing behind them.

CHAPTER FORTY

C'Tan was extremely grateful for her ability to heal quickly with magic. She put out the fire with an inversion spell of cold that sucked the heat right out of the flames, then rested under the trees, sleeping throughout the morning. When she awoke, the sun was high in the sky, and for a moment, she was puzzled by the quiet. It took only seconds to remember what S'Kotos had done. Sorrow and hate filled her like never before. She got to her feet, still sore, but the broken bones had healed at least and she could walk. She dug through the satchels, looking for food, and found it in the form of jerky. She gnawed on three pieces and stuffed her jacket pockets with as much as they would hold before mounting her drake and having him guide the others. She needed access to as much food as she could stomach to replace the energy she had used for healing. C'Tan could hardly stand to look at the piles of dust, bone, and armor that sat beside each dragon. She had to pretend they weren't there or she would fall apart once again, and she couldn't afford to do that where she was going.

"Drake, head for Bendanatu," she called out to the dragon, too tired to mindspeak.

"But Mistress," he thought at her, "they are the enemy. They will kill us on sight."

She shook her head, then realized he didn't understand. "Not today, they won't. To Bendanatu, and land on the other side of the ridge."

Feeling his reluctant assent, she pulled out more of the jerky and a waterskin, continuing to heal herself as fast as she could.

It didn't take long to reach the ridge. The dragons landed, and C'Tan dismounted, feeling much better for the protein and rehydration. With all her soldiers gone, she was extremely grateful that she had trusted Jarin to get Marda here safely. If S'Kotos had seen either of them, it was likely he would have killed her along with the rest.

She walked up the hill to meet her brother and sister-in-law.

"What took you so long?" Marda asked, squinting at C'Tan's bruised eye. At least she assumed it was bruised. It was still tender.

"My master," she spat the word, "decided to teach me a lesson. He didn't like that I was coming here to defend Ember. He is terrified that she will destroy him." She looked away and muttered, "I hope she does."

Out of the corner of her eye, Marda and a very human-looking Jarin exchange a glance, though they didn't say a word. She knew what that look meant. They had hope for her. Hope she would change and come back to the light. She snorted. As if that was possible. She'd condemned herself long ago—but it didn't mean she didn't have a heart.

They hadn't gotten far when a group of six younglings stepped from the trees, arrows aimed at them.

"Hold!" Marda cried. "We're here to help."

"She's not," said the tallest boy, gesturing to C'Tan. "I know who she is, and she don't help nobody but herself."

C'Tan smiled. The boy was right. Usually, that's all she did.

But not this time.

"If you'll just take us to Bahndai, we'll explain everything. Please. He can do what he wants with us after that," Marda pleaded with them.

Jarin stepped forward in all his glowing servant of Mahal glory and backed up the woman who had once been his wife. "She speaks the truth.

We are here on an errand from the Guardian Mahal. Would you deny his messengers audience with your chieftain?"

The boys' and girls' arrows dropped in an instant, and though still casting wary glances over their shoulders at C'Tan, they led the three to Bahndai's cave and surrounded C'Tan while they whispered to one another. She found it funny, but sobering. These younglings were more loyal than any of her guard had ever been. Not a one would have protected her the way these did their chieftain. It saddened her and made her question once again if Jarin and Marda were right. Did she have a choice? Did she *have* to follow S'Kotos?

She couldn't stop asking the questions.

Bahndai turned his attention to her. "C'Tan," he said, his voice full of ice. "To what do I owe this dishonor?"

She gave him a cynical bow. "I wish to assist you in your fight against the Ne'Goi. I have brought my entire wing of dragons to help."

"No men?" he asked, surprised.

She hesitated, then gave him a part of the truth. "Not anymore."

His brows raised as if he was surprised, then lowered them again. "Why would you want to help us?"

She sighed. "Because they are enemy to us all."

He waited.

She continued. "I am protecting an investment."

Still, he waited.

She gave in. "I need Ember Shandae to remain safe so she can collect the keystones and put S'Kotos in his grave."

That wasn't what she had meant to say, but it was the truth, nonetheless.

The boys around her looked up, then at Bahndai and one another. They lowered their weapons once again and left the room.

She was surprised. Evidently, honesty did open certain doors.

Bahndai leaned back in his chair, fingers combing through his beard. "Truly. You wish for this?"

She nodded, her posture stiff and her jaw set. She was sure the anger in her eyes said it all.

"Huh." He paused for a long moment. Then he met her eye and extended his hand. "Well then, I think I'll accept your offer. I don't entirely trust it, but we need the help. Welcome to the battlefront, C'Tan. We can definitely use you."

CHAPTER FORTY-ONE

Kayla wiped her brow, knowing she most likely smeared dirt across it in the process, but she didn't care. Thirty-five pits dug, staked, frozen, and disguised. Brant had been a little over-exuberant in his pit digging. Thankfully, they'd had extra stakes and extra poison. But she was exhausted, and so was everyone else. The pits, the blinds, poisoned arrows and pitched arrows and catapults just waiting for a fiery load—there wasn't much more that could be done to prepare for the enemy.

Finished, Kayla walked with rubbery legs down the hill, carrying empty pots she planned to spell clean for Dawnna. Aldarin's orange tattoos lit up in the distance, like a torch in the night. Curious, she dropped the pots outside the eatery and made her way toward his glowing form.

As she drew closer, she saw him hugging a dark-haired woman so tightly, it seemed her head would pop off from the pressure. He laughed and cried. She cried and laughed. Who was this woman Aldarin cared for so much? A wave of envy so green it was venomous struck her, and right behind that, a wave of grief. She'd lost Brant, and now she would lose Aldarin too. Would she never find genuine love?

She turned, her shoulders slumped, and began to walk away.

Aldarin called out to her. "Kayla! Kayla, come here! Kayla!" She ignored him until pounding feet brought him to her side, where he spun her around, his smile so bright it could lead the way through a midnight cavern. "I want you to meet someone. I—" He must have finally noticed her demeanor and the tears tracking down her cheeks. "What's wrong?" he asked.

She turned away, but he wouldn't let go. Concern lacing his voice, he turned her again, his hands on her arms. "Kayla. What's wrong, Mishon?"

That word. That one word she had so treasured was now a knife to the heart and she hit him in the chest, just above *his* heart. "Don't call me that!" she screamed, then turned and ran. She'd only gotten a few steps when he caught her again, spinning her around, pinning her arms and kissing her soundly.

"You *are* my Mishon," he said when he finally came up for air. "I will never stop calling you that." He brushed hair away from her face and wiped at the smudge on her brow. "Why are you upset, my love? I only wanted to introduce you to the woman who raised me. She's your family too, if I remember correctly."

Kayla froze. "Then, you weren't . . . I mean . . . you two . . . "

Aldarin blinked, then laughed. "Oh, goodness no! She is my mother, though she didn't birth me. Please. Come and meet her." He pulled at her hand, and her feet unwittingly followed.

"But—wasn't she captured by C'Tan?" she asked as they approached Ember's mother, a glowing hawk perched on her shoulder.

"Yes, I was," Marda replied. "Jarin here convinced C'Tan that she needed me—us—when she came to offer her services to the Bendanatu in this battle against the Ne'Goi."

Kayla's jaw nearly hit the ground. "C'Tan. Here. Offering to . . . help?"

Marda grinned. "I know. Hard to believe, isn't it? But something is happening to her. She's not the completely evil person I've seen all these years. She is softening somehow. I don't know why, but I won't reject a good thing."

"Just her, then?" Kayla asked, nervous and excited at the same time. After all, C'Tan had sent Ian Covainis to kill her, even though he assured Kayla he was there to help. She wasn't sure how much to trust *this* offer of help.

"No. She brought all her dragons. *All* of them. Not a one remains at her keep." Marda seemed awed by that somehow. "But enough of that. It is good to see you again, Kayla."

"And you as well. I'm sorry I didn't recognize you. Mother is here too—somewhere."

"I know," Aldarin's mother said. "We've already spoken and reunited. It's you I've been waiting for." She stepped forward and embraced Kayla. Kayla wasn't really a hugging kind of person, but Marda was her aunt. Some of the only family she'd met, besides Uncle Tomas and her evil grandfather. Okay, the only female relative aside from her mother. Hugging Marda was like hugging a grandmother, or at least the way she imagined hugging a grandmother would feel. Safe. Comfortable. A gentle place to stay forever and never get hurt. Kayla stepped back, smiling.

"So, you're my aunt, huh? We didn't really get to talk much before." she looked Marda up and down. "You don't look much like my mother."

The woman laughed. "No. We have always been opposite sides of a coin. She tall, light, and slender, and me, short, dark, and sturdy. I have no idea how that came about."

Kayla tipped her head to the side. "Ember favors you."

Marda's smile dropped at the reminder of her daughter. "Yes. I've always thought so. She certainly inherited my strong will." Throwing her hands in the air, she continued. "And she's in danger again. I hate this. I never wanted her to pursue magic, and now she's the most important magi in three millennia. I'll never be able to drag her from it now." Bitter words fell from her lips.

Kayla didn't understand. "Why would you want to? She has done so much for so many, and she could never have done that without her gifts."

Marda teared up. "I know. The magic has brought a lot of pain over the years. I didn't want that for her."

Taking her aunt by the hand, Kayla spoke softly. "There's something I've learned recently, and maybe it's something you already know, but I feel as if I must share it with you." She hesitated, searching for the right words. "There are very few things in life that are black and white. There are no absolutes. What can create misery for one person creates ethereal joy for another." She met Marda's eyes. "Don't let your terrible experience with magic shape and color Ember's feelings about it. She is very, very good at what she does. With no kind of knowledge about magic, she has fought for us by instinct alone. She has saved the lives of hundreds without knowing the impact she made. I'll bet that right this moment, she is in the cavern holding the Emerald Wolf. She will be back. I have no doubt. If anyone can succeed at the impossible, it is Ember Shandae."

Marda pulled Kayla into her arms once again, a sob escaping as she wet Kayla's shoulder with her tears. "Thank you," she whispered, squeezing tight.

Kayla said nothing. She didn't really need to. Love spoke for itself.

With the sun having set on the exhausting day and dinner served from the sanitized pots Dawnna held dear, Bahndai's family, both by blood and adopted, gathered together around the hearth. Kayla and Aldarin were invited to sit with Bahndai in his home. Marda and Kalandra sat in the corner, heads together like young schoolgirls, giggling and holding hands. The hawk sat in the window now, and Kayla could see his green glow against the dark sky. It made her curious. She turned to Aldarin. "Who is he?" she asked, somehow knowing the bird was male.

Aldarin's voice was full of awe. "That is your uncle, Jarin."

"But I thought . . . I mean . . . Isn't he dead?" she finally asked.

Aldarin nodded.

Further confused, Kayla watched the bird blink and then turn his green eyes on her. It was eerie, the intelligence in those eyes. "He doesn't look very dead to me," she mumbled.

Aldarin snorted a laugh, then covered his mouth with his hand, leaning forward, his shoulders shaking. "I know," he finally got out. "He's dead, but he's not. Mahal brought him back to watch over Ember. He's always been around, but we didn't know who he was until the mage trials, when he saved my father's life."

Kayla's brows went up. "Now that's a story I have to hear."

He looked past her and his face went blank, a guarded mask slamming firmly in place. "Another time," he breathed.

All eyes were on the doorway, so Kayla followed their direction and froze.

C'Tan stood there, her riding leathers blood red, fitting as if they were painted on. Kayla fought warring emotions—one to jump out the window and run away in fear, the other to leap at S'Kotos' greatest servant and beat her black and blue.

Neither was a good option. Nor was it feasible.

"May I join you, Chieftain Bahndai?" she asked, her habitual characteristic of pride distinctly lacking. Was Marda right? Was C'Tan actually changing? Kayla would have to wait for further proof before she could form a valid opinion, but the spark of hope was there.

Bahndai stood and gestured toward the fire. "Please. Join us." Once C'Tan found a place to sit near Marda and the hawk on the windowsill, Bahndai sat. A few more stragglers came in after C'Tan, each stopping, startled, upon the sight of the one they had always thought of as the most evil woman on Rasann.

All but one. One entered with raised brows and C'Tan stood. "Mother?" Lily whispered, sounding nervous.

The woman in red nodded, her hands clasping and unclasping, as if she didn't know what to do with them.

"May I approach?" Lily asked.

Again, C'Tan nodded, glancing at Marda as if seeking her approval. Ember's mother did nothing. Lily walked slowly across the room and stood in front of C'Tan.

"May I . . ." she asked, holding her arms out.

Now C'Tan looked as if *she* wanted to jump out the window. She backed away, but the wall was behind her. Lily dropped her arms in disappointment.

An angry voice came from the doorway. "Celena Tan! You hug your daughter the way she deserves to be hugged! I don't care that you didn't raise her. I don't care what happened. She deserves your love, and she will have it!" Asana entered the room like a cloudburst pouring its rain in sheets. Her emotions pushed outward like a storm.

C'Tan's jaw dropped as she saw her mother, and something shifted. Not anger. Not resentment. Sadness, perhaps. A small seed of love? Kayla wasn't sure, but C'Tan did as her mother demanded and opened her arms to Lily, though they were stiff as wood. Timid, the girl stepped toward C'Tan, whose arms remained open, her eyes on Asana. Lily hugged C'Tan. She looked as if she had her arms around a snake, just waiting to be bitten.

C'Tan stood straight, stiff arms around her daughter, obviously uncomfortable, but obedient to her mother even now. It was strange to witness. When Lily let go, disappointment showed in her face and slumped shoulders. C'Tan ignored her and leaned against the wall, scanning the room and the doorway, never letting down her guard. So sad. Poor Lily. Kayla glanced at the girl who sat quietly across the room, her head bowed and eyes on the floor. It just wasn't right.

The others went back to their conversations. Asana sat beside Bahndai and stared at him. He appeared to ignore her, poking a stick at the fire, but sweat formed on his upper lip. Kayla smiled. He was obviously more nervous than he wanted to appear. After staring at the chieftain for a bit, Asana reached over and took his hand. His entire body stilled for a moment before he turned to face her. Asana let go and reached up with both hands. He flinched, but she placed them gently on each side of his face, then leaned forward and kissed him gently on the lips. He looked flabbergasted. "I missed you, love. More than I can ever express. If you leave me like that again, I will hunt you down and cut away pieces of you and leave them to rot." She held his gaze to prove that she meant it.

He reddened, but clasped her hand more firmly, dropping the stick and twisting his body so he could embrace her. Pulling back, he met her eye. "You have my word, love. Never again. I have missed you, too. I would have returned if you had let me." He looked down. Kayla watched the interchange with fascination.

"I was a fool," Asana admitted somewhat grudgingly. "I should have listened. I was so hurt and angry, there was no room for anything else."

"I understand. There is no blame for that," he said, scooting closer and putting an arm around her. "I was in the wrong for leaving without an explanation. I never had the chance to tell you I was Bendanatu and was afraid that if I did, you would no longer love me."

Asana shook her head, then rested it on his shoulder. "It wouldn't have mattered if you were half cockroach. I would have loved you anyway."

Bahndai laughed, put both arms around her, and that was that. The couple who had been apart for thirty years had reconciled. Who would have thought when Shari Bird threw Asana onto her back to save her that she would bring her back to her one true love?

So many changes that night. So many hearts softened, reconciliations made, and loves kindled. Bahndai and Asana. Shad and Kalandra. Kayla and Aldarin. C'Tan and Lily, in their own odd sort of way. And then Kayla realized why it all happened tonight.

The morning would most likely bring death to them all.

CHAPTER FORTY-TWO

The moment Ember, Tyese, and Keyera stepped through the doorway and into the light, the changes Ember had made to their bodies disappeared. The passageway through the trial of the doors was bright, a tunnel leading only one direction—forward. They put on their socks and boots and kept walking for what seemed an eternity. Each step seemed as if they walked upon sunshine, and yet the floor beneath them, the walls surrounding them, were solid and smooth as crystal.

When at last they reached the end, they found a very ordinary stone door. Ember looked at Keyera on her left, Tyese on her right. Nodding, the three of them pushed on the wolf carved on the left side of the door and it swung open, heavy on its hinges. A horrendous screech sounded from the moving door and dust rained down on their heads. They coughed, waving their hands in front of their faces until the air cleared, revealing the next room. The light from the tunnel shot into the cavern like a spear, hitting a mirrored surface that cast it toward the ceiling, which reflected to multiple mirrors. A practical solution for light in the darkness, rather than using magic like so many did. What it showed took Ember's breath away.

In the center of the room, a short pedestal rose from the floor with a reflected beam bathing it. Emerald eyes shone from the darkened stone. The girls moved into the room and toward the pedestal, Ember's heart hammering in her chest. Emerald eyes? Was it alive? What were they going to have to face now?

As they neared the pedestal, the area around the emerald eyes appeared to grow until she could see they were embedded in the stone head of a wolf. Had they finally found the resting place of the emerald keystone? The closer they got, the more sure she became. This was it! They had found it—or at least its resting place. Now they just had to figure out how to activate it and get the actual keystone from inside.

"Is this it?" Tyese asked, her voice full of awe.

"I think so, yes," Ember answered.

"Then where is the keystone?" Keyera asked. She gently touched the stone pillar, and grinding sounded from within. She jerked her hand back and the sound stopped.

A slow grin spread across Ember's face. "Come on! Let's all touch the stone at the same time and see what happens."

"I don't know," Tyese said, backing away. "That didn't sound good. Not at all."

Ember glanced at Keyera, but the wolf girl only shrugged. It appeared that convincing Tyese was on her shoulders once again. She stepped out of the light and away from the pillar to take the girl by the arm. "Come on, Tyese. Don't be afraid. Something was moving around inside there, that's all. The keystone has to be somewhere, and how are we going to get it out otherwise? Do you want to chisel it out? We don't have any tools, any weapons—nothing but our hands and these divided keystone keys. We can't do it without you."

Tyese trembled under Ember's hand, but she took in a breath and held it, as if to steady herself, then gave a single sharp nod before stepping quickly to the pillar and waiting for Ember and Keyera to join her.

Together, the three girls put their hands on the top of the stone wolf's head, right between the ears, their fingers barely touching the surface. The stone shook and the grinding started again, faster this time. Simultaneously, the individual keystones glowed on Keyera and Tyese's wrists, and Ember's chest where the medallion had embedded itself. The eyes of the stone wolf glowed with them, growing brighter until Ember squinted against the light.

The green eyes melted, the stone liquefying and streaming upward, as if nature's rain had reversed itself in running down a window. The green gathered over the girls' hands, and their individual keystone keys rose to the surface of their skin. Ember felt burning as her medallion drew upward and formed once again into the metal and emerald it had been before. A small stream of green left her necklace and joined the keystone forming over their hands. The bracelets lost their emerald eyes and joined the stream of emerald as well. The light increased until Ember had to close her eyes, the shaking so tremendous that her teeth rattled in her head.

And then it stopped. The light. The shaking. Everything—and a cold circlet fell onto the backs of their hands.

Ember opened her eyes and peered down with surprise. The Emerald Wolf didn't look at all like a wolf. It appeared to be . . . "Jewelry?" she said aloud. An oddly shaped circlet with a teardrop on the forehead. Bracelets of pure emerald, and a long chain that led from the circlet to another smaller circlet.

"This makes no sense!" Keyera said. She pulled her hand from under the keystone. "What use do we have for jewelry? Using it as a key is one thing, but to fight a war? We need weapons against S'Kotos and the Ne'Goi. How is this going to do us any good?" She growled and stomped away.

"Oh, it will do you good. Much good—if you know how to use it," a deep male voice sounded from the darkness.

Startled, the girls turned as one, Tyese giving a small squeak of fear or surprise. An ancient man stalked toward them, the two remaining Ne'Goi boys at his side. "I wondered who would bring the keystone to light. I hadn't expected the Wolfchild to be here." A snarl touched his voice.

"Who are you?" Ember asked, relieved that the fear shaking her core wasn't evident in her voice.

"I? Who am I?" He smirked. "I'm surprised you do not know. Am I not a creature of legend? A nightmare made real?" He held out his arms as if daring them to examine him. The ground shook.

Keyera and Tyese went wolf and growled. Ember held her composure as best she could until the floor held still.

"You didn't answer my question. Who are you?" She lifted her chin and glared.

The man's face darkened as he placed his hands on the head of each of the young Shadow Weavers, now in their Ne'Goi form. "I am the beginning, the fountain of all darkness. I am the creator of void, gluttony, and death. I am Ne'Goi."

Ember cocked her head. "I didn't ask *what* you are. I asked *who* you are."

The man leaned forward as if he were about to pounce on her and roared. Ember held still, though she longed to flee to the lighted tunnel and hide from this beast. Somehow, she knew he would not follow.

His voice rumbled, low and threatening. "I am both *what* and *who*. I am Ne'Goi. Father to all Ne'Goi. The beginning of Ne'Goi, who came from the darkness beyond our skies and fell to Rasann. I. Am. Ne'Goi. *The* Shadow Weaver. Father of all darkness." His chin jutted forward, as if daring her to refute his identity.

She sincerely wanted to.

If what this man said was correct, he was the first Shadow Weaver. Unlike the others who were made here upon Rasann, he came from the night skies, falling to their world . . . A being from somewhere else—somewhere equal to that place where the Guardians lived. If the Guardians were light, this being was their opposite. Darkness incarnate.

No wonder the Ne'Goi ate magic. Magic was light made solid and directed to a purpose.

This was *the* Ne'Goi.

Ember moved slowly toward the pedestal and the green keystone. If she could just put it on, she might have enough power to overcome this creature from her nightmares. With a single raised hand, he tried to stop her with his presence alone. "The keystone is mine," he said.

Ember quirked an eyebrow and kept moving. "I don't think so."

Darkness oozed off him like a poisonous fog, covering the mirrors and reaching with living tendrils toward the girls, who backed away. "It is mine," he said again, his voice deeper, darker somehow. "I have waited for ten millennia in this cave for one to come and open the box which held it. Some have tried. All have died. You are the first to succeed. I need the keystones. All of them," he almost pleaded. "Only the magic of the keystones and the destruction of this world can throw me back to my home amongst the stars."

She almost choked. "No. You would destroy an entire world just to go home?"

"Yes."

That was when Ember knew she didn't just face evil—she was dealing with insanity. All she could do was battle this creature and pray she'd win, though it seemed impossible. If not, they were all dead anyway.

She turned her head to the Bendanatu girls, now both crouched at her right. "Go," she muttered. "Get the keystone and keep it safe." The girls looked up at her, then slunk toward the emerald circlet.

Ne'Goi thrust the young Shadow Weavers forward. "Kill them!" The creatures snarled and leaped after Tyese and Keyera.

Ember faced the original Ne'Goi alone. He braced his legs, then reached, sending tendrils of darkness racing toward her. Ember danced away, fear surging through her veins. How could she fight this being who had the strength of a magic-eating Guardian, but the form of a man?

Desperate, she cast around for the rubble that had dropped in the cavern over the years. She pulled at the surrounding air, at the ground, and levitated the stones. With a thrust of her arms, pointing like an arrow at Ne'Goi, she sent the rubble at him as hard and fast as she could. It hit him nearly at once, thousands of stones plopping as if dropped into thick mud. Instead of penetrating the being, they stuck to him and then sank beneath his skin. Evidently, his human form was but a shape he had assumed. He was completely inhuman.

He grew in size.

Her heart leaped. Magic, fire, and now stones—all absorbed by this monster.

"That was a tasty snack. Anything more for me?" He mocked her efforts, his arms open, welcoming another attack.

Ember did not know what to do. A cry sounded from behind her and she spun.

Keyera had picked up the keystone and placed it upon her head and wrists, the long chain trailing down her back. The emerald sank beneath her skin with a smoking burn, nothing like the usual magical immersion of keystone with bearer. Keyera screamed as her skin blistered and blackened, looking as if it were about to melt. Her lovely brown hair caught fire, and she ran, trying to escape the fire when impossible. Its cause was embedded beneath her skin. Tyese battled the two young Shadow Weavers with stealth and teeth. Smart and fast, she tore one in the hamstring, then the other in the throat. Blood covered her, but there was no telling how much was hers and how much belonged to the young Ne'Goi.

Ember's eyes went back to Keyera. The girl would die. There was no question. She only wished she could put her out of her misery and stop the pain. Ne'Goi's voice sounded from directly behind Ember. "You see? I told you—many have tried. All have died. She is not the keystone bearer, and thus it turns upon her. It will recognize me, as I am brother to its creators, but only one other will it tolerate. You, perhaps?" His lips nearly brushed her ear. "Try it and see," he hissed.

Her run to Keyera was as much to escape Ne'Goi and his laughter as to help the burning girl. If she could get Keyera down the tunnel and open the doors, they would be back underwater and maybe the flame would extinguish. That hope in mind, she finally reached Keyera just as the girl collapsed near the lighted tunnel, still burning and smoking. Ember couldn't tell what part of the charred surface was skin and what was cloth. Her heart aching, Ember knew there was no healing from this. She doubted even the waters would extinguish the magical flame. Instead, she wrapped her cloak around Keyera and turned her over. The girl was barely conscious. Thankfully, the flames had gone out.

Keyera looked as if she would cry, but no tears came from her scorched eyelids. She couldn't see, couldn't move—could barely breathe—but with that breath, she whispered a few words. Ember leaned close to hear. "I thought it was me. I'm sorry. I thought it was me."

And then she was gone.

Somewhere in the moment, Tyese had killed the last two Shadow Weavers and joined Ember over Keyera's body. The keystones lit up with emerald fire. The girls hid their eyes and shrank back. When the light died down, they turned forward to find that Keyera's body had burned to ashes, the keystone pieces amongst the gray like jewels dug from the ground. It was beautiful and terrible all in the same moment.

Laughter sounded from behind them, and Ember's ash-filled heart burned with anger like none she'd felt before. This being, this Ne'Goi, was so callous, he would laugh at the death of their friend? A girl who was strong and brave and kind and had done everything asked of her. Everything. Even die.

Ember stood, her fists clenched, and turned to face the enemy. *He* had to die now. With no thought, only emotion, Ember drew up a fireball and threw it at the beast. It impacted his chest and actually did some damage, though Ne'Goi took the remainder of the magic into himself. It healed what damage she had done. She reached up and pulled the roof down on top of him. It fell, cave spikes and all, covering him with the rubble and boulders.

Laughter sounded from deep in the midst of the mound. It shivered and moved, bursting away from Ne'Goi as if he were a bow and the boulders his arrows. One of the larger pieces barely missed her face. She dodged to the left and then grunted as a head-sized stone struck her right shoulder, another few bits embedding themselves in the side of her head. The impact spun her in the air and she landed on the ground, wheezing. If only she could get to the keystone, she might have a chance. If not, this fight was over. She rolled and crawled back to Keyera's ashes, her hand reaching for the emeralds—but they were gone.

"Nooo!" she cried out.

And then she saw her. A wolf. White, with brilliant green eyes, much like Ember and Shad—like Ember's father had been. The white wolf wore the keystone, and now Ember understood the strange shape. It wasn't made for human use. It was made for Bendanatu. The circlet went around the lupine ears. The bracelets were cuffs for all four legs. The long chain ran from the headpiece down her back to a small ring that circled her tail. "Tyese?" Ember whispered. No, it couldn't be! She didn't look like the girl at all, but she moved like her. Fought like her. Remembering how the keystones had a tendency to change people, Ember believed. "Tyese, it is you!" she cried, sitting up.

The wolf girl glanced at Ember and winked, then went back charged toward Ne'Goi. Every leap doubled her size until she towered over him and nearly hit the tips of the hanging cave spikes. She rammed into Ne'Goi, sending him flying across the room to slam into the cave wall. He embedded in the stone a foot deep. When he pulled himself out of the man-shaped hole, he yelled. No doubting he was angry. That had to hurt. Tyese went on the offensive, darting in with her razor teeth and swiping with her sharpened claws. With the keystone, Tyese's bites were doing more than a little damage. Even her magic was hitting home, somehow unable to be absorbed by the original shadow mage.

As the two of them danced in the darkness, Ember noticed something.

Ne'Goi avoided the light of the mirrors.

Why would he do that? It just made things easier to see. Was the brightness streaming from the tunnel somehow different? Special? Ember puzzled over it for a moment and walked a few steps into the tunnel. White light. Pure, white light. No diffusions. No imperfections. Just the purity of all the colors of magic combined into one—white.

Ember grinned.

Running across the room, she pushed the first reflective mirror from behind. Slowly, ever so slowly, it swung toward the battling duo and finally it struck home, covering Ne'Goi with brilliant white light. He screamed, his body smoking instantly, and darted back into the darkness.

Ember followed him with the light, the mirror moving more easily with use. Again, she struck the being with the pure light and he smoked and charred. He hissed at her, stepping into the darkness and then charging toward her. She could hear his steps come closer, pounding the rock like hammers.

She waited.

Closer. Closer. And then he was almost there. She swung the mirror toward the doorway and stepped into the light, where it was at its brightest. He hissed, cowering behind the mirror, unable to get closer. Tyese stepped into the stream of light and glowed brightly, green and white together. Ember finally understood in that moment the purpose of the tunnel. It was Ne'Goi's prison door. No exit but through that tunnel of unbearable light capable of incinerating him to ashes. The tunnel was long enough that by the time he reached the other side, he would be crispier than a chicken left on the spit overnight.

Tyese stepped to Ember's side and sent thoughts into her mind. *We have to get him into the light. It's the only thing that will kill him. Any suggestions?*

Well, I'm not strong enough to throw him over the mirror and hold him down. Magic won't do much good—

My magic will. Tyese's mindvoice sounded a bit smug. *What if we shut the door and turn off the light, get him where it would shine, and then you open the door while I pin him down?*

It sounded workable. Though Ember didn't know how smooth it would be, it was possible. Running to the door, Ember stepped into the tunnel and pulled the beastly stone thing toward her. It shut with a resounding thud. She couldn't hear anything inside the cavern, but she could still feel Tyese as she battled with Ne'Goi, trying to position him along the light path. Her desperation leaked through and finally Ember heard Tyese cry outside the door. At the same time she screamed in her head. *Now! Now! Open it now!*

Ember pushed as hard as she could, but the door didn't budge. Her eyes welled up with tears. Somehow, the door had locked when she pulled it closed. "Can't something go right?" she screamed at the sky, knowing Mahal could hear her. "I lost my friend and I'm about to lose another because this stupid door won't open. Why? Why did you send me on this quest if everyone I love is going to die? What's the point?"

Sobbing, she sank to her knees. It was pointless. No one was listening. Nobody cared. She was going to die down here as soon as Ne'Goi finished with Tyese. Then, remembering the light that held him prisoner, she realized she'd be more likely to die of starvation, thirst, or lack of air. That only increased her sobs. She became vaguely aware of the brilliant light brightening around her, if that were possible. A feeling of peace and warmth flowed over her—a feeling she knew well.

She raised her tear-stained face just as two hands touched her gently, one on each shoulder. She stood up in a single motion to see two men, or two beings. Mahal and her father stood beside her. "I thought you couldn't stand on Rasann," she said to Mahal, his presence surprising the question right out of her.

He smiled. "This is one of the few bubbles that protect me from Rasann. She cannot feel me here. It is filled with my light and magic, and she cannot distinguish between us. If I stepped into the cave, it would be another matter. It is just like the cavern at the mage academy. This place is special. I created it."

Speaking of the cave brought her back to herself and what was happening. "My friend is dying in there and your stupid door won't open."

"We can't have that now," he said. He reached with his left hand, touched the carved image of a wolf, and the door immediately swung open, the light showing Ne'Goi leaning over an unconscious or dead Tyese. The beam hit Ne'Goi directly, and his skin sizzled. He hissed and tried to retreat into the darkness, but Ember's father leaped past them, turning midair into a giant wolf and landing on the being, holding him in the light. Ne'Goi fought to escape Jarin's weight, and finally threw him across the room. Rebounding off the wall, Jarin landed on his feet, then shook himself. Ne'Goi slunk into the darkness and Jarin bounded after him. Ember couldn't see the battle for a few moments, but she could hear growls, yelps, yells, and screams. It sounded like the battle between the two was pretty even. Finally, Jarin pulled a stunned Ne'Goi into the light, then sat on him. The shadow weaver thrashed and screamed at Jarin.

"Release me, you oversized hound! I was old long before this world was born! Let me go!" Jarin looked at Mahal, who shook his head, his face hard. Ne'Goi must have known it was the end then. He let out a long scream that Ember thought would never end. He smoked and steamed, just as Keyera had done, then burst into black flames that did not touch Ember's father. When it was done and the creature was dead, Jarin stood, shook ashes from his fur, and shrank to a normal size.

"There. See? That wasn't so bad," Mahal said.

Ember looked at him like he was crazy, then ran to Tyese and checked to see if she breathed. A sigh of relief escaped her when she saw that the girl still lived. After that she went to Keyera's cloak, kneeling by her ashes mounded there—all that was left of her friend. Everything was reduced to a pile of ashes, all because she tried to take up a keystone that didn't belong to her in order to save her friends. Mahal stepped up behind her. The earth shook a bit. He stood on Rasann without the protection of his magic, she realized. He was taking a chance. For her.

But she was still angry. "If you could save Tyese so easily, why not Keyera? Why couldn't you step in before? Why did she have to die?" Ember's eyes welled with tears that quickly trailed down her face and dripped off her chin into the ashes below.

Mahal knelt beside her now, his hand over Keyera's ashes. "She has a different path to follow," he said.

How cryptic. "Can you bring her back?" she asked.

He shook his head. "No, I cannot. Not in the form she once was."

Ember looked at him. "What is that supposed to mean?"

He gave her a sad smile and put his hands in his lap, then stood as the room rumbled. "You shall see. I must go before my presence tears apart the world." He walked back to the tunnel. "You are doing well, Ember Shandae. Next, you must go to the MerCats and find the Amethyst Eye, and let your cousin, Kayla Kalandra Felandian, go in search of the Ruby Heart. Time is speeding up, and it is necessary that you part ways for a while. Even while you were here, time has slipped. How long has it been since you left Bendanatu?"

"We left yesterday."

Mahal shook his head. "It has been three days outside of these walls. A battle is raging in Bendanatu. A battle you must join if they are to succeed."

"Three days?" she asked, not believing.

He nodded. "I must go. I leave a parting gift that will help you on your journey. Take good care of her, Ember. She is the only one in the world."

She had no idea what he meant by that, but she nodded anyway, and then he was gone as quickly as he had come. She glanced at her father, who turned human and came to her. "I have no words for you, daughter. Nothing that will give you peace or help you on this journey. I can promise you that I have kept a close eye on your mother and C'Tan. Brina is doing well and is no longer as closely guarded." Ember had to think a moment before remembering her mother was called Brina before her husband died. He continued. "She is treated more as a guest than a prisoner. And C'Tan—" He paused. "C'Tan is not what she seems. There is good in her, Shandae. More than you could ever know or believe. When the time comes, give her a chance. For me, if for nothing else."

Ember nodded slowly, not sure what he meant.

He smiled. "Thank you, my darling girl. I shall go back to your mother and watch over her. Mahal will watch over you. I wish you the best." He kissed her on the top of the head and was gone in a whisper.

Turning back to the ashes that had once been Keyera, Ember was stunned to see them glowing and moving around, forming a solid shape that grew until it was the size and shape of a horse. Magic hung in the air like mist after a summer rain. Before she could blink, a beautiful white mare rolled onto her knees, then stood up. She unfurled dragon-type wings and dipped her horned head several times, as if to test things out. She then turned to Ember, and blue eyes meeting green, the horse thing mind-spoke to her. *Hello, Ember.*

Ember's heart felt as if it surged up her throat. "What . . . Who . . . I . . ." She couldn't find the words.

A silvery laugh in her mind combined with a vocal whinny. *I am called a Pedracorn. Part Pegasus, part dragon, and part unicorn. I am to be your companion and helpmeet. As your cousin Kayla has Thew and your*

DeMunth now has the Phoenixian Ted Finch, you have me. I am the only white companion in the world.

Awed by the beautiful gift of the Pedracorn, Ember sank to her knees. "What should I call you?"

Again, that combined silvery laughter with a whinny. *I am as of yet unnamed, but in the past it was usual for a Pedracorn to be named after the person from which they were born, added to it something completely their own.* The Pedracorn cocked her head. *Keyera was this Bendanatu—am I right? A part of her essence remains with me, along with many of her memories.*

Ember teared up again and nodded.

I think perhaps I will keep the pronunciation of her name, but spell it differently. How does Kierra sound?

As she said the name, Ember saw the spelling change in her mind. A sound, not unlike DeMunth's wordless singing sounded through her head. She took that for a good sign. "I think it's perfect, Kierra. Absolutely perfect."

CHAPTER FORTY-THREE

Kayla woke to a clamoring bell and panicked shouts and screams. She scrambled out from beneath the blanket someone threw over her during the night, made sure the flute was still at her side, and mentally called for Thew.

A familiar voice bellowed with rage, "Where is tiny halfling with sapphire flute? Wyciskalla hungry! Halfling! Come face Wyciskalla!"

The Ne'Goi had arrived.

In less than a minute, every person in the room rose, scrambled from beneath their covers, threw on armor, and raced down the stairs. Thew waited outside the entry for Kayla and she nimbly leaped to his back. He soared into the air to join the Phoenixians and dragons who already battled the winged Ne'Goi.

From above, she could see that they had triggered many of the poisoned stake pits. Ne'Goi bodies hung on the sharpened wood, sometimes two or three per pit. It wasn't much, but every Ne'Goi taken down was one less to fight. The Bendanatu and humans charged against the sea of Shadow Weavers, gnats swarming toward an elephant stampede. Why did she even *think* they had a chance at surviving this battle?

Oh. Because she had hope, and just an ounce of faith that the tide would turn. She couldn't help herself. It was her nature.

The dragons belched streams of flame that took down Ne'Goi by the dozens as their wings caught fire. For the first time in her life, she was grateful to C'Tan. To be honest, if they had any chance at all, their success was primarily C'Tan's doing. Kayla didn't know how that would affect the Bendanatu, but whatever the price, it was worth it to save these people she'd come to love so much.

A Phoenixian danced through the air—Eden, she thought—and dove into the midst of a cluster of Ne'Goi. Kayla feared for her until she saw a brilliant flash of light that turned most of the Ne'Goi surrounding her to ash and burned the others so badly, they fell to the earth in lopsided spirals. Eden soared high to where the rising sun struck her fully. She glowed with the light, and when Kayla thought Eden might explode with it herself, she dove back into another cluster of Ne'Goi and repeated the process again.

Kayla realized then what she was doing—expending her light energy, like little Ezra had done to save his mother. The Phoenixians were creatures of light, just as Thew was a creature of air. When Eden soared high enough for the light to envelop her, she could, in essence, recharge the light she had lost. It was sheer genius, and Eden was not the only one to use it. Dozens of Phoenixians rose and fell, pulsing with light in the depths before soaring back into the sky. It must be standard battle practice. Even Shari Bird battled the Ne'Goi, though she did so with a fierceness that scared even Kayla. Losing Ezra was devastating to her, and now she paid back the creatures who took her son. She healed in her own way.

Kayla accomplished nothing by watching the others. Pulling the flute from her satchel, she called Brant. He answered in a cyclonic explosion that would have blinded her had they been on the ground with dust and rocks. "Yes, Mistress," he said, battle ready. She had rarely seen him like this. Brant was still there, but his upper body was huge—muscles so big they would be near impossible for a human to build. From the waist down, he was a spinning swirl of air, much like a tornado. No doubt he could cause that kind of damage, too.

"It's time for you to fight, Brant." She pointed to the Ne'Goi, both on the ground and above. "If it is dark, it is a Shadow Weaver, the enemy. Watch the energy. It will tell you better than appearance. Black is bad. Kill it."

He grinned, his teeth showing in a not-so-nice way. "Oh, yes, Mistress. It shall be done." Brant dove for the ground, where so few stood against the swarm of evil. He grew in size until his bottom half truly was a tornado swirling among the Shadow Weavers. His power sucked them into his funnel, chewed them up, and spat them out the top, mangled and torn to fall the long distance to their deaths, screaming all the way.

Kayla shivered, hating the scene, but the Ne'Goi would not leave of their own volition. It was death or defeat. She would not accept defeat. Not willingly. The only option was to fight with everything she had.

With Brant having been loosed on the enemy, now it was her turn to do some damage. Kayla played, her focus going to the poisoned arrows that were hidden in batches throughout the woods and behind the blinds. Some of the youngest hid behind those blinds and shot arrows at the enemy as best they could, but she needed the arrows now. Gathering as many as she could find, she raised them all into the air at once, points facing the Ne'Goi that came down the hill. She strengthened the wood and spoke to the air, asking it to guide her arrows true, and with a high trill, shot them forward and into the onslaught of Shadow Weavers.

They fell by the hundreds, the poison doing its job even when the arrow hadn't quite hit its mark. It only angered the remaining shadow weavers. Wyciskalla yelled again. "Halfling! You kill my people. You will pay! I will eat you with your flute and use its power to kill all. All!" Kayla shivered. The moment the never-ending surge of Ne'Goi had been dealt with, she would face the giant.

With a terrible screech, a black-and-red winged man charged her, tackling her around the waist. She twisted sideways off Thew and fell. The Ne'Goi wouldn't let go, his teeth snapping at her neck and face. She barely held him at bay, focusing instead on calling Thew or Brant—somebody to catch her in this long freefall. The air itself took her in its embrace, pulled her away from the Ne'Goi, and carried her back to Thew. She was almost tossed onto his back, and this time she put the flute away long enough to strap herself in. She didn't want that to happen again. Ever.

Just as she buckled the last strap around her thigh, the same red-and-black Ne'Goi charged at her, his mouth open and sharp teeth ready to rake her flesh. He aimed for her face, but as he reached for her, she leaned low over Thew and yelled, "Dive!" The elemental dove while Kayla recovered the flute and began to play. The wind rushed at her, filling her lungs, lifting her hair, and the flute came alive with sound. She aimed a sharp note at the Ne'Goi who chased after her, and icicles arrowed toward the being. He twisted, spiraling between them, and raced on with wretched determination. Why was he so obsessed with killing her? She didn't know him, hadn't had any dealings with him other than these battles. He seemed to have a grudge against her, but why?

He swooped close, poison glinting on his teeth, neck veins bulging.

Kayla sounded a high series of repeated notes. An ice ball the size of her fist appeared and slammed into his forehead. His eyes rolled up in his head and he fell, hurtling toward the ground until Wyciskalla snatched him from the air and laid him down gently. The giant bellowed up at her. "You hurt Laerdish, Halfling! Time to face me! Hungry!"

Black energy sucked her toward the ground, and for a moment she panicked—then fury blazed hot in her chest. "Oh, no you don't," she muttered, pulling on the magic of the flute to strengthen her and Thew, thrusting them up to soar high above the battle. The giant Ne'Goi bellowed, reaching for them, but missed as they shot past.

Far below, he screamed, uprooting trees and throwing boulders, harming his own people in his blind fury. Ripping a pine tree from the ground, he launched it at Kayla, wounding a dragon but falling short of his real target.

Wyciskalla circled far below, waiting for her return to battle—for his chance to devour her and the flute. How could she fight the giant and avoid him at the same time?

As she watched for an opening, the battle raged. She mourned the fall of every dragon, every Phoenixian and Bendanatu as she racked her brain for a way past the monstrous giant. She swooped and feinted, but he shadowed her below, waiting.

There was no way around him. It all came to one solution—one she'd hoped to avoid at all costs.

She must fight and defeat Wyciskalla.

Cut off the head, and the snake would die. If she could beat the giant, the Ne'Goi would likely flee and the battle would be won for today. Maybe even the war. He seemed to be the one in charge, despite his limited ability to think—a figurehead. The manpower behind the assault.

But that didn't mean she had to do it alone.

Calling Brant to her side, she pulled energy from the flute and infused herself and Thew with it, put the flute to her lips, and sent a mental note to Thew. *Come, my friend. It's time to battle the monster.*

A wave of fearful excitement washed over Kayla as they turned and dove toward Wyciskalla. Win or lose, it would be a battle to remember, if nothing else.

She pursed her lips and blew a trilling blast that sent icicles and ice balls toward the monster's face. He bellowed his rage as they struck flesh.

It felt like the beginning of the end.

CHAPTER FORTY-FOUR

Tyese hit the wall a final time with the stone before dropping it and sinking to the ground, exhausted. "I can't do this anymore, Ember. It's too hard. It will take us weeks to get out of here this way. Months, even!"

Ember looked at Tyese and dropped her own stones with a sigh. "You're right. But how else do we leave? We already tried going out through the tunnel. We can't get past the other end. The doors in the magic box have shut again. What do you suggest?" Ember sat on a boulder and leaned forward. She rubbed her blistered hands on her knees, wincing.

"Use your magic!" Tyese said, as if it was the most obvious thing in the world.

"It won't work in here," Ember snapped. "We already tried that."

"Yeah, but not the way you used it at the mage academy. I saw you pass through the walls. Remember? That was a different kind of magic. Wouldn't it work here?" Tyese was either tired or angry. Her voice was getting waspish.

Nevertheless, she had a point. Could Ember travel through stone the way she had at the academy? And more importantly, could she carry the weight of a girl and the Pedracorn with her? What if they were too heavy, and she got stuck? What would happen then? Would they be frozen in stone forever? Dead before they had a chance to live? Was it worth it to try?

That was the big question, but honestly, Ember didn't see any other answers. She stood and wiped her now-sweaty palms on her legs. "Okay. Let's try it, but if you die in there, if we *all* die in there, know I did my best, okay?"

Tyese grinned and jumped up and down. "Okay."

Ember doubted the girl had heard a word beyond Ember's assent to try. Turning to Kierra, she asked, "What about you? Are you willing to trust me enough to try swimming through the stone to the outside?"

Kierra's head came up and their eyes met. *I would trust you with anything, Ember Shandae. You are my companion. My bondmate. Where you go, I follow.*

Ember winced as the weight of Kierra's absolute trust settled over her—hopefully she'd prove worthy of such faith. Walking to the cave wall, Ember raised her hands high and touched the wall, but it wasn't high enough. Frustrated, she dropped her arms and turned. "Kierra, can you give me a boost?"

The Pedracorn scrambled to her feet and trotted over to Ember, then lowered a leg and shoulder to give Ember a step to mount her back. Once astride the horse-like being, Ember balanced her feet on the strong joint of wing to body and reached higher. Using the same magical feelers that had sensed the stone in the mage academy, she reached into the rock to find any fissures or weaknesses that would allow them an easy exit. It took a few minutes, up and down, side to side, deeper and deeper, until she tapped into what she had sensed below.

A crack. A weak place in the stone that carried to the outside. Grinning, Ember dropped to Kierra's back and beckoned for Tyese to hop on. The young girl, who was now the guardian of the emerald keystone, came forward, her eyes big. "You mean we're going now?"

Ember nodded. "Can you think of a better time?" She patted the spot behind her once more.

Tyese came close and tried jumping up, but she wasn't tall enough. Ember gave her a hand, and the second time the girl jumped, she was able to walk up the side of the Pedracorn with Ember's hand holding her safe. Once seated, she wrapped her arms around Ember. "Will this hurt?"

The Wolfchild laughed. "Not if I do it right. Kierra, take to the air, would you, and then charge at that spot I touched, full force. No holding back, okay?"

Now Kierra seemed nervous when she answered. *If that is your wish.*

Ember patted Kierra on the neck. "Trust me, my new friend. We will swim through the stone as if it were mud. There will be no pain—but you might want to hold your breath. Just get as much momentum as you can. That will make my job easier." Sweat dampened Ember's palms, but she gritted her teeth and nudged Kierra. The Pedracorn took off running for the other side of the cavern, lifting them into the air shortly before the far wall. She circled the cavern, gaining speed with each pass until the third time she got to the far side of the cavern, she soared high, picking up even more speed, then dove and beat her dragon-like wings hard and fast. The wall came up sooner than Ember had imagined and she barely had time to get her thoughts in place to soften the wall and say "Change!" before they were immersed in the rock and propelling through it as a hawk diving from the sky.

Ember followed the crack in the stone, using it as a guide rope to lead them outside. They were nearly to the end when they hit a patch of granite that slowed them down to a near stop.

And then they *were* stopped. Stopped and stuck in the mountain just feet from the exit they desperately needed.

Ember would have screamed if she could have. Knowing the other two were starving for oxygen, she racked her brain for a solution and finally found one, but it would be neither easy nor pretty.

Actually, she was about to make a huge mess.

Putting her hands forward and slightly out, Ember solidified her hands into the surrounding stone. She then twisted her hand and popped, but the stone didn't go anywhere like it had at the mage academy. Realization hit and she would have smacked herself in the forehead if possible. Of course, the stone didn't go anywhere. It had nowhere *to* go! The only place that offered any kind of relief was ahead of them. That's where there was space to send the stone. She couldn't chip her way out of this one by the handful. She felt ahead once more. About four feet of solid granite lay between her and the outside. She was going to have to push everything in front of them, make a hole big enough for them to fly through, and shove it into the air on the other side.

The task seemed impossible! But she'd done the impossible before. She could do it again. Besides, it's not like it was a big job or anything. She smirked at the grim joke.

She would have taken a deep breath, but there was no air in the stone. Instead, she focused on the tightness in her chest and let it build, then put that energy into her hands. She reached out, her hands pressing against the granite, and in her mind she yelled, *Move*!

The stone shook around her, creaks and pops sounding, and a little air snuck through, allowing the girls to breathe. Everyone gasped, drinking in the oxygen like water in the desert. Ember tried to ignore her surroundings, took in the energy once again, and sent it forward and out. *I said move*! Again, the stone shook and cracked, but it didn't go anywhere.

This was ridiculous. They'd come this far, spent so long searching for the emerald keystone, had lost a friend, and now they were stuck in the side of a mountain where no one would ever know what had happened.

No! That was not acceptable!

Anger and desperation made Ember pull in more energy than she'd ever thought she could hold—a mixture of orange magic for change, green magic for the land, and red fire for both the anger she felt and to soften the stone. She pulled it in, filling every limb, every cranny, every cell of her body until she quivered with it, and in one tremendous burst of anger and desperate energy, she threw it in front of them and screamed, "MOVE! Get out of the way!"

The side of the mountain exploded outward, and the girls were showered by pebbles and stone, dust filling the passageway with its cold, earthy smell that set them coughing.

But when the air cleared and they could breathe and see, the passage was open and beautiful air circulated around them. Tyese squeezed Ember tight and Kierra twisted her head up to look at Ember with one blue eye. *That was—impressive. Very impressive,* she said, her mindvoice full of nervous awe.

Ember didn't smile. She was too exhausted. "Thanks."

Bit by bit, she pulled energy from the cool stone mountain, filling her depleted reserves with its strength. If there really was a battle out there, and she had no doubt Mahal spoke the truth, she'd need all the power she could get.

It took about ten minutes to fill her energy reservoir to near full. She would have topped it off completely, but Tyese was nervously kicking Kierra in the sides, and Ember could feel the annoyance building in her white companion. It was time to go.

"All right, ladies," she said, straightening her shirt. "Let's head out. We've got a war to fight."

Tyese held still at that, and Ember could feel her smile even if she couldn't see it. Kierra dipped her head in acknowledgement and pawed at the ground, and then with a leap, she jumped to the edge of the hole and leaped again into the clear air. That fast, they were airborne and circling higher. Ember had no idea where they were or where the battle took place, but she felt an incredible pressure to get there fast, to get there now.

Kierra's keen ears pricked up when the noise of fighting first reached them, and without being told, she dipped to their left and over a crest. Ember sucked in a breath. The carnage below was horrific. Granted, most of the dead were the enemy—dragons and Ne'Goi in numbers so great she couldn't count them all—but there were also a few Phoenixians and Bendanatu.

And what in the world were dragons doing here? Dragons meant one thing and one being only.

C'Tan.

C'Tan was here, but was she fighting against or with the Ne'Goi? A few moments later, Ember witnessed a wing of dragons attacking the Ne'Goi and defending a Phoenixian. That simple act proved the dragons fought on the same side as Ember. It seemed impossible to believe, but C'Tan was helping them.

She shook her head. "Kierra, can you take us down to the ground? I'm sure Tyese wants to dismount and help her people, and I want to see who remains alive."

Kierra didn't answer, but dropped from from the sky—a controlled fall that was beautiful as well as thrilling. Grace personified. Kierra's every movement exuded elegance and precision. Awe filled Ember that Mahal had given her such a companion, especially one that was so opposite from the way she saw herself.

The ground came up fast and Ember feared they would end up a broken mess on the rocky ground, but she should have known better. At the last moment, Kierra turned, skimming the surface, then used her wings to slow and land with elegance. Tyese let go of Ember and stood on Kierra's back, balancing with her hands on Ember's shoulders, then leaped to the side, changing to wolf in midair before they ever touched ground. Ember gasped—Tyese's wolf form no longer resembled the mottled brown thing she'd known before. It was pure white, like her father and herself. She'd seen the difference in the cavern, had even taken note of it, but she hadn't really taken it in, hadn't really *seen* it until this moment in the glaring light of day.

Tyese's brilliant white fur took on an emerald-hued glow, and she grew in size to twice, three times, and finally ten times the size of any other wolf. She was huge. The girl engaged the enemy three and four at a time, destroying them with a single savage bite. Ember shivered. Tyese seemed so naïve, so innocent. Watching her fight broke the illusion.

Kierra began to run once more, then spread her wings and soared into the sky. They had their own battles to fight.

CHAPTER FORTY-FIVE

C'Tan led her multitude of dragons directly into the thickest collection of airborne Ne'Goi. She wasn't worried about the Shadow Weavers' immunity to magic. The dragons spat fire—huge spouts which caught the Ne'Goi unaware and sent them burning to the ground below. C'Tan used a bow and arrow, setting them alight with her magic, then sending the flaming sticks out four and five at a time into the enemy ranks.

Hope stirred in her heart. Thus far, the battle had been much easier than she'd been led to believe it would be. The Ne'Goi were weak, foolish beings, and she had no qualms about killing them. Her dragons continued to toast the Shadow Weavers until one fell from above and landed on the back of one of the drakes, arms wrapped around his neck. C'Tan felt something pull—a dark void sucking the magical energy from her drake. The dragon screamed in pain, bucking against the enemy, but it held fast. The Ne'Goi pulled the life energy of the dragon into itself until, with a roar of triumph, he let the drake drop from the sky like a stone—broken, twisted, and already dead.

Rage consumed her as the remaining Ne'Goi followed the first in attacking her wing of dragons and within seconds, an entire regiment perished—dead and headed to dirt.

Realizing there was nothing she could do to stop this massacre, C'Tan called a retreat through her dragon, Drake. The Ne'Goi followed, and she gave instructions for the remainder of the wing to take evasive action. Kill the Ne'Goi, but protect their own lives.

They did their best, but in moments more than half of them were gone.

Gone.

And she sat astride her dragon, helpless. She could not save them, no matter how much she wanted to.

It was the first time in a very long while that she felt her humanity, her vulnerability. She hated it.

And yet, it made her feel very much alive.

CHAPTER FORTY-SIX

Thew dove and spun, taking sharp corners in the air and surging toward the sky, fighting to expose Wyciskalla's weak points—not that there were many. Kayla threw another ice ball at the giant, striking him in the knee. He bellowed with pain and swung at her, but Thew whisked away before the fist came anywhere near. The giant healed as fast as she struck and she screamed in frustration, feeling as if she were a mosquito. She could sting and bite, but she couldn't do any actual damage.

Remembering her confrontation with the group of Ne'Goi posing as Magi at the mage school, she tried the same tactics here, covering herself with an icy shield—but the moment it was complete, Thew gave an agonizing screech and plummeted toward the ground like a stone, his wings beating frantically. Not understanding why, but knowing there was a problem, Kayla let the ice disperse in an instant and Thew regained his equilibrium. Beating hard to gain some height, Thew sent a mind blast toward Kayla—one of few words, but backed by a flood of emotion. Fear, anger, disgust with Kayla. Words muttered in her mind. *Idiot. Think. Air and water conflict.* And then the actual message. *Ice too heavy. Enemy to air.*

Kayla got it and burned red for her actions. She should have realized that adding the weight of ice to an air elemental would be like trying to lift a boulder with a kite. She had *not* known about the conflict between air and ice, though it made sense now that she thought about it.

She was brought back to the moment when an enormous foot came down, caving in the ground where Thew had just been.

How could she defeat this giant when he was impervious to her attacks?

A tremendous explosion sounded from just over the hill, dust rising from the mountainside. Everyone turned to see what had happened, but there was nothing to see but a cloud of dust that shot skyward and then settled toward the ground.

Kayla turned back to Wyciskalla just as his huge fist connected with her body, slamming her and Thew into the ground. The giant was so strong it felt as if she'd been hit by a boulder. She didn't move, gasping for breath for a long moment, before she realized that the agony wasn't entirely her own. Images of pain flooded her mind as the air elemental groaned and lifted his head, only for it to fall back to the ground. She raised herself up on one elbow, oblivious to the surrounding danger, and met Thew's eye. She stroked his head with a trembling hand. "Hey, Thew. It's going to be all right. Just be still. Hang on."

His face turned toward hers and a soft whimper escaped his mouth, a shot of steam whispering from his nostrils. *I can't. I am . . . broken. The monster broke me. I am sorry.* He met Kayla's eyes. *Goodbye, new friend,* he said in her mind. With nothing more, He exhaled and then stilled, his cold body immediately disintegrating. Like a mound of torn tissue in the water, it dispersed, and finally he disappeared entirely, merging back into the air from which he'd been born.

"*No*!" Kayla screamed, then scrambled out of the way as Wyciskalla's foot came from above to squash her like a bug. She could barely see the giant for the tears blocking her vision, but she rolled left and right, front and back. Kayla lurched to her feet and pain squeezed her right ankle as if it were caught in a vise. She screamed, hands wrapping around it as she fell. The pain was exquisite, racing up her leg and into her knee, then surging down into her foot. Something was broken, that much was obvious, but what? She didn't know.

Wyciskalla reached for her. "Going to eat you now, little halfling. You and the flute. You are mine." At the mention of the flute, she knew that despite everything, she had to hold on. He couldn't destroy one of the keystones that would heal the world. She couldn't let that happen. She rolled over the rocks, trying to get out of the way. Wyciskalla followed her, his laughter a deep rumble.

His hand darted toward her, but she rolled off a rock and to the ground, crying out when her ankle bent at an odd angle. For the moment she was protected, surrounded by jutting rocks that kept Wyciskalla's hand away. He began pulling at the stones, trying to move them, and she desperately searched for a weapon. Something, anything, that could help defend her. But there were no rocks, no bow or arrow. Nothing—and then Kayla remembered she had a weapon he did not.

The flute.

Wyciskala finally got two of the spikey boulders out of the ground and eased his hand into the void toward her. Time was up and she hadn't even pulled the keystone out of the bag and put it to her lips. With no other options, Kayla put her fingertips on the bag holding the flute and imagined an icy dome covering her. As quickly as she thought it, it was there, Wyciskalla's fingers bouncing off its surface. He pulled his arm back, shaking his hand, and yelled. His fist hurtled toward the dome and hit it like a boulder dropping from the sky.

The dome held, though it rang like a bell. But the giant's blows did not stop with one. He hit and kicked the ice, biting it with such force, a tooth cracked against the surface and broke off.

And then he stopped and smiled the scariest grin Kayla had ever seen. He got down on his hands and knees, then leaned forward and covered the dome with his body, wrapping his arms around it so hardly any light entered. She wasn't sure what he did next, but the giant began to pull the energy from the flute, like a magical tornado. "I eat you now, little halfling. I eat you and flute." His voice resonated through his chest and into the dome. "Halfling energy taste good. Keystone flute energy taste better." Kayla could imagine his smile as he pulled the magic from her and the flute. The energy floated visibly up and through the dome, collecting on his chest before sinking into his skin. She felt weaker every moment.

A roar came from somewhere near. Not the giant—his roar was like the groaning earth during a quake. No, this one sounded more like a bear. "Brant?" she whispered.

Wyciskalla bellowed as Brant wrenched the giant from Kayla's ice dome. Once the monster was out of the way, the swirling air elemental was revealed. His left side to her, his base spun, angry bursts of lightning surging through the dusty vortex, and somehow he had grown to match the giant inch for inch.

The giant swung at Kayla's hero, stumbling when his fist passed directly through the elemental's cyclonic whirl. The Ne'Goi screamed when rubble in the vortex pierced his hand like shrapnel. It bled, running in rivulets to drop off his fingers. Furious, the beast tackled Brant, arms thrown around his solid torso this time. He skidded backward, grinning—and then his smile turned to a surprised grimace as Wyciskalla held Brant tight against his chest and began the same pull Kayla had felt before. "I eat you, elemental boy. I eat you to nothing," the giant said.

Kayla's fingers shook as she tried to undo the knot holding the flute to her hip. "Come on. Come on!" She snarled at the stubborn leather. She looked up again. Brant didn't even squirm. He looked stunned as the life was drained from him—again. He'd already died once and Kayla had already lost him—she wouldn't do it again. No more loss. She let the bubble dissolve and stood, despite the grinding agony surging through her ankle.

The knot seemed to dissolve, and in an instant the Sapphire Flute was in her hands. She yelled at the giant. "Wyciskalla! Let him go and come face your true adversary. The flute is calling you!" With that,

Kayla put the flute to her lips and played. The giant ran toward her in big, lumbering steps, leaving Brant diminished in size and strength, his cyclone barely moving. But he was alive, and that was all that mattered.

She'd probably die after this, but he would live. Brant would live on in the flute for as long as the flute existed.

Wyciskalla stopped, hovering over her, then reached down and grasped her, arms pinned to her sides, and lifted her to his face. His hand encased everything but her head and her feet. She dangled, trying to breathe in his grip, and waited for death to come.

CHAPTER FORTY-SEVEN

Kierra had taken the images of Ember's friends and family from her companion's mind, and together they had found nearly all of them battling in some way or another. All but Lady Kalandra. She was nowhere to be seen. Ember worried for her, but at the same time had a feeling she was okay. She wasn't the fighting type and most likely had stayed behind to watch the littlest Bendanatu while the older younglings and their caretakers fought. Dawnna and Rhonald she found easily enough and someone had to take their place, didn't they? Still, she would have liked to see her aunt to know for sure.

The greatest surprise had been in seeing her mother there. Marda used her magic to hurl burning, poisoned arrows at the Ne'Goi and did a fair amount of damage. Jarin had grown to massive proportions, just as he'd done in the caves—but now in hawk form. He carried boulders and dropped them into groups of Ne'Goi, crushing them with little effort. Surprisingly, it was the dragons that continued to take the most damage. They were supposed to be strong, untouchable creatures. They could breathe fire—but the fact that they were creatures of magic made them vulnerable to the Shadow Weavers, who sucked their energy and sent their bodies to the ground. She hoped Kierra didn't share their vulnerability.

Having found most of her people and seeing that they were well, Ember turned to the battle, looking for the place where she could do the most damage.

A woman screamed, and Ember scanned the area. When she found the screamer, Ember's toes curled and her fingers twisted Kierra's mane in anger. "There," she told Kierra. "Go fast. Kayla needs us."

Kierra ran through the air, her hooves pounding as if she ran on dry ground, her wings beating in hard strokes that sent Ember through the air as if shot by a catapult. A red-and-black blur pulled up in front of them and Kierra pawed at the air with her front legs, trying to stop. When her hooves landed, Ember looked at what had stopped them and her heart froze in her chest. She'd seen this one before, but hadn't known he was Ne'Goi. She'd thought he was a servant of S'Kotos. The spy within the ranks of the mage council, the man who had tried to take her magic away and punish her for crimes she hadn't committed until she exposed him and escaped through the glass ceiling.

Laerdish.

He grinned at her in his true form, his energy still a patchy red and black that now showed on his skin. "I've been having fun tormenting your cousin, Ember. It's time for you to take a turn."

Ember laughed at him, though she didn't feel it. She was terrified of this man—thing—who hovered before her. "You couldn't match me when you cheated, and I did not know how to use any of my power. How do you expect to beat me now?"

"I don't have to beat you," he hissed. "I just have to drain you of your magic and the fall will do the rest."

She put her arms out, sitting astride the hovering Pedracorn. "Do your best, oh master of deceit. You will not find the scared little girl you once did."

He laughed out loud. "That was but a week ago, my dear. Surely little has changed in that amount of time."

Ember wanted to continue the banter, but Kayla was in serious trouble and Ember needed this to end quickly. "I am truly sorry, Laerdish, but you are wrong. It is time for you to die."

The Ne'Goi who had tortured her so much the week before snorted. Kierra lunged, and Laerdish doubled over, dark red blood dribbling from his mouth. Ember looked down to his midsection and saw that Kierra had taken the initiative and skewered the Ne'Goi with her golden horn, leaving it protruding from his back. He gasped and groaned, then glared at Ember. "You have not seen the last of me, Ember Shandae. I will be back. The Ne'Goi always return once we find a new host to house us." He laughed. Laerdish reborn. The thought was terrifying, and even more so was the rebirth of the ancient Ne'Goi her father had just killed.

Ember reached over Kierra's neck to the still impaled Laerdish and grasped his temples with her palms, forcing his eyes up to meet hers.

"What do you mean, you'll return? How can you do that?"

He laughed, bloody flecks of spittle misting her face. "You'll see, Ember Shandae. You will know when it happens." He laughed again, his insanity becoming more apparent with the draining of his life.

Ember snapped. Angrier than she ever remembered, she fed that energy into Laerdish's head, which began to bubble and boil under her touch. She quickly pulled away and his face continued to morph, one side bubbling out, then the other. Then his head expanded like a sheep's stomach. Ember sent a thought to the Pedracorn. "Uh, Kierra, you might want to—"

"I'm already on it." She pulled her horn from the Ne'Goi, whose head inflated to a monstrous size. He fell, screaming, and was only ten feet away when it burst into fire. A few seconds later, it completely exploded. His body continued to fall, but there was no longer any life within it. Laerdish was finally gone.

Beyond Laerdish's remains, the giant bellowed in triumph as he raised the fist holding Kayla toward his open maw.

Kierra charged at the giant's temple, where her sharp horn could pierce the skin and skewer his brain. The tactic was successful—partially. Kierra hit the soft part of the bone dead on and her horn pierced through skin and bone—and there it stayed. His bone was so thick, she could not reach his brain, and now she dangled from the side of his head while he bellowed and thrashed about, reaching up to take the stinger from the bee in his head.

Kierra sent Ember a quick thought. "*You're going to fall. I'll catch you.*" The Pedracorn immediately transformed from a winged and horned horse to a beautiful, slender girl—more dancer than warrior. As soon as the horn was gone, they fell, but Kierra stretched her arms into a beautiful swan dive, smiling from ear to ear, her dark hair and blue-gray eyes every bit as beautiful as her white equine form. In an instant, Kierra changed back into a Pedracorn and darted beneath Ember in such a way that Ember landed astride her new friend naturally and with no pain.

"Wyciskalla angry! Pain! Who made pain in Wyciskalla's head?" the giant shouted.

Ember had an idea as Wyciskalla brought Kayla up close to his eye, his temple still leaking blood in sluggish spurts. "Kierra, take out the eyes! Blind him and we have the advantage!" Ember tightened her hold on Kierra's mane, her legs pressing against her flanks.

Kierra took them high, really high—above the battling Ne'Goi, dragons, and phoenixians and nearly to the clouds until the giant was the size of a cat. Then Kierra spread her wings and dove toward the giant, making subtle corrections to aim for his left eye.

Once they lined up as perfectly as possible, Kierra tucked in her wings and they sailed toward Wyciskalla with hardly a sound. They struck dead on in the center of his iris, puncturing straight through. The eye exploded and then they plowed in behind it, skewering Kierra's horn into the hole where the nerve came through. The beast slapped both hands over his eye, trapping the girls inside his eye socket.

That was bad. That was very bad. If he had both hands over his eye, where was Kayla? "Kierra! We have to leave! Now! Kayla is falling!"

Once again, Kierra morphed into the beautiful dancer. Running forward, she dove between the gaps in the giant's fingers. Ember followed right behind her close enough to touch Kierra's heels if she reached out. As soon as she began to freefall, Ember's heart raced. She wanted to panic, but that would accomplish nothing. Instead, she focused on finding Kayla, which was not difficult at all. Only a three second lead, but that was enough for her cousin to fall half the height of the giant. There was no way Kierra could reach her in time, but Ember couldn't lose her cousin, one of the few friends she had. She reached out toward the falling girl, much too close to the ground, and sent out a longing so strong, their white heart ropes connected and solidified. Stunned, she did nothing for a moment, and then she dug in her heels and pulled.

Kayla stretched the heart rope, nearly touching the ground, and then rebounded like a pulled-back twig. She flew toward Ember, who stood in the air, her heels embedded in small clouds. She didn't know how she did it, but her magic worked best when things were at their worst. In mere moments, Kayla collided with Ember, who hugged her cousin tight. She could feel the increased strength in the lifeline between them, as well as the agonizing pain in Kayla's ankle that quickly faded as Ember's white magic filled her body. It was nice to use her magic to heal instead of harm. Ember smiled. What she felt for Kayla was almost like having a sister.

Kayla pulled back and looked at Ember, a slow smile creeping across her face. *I hear you! I can hear your thoughts, like Brant's. Who says we have to remain cousins? That may be the line of our blood, but I claim you, Ember Shandae, as my sister. One I've always wished for.*

Ember grinned and replied the same way, taking only a second. *And I claim you, Kayla Kalandra Felandian, as my sister. And friend,* she added for good measure.

They hugged again, and then Kierra dove beneath them so they sat sidesaddle, though Kierra's back was bare. *We still have a giant to be rid of,* the Pedracorn said seriously. *He is blinded in one eye and is thrashing about, harming people and property, trying to find his attackers. He needs to be taken care of now.*

The girls glanced at each other and nodded, then settled down on Kierra's back. Ember was shocked she hadn't heard the giant in trying to save her cousin. Evidently she had tuned him out, she was so focused on the moment.

The Pedracorn ran. Brant rose up, matching Kierra's pace. "Do you need assistance, Mistress?"

"No, Brant. I'm fine," Kayla answered. "I'm glad to see you recovered from your draining."

He nodded once. "Nearly recovered, yes. Are you sure you have no need of help? The Wyciskalla is quite a challenging being."

Kayla shook her head. "No, we can do this." She stopped and looked at him, then at Ember. "Wait! Yes!" She outlined her plan.

Brant took off in a surge of wind that blew him like a hurricane toward Aldarin and DeMunth.

Let us take out that other eye, shall we? Kierra mindspoke.

Ember grinned and leaned forward. "Do it."

From a lesser height, Kierra tucked her wings, flying fast and true.

Swinging wildly in panic, the giant searched the skies with his one tear-filled eye.

The horn found its mark, a sharp jab that tore through the fragile membrane and sliced across the pupil and out the other side. The giant reached for them, his voice deafening, but they were quickly out of reach.

"*No*!" he screamed, bellowing his anguish, both tears and blood streaming down his face. He fell to the earth and writhed around, flattening pine trees and several bushes as he thrashed in pain, his yell a constant grating on everyone's ears.

"I wish we could take out his voice as easily," Ember muttered.

We can, if you wish, Kierra mindspoke. *Though it might be safer to do with the others present.*

As if answering her wish, Brant returned and set down slowly, releasing five people near the head of the giant. Four of them did not surprise her. The fifth made her growl until she remembered the promise she made to her father.

"C'Tan," she spat.

The blond woman turned, her eyes surprising Ember. She had expected to see hatred—pride—but there was also sorrow and pain. She returned C'Tan's gaze with wary consideration.

The enemy, who was currently an ally, nodded to each of them. “Ember. Kayla,” she said, then turned away, her back stiff. Ember doubted she could ever trust the woman and hated having her there. C’Tan had been trying to kill Ember for most of her life.

Ember glanced at Kayla, who seemed as unsure about this uneasy alliance as her cousin. Knowing she could do nothing, she turned to study the rest of the group, but stopped when she saw DeMunth. She rushed to the man she loved for a quick hug. When she tried to kiss him, he pulled back. "Sorry," he said in his metallic-sounding voice. That lovely silver tongue never ceased to amaze her. "Might we . . . uh . . . delay our kiss until you have showered? You are covered with blood and . . . slime."

Ember laughed. She hadn't even thought of that. "It's from his eye," she said, gesturing behind her.

Wyciskalla threw out an arm in their direction, sweeping it along the ground. They danced out of the way. "I hear you, puny humans and halfling. I hear you shifters! You took Wyciskalla's eyes! My eyes! You will pay!" He scrambled to his feet and began to stomp randomly, probably hoping to catch one of them accidentally.

DeMunth and Aldarin looked at each other. "It’s definitely time," Aldarin said. “We need this one gone. I think it will break the rest of the Ne’Goi.”

Kayla said, "The power of three keystones, the magic of a white mage, and orange and red? Strong, all of you. Together we can do what I could not. We have to overwhelm him with magic."

The giant stumbled to a knee and swept the ground, reaching for them as they evaded his grasp, then stood and stumbled backward into a cliff, knocking several boulders loose and battering down more of the forest. A boulder rolled into a pit, the poisoned stakes breaking beneath its weight.

"But don't the Ne’Goi eat magic?" DeMunth ducked under a falling branch as the giant knocked a tree down.

Kayla nodded. "Yes, but I have overpowered them before. If you use the power of magic on physical things, they can do nothing. They also have weak resistance if you use the dark side of your color of magic. Fire using ice. Air using suction. Orange, using stasis instead of change. Do you understand?"

They all nodded, and Ember grinned. The group scattered as Wyciskalla stumbled into their midst, sweeping the ground with broken trees. They regathered behind him, near the cliff where he'd knocked the boulders loose.

Ember looked around at the people with her, noticing one was missing. "Where is Tyese? She has a keystone too."

Kayla's brows rose. "I didn't know. Brant?"

"I shall retrieve her." Wind swirled, and he thrust the giant's fist aside, deflecting the blow meant to crush them all.

"No need," came a small voice from the forest. "I am here." Tyese stepped out from between the trees and joined them. "I saw you and thought to help." She glanced around, her eyes stopping on C'Tan, her breath locked in her chest before it released in an explosive bark. "Why her?" She glared at C'Tan.

"I hear you! I kill you!" Wyciskalla swung, his bloody hands searching.

C'Tan stepped out of his reach. "I came to help."

Tyese exchanged a wary glance with Ember as the group spread itself in a circle around Wyciskalla, colors surrounding him like a rainbow. C'Tan's red next to Aldarin's orange, next to DeMunth's yellow, Tyese's green, Kayla's blue, and Lily's purple. Ember stood between C'Tan and Lily, wedged between her friend and enemy, but knowing that she needed to be at the head of the circle. "Let's do this fast," C'Tan muttered, looking to the Ne'Goi that raced toward them.

Ember swallowed her dislike. "Agreed."

CHAPTER FORTY-EIGHT

Kayla watched Ember war with her emotions on the other side of C'Tan, but the pull on her magic began almost immediately, and without thinking, Kayla tapped in to the power of the flute. She wasn't the only one. She felt yellow and green pass through her as the power in the circle went round and round, building in strength, then climbing higher until the power stood like a wall of mottled color, holding the Ne'Goi at bay, sparks erupting from the magical curtain as the enemy pounded at it.

Ember reached a hand toward the spinning wall and let her fingers trail in the magic. Colors collided with one another, and like bubbles, they combined to form a larger and larger fusion of color until the entire thing was white. White magic holding the Ne'Goi at bay. Ember took a step forward, the others following her action. She took another step, and another, until they stood within inches of the giant's feet. He turned and rammed a shoulder into the wall. A burst of sparks and pain threw him into the wall behind him with more of the same. Tears and blood rolled down his face as he held perfectly still so as to not touch the wall.

"Let Wyciskalla go! Go! Wyciskalla hungry! Must eat!" he shouted in his gravelly voice. He swung out, but hit only the white wall, sending more sparks up his arms and a screeching howl from his throat.

He snarled. "Will stomp you! Must have keystones!" He jumped into the air and everyone scattered to the edges of the wall holding the Ne'Goi at bay. Wyciskalla came down in a thundering crash, then took gigantic steps around the small area, desperate to squash one of his captors.

The giant screamed again. "I will kill you! I must!"

As magic swirled through the circle of keyholders, thoughts drifted together with feathery touches of green, yellow, and red.

The giant came close and Kayla darted out of the way, diving between the giant's legs and rolling to her feet on the other side. Wyciskalla was dangerous, and rather than confining him, the white energy wall confined them all, making them very easy targets. If they didn't do something soon, he would catch one of them. They couldn't avoid him forever. A thought surfaced in Kayla's mind—not her own. *Cousin, would you play him to sleep? I see no other way to subdue him. Will you help me?*

Without a word, Kayla pulled out the flute and played the song she wrote for Brant's funeral. It brought memories that wet her eyes and clenched her heart. After a few notes, she felt Brant's presence behind her as he listened. She hoped it was the Brant she knew who heard, and not the servant of the flute. She wanted so much for him to remember.

Wyciskalla's bloody tears continued to fall as he stormed around his magical cage. He fell to one knee, then the other as sleep stole the fight from his body. A soft smile graced his ugly face as he collapsed to the side and began to snore. She deepened his dreams, relieved that he had stopped trying to kill her at last.

Once sure that he slept deep and sound, Kayla changed her tune and pulled cold from the surrounding air, pushing her magic into his chest, surrounding his heart and lining the arteries that fed it. Continuing to play, she opened her eyes and looked at Ember, giving her a nod. Ember turned to C'Tan. "Your turn."

C'Tan's fire. Oh, what a gruesome image that brought to mind! Kayla closed her eyes once again, focusing on feeding energy into the giant's heart, not freezing it yet, just readying it, like a net around a rabbit.

Kayla, now! Ember's voice shouted in her head. As softly as she could, Kayla froze the blood pumping to his heart, then the arteries traveling from it, and worked inward until the heart itself was a block of ice. It gave one last beat before it froze completely. Kayla opened her eyes, then wished she hadn't. Ember used a beam of energy to decapitate Wyciskalla as fast as any sword, and C'Tan raised her hands, sending huge bursts of fire into the giant's head. A high-pitched keening came from the mouth of the beast, screaming despite having no lungs to breathe. Its empty eye sockets focused on Ember. "You will pay for what you have done, Wolfchild. You will die for this. So says the son of the Master, Ne'Goi. He will know what you have done. He will have your head as you have taken mine." The keening rose to an excruciating screech, then cut off completely.

The silence made their ears ring.

The cries of despair started with the Ne'Goi, those closest vanishing into the sky like a meteor shooting up instead of down. One by one, then in groups of three or four, and finally a mass exodus took place and all the Shadow Weavers fled, leaving only the bodies behind.

Then the cheering began. The Phoenixians, the dragons, the Bendanatu, the humans—it didn't matter the race or what they had done. Everyone shouted their relief and thanks to the Havens, some falling to their knees in tears.

Ember's group dropped the wall that had held the Ne'Goi at bay.

Kayla joined the others in celebrating the death of the lead shadow weaver, winning the battle and perhaps even the war—at least the war the Ne'Goi raged against the Bendanatu. Aldarin ran to her and spun her around with a kiss. When he set her down, she laughed to see Ember looking at them strangely. There would be time enough later to fill her in.

Walking hand in hand with Aldarin, Kayla started down the hill, then stopped, watching with sickening awe as the bodies of the Ne'Goi disintegrated, leaving behind nothing but their clothing and weapons and a greasy black stain in the shape of their bodies.

Even more surprising, the dead dragons burst into flame and burned quickly to ash. C'Tan walked past, putting a hand on the head of one of the black beasts, a tear trailing down her face. Kayla hadn't known the woman could cry, let alone that she had a heart that would allow her to do so. Maybe she was human, after all.

One by one, C'Tan went to each of the dragon bodies, wishing them a private farewell before they burned to ash. Her anguish was obvious, no matter how she may have tried to hide it. Lily walked quickly past Kayla and Aldarin and put an arm around C'Tan. The woman stiffened for a moment, then shrugged her daughter's arm off her shoulder and moved on to the next dragon body, as if the black beast was more her child than her own flesh and blood.

Lily turned and walked down the hill, her head bowed and her steps dragging.

A slow anger built in Kayla as she watched her friend spurned by the woman who should have shown her the most love and kindness. It made Kayla wonder if there was any kindness at all in C'Tan's soul. And yet—as the woman moved from the body of one dragon to another, C'Tan touched them with what seemed like love and grief. Perhaps there was more to her than she showed the world. It was something to think about.

Kayla and Aldarin returned to Bendanatu and reunited with those they had left behind. Kayla greeted her mother with as much exuberance as Aldarin greeted his stepmother. And then they saw the bodies. Not many, but they had lost a few of those they knew in the battle. They had killed three of the Moningers, as well as Justesen and Kymber.

Dawnna knelt, weeping near the five, Roahnald standing with his hand on her shoulder. The seer stood over them, casting last rites and offering comfort.

The Phoenixian Aryana, whom Kayla had first met at the mage academy, had died in battle and gone to the light, but the other Phoenixians survived. Most of them were injured, but they were alive.

Few humans fought, and none of them died. It was amazing how few had been lost, considering the overwhelming numbers they fought against.

Kayla watched C'Tan leave the battlefield as the last of her dragons turned to dust. She walked with her head high, no emotion on her face, but what Kayla had seen as the woman bade farewell to her dragons told her it was a mask. Just as Kayla had done so often among the aristocrats of Peldane, C'Tan hid her true self. Not sure how that made her feel, knowing that she and C'Tan had something in common, she excused herself from Aldarin and her mother and approached the fierce woman. Was she truly evil? Or was there something more?

She climbed the hill toward the dragon lady and as they were about to pass one another, Kayla reached out with a soft hand and took C'Tan's arm. It felt like flesh, just as any other person. That fact alone gave Kayla courage.

C'Tan turned her head and stared blankly. Gathering her courage, Kayla softly said, "We could not have won this battle without you and your fierce dragon warriors. Thank you, Lady C'Tan. Thank you."

C'Tan seemed a bit taken aback by her words, then slowly smiled—a genuine kind of smile that actually reached her eyes. "Lady C'Tan. I like that." She pursed her lips and tipped her head toward the sky. "Tell me, Duchess Kayla. Is it ever too late to change, do you think?"

Startled that C'Tan knew her new title, and even more startled by the question, Kayla stammered, "Too late . . . I mean . . . What . . . Why are you asking me?"

The smile broadened. "Because you took the time to stop and thank me. You looked beyond my past and called me a lady. So I ask you, in your wisdom and kindness, Duchess Kayla, is it ever too late for one to change?"

Cocking her head to one side, Kayla looked at C'Tan—really looked—and saw something behind the mask.

Kayla shook her head, her eyes never leaving C'Tan's. "No. I don't believe it is ever too late to change. It may take a lifetime to do so, but it is never, ever too late."

C'Tan pursed her lips, nodded once and continued into Bendanatu. Kayla watched her go, not sure whether the conversation had given her hope or increased her fear of the woman.

CHAPTER FORTY-NINE

Thje baths were crowded after the battle, but Ember didn't care. She wanted the filth from the caverns and Wyciskalla's eye slime off her, so she bathed in the corners she could find, washing her hair with soapstone three separate times before it felt clean. Her clothes weren't worth saving in their condition. She took a towel and a cotton bathrobe and let that dress her for the moment, leaving her slime-encrusted clothes at the side of the pools.

Ember took the stone stairs up into her grandfather's quarters and sat on a bench in the common area, wanting just a moment alone. A lot had happened over the last week. It felt like three or four days, but according to Kayla, DeMunth, and Aldarin, it had been a full seven. She didn't understand how time could be different inside the emerald maze than it was out here. How could she have lost days?

Something Mahal had said came back to her mind. He'd told her that time was speeding up, that it was already splintering. Was that because Rasann itself was falling apart? Or something else? When next time ran differently, would she lose days, or maybe weeks? Months? She shivered, shaking off the fear that lurked in such thoughts.

Only the keystones could heal Rasann before the world completely unraveled. Mahal needed her to go to the MerCats and find the Amethyst Eye, but why her? Why not send Kayla to the MerCats? She'd been there already and knew them. It only made sense. But the Guardian had been very specific. She wished for time to rest, to train.

But there wasn't any to be had.

The seer popped her head in the room and tsked when she saw Ember. "You can't wear that in the chieftain's presence! What happened to your clothes?" she asked, then stopped. "Ah! You probably ruined them in the battle, and I don't imagine you have many more."

Ember shook her head.

Adrienne gestured. "Come with me, then. We'll get you dressed up properly."

When Ember objected, Adrienne cut her off.

"Nothing fancy. Just clothes, I promise."

Ember grinned and took Adrienne's hand. She led her down the stairs and across the hall into a room with many closets. She looked Ember up and down, then walked across the room and threw open double doors, behind which were stacks of clothes filling cubicles from floor to ceiling. The priestess pulled out a pair of pants and a white blouse and handed them to Ember. "Take these as well." Adrienne offered a bundle of socks, boots, and a second set of clothes. "Our Wolfchild should have more than just the clothes on her back."

Ember's eyes grew wide with the seer's generosity. "This is too much, Adrienne. I can't—"

"Yes. You can," she said, laying her hand on top of the clothes and meeting Ember's eye. "It is a small thing to do to repay the Wolfchild for her gift of service. Please. Take it."

Ember wanted to object, but she needed the clothing. She nodded reluctantly, then hugged Adrienne one-armed. "Thank you."

“I’ll step out while you change.” Adrienne turned before she reached the doorway. “It has been an honor having you among us, Wolfchild. You are welcome in my cave whenever you have need.” She bowed, turned, and left before Ember could answer.

Ember pulled the clothes on quickly, leaving her robe on a hook near the door. She made her way back up to Bahndai's quarters, stopping in her room to lay the clothing and boots on her bed. She'd pack them later. Having just found lost members of her family, she wanted as much time with the people she loved as possible. Packing would not take long, but she would be leaving soon, and she ached for time with her family *now*.

A shadow stretched from the doorway, and Ember spun, her heart racing. An older woman, dressed in clothing much like Ember's own, stood with silvery white hair hanging in a long, thick braid over her shoulder. When she saw Ember's eyes, she smiled and stepped into the room.

Ember stepped back. "Who are you?"

The woman dropped her arms, her eyes showing hurt and confusion for a moment before clarity hit, and she laughed. When she stopped, she was smiling. "They haven't told you about me, have they?" she asked.

"Who?"

"Lily. Bahndai. Kayla. Aldarin. Any of them." The woman eased into the room, put her hands behind her back, and leaned against the wall.

Ember shook her head. "No. I haven't had time to talk to them. I blew out the side of a mountain and flew into the heart of a battle." She wanted to sit on the bed, but she was wary with this stranger in her room and felt safer on her feet.

The woman's eyes twinkled. "Have you ever heard the name Asana?" she asked, looking at her booted feet as if nervous.

Ember straightened. "Yeess," she drawled. "She's my grandmother, but I've never met her. She's supposed to live in the woods and is a magestone miner. Why?" Her heart beat a little faster in her chest.

The woman met her eyes. "I am Asana."

Ember's eyes widened. "You."

The woman nodded.

"You are Asana."

She nodded again.

"My . . . grandmother?" Ember asked, fighting the tears that flooded her eyes.

"Yes," she finally said aloud. "I would have come if I had known of you, Ember. I never knew—"

Ember silenced the apology by racing across the room and throwing her arms around her grandmother.

Asana's arms wrapped around her slowly, and Ember began to sob. She had a family now. A real family. Yes, they were quirky and not the normal family everyone else had, but she had one. Grandparents. Mother. Father. Cousins. Aunts and uncles.

She wasn't alone.

Asana patted her on the back. "Shhhh. There, there. I didn't mean to upset you."

Ember drew back, smiling through her tears. "No, you don't understand. I'm happy! I've wanted to meet you from the moment I learned of you."

Asana chuckled, a deep laugh that rumbled in her chest. "It seems a miracle we all found each other, one I'll be thankful for until the day I die."

They embraced again, then let go, but clasped hands. "Come on," Asana said. "My husband has called a meeting in the common room."

Ember stared at her in shock.

Asana's grin was mischievious. "I would guess nobody told you about that either, since you didn't even know I was here. Bahndai and I renewed our vows."

Ember blinked slowly.

Asana threw back her head and laughed, then threw an arm across her granddaughter's shoulders, and pulled her through the doorway, walking as they talked. "Do you think I'd actually let him out of my sight after thirty years apart? No way in the Havens or Helar. He is mine."

Ember knew what she meant. She felt that kind of attachment to DeMunth. Having been separated through his anger, then unconsciousness, and the emerald maze made her long for the silver-tongued man she loved. She couldn't imagine spending thirty years apart. Grinning, she squeezed her grandmother's hand. "I am so happy for you two!"

A few more steps and they entered the common room, where Asana moved forward to sit beside the chieftain. He leaned over and gave her a kiss on the cheek.

Warmed by their reunion, Ember surveyed the already too-full room, searching for an empty place to sit. DeMunth's wave caught her eye, and she smiled. He had saved her a spot near the window, where her father perched on the windowsill once again.

She reached up and caressed her father's bird-formed head and neck. He pressed into her fingers and she savored the touch.

Bahndai stayed seated, but spoke. "I know the battle is barely finished and you are all exhausted and heart heavy, but I thought it best to meet now rather than later. Ember—" His fierce gaze sought his granddaughter. You always have a home here. Always. But I know you have a mission to fulfill. What do you need from us?"

She'd expected him to ask about her plans, not offer her help. She rearranged her thoughts for a moment, then stood and spoke.

"Before I answer your question, Grandfather, you should know what happened once Tyese, Keyera, and I got through the door to the emerald maze." She was quiet for a moment, making sure she had everyone's attention, and then told them about the trials that had been set for her using all the colors of magic and their inverse power. They gasped at the vines which poisoned her and how she cured herself. Ember spoke of the water test, gills, the stone cube, and the Emerald Wolf. She almost snarled her description of Ne'Goi and cried for Keyera's death. She told how Tyese became the guardian of the emerald keystone.

They whispered in awe as she told of Mahal and Jarin unsealing the door to save Tyese from Ne'Goi. Lastly, she told them about Mahal's gift.

"Keyera's ashes moved, grew, and formed into the shape of a horse, then grew upward and solidified to create the Pedracorn. You saw me flying with her?"

The room nodded as one, entranced by her story. "She is my companion, as Brant is to Kayla, and Ted Finch is to DeMunth." The guardian of light seemed surprised at that. "And someone will be for Tyese."

Uncle Shad spoke up. "That would be me," he said, standing slowly. "I've known for some time that there was more in my future than just to be the son of the chief. This is my calling and duty as well." His eyes met Lady Kalandra's. "I hope you will understand," he said, then sat again.

Bahndai opened his hand. "What can we do, and where will you go next?"

There was the question she'd been expecting. "When Mahal was in the cavern, he told me that Kayla and I must separate again."

Kayla groaned. "Again?"

Ember nodded. "I don't understand why, but he told me to go to the MerCats and find the Amethyst Eye."

A wry grin spread across Kayla's face. "MerCats. I know them. Sarali's parents are kind and good leaders. One of her brothers is the kind of prince every girl dreams will fall in love with her." Her face darkened. "Her other brother, Jihong, is dark and twisted and selfish." Kayla sighed, regret clear in her tone. "I had to kill him."

The room gasped and broke into a round of whispered conversation. When it quieted, Kayla continued. "I froze his body, so it is possible that his brother revived and healed him. I do not know. He took his body back to his home under the sea, and Sarali left for home just before our departure from the mage academy. It sounds to me as if Mahal is sending you to Mercato because he knows that sending me would most likely be a death sentence."

Ember blinked. "Evidently. Okay, then. I understand. So, I will go under the sea and search for the Amethyst Eye—having absolutely no idea where to begin—while Kayla is to retrieve the Ruby Heart."

Kayla looked at her as if she'd grown another head. "But . . . nobody knows where the Ruby Heart is!"

C'Tan stepped through the doorway. Everyone turned and stared. "I do," she said, her voice soft and full of something. Anger? Pleasure? Dismay? Ember couldn't tell.

"Surely not." Kayla faced the woman who had been their greatest adversary. "How can you know when none other does?"

The woman in red leather, still scuffed and stained from battle, gave a smile that could put out a volcano with its cold. "I know, because my master told me."

Kayla visibly gulped. "S'Kotos knows?"

C'tan's smile broadened. "Oh, yes. He knows very well, as it has stayed where he put it since the one-hundred Guardian war. From the beginning of time as we know it," she hissed, her lip curled in distaste.

"Dare I ask where we can find it?" Kayla whispered.

C'Tan nodded. "When S'Kotos' love rejected him and fell from the skies, the pain was so exquisite that he ripped his heart from his chest and hid it for safekeeping. It keeps him alive. Pain free, but slowly dying without his heart, he looked for something to replace it with—something that would keep him alive and emotionless." C'Tan looked around the room, completely silent at her revelation.

“If you seek the keystone, you’ll need my help.” She took a breath, then released it, her eyes boring into Kayla’s. “The Ruby Heart beats within S’Kotos’ chest.”

PRONUNCIATION GUIDE

EMBER'S GROUP:

- Brina—BREE-nuh
- Marda—MAR-duh
- Ember—EM-burr
- Shandae—shawn-DAY
- Paeder—PAY-dur
- Ezeker—EZZ-ick-cur
- Aldarin—AHL-duh-rin
- Tiva—TEE-vuh
- Ren—REHN
- Shad—Shad
- DeMunth—di-MOONTH
- Tyese—tye-EES
- Lily—LILL-ee
- Bahndai—bohn-DAY

BAD GUYS:

- C'Tan—seh-TAHN
- Kardon—KAR-dawn
- Ian Covainis—EE-in co-VANE-us
- Ne'Goi—nih-GOY

GUARDIANS of RASANN:

- Mahal—muh-HALL
- S'Kotos—SKOE-toess
- Bendanatu—behn-duh-Nah-too
- Klii'kunn—klee-KOON
- Lahonra—luh-HONE-rah
- Hwalan—hwa-LAHN
- Sha'iim--shaw-EEM

KAYLA's GROUP:

- Adrienne—AE-dree-in
- Asana—ae-SAH-nuh

- Brant—(as spelled)
- Felandian—feh-LAN-dee-in
- Kalandra—kuh-LAN-druh
- Kayla—KAE-luh
- Sarali—suh-RAH-lee
- T'Kato—tuh-KAH-toe

PLACES:

- Rasann—Ruh-SAHN
- Karsholm—KAR-showlm
- Peldane—PEHL-dayne
- Phoenixia—foh-NEE-SEE-uh

SHAPESHIFTERS/RACES

- MerCat—MUR-kat
- Bendanatu—BEN-duh-NAH-too
- Ne'Goi—neh-GOY
- Phoenixian—foe-NEE-SEE-in

- Ketahe—keh-TAW-hee
- Ketahean—keh-TAW-hee-in

KUDOS

First, I want to thank all of you, my loyal readers, who have waited so long for Ember and Kayla's journey to continue. Without you, there would be no story, for as the infamous Tracy Hickman says, "It doesn't matter if you're published. What matters is if you're read."

As always, I thank my amazing editor and friend, Tristi Pinkston, for her thorough, hilarious guidance, and polishing.You are the best!

Heartfelt thanks to my dear friends, Wendy Swore and Rebecca Blevins, who read my pukey first draft and gave me honest, kind, and sometimes, hair pulling advice. Not only are they great beta readers, but they are world class butt-kickers as well. Thanks, ladies!

This book has over forty people from the real world written into its depths, most mentioned by name, some only they will know, but they are there and I loved every moment of writing them into the story. So, no matter how you got in the book, thank you Abbey, Adrienne, Aislyn, Alexa Jade, Anna (Agrobel), Arianna (Aryana), Ben (Behn), Bill (Justesen), *Blake, Cole, Leighton, Madison, Tatum, and Tayten* (my Moningers who are never called by name), *Cooper, Jarret, Jayden, Logan, and Ryder* (my young Ne'Goi spies, also never called by name), Donna (Dawnna), Eden, Elaisha, Ezra, Hailey, Josh (Wyciskalla), Keyera, Kierra, Kimberly (Kymber), Lex, Lincoln (Lynkyn), Mandalin, Matthew (Thew), Mike (Miek), Rachel (Raech), Ronald (Roahnald),

Ronan, Shari Bird, Tabitha, Ted Finch, Tia, Tyese, and William. You guys made this story extra special.

Special thanks to my husband and sons, for allowing me the time to write, and taking it as seriously as I do. I love you guys!

And most importantly, I thank my Heavenly Father, for without him there would be no life, no breath, no soul from which to write.

ALSO BY THE AUTHOR

The Wolfchild Saga:

The Sapphire Flute

The Armor of Light

The Emerald Wolf
The Amethyst Eye
The Ruby Heart
The Hidden Coin
The Crystal Mallet

Newtimber:

Fractured

The Misadventures of a Teenage Wizard:

Two Souls are Better Than One

Poetry:

And the Mountain Burns

Karen E. Hoover has loved the written word for as long as she can remember. Her favorite memory of her dad is the time he spent with Karen on his lap, telling her stories for hours on end, everything from Dr. Seuss' Green Eggs and Ham (which he thought was disgusting) to sharing his love of poetry in reciting Jabberwocky enough times she memorized it at a young age. Her dad promised he would have Karen reading on her own by the time she was four years old . . . and he very nearly did.

Karen took the gift of words her dad gave her and ran with it. Since then, she's written many novels and reams of poetry. Her head is fairly popping with ideas, so she plans to write until she's ninety-four or maybe even a hundred and four. Inspiration is found everywhere, but Karen's heart is fueled by her husband, two sons and her grandson, the Rocky Mountains, her chronic addiction to pens and paper, excessive office supplies, and the smell of her laser printer in the morning.

WHERE TO FIND ME

Thank you so much for reading The Emerald Wolf! If you enjoyed the experience, I would greatly appreciate your leaving a review on Amazon and Goodreads. It is one of the best and easiest ways to help your favorite authors. There are many more stories about Ember and Kayla and C'Tan to come, and I hope you will join me in continuing their journey in saving their world.

You can find me at the following:

Website: karenEhoover.com

Amazon Author page: amazon.com/author/karenehoover

Instagram: author_karen_e_hoover

Facebook: @karenEhoover

Tik Tok: @keghoover

Goodreads: Karen E. Hoover

Bookbub: Karen E. Hoover

MyBookCave.com: Karen E. Hoover

Sign up for my newsletter to receive behind the scenes content and much, much more! Character and location pictures. First glimpses at upcoming books. The chance to join my street team and spread the word. Games. Prizes. FUN! Come and join me! The link can be found at www.karenEhoover.com.

Made in the USA
Middletown, DE
25 May 2023